DEADLY DECORUM

JACQUELINE VICK

CR

This is a work of fiction. Names, characters, places, and incidents are either a product of the author's imagination or are used fictitiously. Any resemblance to actual people living or dead, places, businesses, or events is entirely coincidental.

The Harlow Brothers Book 3

ISBN-13: 978-1-945403-33-0 (Print)

ISBN-13: 978-1-945403-32-3 (Digital)

Classical Reads 1st edition April 2021

Laughing Loon Press edition March 2023

Printed in the United States of America

Cover Design by James, GoOnWrite.com

For Foster

"My dear, if you could give me a cup of tea to clear my muddle of a head, I should better understand your affairs." – *Charles Dickens*

CHAPTER 1

Some lady writer once started her story with, *Last night, I dreamed I was at...*and then she named the place of her nightmares. Well, this was no dream because I wasn't asleep, but I was back at the place of my nightmares. Inglenook Resort.

I stood inside the front entrance to the former family manor and surveyed the lobby. The dark-wood paneling sucked up the light given off by scattered lamps and torch-shaped sconces that lined the walls, reminding me of those moodily lit restaurants where you couldn't be certain the table was clean.

Inglenook's guests hadn't gotten any younger or more attractive since our last visit. The average age was sixty-five, almost three decades older than my brother and me.

To my right, a few guests climbed the wide marble staircase to the second floor, while the less athletic waited for the gated elevator installed eons ago when the original Inglenook became infirm.

We were back for a charity fundraiser for Tea for Teens featuring my older brother, Edward, as the celebrity guest.

The kickoff was the masked ball tonight. Tomorrow, an expert would talk about types of teas, their proper preparation, and the tools involved, and then Edward would lecture about the dance etiquette of days past. That seemed pointless because by the time his talk took place, the ball would be over.

The last day, Sunday, would find him supervising a demonstration of an afternoon tea featuring two of the teenagers from the charity.

If you're wondering what business a six-feet-two former college linebacker with dark hair that tends to curl, gray eyes, and a Van Dyke goatee has mingling with tea drinkers, my brother writes the Aunt Civility etiquette books.

His fans thought he was just the public face of the allegedly agoraphobic Auntie, probably because that's what it said on the inside flap of the book cover. Yet those same fans, at least the females, swooned over him as if he were the actual author. Which he was.

For the record, I'm a few inches shorter and have the same dark hair and gray eyes, though I skipped the beard. I played halfback.

If you're also wondering why I, Edward's secretary, factotum, and general dogsbody would agree to come back to Inglenook after our last experience here involving multiple murders and a near escape from death by yours truly, Edward needed the publicity.

His sales had hit a slump.

This winter had brought with it a particularly nasty flu. People weren't interested in throwing parties. They weren't interested in being polite, either.

At the beginning of the epidemic, there had been fistfights over toilet paper, of all things. I was certain his sales would rebound, especially if he finished his latest dealing with the difficulties of picnicking, a manuscript now six weeks overdue.

Surveying the room, my gaze stopped on Claudia Inglenook working behind the front desk. If Inglenook was my nightmare, Claudia was the Hellhound that kept me from waking up.

Standing behind the polished dark-wood counter, she tossed her auburn locks over her shoulder as she dealt with an incoming guest. The half-owner of Inglenook gathered her dark brows together in a frown as she worked on a problem, and then her full lips revealed straight white teeth as she smiled, victorious.

She was mid-thirties and, though her exterior gave the impression of a woman so sweet-natured she dined on strawberries and cream for breakfast, on the inside, she had the soul of a harpy.

When Edward and I stayed here the first time, she came bleating to us for help when a murderer ruined the resort's opening weekend. Along the way, she and Edward fell for each other. My older brother, who was hard enough to control when his spine was straight, wrapped himself around her crooked finger and fell over his feet to do whatever pleased the wench. Like come to Inglenook for a charity fundraiser.

A cold spray of drizzle hit my neck, and I stepped aside and held the door open for a woman in black. Black wool jacket, black boots, and black knit cap with her hair tucked under. She walked through without acknowledging me. Not that I expected a fan letter, but a simple thank you is just as polite as the act of opening the door. Working for my brother had made me sensitive to rude behavior.

"You're welcome," I called after her, but she didn't bother to look back and took her place in line.

The doorman, Alfred, dressed in his red uniform and

black top hat, stared me down, waiting for a tip. He'd only grabbed the handle after I'd pushed the door open myself, but as I might need his help later, I handed him five bucks.

Since we'd met before, I felt entitled to ask him a question. "What's the deal with that getup? Do they force you to wear it?"

He sucked his teeth. "Nah. It was my granddad's. He was a bellhop in the twenties. I added the hat for class."

"It suits you."

Since Inglenook didn't have a bellhop, I picked up our luggage and headed for the counter.

In honor of the event, the Inglenooks had decked out the lobby with an obnoxiously cute welcome banner featuring a couple of field mice in dresses drinking tea in a garden. Glass bowls of candy and vases of white roses sat on each of the mismatched tables next to chairs that looked as if they had been salvaged from the original Inglenook Manor before it became a commercial enterprise out of necessity, because they were.

The fresh scent of rain lost something after being dragged inside on damp coats and boots, and the lobby smelled like a locker room.

On my way to the front counter, a large oaf rammed into me, causing me to slip on the damp marble floor.

"Excuse me," I called out after him once I caught my balance, but he and his brown cashmere topcoat kept moving.

The guy with him, tall and slim and walking a step behind, looked back at me. Since his expression said he hadn't had a good day in years, I let it go, but I noticed when he approached the woman in black. She was being helped by Claudia Inglenook. He whispered something in her ear, and the woman looked up at him with a scowl. He smirked and walked away.

"Next, please."

I handed Robert Inglenook, Claudia's brother and the owner of the other half of Inglenook Resort, the company credit card.

"It's good to see you, Nicholas."

I nodded. "How's tricks?"

He grinned back. "We're kind of crowded. Let me check if we have two rooms available."

Robert was joking about our first trip here. They'd over-booked, and they had forced Edward and me to share a room. At least, I hoped he was joking.

Once he printed off a form and held it out for my signature, I double-checked the number of rooms and wrote my name on the dotted line. He slipped me two keys. They hadn't yet updated to electronic cards.

I looked at the name on the keys and gawked. Darling Daisy and Blue-Bell. "You've got to be kidding."

"What?" he said innocently.

Pushing the keys back at him, I said, "Try again."

We'd stayed in Blue-Bell last time, and a charming killer had nearly brained Edward in Darling Daisy. Bad memories. That was not how I intended to start Edward's comeback weekend.

"Sorry. We're booked. There are two rooms available in opposite wings, but I thought you wanted a connecting door."

After a brief debate, I decided that keeping close tabs on Edward got top priority. After all, he hadn't been in Darling Daisy for more than ten minutes, and he'd enjoyed being the hero who captured the killer. I took back the keys.

Robert slid a glance toward his sister and leaned forward, casually. "We'll catch up later in the bar."

As the siblings of Romeo and Juliet, we suffered the same pains every time the couple hit a rough patch.

I agreed to the plan and carried our luggage to where Edward waited impatiently.

"Maybe we should go to our rooms and unpack. Freshen up."

As expected, he kept his love-sick gaze on Claudia and said, "You go."

"Nope. I'll wait for you." I set down the luggage and stretched. "You know what today is?" When Edward grunted, I said, "March fifteenth. The Ides of March. Maybe Claudia should have hired actors to play out the assassination of Julius Caesar. That would have pulled them in."

He snorted out a laugh despite his efforts to ignore me.

"Mr. Harlow!"

An elderly woman in a fur coat and her two friends closed in on him with pleased smiles. Edward hated to mingle with the public, but these people had come all the way to a resort in Northern Illinois to learn how to fill a teacup. He was stuck.

After bowing his head in their direction, he listened as they told him he flew with the angels because he supported their charity. He didn't even wrinkle his nose at the wet-dog smell coming from the lady's animal rug.

"It's my pleasure. Tea for Teens is a worthy cause."

The woman rested her fingertips on his bicep.

"We were just talking about how wonderful it must be for your aunt to have such a handsome assistant and how much we would love to have one of our own."

The shorter woman, the one with a pug nose, giggled. "Like those cabana boys that bring the drinkies! They probably think I'm a lush, but really, I pour my drink in the sand so I can get them to come back. I feel guilty sometimes, making them work so hard."

"I've warned you about that," Fur Coat said. "They probably spot the puddle and think you're incontinent."

Pug Nose gasped.

I'd heard about cougars. Older women who preferred the company of younger men. My first exposure to the species disappointed me. I'd always imagined they'd resemble actress Susan Sarandon.

My brother didn't know whether to send them a frown of chastisement or let loose a strangled laugh, so he went with the polite response. "Er, thank you."

The third woman spoke up. She had ramrod-straight posture, and her thin lips refused to move when she talked.

"Seems to me there's not a lot of work involved in your job. You get to travel, show up at nice places like this, and talk a little. Maybe you do some memorization, but you can always refer to your notes." She shrugged her shoulders and sniffed. "Your aunt is the one who has the proper job, though writing things down doesn't sound very difficult, either."

That wasn't fair. I knew how much research Edward put in to get the details right so the average person could make a good impression on the boss or the in-laws. One celebrity, who the press regularly described as *charming,* owed her success to *Behave Yourself: Make a Lasting Impression Through Repression.*

Fur Coat decided her friend had pushed it too far. "It's nice of you to help her out with the extra chores."

"I wouldn't dream of allowing my aunt to handle anything beneath her dignity. That's what I'm for." My brother got a glint in his eye. "To be her cabana boy."

They giggled, but I recognized the signs of a coming fit and grabbed his arm to extract him from the conversation. "We should get you to your room."

The women took the hint and agreed that travel equaled the fifth level of hell and needed recovery time. When he said he hoped to see them at the masked ball tonight, his comment met with more giggles and coy smiles.

"What costume will you be wearing?" Fur Coat asked.

He gave them a genuine smile. "That would ruin the surprise."

Thin Lips had two more cents to offer. "I hope it's nothing that would embarrass your aunt. You have an obligation to represent her in the best light possible."

The glint was back in his eye and made a mockery of his friendly smile.

"What would *you* suggest? I can imagine what you'll be wearing."

With one hand, I waved at the women. With the other, I dragged my brother away. "See you tonight, ladies."

Edward jerked his arm from my grasp. "Would you like to explain why you embarrassed me in front of my fans?"

"To keep you from embarrassing yourself. Let's leave it as you're tired after your trip."

"I'm not." He ground his teeth. "I feel fit as a fiddle."

"Fit as a fiddle and ready to fight. You've already insulted one old lady this month. That's your limit."

A few more fans, seeing that Aunt Civility's public face didn't bite—that they knew of—gathered around him. I stepped out of the way. After watching to make sure Edward was behaving himself, I let my mind work on a greeting for Claudia that would cut her to pieces.

One man shook Edward's hand and said something that made my brother grimace. I moved closer. They were talking about Northwestern's chances in the NCAA tournament. My brother and I favored Duke, and it wasn't just because the Blue Devil's coach, Mike Kzyzewski, had impeccable manners.

"You're betting on the wrong team," the guy said, grinning. "But I could use a few extra bucks. Want to back up your pick with a small wager?"

Edward's love of physical competition was as natural as

his hair color. He tried to convince me he no longer had an interest in sports as they didn't fit in with his image, but he casually dropped by my room whenever I had the games on TV. That meant he had a handle on each team's strengths and weaknesses. He probably had a chart hidden on the back of his bedroom door to track each player's performance. If he gave up the Aunt Civility gig, my brother could make a living accepting bets from guys like this.

Edward's jaw muscle twitched as he controlled his impulse to wager.

"I'm afraid that wouldn't be appropriate."

"Appropriate?"

He cleared his throat. "My aunt, Aunt Civility, might not approve."

The guy's eyes opened wide, as if my brother had suggested that all men should shave their legs. Then he shook his head at the wonder of a grown man afraid of his aged aunt and left us. Edward watched him walk away with an expression of envy.

The situation called for a distraction.

"I'm telling you. You're a hit with the ladies. They'd probably be thrilled to find out you were Auntie. Women would love to hear the male perspective on manners."

And it would make running his social media sites, something he refused to take part in, easier because I wouldn't have to pretend to be a sixty-something-year-old woman. Since I made the suggestion about once a month, he ignored me.

The harpy behind the front counter tittered at a customer's joke, and my jaw clenched. My brother's long-distance relationship was a distraction, and not the pleasant kind. His need to talk to Claudia every day, his growing desire to get her opinion and approval before he brushed his teeth, and the occasional tiffs brought on by the frustrations of distanced-enforced celibacy all made him difficult to handle.

Last week, for the first time, he'd taken his mood out on his fans. At a reading for a gardening society, he'd told the president to soak her head after she expressed disappointment that Auntie couldn't be there in person. It had taken all my skills as a fibber to get her to believe he was passing on the author's advice to soak the heads of the roses to make them bloom faster, *head* being her own homey term for the flowering bits.

He met further attempts at conversation with grunts, so I was happy when the female Inglenook finished checking in her last guest and left Robert holding the fort. I'm positive my brother, the romantic, had envisioned this moment since I booked our reservations. He probably saw himself sweeping Claudia into a tight hug as the music crescendoed until, violins screeching, he kissed her with a passion that would have the rest of the guests swooning.

Someone else got there first.

Just as she stepped out from behind the counter, a man about Edward's height with long blond hair tied back in a ponytail swooped Claudia into his arms and kissed her right on the mouth.

Edward, about to step forward, froze.

"Claudie! So good to see you."

Claudia blushed a pretty pink and glanced at my brother. "Edward, this is my friend, Joshua Breen. He's offered to photograph the events this weekend for the Tea for Teens newsletter."

A tall lady chatting with her husband turned around and gaped. "Not *the* Joshua Breen. The one whose photographs have been in *International Geography* and *Exploration Times*?

Everybody knew Joshua Breen, including me. I gave

Claudia a look that said I was impressed, with reservations. She stuck her tongue out at me.

The photographer grinned, showing a fantastic set of white teeth. "Guilty."

The lady's husband joined her. "How did you get that shot of the Northern ghost bat hanging from the stalactite?"

"Carefully," he said with a chuckle, and everyone tittered along with him except Edward, though he kept his features friendly. "I take time to observe my subject before snapping pictures. It's my favorite part, aside from the finished product. It relaxes me."

"Did you use a zoom lens?"

"Rappelling equipment."

Joshua's smile turned modest as the man went over some of the photographer's known heroics, such as trekking up Everest to snap pictures of a Himalayan tahr and swimming off the coast of Australia for some close-ups of Great White sharks.

While Claudia beamed up at her famous friend, Edward had an unreadable expression on his face. And since Claudia didn't introduce me, I took care of that myself once his fans had dispersed.

"I'm Nick."

He grinned. "Ed and Nick. I've heard a lot about you."

Edward raised a brow in Claudia's direction, and Joshua caught it.

"Claudie and I go way back. But I'm sure you've heard about me as well, seeing as how I was going to marry her. Wasn't I, Claudie?" He bumped her with his hip and grinned. He grinned a lot.

Though Edward's expression didn't change, I sensed him stiffen at my side.

Claudia brushed her hair back nervously. "They're not interested in all *that*."

I raised my hand. "I think it's interesting."

She glared at me, and I held back a grin. My desire to keep Edward calm was duking it out with my desire to irritate Claudia.

Joshua's expression turned serious. "Uh-oh. Did I stick my foot in it? Honestly, that wasn't my intent. I'm just buzzed at being back here and seeing Claudie and Rob again."

"Not at all," Edward said. "You're a photographer, Mr. Breen? Do you specialize in wildlife?"

My brother knew damn well Joshua Breen's talents extended to anything of interest, including sports. His photos had graced the covers of several athletic magazines over the past ten years, magazines Edward picked up on the sly and kept in his room. I borrowed them regularly.

"It's Josh. Please."

"And I prefer Edward. Please." He glared at me. "You can call my brother whatever you wish."

Which meant my brother was calling me all sorts of names in his head.

Josh leaned against the counter. "I go where I'm called. You know what it's like. If an editor wants a Northern ghost bat, it doesn't matter if I'd prefer a Golden Capped fruit bat. I pack my bags and head out. And if I'm more interested in exposing the Muslim concentration camp in China and the editor prefers me to cover the dancers in *Mulan* being filmed a few hundred yards away, I grit my teeth and give him what he wants."

"Sounds like a tough life." I meant it as a joke, but he surprised me.

"It's lonely." He reached out one muscled arm and pulled Claudia to his side. "That's why it's nice to touch base with old friends. They help keep me grounded." He smiled down at her. "And sometimes it's nice to be with people who know the real you."

Claudia's cheeks turned a flaming red. She covered her embarrassment and pleasure by turning the conversation to housekeeping.

"We've run into a slight problem. The shop we ordered the guests' costumes from has a broken pipe. Much of their stock suffered water damage. They're scrambling to come up with enough outfits to meet our needs. I'm afraid some guests will be disappointed. They may not get what they ordered."

Edward nodded at the horrors of unscheduled floods. "I leave nothing to chance. That's why I special ordered ours. Did they arrive?"

"Oh, yes. Yours are here. I'll have them sent up to your rooms."

He continued to stare at her. It surprised me to see Edward looking awkward. Normally, he's the proverbial bull who crashes through the china shop on his way to his goals. He seemed to be willing Claudia to do something. Or say something. Whatever he hoped she would do or say, she wasn't cooperating.

"Then I will see you at dinner. Claudia. Joshua."

As he turned and headed for the stairs, I added another problem to my list. *Keep Edward and ex-boyfriend apart.* Leave it to Claudia Inglenook to add to my stress.

CHAPTER 2

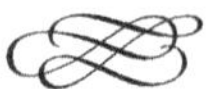

At the top of the stairs, I turned left and headed to our wing. As I entered the corridor, the first door to my left belonged to the staff member assigned to us, the room where she would go to restock her cart supplies. When I walked past, I paid my respects to Maggie, the maid who had died at the hands of a killer last year.

I'd liked Maggie and her dark, curly hair and crooked smile. She had a quick laugh and big dreams of owning her own bed-and-breakfast. Unfortunately, she saw a shortcut to making that dream come true; however, blackmailing the killer hadn't turned out well for Maggie. A wave of sadness slowed my steps until Edward called out to me to hurry.

I stood before Darling Daisy and unlocked the door. "I'll take Blue-Bell."

Edward grunted. "I'm not surprised you don't want to go back into Darling Daisy. Not after your last experience there."

Funny, but I hadn't thought about how a return to Inglenook might affect me.

"I don't even remember," I lied, handing him his key. "The entire weekend is a blur. You should forget it too."

He strolled into the room as if he owned it. I followed behind with his suitcase, left it at the foot of the spare bed, and proceeded to the Blue-Bell Room next door.

After closing my door behind me, I took a deep breath. My last memory of being here was waking up in bed after being drugged and nearly brained by the killer. I shook off the ominous atmosphere and tossed my suitcase onto the closest bed.

Various shades of blue shrieked at me, from an over-stuffed love seat resembling a ripe blueberry to the wallpaper smothered in cascading bluebells. Claudia's decorating choices lacked subtlety.

The other rooms in this wing included the Tulip Room, the Red Rose Room, and the Birds of Paradise Room. Thinking of Birds of Paradise and its hellish combination of oranges, I acknowledged I got off easy with cascading bluebells.

The rain had stopped, and the sun braved an appearance through receding gray clouds. Past the mini-bar and the second bed stood a writing desk set into a recess. An enormous bouquet of gardenias sat on top. I opened the balcony door and stepped outside for some fresh air, taking the vase with me.

I hate the cloying smell of gardenias.

After setting the vase on a small wicker table, I leaned against the railing and took in the huge expanse of lawn that stretched out to a tree line of oak and maple struggling to get their buds going for summer. Last time, the view had been under a blanket of snow.

High heels clicked on the walkway below. I leaned forward in time to see a woman dressed in a black-and-white server uniform disappear through the doors leading into the

Ballroom below. Since the temperature had only hit the upper forties, I went back inside, closed the doors, and got moving.

This wasn't a vacation, so I put my suits and necessities in the armoire—the room didn't have a closet—and set up my laptop on the writing desk. When I put my toiletries in the bathroom, I noted that having the room to myself during this trip meant I wouldn't run out of towels. Now it was time to take care of Edward.

When I turned the knob on the connecting door, it didn't budge. After knocking, I called out. "I need to unpack your things."

"It's already done."

I took a step back and stared at the door. On business trips, Edward expected me to handle the menial tasks. I chauffeured him, even opening his door when fans were present. I made the bookings, checked us in, and attended to all the details, including his unpacking, while he concentrated on more important tasks like being a celebrity.

Before I could consider my next step, someone knocked on my door. I opened it to find a square woman with rounded shoulders and a gray head of hair.

In a nod to bygone days, the Inglenooks dressed their employees in old-fashioned outfits consisting of a black dress that came below the knees covered by a white apron. Her appearance gave me a shock because all the Inglenook maids I had met previously were comely young women. This one resembled a gargoyle.

She held out a large box. "Miss Inglenook sent this up."

The costumes. I took the box but stopped her. "Someone has opened this box."

"Want me to return it?"

"I want to know who opened it."

She responded with an impressive shrug, though her

shoulders were a little stiff. "What do I know? Maybe security checked to make sure it's not a bomb."

I dug into my pocket for a tip, not expecting a thank you. I didn't get one. Edward had been secretive about the order, so I set the box on the spare bed next to my luggage and rummaged through the packing material.

The first costume I took out was Edward's. I knew this because it brought to life all his romantic fantasies. Zorro. I set out the pieces to make sure they were all there. A heavy black wool cape, loose black pants, black shirt made of a lightweight material all the better for billowing during sword fights, black knit headscarf, flat black hat that might have been felt, and a red waist sash.

Then I pulled out my costume and gaped. Robin Hood. I rubbed the soft beige tights between my fingers. They weren't see-through, but there wasn't a chance I'd put them on, even with the mask. I dumped my costume back in the box and put the box in the corner.

"I'm surprised at your choice of costume, Edward," I called out in a loud voice. "Transvestite hooker doesn't suit you."

The lock turned, and he yanked the door open. When Edward saw the Zorro costume, he scowled. "Very funny."

I held it up so he could inspect every inch for wayward wrinkles or separating seams. Instead, he turned and walked back to the writing table in the corner and left me with the honor of hanging it up along with the rest of his suits, which were still in his luggage.

When I saw the vase of roses on his writing table, I skipped a comment about favoritism and instead attempted to set an upbeat tone, one I hoped would last the weekend.

"With the common daisy wallpaper, this really is a pleasant room. Kind of soothing. Claudia could have made it a psychedelic nightmare if she'd included Gerber daisies, but she showed surprising restraint. Did you know daisy comes from the phrase *day's eye*? The flower closes at night and reopens in the morning. That makes it a practical flower since most people aren't looking at their gardens in the dark, so why waste effort? The yellow centers give the room just enough color."

I'd finished sharing my limited knowledge of daisies when I noticed Edward was staring at a letter. I held out my hand, assuming it was another request for help from Aunt Civility's fans.

"I'll put it with the others."

Startled out of his thoughts, my brother folded the page and glared at me. "This isn't for you."

"Then I'll file it, like I do all your letters."

"Not this one."

He tucked it back into a thick manila envelope, slid the envelope into a drawer, and locked it. Not smart. My brother should know that would only pique my curiosity. I made it a point to never leave my curiosity unsatisfied. Already he had me wondering what could be so sensitive that he wanted to keep it from my eyes. And the move irritated me and brought up a discussion I'd been planning to save for later.

I put my fists on my hips and glared back. "Maybe we should clarify my role. Am I or am I not your secretary? I admit the term doesn't cover half of what I do, which includes duties no secretary with dignity would perform, but I like to do any job I take on well. Yet you keep getting in my way. You're big on examples, so here are a few. Racing me to get the mail every day and going through it instead of letting me sort it. Locking your office door, which makes it difficult to get to the files. Snatching the phone on the first ring instead of letting me answer, 'Edward Harlow's office,' in soothing yet manly tones. If I didn't know better, I'd say you were angling for my job."

"Your job is to do what I tell you."

"Okay. What do you want me to do next?"

He immediately contradicted himself.

"Do I have to spell out everything? Are you helpless?"

I set my jaw. "Yeah. That's me. Mister Helpless. I got that way working for a guy with control issues. Don't forget we need to meet the charity director in the ballroom in an hour."

I slammed the connecting door.

Edward must be sulking about the kiss.

My brother had come a long way since the days after college when he wanted more than anything to sit in a press box and drool over baseball. Or football. Even basketball. Heck, I'd even seen him watch golf.

After hiring Edward to write the Aunt Civility series, Classical Reads helped polish his rough edges to reveal the diamond underneath. He spent less time attending games and more time brushing up on etiquette and manners until he no longer had to slip into his public persona because he wore it all the time.

I was proud of Edward, and I didn't enjoy watching him fumble his career because of his attraction to the Inglenook woman.

It took little thought to decide what to do next. I grabbed my key and set out to deal with the Gold Room, since I knew that's what my brother would tell me to do once he stopped being a jerk. And sooner than later, I would discover the contents of that envelope because no one could convince me it held good news.

CHAPTER 3

When I flipped on the light in the Gold Room, the first thing that drew my eye was the ten-foot-long conference table dead center of the room. That and the podium were additions since we were last here, as well as a small side table with an electric kettle and a basket of instant coffee and teas and such. The dull off-white paint was the same, as was the hotel regulation beige carpet. I wrinkled my nose. A carpet the Inglenooks had recently cleaned.

Last time we were here, this was where Edward was supposed to give his talk to the Victorian Preservation Society. We got snowed in before the VIP gang made it, so he never had the pleasure of lecturing the masses. However, I had checked out the facilities back then and knew what I was up against.

In my room, I had a portable microphone with a headset and a small projector that would hook up to my laptop for Edward's slides. We'd have to settle for projecting them on the wall unless I could get Alfred to help me hang a sheet. At least the podium meant a place where I could set up his notes.

I eyed the table with disfavor. It was too big to get through the door, but if I turned it sideways, I could push it against the back wall and leave room for chairs. I had no idea how many people to expect, but I thought the room could seat eighty if half of them stood and agreed not to breathe.

Since moving the table was a two-man job, and there was only one of me, I shimmied it. Grabbing one rounded end, I discovered the Inglenooks had purchased quality. Solid mahogany weighing about three hundred pounds. I'd just got the front of the table pointed toward the exit when a voice called out, "Please don't do that."

In the doorway stood a severe woman about my age with shoulder-length, auburn hair the color of Claudia's. She got her black suit from the same guy who outfits funeral directors, the ones that used to pull their hearses with horses. Her long black jacket buttoned in the middle, revealing the neckline of a black knit turtleneck, possibly a body suit. Her pants were slim cut and tucked into knee-high boots. Leather.

She could have been pretty, but she looked like a ghoul with her pale skin, sharp green eyes emphasized by kohl liner and fake eyelashes, and a slash of dark red lipstick that might have been blood. I'd have to wait until she smiled to see if she had fangs.

"You're welcome," I said, recognizing her as the woman who had declined to thank me for holding open the door.

"What do you think you're doing?" Her voice had a scratchiness to it that made me wonder if she had a cold.

I stood straight. "Are you newly employed by Inglenook resort?"

She scoffed. "Hardly."

"Then take it up with management."

I moved to the end of the table farthest from her and

swung it a few feet toward the back of the room. Then I repeated with the other side.

She closed the door behind her and lowered her voice. "Mr. Hamilton needs that table. Mr. *Benedict* Hamilton."

"He's welcome to it." I opened the door. "It stinks of carpet shampoo in here. Let it air out."

She must have smelled it too because she stepped farther in without messing with the door.

"You're not listening. He needs to use this room for an important conference. You can't expect him to hide in a corner."

I leaned against the table. "Look, what's your name?"

"Why?"

"Because I don't like to think nasty thoughts about someone unless I know his or her name."

She considered this reasonable because she told me her name was Jennifer.

"I'm Nick. Not that I think you're sending bad thoughts my way."

When she smiled, her eyes crinkled, making her look human. No fangs. "As I said, my boss is Benedict Hamilton."

She waited for me to be impressed, so I told her I wasn't from these parts. She nodded as if that explained why I hadn't swooned. "Mr. Hamilton is the largest developer in Northern Illinois. Private developer, that is. He plans to use this room for a conference this afternoon, and what Mr. Hamilton wants, Mr. Hamilton gets."

"He can have the room, but the table is going to be against this back wall, and I'm setting up chairs. *My* boss needs this room ready for his lectures and demonstrations this week-end. He's the celebrity guest at the fundraiser."

"Mr. Hamilton is on the board of Tea for Teens and a *very large* donor."

Since she thought this was a contest, I said, "You win."

"Who is your boss?" she demanded, opening her notebook as if she thought the information would be in her notes.

"Well, *his* boss is Aunt Civility."

"So, you work, indirectly, for a woman. That's good. I'm incredibly supportive of women-owned businesses."

"You could say that." Edward behaved like an old lady sometimes.

The guest in the room above us jumped off the furniture. At least, I assumed that's what shook the ceiling. Heavy footsteps followed. I fervently hoped the residents above planned to vacate the room to attend Edward's lecture.

As I walked to the other end of the table, I saw her lips part with another protest and cut her off. "Look. Once the table is back against the wall, your boss can pull up chairs. If he sits with his back to the door, it will give the illusion of privacy."

"Mr. Hamilton likes to face the door, and what Mr. Hamilton wants—"

"Mr. Hamilton gets. Yeah, I've heard. He can sit at the end facing the door and leave his client with his back unprotected. That way your boss can give his client intimidating stares, while you sneak up on him."

The latter scenario appealed to her. "That would work. Please take care of it. How long will you be?"

Not being employed by Benedict Hamilton, or her, I bristled. "The more help I have, the sooner I finish."

She looked down at the heavy table. "I'm the personal assistant of the largest private developer in Northern Illinois."

"So you said. I like the sound of that. Personal assistant. Sounds better than secretary. I'll have to talk to Aunt Civility."

"It's not my job to move furniture."

I gave her a withering look. "Just like a woman. When a job is tough, you get a man to do it."

Pressing her lips together, she reached for her end of the table. I let go of mine, crossed my arms, and shook my head.

"I was talking about the chairs. I don't want to be responsible for your hernia. I had an aunt who lived on a farm and did a lot of heavy lifting. It shifted things inside her and she had troubles later in life."

Her jaw dropped, and she took a step back. "I'll get the chairs."

Which was simple since they rolled. Alfred had promised to load some extra folding chairs onto a trolley that I could attend to later.

As she left the room, I grinned. I'd lost score, but the battle had improved my mood. I'd also eliminated one of Edward's gripes. He might even feel calmer with this chore out of the way. Amazing how much I pampered him so he could feel important.

Yes, things were moving in the right direction, toward a peaceful weekend that would push my brother back on track.

At least that's what I thought.

CHAPTER 4

By the time I got to the Ballroom, Edward was already there and conversing with the late Maya Angelou. At least it looked like her.

The woman wore a loose tunic in a pattern of muted orange, yellow, and blue squares over a pair of yellow slacks. Her necklace and earrings, made of large round wooden beads, matched the blue in her tunic. Two teenagers flanked her in matching yellow tracksuits that had a Tea for Teens logo on the back.

The stocky boy, about sixteen, had a tattoo on his neck, and the girl, taller but maybe a year or two younger, wore her hair in a large afro.

This room served as the resort's main dining room.

Mrs. Beckwith, Inglenook's cook, had already made headway on my next meal, which the schedule said would be early so the staff had time to clear the way for dancing on the black-and-white checkered floor. The smells of roasting meat and garlic wafted through the double doors leading to the kitchen where the clatter of cookware made my stomach growl.

A few employees were shifting a backdrop featuring an English garden in front of the double doors that led to the kitchen to provide cover for the servers as they entered and left the room. To the left, two men wrestled with a tabletop fountain, trying to place it near an outlet in the wall. Other staff busied themselves setting the tables, which had been pushed close to accommodate the decorations along the walls.

The sun shone fully through French doors that led outside to the courtyard. It illuminated the party as they stood next to a raised platform where the band would play.

I hummed as I skirted the tables. The hustle and bustle promised an exciting event, one that Edward would enjoy if I had to force him.

When I arrived, Edward turned. I was happy to see he seemed pleased with the organizer.

"Ms. Latoya St. Armand, Miss Makayla, Mister Brandon, may I present you to my brother, Nicholas Harlow."

My brother was stretching the point, since young men aren't typically addressed as mister until they reach eighteen, but the other option for a title, Master, wasn't used on a boy over twelve unless he was the oldest son of a Scottish viscount or baron, which did not apply in this case. Amazing the useless facts I carried in my head since working for Edward.

Both kids seemed shy and gave me tiny waves, but the organizer took my outstretched hand. She did it like a lady would, by turning her hand and grasping my fingers, the purpose being that a man should not crush a lady's hand in a contest of strength but gently squeeze her fingers. It reminded me of the days when a man would have bowed over her digits. I wasn't sure she would appreciate that. Or she might think I was making fun. Today's casual manners are making simple, polite gestures awfully complicated.

I nodded, which is kind of a bow. "A pleasure."

Her smile used all her features. You felt she meant it, so I grinned back.

"I can see the resemblance." She gestured toward my chin. "The shape of the face. The coloring." She looked at Edward. "Is this what you would look like without your beard?"

Edward shuddered. "Perhaps."

Her voice had a richness edged by a vague accent I couldn't place. When she laughed, it came from the belly. She waggled her finger at Edward.

"You should appreciate your brother. Family means everything, both blood relations and those family bonds you form on your own." She gestured toward the teens and they glowed.

Edward swept a hand toward the organizer. "Ms. St. Armand is the executive director of Tea for Teens, but more than that, she founded the charity and built it from the ground up into the wonderful organization it is today."

"I didn't do it single-handed." She nodded slowly. "But you're right. My sweat and blood are in it. It's a part of me just as my right arm is part of me." She smiled. "I've got something to show you."

We followed her to the cardboard box sitting on the bandstand. She pulled back the flaps and, for a minute, I thought she was going to ask us to close our eyes so she could surprise us.

"Look at this." She pulled out a delicate teacup with a pale-pink rose pattern and gold edging. "I got an entire set, including a teapot, sugar bowl, and creamer especially for the demonstration. I've been using the same set since I started the organization, and they were old then. Some were chipped, and—" She grinned like a naughty schoolgirl. "What can I say. I just wanted them."

It was a pretty cup, but when she insisted Edward hold it,

he took the handle in his big fingers and rested the bowl in the palm of his hand with plenty of space leftover.

"Be careful!"

I turned to see the large man who had bumped into me in the lobby. His pale scalp showed through his thinning light-brown hair, and thick lips pointed down at the edges in a perpetual frown. "You'll break it, and they were expensive. An unnecessary expense, not that anyone asked my opinion."

When she greeted him, an expression of resignation replaced Ms. St. Armand's friendly smile.

"Edward Harlow, Nicholas Harlow, this is Benedict Hamilton, one of our board members. And the man next to him is Frederico Agosti, his private secretary."

Frederico Agosti was the man who'd held eye contact with me after Hamilton bumped me in the lobby. The happiness bug hadn't bitten him since then, but after a closer look, I decided his eyes weren't sad but soulful. The type of dark, intense orbs that make women think a man has led a tortured life and only they can help him snap out of it.

I held out my hand. "Benedict Hamilton? The private developer? I've heard of you."

Edward raised a brow in my direction. It was just as well he distracted me, because Hamilton made no move to greet either of us, and private secretaries apparently weren't allowed to shake hands. The kids must have met him before because they melted away.

"I need to speak with you, Latoya," he said.

"We're busy setting up for tonight. Why don't we have coffee later?"

Edward interrupted. "Excuse me, but Ms. St. Armand was just about to show me where to set up my book table."

Hamilton smirked. "It's already set up." He pointed toward the back corner of the room next to a portable bar. "Out of the way."

My brother gaped.

Latoya St. Armand met Hamilton's gaze. "Mr. Harlow should be at the front of the room by the photographer. He is our guest of honor. People might want a picture with him."

"Stop trying to be nice and use your head, Latoya," Hamilton said gruffly. "There will probably be a line of people getting photographs with the backdrop. Anyone crowding around his table will get in the way. Besides. It's not as if he's a famous author. He's just the publicity man."

Hamilton had a point about backed up lines, but I didn't like the way he phrased it. Latoya St. Armand wrinkled her brow and glanced at Edward, who was doing her charity a favor by being here. Responding to her distress, he immediately smoothed out the creases in his expression and put her at ease.

"Please don't give it another thought."

She smiled, relieved, but her happiness was short-lived. Hamilton took hold of her elbow and leaned in.

"More important, I have the votes. I'd like to make an announcement tonight."

Her eyes narrowed. "You wouldn't dare."

"Is there something we can help you with, Ms. St. Armand?" Edward asked.

Hamilton frowned. "We're discussing a private board matter."

Frederico stepped forward and offered to show us to our table.

"They'd have to be blind to miss it," Hamilton said, but then he reconsidered. "Good idea. This isn't for your ears, Rico. Meet me in the bar in fifteen minutes."

Latoya St. Armand broke out her smile again, though it didn't make it to her eyes. "It has been a pleasure meeting both of you. Until tonight?" She bowed her head, and we took the hint.

The three of us walked to the back of the room, pausing by the barren, eight-foot-long table Hamilton had assigned to Edward. The tabletop had scars and stains, as if the staff had found it languishing in the basement. When I rested a hand on the rough corner, the table wobbled.

Rico swept out a hand. "Here we are." He smirked. "You should be grateful. Ben wanted to put you in another room."

Grateful my hind end. Though Edward had done his best to sooth Latoya St. Armand, his typical reaction to being slapped in the face included pounding the slapper on the head. Like a nail. Rico, like me, was a minion, and it wouldn't be fair to take his boss's failings out on him. I set out to make the situation better.

I folded an arm over my chest and rested the finger of the other hand against my lips, nodding. "Excellent."

Edward shot me a perplexed look. "It is?"

I patted his shoulder. "You're right by the entrance, Edward. It's like you're the ambassador for Tea for Teens. Also, you're next door to the busiest location in the place. The bar. I couldn't have picked a better spot if I'd tried."

Rico's eyebrows went up, surprised by my sunny tone. He'd be even more surprised if he knew me.

I approached a harried employee and asked her if she would please make a tablecloth available. After receiving her assurance, I grabbed some coasters from under the bar and slipped the necessary number under the table leg until it was even.

Once I added the white tablecloth brought by the employee, I caught up to Edward in the lobby in time to see Rico disappear into the bar to wait for his master like an obedient servant.

CHAPTER 5

Claudia met us at the bottom of the staircase. In deference to her, Edward called for the elevator instead of taking the stairs.

Her perfume, something flowery with a subtle hint of musk, would have been pleasant on any other living woman. On her, the mixture carried the additional odors of false sweetness and rotten heart that seeped from the wench's pores.

"Nice perfume," I said, sneering down at her.

She narrowed her eyes. "You like it?"

"I'd buy some for my pet monkey if I had one, but he might choke on it."

"I thought *you* were the pet monkey."

The elevator came, and we stepped inside. We were silent on the ride up. It was obvious Claudia wanted time alone with Edward, especially when the doors opened and she said, "Nicholas, if you could excuse us."

Aware that Claudia might have another curve ball up her sleeve, I wasn't eager to leave them alone. I took a page from

Joshua Breen's book and observed nature: the communication habits of a pair of knuckleheads in the wilds of the Inglenook hallways. No photos necessary.

When I closed the door to the Blue-Bell Room behind me, I kept the nob turned so it wouldn't latch and then let it creek open a hair in time to hear the female of the species issue a challenge.

"—and then you ran off before I could say hello."

"You were busy with Joshua Breen."

I recognized the sulk in Edward's tone.

"Josh is my friend. I've known him since I was sixteen."

"Is that when you became betrothed to him?"

Sulk had moved on to sarcasm. Always a sign of recovery.

"Edward. It was a joke. I had a crush on Josh, and he used to tease me. *Someday, I'm going to marry you, Claudie.* It meant nothing."

Silence as they reevaluated their approach.

My brother cleared his throat. "He's done very well for himself."

"Yes. He has."

"And he's quite well known."

"It tickles me to think someone I know is a celebrity." Claudia sounded pleased and completely innocent of any irony. Silence followed her agreement as her partner decided whether to abandon the ritual and adapt to a single life.

"Will you save me a dance, sir?" She made the request in a coquettish voice that I assumed was accompanied by fluttering eyelashes.

"I'll be working."

An impatient sigh.

"Let Nicholas cover for you. You're only handing out books. Even he can handle that."

I smothered a growl.

My brother sighed like a big, sad bear. "Yes, I suppose he could. It's not as if it requires skill. Or talent. A six-year-old child could do it, or a person with limited mental abilities. They could also be physically impaired, as sitting behind a table requires no exertion."

The natural response would have been to ask him what was bugging him, and the answer might tell me why he'd been behaving oddly of late. Instead, there was another moment of silence until she said in a strained, happy voice, "Then I'll see you tonight."

Unless they had been communicating through ESP, they hadn't touched on anything of interest to me, so I closed my door. I gave it a few minutes before knocking, and as I entered his room through the connecting door, I received the full brunt of my brother's anger.

"Where were you? You were late meeting Ms. St. Armand. I don't have time to go searching for you."

"I set up the Gold Room. I got everything in place except the portables. You know, the microphone and the projector. I'm waiting for the rest of the chairs, but that's on Alfred. Anyway, someone needs to use the room for an afternoon meeting."

Edward frowned. "Who?"

"Benedict Hamilton wants to annex a small country for his development company."

"What kind of meeting is it?" he demanded. "How many people will be there?"

"I didn't get an agenda."

"That man has no business using the Gold Room this weekend."

"I know. Not after we called dibs. Will you listen to yourself? It's a public room. Who cares?"

"He'll probably leave coffee cups and trash and move the

furniture to suit his convenience." He slammed his fist on the table, making his pens jump. "Use of the Gold Room is the only request I've made. But I suppose I can't expect anyone to respect my wishes. I'm supposed to be the polite one who cedes to everyone else's desires in order to keep conflict at bay. Essentially, I'm a doormat."

"Don't doormats usually say *Welcome*?"

He growled.

"Look, Edward. This is a big weekend for you. Hundreds of guests are coming tonight, and if they like your book, they may buy the next one. Or go back and pick up copies of the older books. Sales."

"That's all I am. A dollar bill."

"You look fetching in green."

He picked at the corner of his desk. "What about what *I* want? Doesn't that matter?"

"You mean you don't want your books to sell?"

"Of course I do," he mumbled.

"Look. I can't help you if you won't tell me what's on your mind. I agree Hamilton needs a kick in the pants for treating you like you're the hired help, but that doesn't explain your behavior or your attitude lately. Bouncing from snapping at harmless but annoying old ladies to looking like the sun will never shine again. It's like living with Dr. Jekyll and Mr. Hyde, but only if Jekyll wasn't that nice to begin with."

I shouldn't have brought up Hamilton because he got stuck on that.

"Only the publicity guy. I think that's how he referred to me."

"Do you want me to find him and drag him in here so you can teach him some manners? If his sidekick comes along, I'll hang onto him."

The suggestion made him feel better. He almost cracked a smile, so I asked if he'd be changing for dinner.

"There doesn't seem to be any point. We'll have to dress for the masked ball shortly afterward."

I gave him a minute in case he wanted to share anything else, but he shuffled through his papers, ignoring me, so I left to take a quick nap before dinner. Maybe a way to make this weekend work would come to me in a dream.

CHAPTER 6

I didn't take a nap after all. I was worried about that stupid Gold Room. More often than not, I ignored Edward at my peril. So, I jogged down the steps to the first floor to make sure Hamilton hadn't trashed the room.

Past the conference room and some doors marked utility were additional guest rooms. The hallway bustled with maids delivering costumes nestled in clear plastic suit bags to the people attending the masked ball. One young woman carried an enormous pair of wings tucked under one arm.

She winked at me as I stared. "Some people."

That summed it up. I was still distracted by the wings—and the shapely woman carrying them—when the conference room door flew open and Claudia Inglenook burst out. She looked back into the room and said, "Over my dead body. Or yours!" She didn't even look up as she charged past me.

I peered inside. Benedict Hamilton sat at one end of the conference table wearing a smirk. Even though I had no idea what they'd been talking about, I wanted to wipe it off his face.

Alfred had delivered the chairs. They were still on the cart, so I set out to unload them and line them in rows, ignoring the developer while he gathered some papers together and put them in a brown leather briefcase. He glanced my way a few times, trying to decide if I was worthy of a confidence.

A burst of giggles came from the hallway. The maid who'd been carrying the wings walked by with another member of the servant class. She turned her head and winked again as she passed.

Hamilton harrumphed. "Women. They're too sentimental to be any good at business. Don't you think?"

I finished unfolding a chair and stood. "Wait while I wipe away this tear. I was thinking of my mother."

He made a noise of disgust and strode out of the room. Having bested both a business tycoon and his personal assistant in one day improved my mood. I finished in twenty minutes. As a bonus, the room no longer smelled like carpet cleaner.

As I headed upstairs to shower, an uncomfortable sensation niggled at my innards. Benedict Hamilton was a private developer. Logic said he developed properties. Why was he meeting with Claudia Inglenook?

I stopped walking. Were the Inglenooks planning to sell? Maybe her snappy comment was a haggling tactic over an unacceptable price offered by the developer.

Before this place was a resort, Inglenook had been the family home. The remaining Inglenooks still lived here. If they sold the mansion, where would they stay? Was she angling to move in with Edward?

Temporary arrangements had a habit of becoming permanent. And would she bring her crazy Aunt Zali? Icy fingers traveled down my spine. In the words of Claudia Inglenook, *over my dead body.*

I took the stairs two at a time.

Back in my room, Edward had placed a manila file with answered letters on top of my laptop. I took this as a signal that my brother's mind was back on business. I still had time to type them up before I got ready for dinner. Since I didn't want him to lose momentum, I settled in at the desk.

After flipping open the laptop, I let it fire up while I pulled out the top letter. Edward liked to jot notes in his own version of shorthand before handing them off to me to type the response. The first was simple.

Aunt Civility,

My mom's having a fit because I want to invite people to my wedding through social media. It's cheaper. What's wrong with it? I'm saving my money for stuff I want to buy for the house. Stuff that means more to me than fancy invitations. I was going to include an explanation in the post to make my mother happy. It doesn't matter what you say because I've made up my mind. I'm writing to you to shut my mom up.

Princess

His response, by the time I interpreted it, read like this:

Dear Letter Writer,

I looked you up. As no known country has crowned you, I refuse to address you by that ridiculous moniker. By all means put your cheap invitations on social media. You will set the tone for your wedding. Your guests will be grateful that expectations are low when they decide what to spend on your gift.

And since you will have made it clear through your explana-

tion that "stuff" means more to you than the human beings who are being called to witness your nuptials, you may find yourself lucky not to have to go to any expense when they decide not to show up.

Sincerely,

Aunt Civility

P.S. If you are serious about saving money, you could hand-write your invitations. It will take effort, but as you are old enough to marry, you are old enough to put selfish concerns aside and make your guests feel welcome.

Aside from ending a sentence with a preposition, I thought it was a fair response. However, I'm not paid to like Edward's answers but to keep up his image. This didn't sound like a response from an elderly lady interested in leading her followers to their better selves. A snippy older sister, maybe.

I saved the letters under *princesscheap* and sent it to a hold file where I put letters Edward might want to review once again before they became permanent. When I viewed the list of letters previously banished to the hold file, I rubbed the back of my neck. That file was getting pretty fat.

Sometimes the letters spilled over from etiquette advice to just advice, like the next one.

Dear Aunt Civility,

I have a dilemma. My parents want me to work over the summer at the family mini-mart to earn money to pay for my football uniform next year. It's a bore. I've been helping them every holiday since I was ten. My parents would have to hire someone to replace me, but that's business, right? I think it's time I do what I want with my summer vacation. I earned it. I'd rather be a lifeguard at the pool for obvious reasons. If you want to know why a normal teenager is writing to you, my mom likes to read your column, so she'd probably go with what you say. Help me out, okay?

Wannabe Lifeguard

It took me longer than usual to type the response because Edward had done a lot of underlining and crossing out.

Dear Wannabe,

Tough. Life is tough. You are entering adulthood, and being a man means doing things you'd rather not because you must. Every person you pass on the sidewalk, or drive by on the street, or sit next to on the bus, has dreams.

Do you think the person checking you out in the grocery store has longed to do a price check on your potatoes? Or that the school janitor, performing a necessary and underpaid job, dreamed as a child of cleaning up after a bunch of snotty teens? Or that your mother celebrated with fits of joy when you woke her from desperately needed sleep so she could change your diaper?

You would prefer to sit on your posterior and ogle girls all summer. Start using your brain instead of your hormones.

Your parents depend on you. They feed you, house you, and pay for your education, and they ask you to relieve that burden by working in the family-owned business, where you are most likely treated better than you ever will be at any other job you hold throughout your entire life.

Someday, others may depend on you. If you're any kind of man worth knowing, you will do whatever it takes to make them safe, healthy, and happy, even if it sucks the joy from your very soul. Self-sacrifice is underrated.

Man up and stop whining.

Sincerely,

Aunt Civility

P.S. It is right for you to pay for your own uniform because playing high school football is a luxury, not a necessity.

I stared at the response for three minutes, running my bottom teeth over my upper lip. This was bad. This was very bad.

Deep down, Edward respected his fans. If my brother hadn't inked the response himself, he would have had stern words for the person writing them. If this kept up, I'd be editing foul language out of his next book.

That letter, as well as the next three letters, went into the hold file. I decided not to waste any more time typing what my brother would likely change once he pulled out of the moody mire that had him by the ankles. That shows I still had some optimism in reserves.

After closing my computer, I got scrubbed for dinner, and while washing the grime of travel down the drain, Edward's second letter crept up on me.

He talked about dependents as if he weren't a single man. Did he consider me a dependent? I worked my fanny off for him for a paycheck and room and board. That didn't sound dependent to me, so I dismissed the thought and wondered what else might suck the joy from his soul.

Joshua Breen's perfect interception of Claudia's kiss might irk him, but his tantrum started long before this weekend. I dismissed his run-in with Benedict Hamilton as unworthy. Edward wouldn't put energy into acknowledging the ape. His Classical Reads contract wasn't up any time soon, so he wasn't feeling under-appreciated by an insulting offer from the publisher. Mom remembered his birthday with a nice card and a set of engraved pens, so he wasn't suffering from perceived neglect. Besides. He was a grown man, so I crossed off that possibility with a snort.

By the time I finished shaving, I'd run out of possibilities. When I stepped out of the bathroom, moonlight reflected off the glass patio door. Too much thinking had made me dawdle. I was running late.

I didn't want to be late because tonight called for special handling. With donors and bigwigs making an appearance, Edward needed to make a good impression. I put on my light ash-gray suit and double-timed it to the Ballroom.

CHAPTER 7

The traffic headed into the Ballroom was at a standstill. The blame for the backup belonged to an elderly couple up front who decided they didn't like their seating assignment. They argued with the maitre d that people of a certain age should sit at an outside table rather than push through the center where, admittedly, the close quarters might make their fannies rub up against the back of people's heads.

Finally, unable to stand it, I scooted to the front of the line, said, "Excuse me," and gently took the list away and scanned it. I remembered to smile when I handed it back, though I hadn't received good news.

They had placed Edward at a table with Hamilton and me at the next table over, where I might be too far away to chaperon. I sidestepped my way to my assigned spot next to Edward's group without my fanny getting on a first name basis with the seated guests, though I tripped over the purse one lady had left on the floor.

Latoya St. Armand sat on the far side of the VIP table facing the door. She'd already changed, and her silver gown brought out a few silver strands in her hair that I hadn't noticed before. A long necklace of pearls finished the outfit.

There were two empty seats on her left, and Edward sat on her right. Benedict Hamilton and a couple of people I didn't recognize filled in the rest of the chairs. I assumed they were large donors or board members. Or both.

I let out a relieved sigh when I spotted my table next door. There was just enough room to pull back my chair and squeeze in. Edward sat so close we could have filmed a Grey Poupon commercial, which suited me fine.

"Good evening," I said with a nod to those already seated around me as I spread my napkin over my lap.

Jennifer the Personal Assistant took charge and introduced me to the rest of my table mates as Edward Harlow's brother and secretary, Nicholas. I'm not sure if it was to make me sound important or to put me in my place.

"This is Frederico Agosti, Benedict Hamilton's *private* secretary."

Since we'd already met, he merely nodded. "Call me Rico. Everybody does."

I assumed from his unwillingness to shake hands earlier that the private secretary would have a snooty disposition and an uptight carriage. This guy leaned back in his chair, relaxed, in a navy-blue Canali suit. His expression and the casual way he spoke made him seem more like a henchman than office barnacle.

"Mr. and Mrs. Hall are on the Tea for Teens board, as are Mr. and Mrs. Jarvis." Jennifer gestured to two pleasant-looking couples in their sixties.

"Finally, this is the world-renown photographer, Joshua Breen."

Josh grinned at me. "Makes me sound important, doesn't it?"

My reply didn't make it out because Benedict Hamilton

barked out a laugh. I jerked my head to see Edward's reaction, but he had a polite, disinterested expression on his face.

"We rarely come to the charity's social events," Mrs. Hall said, and I turned my attention to her. "Jeff is out of town a lot, and I hate to go alone."

"Blame it on me." Her husband said it with a smile.

"I wouldn't miss one," Mrs. Jarvis said. "Latoya outdoes herself every time." She glanced appreciatively at Edward. "I'm especially excited to meet the guest of honor, though I wish his aunt could be here. She has my sympathy. I understand how limiting physical problems can be."

"Agoraphobia is mental," I said. "Not that the author is a mental case."

"Nicholas works for Aunt Civility," Jennifer said.

Mrs. Hall leaned forward. "I love her books. They've changed my life. Really, they have. Once you have a manual for how to do things properly, you can stop worrying and enjoy yourself. I wish I could have a conversation with her."

"I will pass that on to the author, but anything the author knows, Edward knows, too. That's what he's here for."

"What was it like growing up?" Mrs. Hall grinned. "Was your auntie always correcting you and your brother?"

Edward's publisher, Classical Reads, had put it out that Edward, the public face of the agoraphobic Aunt Civility, was her nephew. That made her my auntie, too.

I cleared my throat to give me a moment to think of something benign to say about a woman who didn't exist. "My aunt is funny. Humorous funny. Not touched in the head. Except the agoraphobia. Mostly, she left us alone, but if we got into trouble, as Edward did a lot, she let us know she wasn't happy. You should ask him about some of his antics. They're pretty amusing."

I nodded my head in his direction and frowned. He didn't look amusing as he absently rearranged his silverware.

Mr. Hall poked his wife. "Did you hear that? She didn't nag."

She giggled, so I assumed it was an inside joke.

Jennifer looked at me over the rim of her glass as she took a sip of wine. "You didn't tell me you were related to the boss."

The way she said it made it sound like she was making a case against nepotism. To be fair, I wouldn't have wound up assisting an author if that author weren't my brother. "You didn't ask."

Her snooty attitude begged me to teach her a lesson. "So, what's a guy need with a personal assistant *and* a private secretary?"

Rico only gave me a lofty smile because he knew I was baiting them, but Jennifer leapt for the hook.

"A man as important as Benedict Hamilton needs people to handle the menial tasks."

Rico frowned at that description.

"He also has an executive assistant to help him in the office. He brought us both because, even when he's on vacation, Benedict is working. I can't imagine a job anywhere else. Or with anyone else. Ben has vision, and he's making his mark. People are going to know his name for years to come. I get to be part of that."

They all turned their heads toward the crash of breaking plates. A waitress had misjudged the space while maneuvering around the backdrop on her way to the kitchen. Fortunately, she'd only been transporting a few salad plates. Also good, the clatter broke off Jennifer's ode to Benedict Hamilton.

When I leaned in to catch the conversation at the table next door, Latoya St. Armand was offering her guests a preview of the coming attractions this weekend. When she mentioned the free books Edward would give away tonight, Benedict Hamilton snorted.

Scooting back in case I needed to make a quick move, my chair legs didn't cooperate, and I almost tipped. I had to grab the edge of the table to right myself. Josh and Rico grinned and clapped. Jennifer laughed out loud. The noise made Edward look over, and even Hamilton sent a quick glance over his shoulder.

My brother raised his glass of wine to his lips, which meant he would let Hamilton's derisive snort pass without comment. But then he gave the developer a pained smile.

"You seem to be at the top of your field, Mr. Hamilton. At least in Illinois. Do you tend to every detail yourself? Or do you have trusted employees who help you get the word out about BenHam, Incorporated?"

So, Edward had done his research on Hamilton and knew his company's name.

"I don't send lackeys to represent me at important events."

Latoya St. Armand gasped, and my leg muscles tensed. Rico leaned back and put a hand on Hamilton's shoulder.

"You're being rude, Ben."

A bold statement for an employee.

Hamilton raised his eyebrows in surprise. "Am I?" He grinned. "Maybe you're right. I'm too direct, not that I consider that a fault, but most people don't appreciate honesty." He nodded to his table mates, lingering on the two couples I assumed were on the board. "Sometimes my desire for what's best for Tea for Teens takes hold of me."

His glance flickered over my brother. "I apologize if I hurt your feelings."

"An unlikely scenario, as that would mean I valued your opinion."

Rico covered his mouth to hold in a guffaw.

"That looks wonderful!" Latoya St. Armand drew everyone's attention to the servers distributing the dinner plates. "Pork medallions are one of my favorites. And are those sweet potatoes?"

Everyone's attention turned to dinner except Rico's. He sent me a look that said he was impressed by the way Edward handled his boss.

A female server set my dinner in front of me. I took satisfaction in knowing the important private developer was eating the same mushy peas as the rest of us.

We moved through dinner with the usual light chit-chat of people who have never met, though I almost missed my mouth a few times trying to keep an eye on Edward.

CHAPTER 8

I didn't even taste my dessert, which was served in a cup. It seemed a shame, as it looked tasty with the berries and cream. My fork made it to my mouth methodically until I went for more and hit the bottom of the glass.

I pushed it away, dabbed my lips with my napkin, and moved to stand up, but the servers arrived just then with coffee.

Compared to the brew Mrs. Abernathy made for us at home, it was swill. Bland and just the other side of lukewarm.

At the VIP table, Edward listened attentively to Latoya St. Armand. He held the cup up as if the only thing keeping him from taking a sip was a desire to catch her every word. My guess is that he'd tried it and was grateful for a reason not to drink.

Mrs. Hall and Mrs. Jarvis started in on Josh, and I tried hard to look interested.

"I'm afraid I'm not familiar with your work," Mrs. Hall said with an apologetic nod.

"Oh, Freda. You must be joking." Mrs. Jarvis heaved her

bosom in the photographer's direction. "I've heard rumors you're getting your own television show. Is it true?"

Josh grimaced. "It's true there are negotiations going on right now, but you know how it is. I'd love to say we start shooting tomorrow, but until we sign the contract, who knows?"

With a pang of jealousy, I wondered how Edward would fare on television. He had the looks, but I got an image of him explaining how to determine who sits where at an important dinner, and my eyes glazed over. He would look ridiculous, and I'd punch anyone who laughed at him, which would mean punching every man breathing. Shaking the thought away, I focused on the conversation.

Mrs. Jarvis had memorized Josh's portfolio and subjected us to detailed descriptions of her emotional highs upon encountering her favorite photos.

She used words like *pure* and *magnificent* a lot and declared that a picture of howler monkeys was an allegory for the repressed voices of...I missed who because I'd lost interest by then. I preferred to study Jennifer's reaction.

The more praise Mrs. Jarvis heaped on Josh, the more agitated Jennifer became. The conversation was over her head, just as it was over the head of anyone with a functioning mind, but what really bugged her was the idea of compliments floating around the room that weren't directed at Benedict Hamilton. She finally busted loose.

"Mr. Hamilton has many pieces of original artwork in his home. He has contemporary artists such as Liu Xiaodong as well as older artists like—"

"People don't want to hear about Ben's *private* home." Rico shot her an annoyed glance and then slipped on the charm for Joshua Breen. "What is your next project? Outside of television."

I imagine life with the personal assistant was a lot like cleaning up after an enthusiastic puppy.

As Josh told us about his hunt for a rare Pangolin, which was rare because the Chinese and Vietnamese considered it dinner, I turned to Jennifer.

"What's the pecking order? Are you Rico's boss?"

I had my answer by the way the Italian American smirked, though he kept his eyes on Josh.

"Well, no," she said, her voice considerably lowered. "We work independently."

"Say you needed help. Would you delegate to Rico? All this private and personal stuff has me confused. Like when you came to the Gold Room. Were you acting in Mr. Hamilton's personal interests or private interests?"

Rico jerked his head toward her with an irritated glare. He didn't know about the Gold Room episode.

Until then, I was enjoying myself in my own sadistic way. Since I didn't want to get her in serious trouble, I waved my hand. "Forget it. It's over my head."

Josh leaned in. "You like to stir things up."

I grinned. "My life isn't nearly as exciting as yours."

"Tell us about Aunt Civility's next project," Mrs. Hall said. "The inside scoop."

Glancing around the table, I caught Josh's interested expression and Rico's smirk, and something happened. For the first time, I felt embarrassed about my brother's books. A tome on the proper way to picnic didn't warrant their level of excitement. I couldn't even get the word *picnic* out in front of the men. So, I lied.

"She's experimenting with a new idea, one with a broader appeal that includes the men."

The ladies oohed. Mr. Hall said it was about time, since she seemed to write her current books for women.

"How does your brother cope with being a man in a

woman's world? I suppose it helps you're there to support him."

"Thanks for the compliment. You know, there's more to my brother than fancy manners and the work he does for Aunt Civility. A whole other side people don't see. For instance, he was the defensive MVP two years running in college."

Mrs. Jarvis purred and sent him another appreciative glance, while her husband stopped looking bored and sat up.

"What position?"

"Linebacker."

As I related some humorous anecdotes about Edward making mincemeat of other players while always helping them to their feet after the play—I added that bit for the ladies—I couldn't help but brag about his incredible memory for stats.

"Go ahead. Quiz him. I dare you to trip him up."

Mr. Jarvis declined on the basis that he didn't have a head for numbers and the only thing that mattered to him was if what happened on the field increased the contents of his wallet.

We had moved on to baseball and the upcoming training camps when Claudia wandered up on her hostess rounds. She handled both our tables at once and stood on an angle between my chair and my brother's.

Edward led the men at both tables in standing. Benedict Hamilton dabbed his lips with his napkin before making his move. When he rose, he bowed slightly to our hostess with a mocking smile.

Claudia insisted we all take our seats, and as Benedict sat down, he looked our way. When his gaze landed on Joshua Breen, his eyes opened in surprise.

I glanced at Breen, and his lips curved in a slight smile. His green eyes reflected a hunter's gleam.

"I hope everything was satisfactory." Claudia employed her best hostess voice.

"As always," Edward said, matching Hamilton's bow but skipping the smirk.

"You must let me have the recipe for the raspberry dessert," Mrs. Hall gushed. "So scrumptious."

My brother looked at her. "The fool."

"Edward," I hissed, ready to believe he had transformed into Mr. Hyde.

Her smile slipped. "I beg your pardon?"

Perhaps realizing he'd left room for misinterpretation, Edward cleared his throat. "The dessert. The dessert was Raspberry Fool."

Claudia jumped in. "It's one of Mrs. Beckwith's specialties. I'm sure she'll be happy to share the recipe. I'll make sure you get it before you check out."

"*Mrs.* Beckwith," Benedict Hamilton stressed.

"Our cook." Claudia lifted her chin in a challenge.

Hamilton looked around at his table mates as if he couldn't believe what he'd just heard. "Cook? Not a chef? Where did she receive her training?" He raised his index finger. "Wait. I interviewed her."

"You what?"

Hamilton held up a hand as if Claudia's reaction weren't important.

"She learned at her mother's knee. Quaint, but hardly up to resort standards."

Rico leaned in, attentive, as if the boss might expect him to take notes.

"I notice you cleaned your plate," Claudia said, getting snippy.

Latoya's smooth alto intervened. "I like the term cook much better than chef. It's personal. Homey. Whereas chef…"

She turned her hand palm up as if weighing the title of chef and finding it lacking. "It's too sterile for me."

Mrs. Hall agreed. "I'd much rather eat home-cooked meals."

Latoya smiled. "The best cook I know is my mother, and she had no formal training."

"Who's talking about Mama Babsy?"

Latoya rose to her feet and flung her arms around a beautiful woman who reminded me of Jada Pinkett-Smith. It was the warm hazel eyes, delicate features, and toned arms revealed by her sleeveless sheath dress. I'd fallen a little in love with the actress when she appeared on the television show *Gotham.* I'd rooted for her to take over the city, and when her character died, I stopped watching.

Naturally, Edward stood at the arrival of new guests, as did the other man, the one who wasn't Benedict Hamilton.

Latoya chuckled, delighted. "You made it."

My eyes moved to the man standing with them, and my jaw dropped.

"Jumping Jezebel!"

Joshua Breen looked up with interest.

"Nicholas. Watch your language. There are ladies present."

Edward turned to apologize and froze. "Good gad."

Latoya beamed at us. "I'd like to introduce you to my dear friend, Shauna, and her husband—"

"We've met," I said.

"Indeed, we have," Edward muttered.

Staring back from across the table, Detective Jonah Sykes from the San Diego County Sheriff's Department lost his smile. The same Detective Sykes who had investigated the death of Professor Jonathon Taylor in Citrus Grove last year. He had considered Edward a suspect for a while, though the detective had relegated me the minor role of accomplice.

If I had to describe him, I would say he was Edward's twin, except for being black. At six-feet-two-inches, he stood just as tall, had the muscular physique as if he, too, had been a linebacker in college, and he wore a trim goatee. Their eyes differed. His were topaz, not gray like my brothers, but they had the same intensity. In Edward, I called it arrogance. I didn't know Sykes well enough to say for sure.

Sykes' wife looked at us with interest. "You know these people, Jonah?"

He forced out a smile. "We've met a few times. This is Edward Harlow, official representative of the author Aunt Civility, and his brother, Nicholas."

Detective Sykes stressed the words *official representative*, as he'd never found proof that Edward *was* Aunt Civility during his investigation. At the time, he thought it mattered.

"Edward Harlow is our guest of honor," Latoya said.

With the way they had arranged the seating, Shauna Sykes was the guest of honor, as they had placed her on Latoya's right. I'm sure it wasn't intentional.

Shauna slid her glance up at her husband and smiled flirtatiously. "You never told me you hung out with such famous people."

So, he didn't want his wife to know we'd been suspects in a murder investigation. That suited me fine, and Edward followed his cue.

"Auntie is the famous one." Edward gestured toward me. "We're lucky enough to be related."

I'd never noticed before how Edward's moniker had robbed him of the simple pleasure of receiving a compliment, since he always had to volley it to Auntie.

"It's nice to have celebrity friends." Shauna squeezed Latoya's shoulders, and the organizer responded with modesty.

"I'm only known among the people my charity helps and

by the donors I regularly apply to." She shook Shauna's arm. "And the people who pitch in and make my life easier."

Perhaps feeling no discussion about famous people would be complete without mention of private developers, Benedict Hamilton cleared his throat.

Latoya introduced the others at their table first, saving him for last. "And this is Mr. Benedict Hamilton, one of our board members."

When Shauna and Sykes looked at Benedict, their gazes landed on the famous photographer at my table.

"Oh my gosh." Shauna swept around the table to the back of Josh's chair. He stood as did I and the male half of the Hall and Jarvis team, since the Sykes were now new arrivals at *our* table.

"Joshua Breen." She said his name in a sigh.

"The photographer?" Sykes joined her and shook his hand. "You've made quite a name for yourself. I've tried my hand at some outdoor photography. Birds and little things like that. My equipment isn't very advanced." He chuckled, embarrassed.

"You have to start somewhere. I remember my first photos. I took them with a Kodak disposable."

Sykes lowered his voice. "How do you get your subjects to hold still?"

While they gushed over him like a couple of schoolgirls, I smirked and made eye contact with Edward. He didn't return the smile.

Claudia excused herself and stepped up to the microphone on the bandstand, where a backdrop of pink balloons shaped into a heart provided background. It reminded me of my high school prom.

The chatter had increased as diners finished eating, and she had to shush them several times. Once she had everybody's attention, she requested we adjourn to our rooms and dress for the masked ball. Coffee service would continue in the Welcome Room.

My brother tossed his napkin on his plate, nodded to his fellow guests, and strode out of the room. When I moved to follow, I got trapped in a conversation with Mrs. Hall about Edward's last book on bringing back the family meal as an alternative to fast food dining.

Since my brother insisted we treat the fans like royalty, and I couldn't imagine telling the queen to save it until next we met, I answered her questions based on my detailed knowledge of his books and lectures.

By the time I made it out of there, most people had finished coffee and were headed back to their rooms to change for the ball.

Jennifer the Personal Assistant walked side-by-side with Rico Agosti, probably working out how to do Hamilton's breathing for him just to make his life easier.

Joshua Breen seemed in a hurry. Maybe he needed to polish his camera lens before the event.

After knocking on the connecting door and receiving no answer, I went into my brother's room. He was in the shower and called out that he'd meet me downstairs.

I stood in my room and considered my own costume options. It took me about two seconds to decide I wasn't wearing tights. Ever.

CHAPTER 9

Edward stood just inside the doors to the Ballroom, the legs under his loose-fitting trousers spread shoulder width in a combative stance and one leather-gloved fist rested on his hip. This pulled his cape back and exposed an impressive leather scabbard with intricate detailing that held the sword at his side.

His flat, brimmed, black hat covered a black headscarf tied at the base of his neck that went over his eyes, except for two holes so he could see. The only hint of color was the red sash tied around his waist.

The romantic in him had to be thrilled with the manly figure he presented, but the corners of his mouth pointed down in a frown.

He turned his head. His gray eyes, emphasized by the scarf, scanned my navy-blue suit. "You didn't change."

"Obviously."

"What happened to your Robin Hood costume?"

"It got lost in the mail."

"Well?" he demanded with more force than necessary. "Who are you supposed to be?"

"A man."

When I scanned the ballroom, a pattern emerged, and I understood Edward's disappointment. In one quick glance, I counted six Zorro costumes not including his.

"You're a popular guy."

"The costume shop Claudia used suffered a flood."

"I heard."

"The back of the storeroom was spared."

"And that's where they kept the Zorro costumes."

"It would appear."

"Yours is nicer."

He grunted an acknowledgment.

It wasn't hard to see what else the costume shop kept in their back room. A large proportion of guests wore pirate costumes, flapper dresses, Dracula outfits, and medical scrubs with plastic stethoscopes.

Looking them over confirmed my feeling that grown adults shouldn't play dress-up. They overestimated their attributes and wound up looking silly.

I did a double take when I saw Claudia Inglenook's costume. Now I knew who belonged to the wings. The leaves of the green felt Tinker Bell skirt came just below her fanny in points and was paired with matching tights and moccasins.

Then she turned to give me her profile. It wasn't Claudia at all. The auburn hair belonged to Jennifer the Personal Assistant.

Other than the guests, the Ballroom presented an impressive site. Claudia and Robert had spared no expense to make sure the donors felt they were getting their money's worth. I hoped those donors would cough up hefty checks made payable to Tea for Teens.

They had pushed all the tables from dinner into clusters along available wall space, leaving the main floor clear for dancing and socializing.

Male and female waiters in black pants, white shirts, white vests, and bow ties wove in and out of the crowd with trays of champagne glasses filled to the brim, while others tempted the guests with little paper cups filled with stuffed mushrooms, baked Brie, and other finger foods.

The French doors stood open and led to the large courtyard patio, about an eighth of a football field in size, and I could see people mingling next to heat lamps.

Our book table, in its spot against the wall on the other side of the portable bar, might have been invisible. Anyone walking in would have to look over their shoulder to spot us. But there was hope.

Next to our table, a cluster of people dipped strawberries into a chocolate fountain. Maybe some of them would wander over. I just wouldn't let them handle the books until I checked their fingers.

Though I hated to give Hamilton credit, he was right. A long line formed in front of the English garden backdrop and wound along the wall to behind the bandstand.

Someone had placed a table and two chairs in front of the English garden backdrop and surrounded the edges with several large potted plants from the Atrium to bring the garden to life. The Wicked Witch of the West and Dorothy from the *Wizard of Oz* sat and posed with teacups raised. I noted the photographer, dressed in a tuxedo, was not Joshua Breen.

A short squat Dracula and a woman dressed as Queen Elizabeth, an assumption I made because she wore a sparkling sheath dress in muted mauve with her tasteful tiara, approached Edward and expressed their appreciation of Aunt Civility's books.

"Your aunt is a wonder," the female half said. The band started a number, so she raised her voice. "I'd love to meet her in person to see how she acts in everyday situations. You wonder if someone that savvy about etiquette worries in social situations."

"It becomes second nature," Edward said, and then he caught himself. "At least, that's my understanding."

The man didn't agree. "She'd make me nervous. I'd worry about her studying me like a specimen and judging my every move."

His wife nudged him. "It would be good for you. Maybe you'd hold open the door for me once in a while."

"I would if you didn't charge ahead of me all the time."

The argument ended on an up note when she smirked at him. "Learn to keep up."

The band members, decked out in pink jackets, played a jazzy version of a waltz. I'll admit the people who took to the floor knew what they were doing. One couple dressed as Calamity Jane and Wild Bill Hickok did the Texas Two Step and fit right in. Not that any of it looked like waltzing.

Benedict Hamilton, also dressed as Zorro, twirled Cinderella around the floor, and a guy dressed as the top vampire looked as if he wanted to sink his fangs into his partner's neck.

Another couple floated around the edges of the dance floor. Claudia wore a green ball gown from the era where the women looked like bells. The dress pushed her breasts into cleavage I didn't know she had, since she usually wore demure dresses. Her long, satin gloves reached the middle of her upper arm. Like many of the women, she held a mask on a stick in one hand.

She was dancing with yet another Zorro. That wasn't a shock, since the odds of finding one were in her favor, but when they turned, I saw a hint of blond hair under the head-scarf. Edward saw it, too.

"Want a drink?"

Edward hesitated. "No. I have to greet the public when I hand out my books."

"Yeah. Hand them out. Free."

"It's for charity, Nicholas."

"You could have given them a percentage of your sales."

"And looked cheap. That's not the impression I want people to have of Aunt Civility."

I felt a sharp pain in my thigh. "Ow!" I rubbed the spot, and Edward adjusted his scabbard. "Is that thing real?"

"I told the costumers I was striving for authenticity. I didn't want to wind up with a plastic cape and a child's toy."

"Yeah. Where's the fun in that? Are you bonded?"

He grabbed the scabbard and shook it. "It's a nuisance. It's heavy, and the damn thing keeps getting caught on things."

"Well, stop fiddling with it before you hurt someone. And don't swear in public."

My brother took one last look around the room and sighed, resigned. "Let's make sure the books made it here without damage."

What he meant was I should check the books for damage while he looked over my shoulder and made comments. Under his supervision, I unloaded our stock into stacks on the table. They looked fine to me, but darned if Edward didn't recheck every book and rearrange my piles.

Latoya St. Armand spotted us and lowered her mask. I would have recognized her anyway by the silver dress. She worked her way through the crowd, stopping to say a few words to people who demanded her attention. When she got to us, she dragged her toes the last few steps and laughed.

"I'm already worn out, and we've only just begun." She stepped back to admire Edward's costume. "It suits you. Very romantic."

He bowed. "Thank you."

She didn't comment on my lack of costume, probably because she'd skipped out on wearing one, too.

"I took a head count from the RSVPs, but sometimes people drop in. You can't exactly toss crashers out of a fundraiser. It doesn't seem charitable. Do you have extra copies just in case?"

I answered because Edward wouldn't know. "I brought a box on the plane, just in case. I miss the days when you could check luggage for free. They're in the trunk of the rental car."

"A man after my heart. Organized. One less thing for me to worry about."

"Is there anything else I can do for you?" It wasn't because she'd just complimented me, though it helped. I liked her. She was a nice lady. Unlike Edward, she'd appreciate my efforts.

She glanced around the room and waggled her finger as if taking inventory. "No. I think I'm good." She raised her eyebrows at me and cocked her head. "I *know* I'm good. I must be to keep on top of the paperwork, the teens, the donors, the guests, the parents, the events. You name it, I'm in charge of it."

"Sounds like a heavy load."

She nodded at me. "Fortunately, I love what I do." Someone called her name, and she lifted her shoulders, took a deep breath, and let them drop with her exhale. "I love what I do with my teenagers and how it impacts their lives. The rest is…necessary." Then she put on her brightest smile, turned, and greeted the latest guests.

Claudia waltzed up just then—figuratively, not literally—with her hand resting on the arm of her dance partner.

"You're here."

Edward's mask hid his eyebrows, but I'm sure he raised them. "Of course."

She giggled. "I wasn't sure with all the Zorros in the room."

"You're quite the dancer," I said to Josh.

"If we looked good out there, it's all because of Claudie."

Josh being modest again. I might wind up liking him.

My brother pulled his watch from his pants pocket and glanced at it. "It's almost time for Latoya to make her speech."

"Did Zorro have a timepiece?" I said. "Wouldn't it have been on a chain?"

Josh laughed, but I heard the growl at the back of Edward's throat and decided to check my humor for the night.

"Hey, Red!"

There's something about the sound of a raised, slightly drunk, female voice that gets on my nerves, and from her reaction, Claudia felt the same way. She jerked, her shoulders scrunched, and the edges of her mouth pulled down into a frown that bared her teeth.

The source of the shout came from either the slim female Dracula or the woman in medical scrubs, both approaching the table.

Dracula had short, brown hair slicked back and a set of rubber fangs protruding over a full bottom lip. The nurse had her Afro pulled back into a bun. Her attributes included long legs, deep dimples, and almond-shaped, hazel eyes.

Claudia turned. "Rhonda? Tiffany?"

The creatures gathered around the half-owner of Inglenook with girlish giggles and shrieks. Claudia responded in kind, though hers seemed forced. I thought it would be interesting to see how she introduced Edward and Josh to her friends, but the matter didn't come up. She didn't introduce any of us.

"When we got the invites and saw your name, we couldn't believe it." Scrub Girl, who I later determined was Rhonda, delivered her line with her hand spread over the center of her chest as if reliving the shock.

"And we—" Tiffany, slurred. She made a noise of disgust and yanked her fangs out. "Can't talk with these things in my mouth. We had to come!"

Not drunk then.

The three women had a group hug, with Rhonda and Tiffany bouncing on their toes. Claudia didn't have any bounce, but maybe dancing had tired her out.

"You're still stuck here?" Rhonda asked. She grabbed Claudia's hand and squinted. "And still single, I see. Brad and I finally got married."

"Did he finish his residency?" Claudia asked.

Tiffany put an arm around Rhonda's shoulder. "Doctor Brad is a surgeon. Who'd have thunk? Although, girlfriend here always said he had amazing hands."

Female Dracula and Scrub Girl chortled, while Claudia joined Josh, Edward, and me in our embarrassment. Talk of sex had Claudia's friends eying the males around our table. Suddenly, Tiffany's eyes boggled. She swept up to Josh.

"You are Joshua Breen."

He held his ground. "I am."

Rhonda forgot about Dr. Brad in her rush forward to grab the photographer's hands. "You took the picture of Michelle Obama feeding ducks. The one that wound up on *Hour Magazine.*"

"I did."

Josh kept his answers short in self-defense. Every time he spoke, they squealed. The noise was getting on my nerves.

Tiffany smirked at Claudia. "You always did like them blond."

Edward darted a glance at Josh, but when he caught me looking, he pretended an interest in the chocolate fountain.

"Remember Guy Wallers?"

Claudia blanched. Tiffany nudged Rhonda, and the two of them giggled like hyenas.

"Red here thought he was hot," Tiffany explained, including Edward and I in the conversation. "He came across as such a nice guy. Didn't he wear glasses?"

Rhonda confirmed this as if astigmatism came with a set of manners. "Girl, what you did to him is legend. They're still talking about it in the Alpha Gamma Theta newsletter."

Tiffany noted our blank expressions. "Red and Guy went on a date."

"They don't want to hear this," Claudia pleaded, but Tiffany forged ahead with relish. When a waiter passed, Claudia lunged for him, grabbed a flute of champagne, and downed it.

"Oh! Me too!" The sorority sisters helped themselves, and after a sip, Tiffany continued. "By the end of the night, Guy turned into a pair of hands. Our Red had to teach him a lesson. It's a good thing that the vase was handy. Get it? Handy?"

Edward growled. Rhonda looked at him in surprise. "Brad said it was only a minor concussion."

"It would have been worse if we hadn't pulled you off him." Tiffany nodded. "You just kept hitting and hitting. It looked like a massacre, but all that blood came from his broken nose."

"Broken noses bleed a lot," Rhonda said, passing on wisdom she'd picked up from Dr. Brad.

Claudia clutched their arms. "That's history. What are you both up to now?"

Tiffany narrowed her eyes. "After that, you moved out of the sorority and stopped coming to parties, not to mention meetings."

Rhonda snickered. "Our meetings *were* parties."

Her counterpart grinned and nodded. "Yeah."

Claudia shoved her bangs off her forehead. "Too much on my plate. You know how it is. But what have you two been up to?" she asked again, more forcefully this time.

While Female Dracula and Scrub Girl bragged about their accomplishments, the two men watching them drew my gaze. I assumed the square guy of medium height with bushy sideburns belonged to Rhonda from the way he held his wine glass in slender fingers. A surgeon's hands.

The other guy was over six feet tall with thinning blond hair. Both had a start on pot bellies.

The band ended their song, and Latoya St. Armand stepped up to the microphone. Female Dracula and Scrub Girl, after a whispered goodbye with muted squeals, returned to their mates.

"Excuse me, everybody. Could I have your attention?"

The chatter died down, and Claudia and her blond sidekick moved forward to get a better view.

"Thank you all for coming to the first Tea for Teens Masked Ball."

She waited for the applause to die down and continued. "I began Tea for Teens seven years ago with the help of three women, including my good friend, Shauna, who's here tonight."

She gestured to Cruella De Vil. I did a double take. Detective Sykes wore a Dalmatian costume, though if the Dalmatians in the movie had been that large and muscular, it would have only taken one pup to wipe out Cruella and her entire gang. That man must love his wife like nobody's business. Then again, if my wife resembled Jada Pinkett-Smith, I would have worn the Robin Hood costume.

"We held our first tea in December of that year, and we've been changing lives ever since. I'd like to introduce you to two of our graduates who will take part in the demonstration on Sunday at ten A M in the Gold Room. Meet Brandon and Makayla."

The teenagers had changed into nice jeans and yellow polo shirts bearing the charity logo. They waved from the side of the stage.

"As for their stories," Latoya continued, "that's none of your business. I will tell you their help is of immeasurable value to me. I rely heavily on these two young adults, and they are up to the challenge."

Both teens tried unsuccessfully not to grin at her praise. Everyone cheered them, and they waved again.

"Now I know you all are itching to dance. You'll hear my whole spiel on Tea for Teens at my talk on Sunday after the tea demonstration." She smiled at the crowd. "You should have received a schedule of events in your package, including a talk by Brenda Peters about finding the perfect tea for your personality and how to brew it to perfection. That takes place back here tomorrow morning. You don't want to miss it because there will be gifts and a drawing for prizes. In the afternoon, Edward Harlow, Aunt Civility's nephew, will tell us all the rules that used to apply to formal dances. Consider yourself lucky we didn't impose them tonight."

As the crowd chuckled, she looked to the back of the room and motioned to my brother. Heads followed her gesture. "Mr. Harlow is waiting to hand out your free copy of Aunt Civility's book, *Will You Play Mother? Bringing Afternoon Tea into American Homes.* Aunt Civility donated the signed copies."

There were a few oohs and aahs and a smattering of polite applause because cheering for free stuff would have been vulgar. Josh and Claudia clapped and smiled along with the others, but instead of appreciating his girlfriend's loyalty, Edward averted his gaze.

"One moment, please."

Benedict Hamilton climbed onto the stage. The black sash of his Zorro costume emphasized a small paunch.

Latoya put her hand over the microphone, but I still heard what she said. "This is not an appropriate time."

He brushed her aside and snatched the microphone. "Could I have a show of hands from the board members in the room?"

After exchanging wary glances, several people's hands went up including Mrs. Hall, Mrs. Jarvis, and Cinderella.

"Six. Excellent. We have a quorum. If we could meet tomorrow morning in the Gold Room at eight on the dot, we have an important decision to make." He glanced at the faces staring back at him—some annoyed, some bored—and kept it short. "I'll see you then."

Stuffing her emotions inside, emotions that probably ranged from embarrassment to fury, Latoya wrapped things up and everyone returned to drinking, dancing, and chatting. I wandered behind the table.

"That was awkward."

"The man's an ass."

"I wonder what's so urgent."

"To a man like that, everything is urgent. That's what makes him an ass."

When Benedict Hamilton came down from the stage, several men approached him, some of them also in Zorro costumes. They conferred with their heads together. It looked ridiculous, like a pack of caped crusaders ready to defend the commoners against the corrupt government officials. They'd need more Zorros.

Then their voices got loud. The conference broke up when Hamilton walked away. That's when I noticed I wasn't the only one interested in the private developer.

A bald guy in a gray pinstripe power suit stood off to the side, hands in trouser pockets, watching Hamilton like a cat watches a mouse. I couldn't read the expression in his eyes because of the black-framed glasses he wore, but his lips were flat-lining, neither lifting in friendship nor drooping with displeasure. Joshua Breen walked by the man, cutting off my view, and by the time he passed, the guy had turned away.

"For a photographer, Joshua Breen hasn't been taking many pictures."

We both stared at the famous man. He approached Claudia, who was talking to a group of guests, whispered something in her ear, took her hand, and led her back to the dance floor. The band's musical selections had moved forward a few centuries, since you can only do so much waltzing before a desire to start a revolution kicks in.

Benedict Hamilton seemed to be working out his aggression. He had Cinderella by the hand and twirled her. It was the same woman he'd danced with all night. I'd noticed her because I always thought Cinderella had black hair. Raven black. Hers was mousy brown. Under the wraparound mask I could see a set of small, white teeth when she smiled, which she did a lot. At least one person liked the local developer.

My mistake. There were two. As the dance ended, Tinker Bell approached and held out her hand to Hamilton with a shy smile. He only shook his head and laughed before escorting Cinderella to a chair. Tink took the public snub by glaring at Cinderella before slinking away, dejected. Some guy in hospital scrubs offered his services, but the fairy turned him down and went to a corner table to sulk.

Since Aunt Civility had already signed the books, most people filed by and grabbed their copy with a nod or a quick hello before returning to the dance floor. Every time a woman walked up, Edward stood, and every time he stood, his sword bumped against the table. When he finished with his latest non-paying customer, he wrenched the sword in its scabbard from his waist and slid it to the far end of the table, muttering, "Damn thing."

"Save the language until you get back to your room."

I only put half an effort into my admonishment because I didn't want to wave a red cape in front of the bull.

"Is it any good?" A genie, or maybe a fairy godmother, with brown skin, long black curly hair, and a Hispanic accent held up Edward's book.

"His best, so far."

She sipped the cocktail she held in her other hand. "You have to say that, don't you?"

"I'm only paid to lie on Tuesdays. Never on Friday."

She took another sip from her drink "It's free, right?"

When I agreed, she condescended to take a copy, though I noticed she set it down on an unoccupied table along with her empty glass and abandoned them there.

A couple dressed in matching pirate suits approached. Edward plastered on a smile and greeted them. I could tell it took effort. A few more people lingered to hear about the famous author. Auntie, not Edward. When he launched into a story, they leaned forward, rapt.

My brother had a talent for weaving a tale. He could make it up as he went along. I found myself drawn into a scenario where young Edward had suffered Auntie's disappointment when she caught him walking with a girl. He had allowed the young lady to walk curbside, and a passing car had splattered her with muddy water from a puddle.

When Claudia's voice reached my ears, I stuffed down my irritation because I wanted to hear how the story ended.

She tried to catch Edward's attention by standing there and looking beautiful, but my brother, who was now speaking with an elderly woman, wouldn't dream of not giving his guest his undivided attention. So, Claudia turned her attention to me.

"Are people taking the books?"

The question didn't deserve an answer since she could see half of them were gone.

"What's your secret?" I asked the photographer.

"What secret?" he said, the eyes peering out from his mask wary.

"How do you take pictures without a camera? Aren't you the photographer for the event?"

Claudia came to the rescue. "When Josh unpacked, he found his camera's sensor was damaged."

Blond Zorro reached under his cape and pulled out a cell phone. "I've had to make do with this."

"I haven't seen you take any pictures."

He grinned, strolled over, and flipped through some candid shots of guests. "That's part of the secret. Being subtle."

I had to admit they were excellent. In a black-and-white shot of Latoya St. Armand and her teens, you got the feeling of expectant change, as if they were baby birds preparing to leave the nest to embark on lives of their own. Her expression reflected a mother's warmth. Proud of their development yet kind of sad that they were turning into adults.

Another, in color, made the dancing Tinker Bell and her partner, Dracula, look like they were taking off in flight in some fantasy world.

"Those are incredible. I usually get candid shots of my feet."

Breen's laughter came out deep and full. Edward broke eye contact with his fans and looked up. He quickly returned his attention to the couple in front of him, but his smile strained around the edges.

This wasn't like him. A shot of annoyance would have been more in line with the brother I knew. It worried me.

Once Edward was free, he sat back and closed his eyes. I

leaned against the table, intent on cheering him up. "You were right. Your fans seem pretty pleased with the free book."

His eyes stayed closed. "That's nice."

"And the charity ball seems to be working out fine for Latoya St. Armand. Maybe she'll pick up a few sizable donations."

"Let's hope so."

It took Claudia's request for a dance to wake him up. He shook off whatever cloud was hanging over him and gave her a gentle smile that seemed to be considering some aspect of her he couldn't name. She looked down, embarrassed, and repeated her request. When it looked like he would decline, I stepped in.

"Move. Let me take over for a while." I nudged him off the chair. "I don't feel like I'm earning my keep, and if anyone has a question, well, I've been over your books and lectures so often I can answer them in my sleep."

He stared at me, and I got the feeling I'd unintentionally stabbed him in the throat. The cloud came back, but I steered him out from behind the table. "Miss Claudia Inglenook, may I present Mister Edward Harlow. He's not much to look at, but maybe you can have pity on him and partner up for the next dance."

"Well, sir?" She held out her hand.

When he bowed and kissed her gloved hand, she giggled. Edward escorted her to the dance floor, where they melted together for a moment before launching into the dance.

Having taken ballet classes to help with his execution on the football field, my brother moved with the light dexterity of a pro. He held her hand in his big paw with the other resting on her waist, twirling her to the one-two-three tempo of a traditional waltz while other couples made room.

His cape and her dress flew out with each turn, making it

seem they were spinning at high speed, and when the song ended, the guests applauded. Edward bowed to his partner, and Claudia's cheeks were still flushed a healthy pink by the time he escorted her back to the table.

For just a moment, he looked happy. Then his gaze landed on his books and his features firmed up and settled into the expression of polite interest he wore in public. He thanked her for the dance, and as the band moved to the next selection, she grabbed my hand and yanked.

"You haven't danced with me yet, Nicholas."

She looked up at me with her lying green eyes, and I looked down at her with my frank gray eyes, both of us trying to disguise our mutual dislike.

"I should stick around in case I'm needed."

"For what?" Edward rumbled. "I don't need a babysitter."

After I led her to the dance floor and got my hand on her waist and her free hand in mine, she went straight to the point.

"What's wrong with Edward?"

"What do you mean, wrong?"

"Don't be obtuse."

"That's a big word. Do you know what it means?"

She accidentally stepped on my foot with her heel, and I mistakenly swung her into a dip without warning, pulling her up at the last moment. While she clutched my hand and jacket tight and caught her breath, I debated whether putting our heads together might not be a good idea.

"Okay. He's not himself."

As I swung her around, she twisted her neck to get a view of my brother. "How long has this been going on? Last week he mentioned a missed deadline, but he wasn't anywhere near as down as he's been since he arrived. He's not himself. I don't like it."

"Boo-hoo for you—ow!"

I shook my index finger. The one she'd bent backwards.

"Is there something specific that's happened lately?" she asked. "Something to do with his books?"

"If you mean one incident, no."

A sigh escaped her lips. "He's lost his confidence."

I pulled back my head and looked down. "Keep searching because that's not the answer."

"Fine. He's—he's sad."

When she said it out loud, I knew she was right. Hurrah for women's intuition. Of course, being a man, I recognized the symptoms just like she had, only I wouldn't have used a soppy word like sad.

"Are the two of you having a spat?" I demanded.

"We don't have spats. We discuss things."

"Lying banshee."

"Ignorant twit."

"Have you picked out your next victim, Red? There's a handy vase in the library."

She firmed up her jaw. "I hope I'm there the next time someone from your past embarrasses you."

Since I had an extensive list of things I'd rather not have known, I conceded the point and apologized. The music ended, and as I led her back to the book table, we agreed to keep our eyes and ears open for the reason behind Edward's, um, sadness.

"Interesting dance routine," Josh said, holding out his hand to offer my partner a port of safety from me. "I don't know if I can top that," the photographer said as she accepted his offer.

"Thank heavens," Claudia mumbled.

Crowded with moving bodies, the room had gotten noticeably warmer, and the brief exercise had made me sweat under my jacket. I kept going past the table to the bar and got myself a scotch cut with water, which I know is akin to heresy, but I wanted to keep my head clear. This wasn't the time for nosing the dram, but I did sip and chew before I swallowed to a burst of pepper.

As I wandered the room, I tried to recognize the faces under the masks. The women were easy, as many of them had masks on sticks that they held up to their eyes when they wanted to disguise themselves, which was pointless, since the people they were hiding from were the same ones they'd just been talking to sans mask.

Mrs. Hall had on a flapper dress in dignified black that revealed her thick ankles, but her feather boa covered the wrinkles in her neck and cleavage.

Her husband hadn't been so lucky. Though his medium height and thick build weren't repulsive, his pirate costume did nothing to compliment his figure. It consisted of red-and-black striped pants, a white, puffy shirt, black vest, and a black scarf tied over his head. It might have passed except for his black dress shoes and socks.

They were laughing with a couple in evening dress who had skipped the costumes except for masks—his a black wraparound and hers a sparkling royal-blue handheld. They had matching jowls. If it's true that people look like their pets, they owned a couple of bulldogs.

Flapper dresses shimmied off some who had the figure and some who didn't. A pirate costume looks good on no one. The hospital scrubs didn't look so bad on the various sizes, shapes, and colors of the guests. Even Mrs. Jarvis squeezed her poundage into one.

The most complimentary costume belonged to Dracula because the long black cape forgave a lot of pot bellies and big bums.

Having made my way to the French doors, I stepped through and sucked in a lungful of fresh air. The Inglenooks had lucked out on the weather. Enough of the rain had dried so I only had to skirt one puddle, and the tall heat lamps scattered around the cocktail tables made the patio an okay place to escape the noise, or have a smoke, or steal a kiss like Cat Woman and Superman were doing in the corner.

The staff had waited until after the rain to set out the tables and chairs, so they were dry. Seated at one table, a suave, dark-haired Dracula with slicked-back hair typed into his cell phone. He looked up when I snorted, and then Rico Agosti glanced down at his phone and sent me an amused smirk.

"No, I'm not playing games or checking social media. All my important documents, notes, and follow-ups are on here. I was looking over the agenda for tomorrow."

Outside, we didn't have to raise our voices to compete with the music. When I moved to join him, the legs of the chair scraped against the cement patio. I sat and stretched out my limbs. "What's the deal with your boss?"

He shrugged. "You mean the announcement? Not in the best of taste, but effective, and that's his chief concern."

"Do you know what it's about? I mean, what business could be important enough to make him interrupt a charity ball."

"You heard Ben. It wasn't for my ears." Rico turned off his phone and shoved it into his pants pocket. "Look. I hope Jennifer didn't harass you about the Gold Room. She is... enthusiastic. I advised Ben not to hire her, which was a mistake. He probably wanted to prove me wrong. She's too inexperienced for the job. She gets overwhelmed. And overawed."

"No harm done."

His gaze traveled over my tailored Brioni jacket. I caught a spark of envy. Since I'd seen him in a Canali this afternoon, I knew that look wasn't because he wanted to swap information on designers.

"If you don't ask," I said, kindly, "they can't say no. I just showed up without a costume, when it was too late to argue."

"Ben would have sent me back upstairs to change." He leaned forward and folded his hands on the table. "What's it like working for your brother?"

"Do you mean working for a brother in general? Or working for Edward?"

"Both, I guess."

"Just curious?"

He nodded. "I would think it would present problems. I mean, it's not as if you're partners in a business. Equals."

"No. Not equals. But why should we be? He's the star of the show and I'm the secretary." As much as Edward gives me a pain in the side, that's between us. "There are pros and cons. For instance, I can say a lot to him I couldn't say to a regular boss, but that goes the other way, too. He expects a lot from me, probably because he can tell mom on me if I slack off."

He didn't smile, which meant he wanted a serious answer.

I leaned back and considered him. "I'm not sure what you expect me to say. It depends on the brother. Edward and I get along, so it works."

With my back exposed to the elements, I felt the chill of damp air, and I shivered. I finished the last of my scotch and set the glass down. "One advantage to your costume is the cape will keep you warm." I stood. "See ya around."

Passing back through the ballroom, Tinker Bell approached me.

"You haven't seen Ben, have you?" Rico was right. Jennifer was in awe of her boss, maybe something more, and she was too inexperienced to go about it subtly.

"He's not outside. That's all I can tell you."

A waitress passed by with champagne, and I grabbed two glasses. It wouldn't go with the scotch I'd just finished, but

Edward won't drink alone. If anyone needed to loosen up, it was my brother.

Using my pinkies, I snatched a few appetizers from a passing tray to go with the drinks. When I got back to the table, I held one glass out and insisted he take it. I thought it would do him good, but I changed my mind when he tossed it back in one swallow.

I set my glass down, untasted, and popped a miniature baked Brie in my mouth. "You were meant to sip it." The oozy cheese went perfect with the chopped walnuts. I handed him one.

Benedict Hamilton rapped on the table with knuckles encased in the black gloves of his Zorro costume, calling for our attention. He immediately got on my bad side when he gave us a toothy smile and said with a hearty chuckle:

"So, you're Aunt Civility's public minion."

He was looking at Edward, not me.

"You're confused," I said. "I'm the only minion around here."

His gaze landed on me. "And you're the minion's secretary."

"*Private* secretary. I've been promoted."

Hamilton picked up one book and flipped it over. "Why didn't we book the author herself?"

"She's unavailable for public appearances," Edward said.

The developer nodded, showing he already knew this. "It would have been a bigger draw. No offense meant to you. I'm sure you're competent at your job or such a famous woman wouldn't employ you, relative or not."

"Can I help you with something, Mr. Hamilton?" Edward asked, resigned. When he abruptly got to his feet, Hamilton took a startled step back.

"What the—are you challenging me to a duel?" He gave a nervous laugh, but he looked wary. The woman behind him, waiting for her drink at the bar, tittered. Her companion looked our way.

My brother's standing had been a reaction to Claudia's appearance. The couple had finished their latest dance, and while Josh hung back, our hostess approached the developer, her smile forced.

"Are you enjoying your evening?"

"I have to admit some concern. Is the charity paying for his room this weekend?" He jerked his thumb in Edward's direction.

"You big baboon," I growled. "Who do you think you are?"

Claudia flushed. "Nicholas! Behave yourself."

I gaped because she sounded just like Edward.

Suddenly, I felt a presence behind me. "What's the matter, Claudia?"

"Your brother is being rude."

"Were you, Nicholas?"

"Perhaps a tad."

Hamilton held up the book. "I realize this fits the theme of the event, but we need to be careful how we spend our money."

"The books are free," I snapped.

Edward sent a glance Josh's way, and the latter gave a small nod. The photographer bent down to whisper in Claudia's ear. "Maybe we should leave them to discuss it." She went reluctantly, but she went.

"As a board member," Edward began in a deadly calm voice that meant he was controlling a powerful emotion, "I suppose you have a right to ask, as offensively as you phrased it. Nicholas and I booked our own rooms."

I raised a finger. "Technically, I booked them, and you paid for them."

The developer nodded and smirked at me. "That wasn't

so hard. I may not have your boss's manners, but I get results."

"A duel." Edward nodded. "It's an interesting idea. Two men, with just their wits and their weapons. How do you think you'd fare?"

Edward's Zorro costume added menace to his words. Hamilton paled. But the developer wasn't used to walking away without the last word, so he tossed the book on the table, said, "Any time. Any place," and strolled away. Dueling hadn't been popular since the Civil War, so he probably felt safe making the challenge.

I turned around. Edward had his hands clasped behind his back, and his expression lacked friendly feelings.

"I don't remember promoting you."

"Yeah. We need to discuss that later."

With another dance ending, a crowd surged over to our table. It took ten minutes to get rid of them, and then we experienced another lull. Edward stood.

"I'm going to stretch my legs."

Instead of mingling with the donors, Edward walked out of the ballroom.

A few more guests came up to the table, disappointed not to meet the famous author's representative, but I handled them. As they walked away, I decided I was through dancing around my brother's mood swings. It was time for direct questions. I'd run out of ideas. That and I wanted to keep him from doing something stupid.

Even though I was a minion's assistant, manning the book table wasn't one of my duties, so I followed Edward, determined to get some answers.

CHAPTER 10

Claudia and Josh reached the door the same time I did, so I stepped aside and held it open on behalf of the lady. In the lobby, a few resort guests who weren't part of the festivities moved around. The lobby also attracted those who wanted to step out of the Ballroom but weren't up to freezing their fannies off on the patio.

The Halls and Jarvises were deep in conversation. Someone mentioned Benedict Hamilton. He'd guaranteed himself top spot in tonight's gossip.

Through the glass windows behind the check-in counter, Robert Inglenook beckoned from his office. Up close, he looked tired around the eyes, but he had a smile ready. He leaned back in his chair and tossed his pencil on the desk.

"How are the festivities?"

"Festive. Did you draw the short straw?"

He grinned. "I have no desire to walk around a bunch of strangers playing dress up." He nodded at my suit. "I see we share the same opinion."

"How did the masked ball wind up here? Are the two of you involved in the charity?"

"That's all Claudia's doing. My sister has a knack for finding opportunities. It's part of her charm."

"Which she is lavishing over Joshua Breen."

Robert grinned. "Good ol' Josh."

I made a gimme motion with my fingers. "Spill."

He nodded thoughtfully. "We met in college and became fast friends because neither of us took the college environment seriously. Who spends the money on higher learning just to specialize in beer bongs and antipathy? Not us. We had bigger plans for our lives. So, I used to bring him back here on holidays. Claudia was just a kid in high school, and Josh was as good-looking and talented as he is today. Naturally, she developed a crush."

"I can see why. You make me want to date him."

I was glad to make Robert laugh. He looked like he needed a good chuckle. I didn't intend to be nosy, but when I glanced down, a lot of red overdue stamps stared back at me. Robert noticed me noticing.

"It's our slow season."

"Sure." I turned my head in the Ballroom's direction. "Do charities pay much?"

"We're booked this weekend. Paying guests."

"Hamilton just accused Edward and me of being freeloaders. And speaking of Edward, did you see him pass by about five minutes ago?"

"People have been moving through the lobby all night. Wasn't he in a Zorro costume? I only glanced up, so I can't swear it was him."

"That's Edward. I better go find him. He's in a strange mood. Which way?"

He directed me toward the Gold Room.

The Halls and Jarvises were still in the lobby along with a few other guests. Someone pushed through the doors of the

Ballroom, spilling music into the lobby which faded as I headed down the hallway.

One of Inglenook's employees gave me a nod as she passed. Since she had a few years to go until she met my minimum age requirement, I merely nodded back.

The light was on in the Gold Room, and though the room was empty, someone had been here since I set up the chairs. There was a gap in the front row. I found the missing chair resting against the opposite wall, leaning on a bent leg. When I picked it up, I exposed a gash in the drywall about three inches long. Nudging the pieces of drywall on the rug with the toe of my shoe, I thought *Edward*.

Should I be happy my brother had gotten his frustrations out of his system? Or was this a precursor to a full-blown public fit?

I carried the damaged chair to a back corner where no one would be likely to use it and moved one from the back row to the front to even things out. Looking around for a way to hide the gaping hole, I put a functional chair in front of it in case someone sat down. On my way out, I turned off the light.

On a hunch, I headed for the library. Not a lot of guests bothered with the library, so Edward could find solitude there when he needed a break. Or a sulk. Still, I like to be thorough, so after crossing the lobby again with a wink at Robert who was helping an elderly guest, I stepped inside the first door I came to and scanned the barstools, booths, and tables without luck. Then I moved on to the Welcome Room.

The scent of sugar and spice confirmed Mrs. Beckwith had kept up the tradition of serving freshly baked cookies at the end of the night. One man grazed at a side table. I thought about joining him until he picked one up in his fingers, saw something he liked better, and returned it to the plate.

A few people sat on the couch in front of a gigantic television. The tops of their heads stuck above the couch. The guy wearing a Cubs hat craned his neck to give me the onceover.

"We can just about squeeze another person on here if you're interested."

"No thanks. I'm looking for someone."

"Aren't we all?" His fit of wheezy laughter stopped when his eyes landed on the guy with the sticky fingers. He curled back his upper lip in disgust.

As I turned, my foot slipped, and I had to grab the door frame for balance. Someone in a hurry had spilled on the floor. Weak tea by the looks of it. Remembering the aged people on the couch, I hoped it wasn't something worse.

It is a natural impulse of human beings to not want an audience when something undignified happens, and I'm fully human, so I sent a covert glance around the area while trying to look as if I didn't mind almost landing on my sitter. I wasn't alone in the hallway.

Claudia stepped out of the library. She had put on a black cape, making her look more witchy than ever. After a few steps, she stumbled and pressed the wall with one hand as if holding herself up. Her body jerked as she let loose a sob.

Though she wasn't my problem, I don't like to see women cry. When I was a foot or two away, I said her name. She looked around, dazed, and for a moment, our gazes locked. Then she picked up her skirts and ran toward the private part of the wing where she and Robert had their apartment.

Great. The happy couple had had another blowup. My brother's mood would be somewhere between foul and murderous. I'd have to thank her later.

The library lights were off, and I assumed I'd find Edward sulking in front of the fireplace. Moonlight bled through the curtains. Two steps into the room, I froze. I'd found my brother. He was face down on the rug with his arms and legs akimbo. He might have been sleeping except for the sword buried between his shoulder blades.

"Edward," I choked out. My lungs stopped functioning, but my heart raced. I ran to him and knelt at his side. It was my fault. I shouldn't have let him out of my sight. Not in his current mood. Hamilton's face popped into my head, and I swore I'd find the man and kill him.

My hands trembled as I grasped my brother's shoulders, and then I let out a frustrated groan. I couldn't turn him over. Not with that sword in his back. I touched his neck, feeling for a pulse, but he was gone.

"Who the devil is that?"

I yelled.

The voice coming from over my shoulder belonged to my brother.

"Edward?"

My voice cracked, and I cleared my throat. I'm not easily spooked, but I couldn't make my head turn to see if it was really my brother standing over me. My hands and legs wouldn't cooperate, either.

"Well? Take off his mask."

He took exactly the right tone. Following his instructions came as automatically to me as manners were to him. I turned the body's head and peeled back the mask. My fingers brushed his face and my belly muscles tightened. He was still warm.

The face staring back belonged to Benedict Hamilton. I owed him an apology.

Jumping to my feet, I trotted into the hallway, making my way to the lobby. I wasn't even sure what I was looking for. Maybe someone in a hurry.

Joshua Breen stepped out of the men's room just before I got to the lobby. We collided, and while we straightened ourselves out, the man in the power suit exited the washroom and scooted around us.

"Who else is in there?" I demanded.

Josh looked over his shoulder. "I don't know. I didn't ask."

I pushed past him and flung open the door. "Health Department." My voice echoed off the tiled walls. "We're taking inventory. Who's in here?"

"For heaven's sake!"

The voice belonged to Mr. Hall. I banged the other stall doors open and found them empty.

"All clear."

"For heaven's sake," Mr. Hall repeated.

In the lobby, most of the guests milling around were people in weekend clothes, not part of the festivities, although I spotted Female Dracula and Scrub Girl gossiping in the corner. I glanced in each room as I made my way back to the library, and once there, I crossed to the French doors and looked outside.

"What are you doing?" Edward said.

The chances were fifty-fifty that I'd choose the right direction. One way led to the patio outside the Ballroom, the other to the front door. I turned left and made my way around to the entrance.

Now that the moon had hidden behind the clouds, the security lights on the side of the building and the dim lamps along the walkway didn't make a dent in the surrounding landscape. My senses were on high alert, and I scanned the dark expanse leading to the tree line beyond the lawn.

I held my breath at faint sounds of movement. When a fox screamed in the woods beyond, I twisted my ankle spinning toward the sound. After hopping a few steps, I put my weight on that foot and decided I'd live.

That forty-something degrees felt more like thirty away from the heat lamps, and by the time I walked in the front doors of Inglenook, I had to rub my arms to get the blood moving.

"Did anyone come in this way recently?"

Alfred narrowed one eye at me. "You did."

"Before. Before me."

"I haven't seen anyone. Why?"

I left him wondering and returned to the library, closing the door behind me and switching on the nearest lamp. Edward still stood over the body. In deference to the corpse, he had taken off his hat and mask.

He turned his head. "Robert is calling the police."

"Did you do it?" I demanded.

His eyebrows went up. "Do what?" He looked down. "This?"

"He's been riding you since you met him. Your last conversation involved mention of a duel."

He made a face. "A duel involves pistols, and even if it didn't, it would hardly be a fair fight to stab a man in the back. I can't believe you asked."

"I had to, didn't I?"

He glanced down at the body. "Yes. I can see that you did."

"There's something else you need to know."

But Robert Inglenook stepped into the room just then and, after a glance at Hamilton, averted his eyes to address us. "The police are on their way. Alfred will guard the body. Come on. I'd say you both need a drink."

As we left the room, I thought once more about the curse of Inglenook Manor. No one would convince me one didn't exist.

CHAPTER 11

Normally, I'm a sharp observer. I remember people's words, expressions, and tones. A subtle change in voice or a surreptitious movement can't happen without my noticing. And I remember.

That night, I went into hyper-drive.

Edward and I sat in Robert's office while the half-owner of Inglenook poured out scotch for all three of us. No water.

My brother had removed his hat, mask, and gloves, leaving his hair disheveled. When I got my drink, I swallowed in one go, feeling the burn, and set the glass on his desk.

My brother sipped his. "Will you stop staring at me?"

I moved my gaze to the floor, but my eyeballs traveled back to his face without my instructing them to.

"What's the matter with you?"

"I thought you were dead."

He grimaced. "Well, I'm not."

"Be reasonable, Edward." Robert gestured at me with his glass. "Your brother has had a jolt. Can you imagine if you found him murdered? Or thought you had?"

He gave me a quick glance and fiddled with his cape. "I'd have to come up with an alibi." His tone had softened, so I knew he understood.

"Ms. St. Armand is making sure no one leaves the Ballroom, but they're all so shocked I don't think it has crossed their minds."

Someone rapped on the door, and in walked Harlequin. He wore a loose garment of yellow, blue, green, and red diamond shapes and a jester's hat. The character was supposed to be some kind of funny servant. At least the Italians and the English thought he was funny. To me, he looked like a menacing clown.

Robert stepped forward. "This is a private office."

"I know. I've been in it before."

I recognized the voice, and with that sharp tenor went all my hopes of recovering the weekend.

Detective Timms, first name unknown, pulled off his mask and nodded to us. Behind the bulbous nose, his face looked as if he'd lost a few pounds since he'd headed the investigation last year.

"Eddie. Nicky. Mr. Inglenook. I've called for Michaelson and the team."

By Michaelson he meant David Michaelson, the stoic sergeant who prided himself on keeping his reactions private. I assumed the team meant forensics and a few patrol officers to keep us in line.

"Were you expecting trouble?" Edward nodded at the Harlequin costume.

"I won tickets in the football pool."

Robert moved aside and let Timms take a seat behind his desk. When the detective pulled off his jester cap, the ginger hair that ringed his head stood on end and reminded me of the Heat Miser.

"Well? Tell me what happened."

He naturally looked to Edward for an explanation, but my brother deferred to me. It was like someone released a rubber band.

"I watched Edward leave the Ballroom. I'm afraid I didn't look at my watch, so I don't know what time. I followed to—to see if he needed me to take care of anything. As I crossed the lobby, I caught sight of Robert in this office. He invited me in. He was working on paperwork. On top was a bill from Wauconda Industrial Cleaners, an invoice from a wholesale restaurant supply store—the name was covered by the cleaning bill—and a grocery list. The list was for half-and-half, coffee, bread, aspirin, and antacids, so I assume it was for personal use."

Edward stared at me.

"We chatted for about seven minutes, and then I asked if he had seen Edward. He had seen someone in a Zorro costume pass by about five minutes earlier, and that sounded like Edward, so I asked which direction. He thought the Gold Room. There were a few people in the lobby. Mr. and Mrs. Hall were talking to the Jarvis couple. She, Mrs. Hall, made a joke about hot flashes, which was funny since I doubt if she's had one in decades."

I took a breath.

"Down the hallway to the Gold Room, I saw two people, not in costume, enter their guest room. A man and a woman. Middle forties, I think. They were at the end of the hallway. So, I might be wrong about the age. Then I passed a maid. On the young side, mouse-brown hair cut into a bob, crooked incisor—she smiled at me—and about five-foot four inches and one hundred and thirty-four pounds. Maybe thirty-two. She was carrying towels. White towels. She had a run in her right stocking. My right. Her left."

"Miranda Evans," Robert murmured. "The description's perfect."

"The Gold Room was empty, but someone had been there."

Edward made a small noise.

"How do you know?" Timms said.

"The lights were on. I turned them off. Then I decided the most likely place for Edward to escape to—"

"I wasn't escaping. I was stretching my legs."

Timms, afraid the interruption would stop the flow, held up a hand. "We'll get to you in a minute, Eddie."

"I thought he'd be in the library, so I went there, passing Robert and an elderly guest on my way. A man. About five-foot-six and balding."

"Mr. Tucker," Robert volunteered.

"I looked in the bar to make sure Edward wasn't there. In the booths from the entrance moving to the far side were a middle-aged couple, an empty booth, a threesome of elderly women, elderly meaning eighties or more, three more empty booths, a couple in their twenties who appeared to be arguing, or at least discussing something serious, and a group of four men in their fifties. Three men sat at the bar, and there was a single woman at a table in the middle of the room. The Welcome Room had a guy with sticky fingers and three television viewers, one with a Cubs cap and two elderly persons with white hair."

I hurried through the rest, skipping my meeting with Claudia. "Then I headed for the library." I shrugged. "You know what I found."

"Were the lights on or off?"

"Off." My throat got tight, so I coughed. "Otherwise, I might have noticed it wasn't Edward."

"You didn't mention seeing anyone in the hallway on your way to the library. There wasn't anyone else? I find it strange that they were all tucked away in their beds at—" He pulled back the sleeve of his costume, revealing a watch. "It's nine now. Say eight-fifteen."

My brother sensed I was stalling.

"Just tell him the truth, Nicholas."

I looked him in the eye and held his gaze. Any mention of Claudia and his brain would empty. Emotions would take over. For the love of Mike, he was wearing a Zorro costume, and what better way to be a hero than rescue the damsel in distress?

Turning my head to look at Timms, I lied. "I saw no one. You know how you spot an empty drive-through, and as soon as you get close, six cars pull in ahead of you? It's called a herd instinct. This was a reverse herd instinct. Everyone got the idea to return to their rooms all at once. And I mentioned the guy at the counter. Doesn't Mr. Tucker count?"

In hindsight, it was stupid to lie, but I'd replayed the moment in my head and couldn't remember any witnesses who might contradict me.

Not being a pushover, Timms kept his eyes narrowed at me for a full minute, but I didn't squirm.

"Did you touch the body?"

My stomach muscles tightened. "I felt his throat for a pulse, and I removed his mask to see who it was. Other than that, no. He was warm. As in not dead long."

"And where *were* you, Eddie?"

Edward shifted in his seat. "I went for a walk. I'd been sitting for over an hour and needed to stretch my legs. I went to the end of each hallway and back. Lower level only."

The detective angled his head to look up at Robert. "Do you agree with everything you heard?"

"I do."

"What about your sister?"

"She was at the masked ball. I had desk duty."

Timms hadn't closed the door all the way when he came in. It creaked open now, revealing a humongous Dalmatian.

"My wife asked me to find out what's going on."

Edward, feeling introductions were necessary, stood.

"Detective Timms, this is Detective Jonah Sykes."

The local detective narrowed his eyes. "Detective?"

Sykes stepped forward and held out his paw. "From San Diego. I'm here for the fundraiser."

Timms' brow cleared, and he stood and shook hands with his fellow officer.

Scooting behind the gigantic Dalmatian to the door, Edward said, "You don't need me. I'm going to check on Claudia."

He may have been our acquaintance, possibly he considered himself our friend, but foremost, Timms was a detective. "You stay put. We'll talk to Miss Inglenook soon enough."

Sykes gestured with one paw. "I know I'm out of my jurisdiction, but I wondered if there was anything I could do. My wife is friends with Latoya St. Armand."

Timms whistled. "Her donors got more than they bargained for." He looked around the office and his gaze rested on the glass windows that faced into the lobby. Several faces peered in from the other side of the counter. "This place won't do. We used the Gold Room last time."

Edward crossed his arms over his chest. "You don't need me. Just because we helped last time—"

Sykes jerked his head toward my brother, which made his ears flop. "Last time?

"Sorry to inconvenience you," Timms said, not meaning it. "Let's go."

CHAPTER 12

On the way over, Timms recounted to Sykes his last case at Inglenook. The San Diego detective's glance lighted on Edward and me more than once, as if reevaluating the coincidence of finding us on the scene of another murder.

Once we made it to our destination, Timms said we should give the room a thorough going over in case the Gold Room figured into Hamilton's movements tonight.

I found it interesting to see the different ways the detectives worked.

Timms wandered the room with his head down like a hound on the scent and checked out the rug, the corners, the conference table, under the conference table, and even the two shelves at the back of the podium.

Someone had left their notes from a staff meeting, but unless I wanted to get a job at Inglenook, the notes weren't useful.

Sykes took in the same information but from his position inside the door. He scanned the room like a hawk searching for prey. I thought he probably saw as much as Timms without moving, except for the papers behind the podium.

"Someone had a fit." Timms moved the chair and exposed the hole in the wall.

I raised my hand. "I noticed that before."

Timms cocked his head in my direction. "Before what?"

"Before now." I'd meant to disassociate Edward's tantrum from Hamilton's murder, but I realized too late I'd slipped up, so I wriggled. "You know. Earlier today. Before all this happened."

He accepted my explanation, and the two colleagues met at the conference table.

"Can we move this thing away from the wall?" Timms asked.

"Why?" I demanded. "I just got it hauled back here. If you want to face your subjects when you interview them, you can sit at either end."

"Too far away."

The two detectives locked gazes—the Harlequin and the Dalmatian—and they both laughed.

Timms held up a foot and shook his baggy pants. "I think we should change, don't you?"

"Agreed," Sykes said.

Timms looked at us. "You two hold down the fort. And that means stay put. And while you're at it, Nicky, make us some coffee."

After finding a sink in a utility room, filling the electric kettle, and flicking it on, I strolled over to Edward and waited for instructions, since I assumed we would ignore Timms.

"That was an impressive display of memory, Nicholas."

"Thanks."

"Except for the bit you tried to cover up."

"Don't know what you mean."

"You hesitated when Timms asked if there was anyone in the hallway."

"I must have been taking a moment to think."

"Nonsense. You held something back. Okay. Maybe it's something you don't want the police to know, but this is me. Your brother."

"Sorry, Edward. I could make something up if it would make you feel better."

A growl started at the back of his throat, but I headed it off.

"I picked up your chair for you. Did you throw it? Or kick it?"

He didn't bother to deny that the overturned chair I'd found here earlier was the result of a temper tantrum.

"And speaking of sharing information, are you going to tell me what's going on with you? The answers to your fan letters were a might testy."

"No."

Not *there isn't anything wrong,* or even *I don't know what you're talking about.* Just no, which was hard to take.

"You acknowledge there is a problem, but you're telling me it's none of my business."

"Well put."

About to throw my own tantrum, our detective team returned just then. Sykes looked sleek and professional. He had on a dark brown double-breasted suit and cream shirt. His tie was an explosion of colors, but it looked good.

When Timms followed him in, I let out a low whistle. Last time I'd seen him in a suit, he looked like he'd slept in it. He'd gone shopping since then, because this suit was tailored to fit his round shoulders and thick middle, and the medium brown complimented his coloring. The tie was a soft cream-and-brown stripe that went with his cream shirt.

"You're coordinated."

They looked at each other, confused.

"You're both wearing brown. Though Sykes wins on the tie."

"Oh." Timms nodded. "I get it."

Sykes gave me a dirty look before moving to one end of the table. Edward grabbed the other side and helped him move it away from the wall about ten feet. Before they lifted, Edward nodded at me, so I hauled the chairs out of their path and stacked them in the corner.

When we finished, Sykes said, "Thank you." He paused halfway to his chair. "We won't be needing you two any longer."

Edward made it halfway across the room before Timms spoke. Perhaps because he liked us, or maybe he didn't appreciate an out-of-state detective ordering people around on his turf, but the local detective told us to stay put.

"They helped me out last time when we were short-handed. Nicky can take notes until my sergeant gets here, and Eddie has some unique insights."

Sykes bowed his head. "It's your call."

"Get the coffee, will you Nicky?"

Since I had no intention of leaving, I willingly took their orders for sugar and creamer and served them.

To support Timms' statement, I pulled the notebook and pen I keep on me for to-do items out of my pocket and clicked my pen. Before the detective could give me anything to write, the cavalry arrived.

Michaelson nodded to his boss. "I thought you'd be in here." He took us in with no indication of surprise, but that was one of his assets. He didn't show what he was thinking, though when his gaze landed on Sykes, his eyebrows inched up.

"This is Detective Jonah Sykes from San Diego. He was at the party. He's helping in an unofficial capacity."

The two men shook hands.

"How many officers did you bring?" Timms asked.

"Three."

"How are we supposed to take statements from two hundred and fifty people? Not to mention the rest of it. I suppose they expect me to track down interviewees and check out Hamilton's room at the same time. Multi-tasking. It will be the death of detective work."

I knew darn well Michaelson would do the running around if no one else was available, but Timms seemed to feel better having got his complaint off his chest.

His sergeant put some sympathy in his voice. "I'm lucky I got them. This is the weekend of the rally."

"Aw, crap." Timms explained. "Schoolteachers. That's the third rally they've had in as many months. I wish they'd spend more time teaching. Maybe we wouldn't have so many morons running around."

Having dated a schoolteacher, I knew there were those who busted their hump to get their students into the next grade. I assumed he was talking about the union leaders.

Michaelson dragged a chair to a spot where he could hear everything but wouldn't be in the way.

"Your sergeant has arrived." Edward nodded at Michaelson. "I assume we can go now."

I leaned in and lowered my voice. "What's your hurry?"

Timms held up a hand. "Hold your horses, Eddie. I need you to stick around. Have a seat."

"I don't see why I should. What can I possibly contribute?"

Timms held his gaze. "You'd be surprised."

Reluctantly, Edward pulled a chair over by Michaelson's and sat down. I preferred to remain standing and leaned against the wall.

"The papers are going to be all over this one," Timms said

with an exaggerated shudder. "Benedict Hamilton was a big cheese in his field. Did you two notice anything about him this weekend you'd care to share?"

Edward's cape fell forward. He yanked it off and smashed it into a ball. "Such as?"

I raised my hand. "He brought a personal assistant and a private secretary along for the ride. Jennifer something and Frederico Agosti. He's also on the charity's board. And he was dancing with Cinderella all night. I have seen no glass slippers laying around, so she's probably still here. She should know a lot about him. They looked cozy."

In my time, I've earned dirty looks from people on the other side of the conversation. Nothing I'd said warranted the filthy look Timms gave me.

"Give her a minute to get over the shock so she makes sense," he growled. "I don't want any hysterical witnesses. Not tonight."

It wasn't my place to pursue the subject, but the unearned glare miffed me, and I wanted to irritate him back. "But that's when she might give you the most information. Not only that, but if they're sharing a room, which these days I assume they would be, she could be destroying evidence as we speak."

He ignored me, but Sykes didn't. He settled his gaze on Timms as if trying to work out a puzzle.

A female officer knocked on the door. She'd brought a guest to the party. Jennifer's face, framed by her Tinker Bell wings, peered over the officer's shoulder. The woman nudged her back.

"This lady would like to speak with you, sir."

"Just a minute. Michaelson, tell whoever is in the Ballroom—"

"Davis and Keller."

"Fine. Tell them to get the names and addresses of anyone

who drove to the event and let them go. The rest can go back to their rooms and we can get to them when we need them."

"Are you going to search the rooms?" I asked. "I have some things I'd like to hide."

"Why would we do that? We have the murder weapon. And Michaelson? Get me the list of attendees from the organizer so we can match it with those who came."

Michaelson spoke into his radio, and when Jennifer walked into the room still dressed as Peter Pan's favorite fairy, Edward and I stood. Timms, Sykes, and Michaelson kept their seats. Probably as officials they were exempt from having manners.

When I grinned, she frowned and pulled on two shoulder straps to remove the wings. Then she rearranged her features into haughty disapproval and snubbed me, an expression that didn't go with her outfit.

I wondered why Benedict Hamilton had rejected her request for a dance and decided he disapproved of fraternizing with the staff.

Timms gestured toward a chair, and by swiping her hand over the skirt as she sat, she got in place without exposing her rear end.

Timms began with the usual questions. "Your full name, please?"

"Jennifer Proctor."

"Mr. Hamilton employed you as his personal assistant?"

She frowned. "I am employed by Ben." She searched our faces. "What's happened? I came here because they said he had been in an accident. When I couldn't find him…"

Sykes and Timms exchanged glances.

"I'm sorry to inform you that your boss is dead."

She thought she would get to her feet, but her body didn't agree. Instead, she slumped in a faint, dropping the wings on the floor.

"Aw, jeez." Timms pointed at the officer. "You're Williams, right?" When she agreed, he sent her for some water.

I got up, strolled over, and took her wrist between my thumb and index finger.

"Her pulse is fine. She'll be okay."

I stood over her and waited until she came to in case she made a wrong move and tumbled out of the chair, but she didn't. Raising her face to mine, she stared for eight seconds before the waterworks started. I handed her the handkerchief from my top jacket pocket, picked up the wings, and backed off to give her space while she covered her face and let the sobs come.

Officer Williams walked in with a plastic cup of water, the kind you get from an office water cooler. She took in the scene and set the water in the center of the table.

Jennifer earned my admiration for the speed with which she shoved her feelings back inside and got practical. After pressing the hankie to her face for one last hiccup, she straightened her shoulders and clenched her hands, ready to cooperate.

"I-I'm sorry." Jennifer's brow wrinkled. "What happened? He worked too hard. And I told him he needed more exercise. Was it a heart attack? A stroke?"

"Someone stabbed him in the back with a sword."

She recoiled against the back of her chair.

"Unless you want her to swoon again, use some tact," I snapped.

"Miss Proctor." Sykes set his smooth baritone on comfort mode. "We realize this has been a shock, but we need your help to find whoever killed Benedict Hamilton."

After Sykes repeated her name several times, her eyes came back into focus and she stuck out her determined chin, back in personal assistant mode. "Ask me anything you want."

Timms muscled his way in. “When did you last see your boss?”

“When he was onstage tonight. When he called for the meeting tomorrow morning.”

“That’s not technically true.” I spared her the embarrassment of being rejected and left out the details. “You saw him on the dance floor.”

“Maybe I did,” she said, and the glance she shot me lacked gratitude.

“He got on stage and called for a meeting tomorrow morning. Do you know what the meeting was for?”

Her lips parted, and her expression said she desperately wanted to know. Finally, she admitted she didn’t.

“That’s right. You’re the personal assistant. I’ll stick to your area of expertise.”

I couldn’t help grinning as I thought of the Gold Room incident, but I wiped it off when I caught Sykes looking at me.

“Did your boss have any personal enemies? Or any enemies that you know of?”

“I’m sure the competition didn’t appreciate his success. He is—was a tough negotiator and often got the better of people.”

She said it with pride. You’d think he was her very own bully.

“What did you do for him?”

“I executed his orders with precision and dedication. I made sure his life ran smoothly and even anticipated his needs. Rico took care of the rest.”

She made the rest sound as if the Italian American darned his boss’s socks and washed dirty dishes. Then she seemed to feel the need to assert herself and stepped outside her area of expertise.

“I wasn’t kept completely in the dark. Sometimes I heard

things, even if Rico treated me like I wasn't in the room. If I had to guess, just from things I overheard you understand, I would say Ben intended to force a vote at the meeting that would replace Latoya St. Armand as head of Tea for Teens."

"With whom?" Sykes asked.

"Benedict, of course."

Sykes controlled his expression, though it got rigid around the edges of his mouth and eyes.

"It wasn't just a power move. He had some wonderful ideas for the charity. Ways to make it more appealing to donors. He thought Tea for Teens had the potential to go international." She realized she was gushing and pulled back to an officious tone. "Benedict knew his business. Whether he planned to go through with it, I don't know."

Sykes spread his hands. "Why not expand it throughout the United States? We have plenty of poor teens here."

She gave him a thin smile. "You could ask him, but he's dead."

Before transferring her gaze to Timms, she softened it. "You have to understand. Benedict always thought big. You've seen some of his commercial projects. The Avalon Theater. The Cotton Blossom."

Timms leaned his head back toward us. "That's a riverboat with shows and gambling he installed on the Fox River. Stays docked all the time but gets around the gambling laws that way. I don't get the name."

Edward cleared his throat. "The Cotton Blossom was the showboat in a movie of the same name."

"Gotcha." He straightened up. "Was your boss working on anything special?"

"Well, Inglenook."

Naturally, after witnessing the scene with Claudia, I saw it coming, but the news must have broadsided Edward.

Anyone else might have mistaken the twitch in his upper lip for a need to sneeze.

"The Inglenooks are planning to sell?" Timms looked at us, but by then we both had blank faces. I answered for both of us.

"Not that we're aware."

Jennifer brushed aside our ignorance with a wave. "She would have. Once Benedict decided, he always got what he set his sights on."

She'd said the same thing to me about the Gold Room. "Was it his charm?" I asked politely.

She didn't bother to acknowledge me. "Benedict didn't go into a situation without researching his subject thoroughly."

I didn't like being ignored. "Research. Sounds like a job for a personal assistant." And uncovering people's secrets sounded like an excellent motive for murder.

She picked at her skirt. "I didn't help Benedict with the research. That was Rico's job. He dove pretty deep, and he didn't want to cause unnecessary problems for people, so Ben didn't share that information. Not even with me."

"What a swell guy. You mean he wanted to reserve any juicy bits so he could blackmail people to gain his objective." And that made me wonder what he could have found to hold over Claudia Inglenook.

About to defend Hamilton, she changed her mind. "Business is tough."

"But there *were* negotiations?"

Timms' interest seemed to worry her. She changed her declaration into a suggestion. "I believe this was only his second visit. Maybe he hadn't decided yet."

"He'd been here before?"

"Yes. Three months ago. He talked about the place. Said it could be a profitable business with a few improvements."

I looked at Edward to see how he was taking it, but his eyes were closed. I leaned over. "Are you asleep?"

He opened one eye to glare and closed it again. He was taking in every word.

"How long have you worked for Mr. Hamilton?"

"Six years."

"Was he a good boss?"

"The best." She sucked in a breath, and I thought she might break down again, but she controlled it. "I can't imagine working for anyone else."

She looked at Sykes, who grabbed the chance to stretch his detective muscles.

"What kind of man was he? Did he have a lot of friends? Get along with people?"

"He was more of a loner. There were very few people he confided in."

It was like watching a puppy protect her squeaky toy. She wanted us to think she was one of the chosen. Maybe she was.

"What about family?"

"His mother died a year ago. I don't know about his father. I got the impression they didn't get along. I only saw him once or twice when I first started working for Ben." She touched her chin. "I once heard about a half-brother or half-sister. Someone he lost touch with after his mother divorced and remarried. That was ages ago when he was just a kid. His mother wasn't the kind to keep in touch with an ex-husband."

"Do you know who stands to inherit?"

"I wasn't privy to that kind of information." She parted her lips to add something but nixed the idea.

Sykes folded his hands. "It would be helpful to know the name of his lawyer."

"I can give you the name, but he just fired the man.

Melvin Gardner. I'll get you his information if you think it will help."

Timms jumped on that. "Why did he fire him?"

"I don't know." She hesitated. "Benedict and Melvin started out in the same building years ago, and he'd used Melvin's services ever since. I don't know why he fired him, but it must have been serious."

"Only a few more questions. Where were you tonight around eight? After your boss's announcement until you heard he was dead. Or had an accident."

"I was in the Ballroom most of the night. I wasn't feeling too good. The noise got to me, but I thought I should stay there in case I was needed. I found a table at the back of the room as far from the band as possible and sat down. If you like, I can point it out to you. I was still there when I heard there had been in an accident. They didn't specifically say it was Ben, but I hadn't seen him and wondered."

"Do you know where the private secretary is? I'd like to talk to him, too."

"I have no idea. I don't keep track of Rico."

"I saw him on the patio," I offered, "but that was a while ago."

She gave a little gasp. "I have to tell him what's happened. I should do that right now before he hears from someone else. Is that all?"

When she squirmed with impatience at the idea of having one over the private secretary, it was understandable, but unsettling. The atmosphere in Hamilton's home must have been fun with the two of them jockeying for position.

"Did you see anything suspicious or odd tonight?"

"After Benedict made his announcement, the board members weren't happy with him. I heard some of them talking about getting rid of him."

Timms' brows went up. "They said that?"

"Yes. But they were probably talking about voting him out, not killing him," she admitted.

"I want their names."

Michaelson readied his pen.

"Mrs. Hall and Mrs. Jarvis. They were with their husbands."

Acting on a hunch, I raised my hand. "Excuse me, but if you didn't leave the Ballroom, how did you hear the Halls and the Jarvises talking in the lobby?"

Reading her expression, I could see she was working out exactly what she'd told Timms. I approved. It doesn't do to let your lies get tangled up with the truth.

"Well, I might have stepped out for some fresh air and quiet, but I came back right away, so I didn't think it mattered."

"It does," Timms snapped. "Who else did you see in that brief moment?"

"You understand, I only stepped out for a sec, so I wasn't paying attention. I saw Mr. Harlow," she nodded at me, "cross the lobby and go into the office behind the front desk with Mr. Inglenook. And I thought—" She raised her fingers to her bottom lip. "I could have sworn I saw Benedict enter a room down the hallway, but there was something about him that made me think it wasn't him." She shook her head.

"Was he alone?"

Her eyes moved back and forth, like she was watching a scene play out. It wasn't a cheerful scene because she got a furrow between her brows and her lips pressed together in grim concentration. She nodded. "There were other people around. No one important. No one who was with him."

Interesting. My impression of her said she wouldn't pass up a moment to be alone with Hamilton. She really thought it had been someone else. Someone else in a Zorro costume. Like Josh. Or Edward. As for the unimportant people, I got the impression everyone other than Benedict Hamilton fell onto that list.

Timms instructed her to give her details to Williams.

A man in sweater and slacks let the women pass through the door before entering with a bundle in his arms. He carried it in front of him like an offering, and after greeting Timms, deposited it on the table.

"What'cha got for me, Jimmy?"

"These are all the swords we collected from that group of fools." He shook his head. "Grown men in costumes." He shared his laugh with all of us but choked it back when he spotted Edward.

My brother looked like a regular guy in a black silk shirt, open at the collar, and black slacks, but the red sash gave it away.

Jimmy unbundled his package and set one item wrapped in plastic to the side. Then he laid out an assortment of swords side-by-side and stepped back.

Timms leaned forward, and Sykes got up and moved closer. Michaelson, Edward, and I joined them.

"As you can see, the theme is plastic." He picked one up. "Cheap. A kid's toy. These came from seven Zorros, one Scarlet Pimpernel, and a Phantom of the Opera."

"I didn't see the show," I said. "But I don't remember a weapon."

"Search me. We just took it off the guy." He slid over the plastic bundle and unrolled it. The weapon was in two pieces. The blade and the handle. "This, on the other hand, is the real deal. For a fake, it's a beaut. It's made of stainless steel, for show. It's not meant for...well, for the way it was used. That's why when we removed it, it broke at the tang. We've dusted for prints. None, as you'd expect, but there's plenty of the victim's blood on it."

I rubbed the back of my neck, something I do when I'm nervous. "Edward, where did you leave your sword?"

He pressed his lips together and exhaled through his nose. "I left it on the book table. I'll get it."

Before he took two steps, Timms said my brother could stay where he was, and Michaelson would retrieve it.

"Another thing you might want to know," Jimmy said. "Before the guy was killed, someone gave him a good punch. His jaw is red." He pointed to the edge of his jaw. "Could have hit it on something else, I'm sure the doc will have more to say about it, but there isn't anything around the body that he could have hit his face on when he fell. My opinion, for what it's worth."

After ten minutes of awkward silence, the sergeant returned holding the scabbard in a gloved hand. He was accompanied by a man in a white shirt, black pants, and red bow tie.

"This was on the book table." Michaelson handed it to his boss. "It's empty."

"That's mine," Edward said.

"Dammit!" It slipped out. Everyone looked my way, including the man who'd come in with the sergeant.

Timms pointed at the new arrival. "Who's this guy?"

"The bartender. Mr. Harlow's book table is in a corner next to the bar. I thought you might want to talk to him."

Timms motioned to the chair, but the guy balked.

"I have to get back. Those people are restless. They almost rioted when I left."

Timms jabbed a finger at the scabbard. "Did you see anyone messing with this?"

"A guy in a Zorro costume."

Sykes nodded at Edward. "This gentleman?"

"Could have been. Without the rest of the outfit, it's hard

to tell. Besides. I was busy, and there were people surrounding the table grabbing free books."

"What time did you see Zorro?"

"I told you. I was busy." He relented and guessed it was around the time some guy took the microphone from the lady onstage.

Edward spread his hands. "That was me. I was still at the book table."

"This isn't a small sword, Eddie. How did someone remove it from the table right under your nose?"

I objected. "People were crowding around on and off all night."

Edward couldn't take his eyes off the sword. "Once I discarded it, I forgot about it."

Timms gestured at the weapon. "It's a nice-looking sword. The detail work on the leather is beautiful. Why'd you take it off?"

"Because it was a nuisance." Edward looked up and snorted with impatience. "I don't see why everyone is surprised the killer used my sword. If he intended to impale his victim, he would have been a fool to try it with one of the plastic toys."

While the cops seemed startled by his blunt delivery, I got the point. "You mean this murder was planned."

"Not necessarily planned but premeditated. The person intended to kill Mr. Hamilton when he or she followed him to the library, and my sword provided the perfect weapon. Who knows what he—or she—would have used if I hadn't insisted on authenticity? A kitchen knife? A broken beer bottle?"

Timms consulted Sykes. "What do you think?"

"He has a point."

Slumping back in his chair, the local detective blew out a stream of air. "Something tells me this case is going to stink."

He gestured toward the chair recently occupied by Jennifer Proctor. "Did you believe her?"

"You mean about what she saw?" Sykes considered the question. "She lied about going into the hallway. Maybe that's not all she's lying about."

"You think she saw who killed Hamilton?"

"I think she saw *something*, but she's not telling us until she figures out what it means."

"I wish she'd let us do the thinking." Timms turned his head toward Michaelson. "What about you?"

"She admitted she isn't as in the dark about Hamilton's business as Rico and Hamilton would believe."

"You mean how she suddenly knew about Tea for Teens?"

"And Inglenook. My impression is she likes having her secrets. Some people like to make out they don't know anything just to hear what you have to say about it. It's a kind of power trip. And I don't believe she didn't have access to Hamilton's research into people's backgrounds."

Williams returned just then. "Sorry, sir. I couldn't find Miss Inglenook. I knocked at her apartment, but no one answered."

Edward and I exchanged a glance.

"Keep looking." Timms stood. "I want to see where you left the sword, Eddie."

When my brother stood, letting the black cape drape from one hand, he looked like a bullfighter who'd forgotten that bulls like red. I pressed my lips together to keep from yelling.

"Do you have something you wish to say, Nicholas?"

"Congratulations," I growled. "Your sword is the murder weapon. We're in it."

"Indeed, we are."

I controlled the urge to kick him as he headed for the door.

CHAPTER 13

When they left, Edward went with, but I remained behind and set the room back up for tomorrow's lecture because someone had to care.

On my way back across the lobby, a short square woman wearing a calf-length dress in a print of little flowers, a bucket hat piled high with roses, and sensible shoes joined me.

The men stood around the front counter, probably preparing a plan of attack. She walked straight up to Edward and grinned. It was Robert and Claudia's crazy Aunt Zali. Maybe not technically crazy, except for that time she spent in care after attacking a man with gardening shears. Originally, Aunt Zali scared the socks off me, but I'd slowly let down my guard around her and was now merely wary.

"I came prepared this time, Eddie." She stepped back and twirled.

"Yes. I see. Do you know where your niece is?"

As out of touch with reality as Aunt Zali seemed to be, she had moments of sharp insight. "Ever since the nurses at the home used to follow me around and not give me any privacy, I decided I would never keep track of anyone, or if I did, I'd forget where they were."

"Did you forget where Claudia was?"

"I did. As soon as I saw her changing out of her costume in her bedroom, I said to myself, I'm going to forget I ever saw you. And I did."

Timms gave Williams a nod, but Edward intercepted her.

"Claudia might not answer the door if she doesn't know who it is. After all, that's the only private place the Inglenooks have, and they don't like to be disturbed. She probably hasn't heard about what happened and isn't aware she's wanted. However, she'll open the door for me."

I glared at him because his being so obvious about wanting to see Claudia before Timms got to her was getting on my nerves.

The detective shook his head slowly. "I want you here with me. Williams, don't come back without her."

Edward watched her walk away. Zali nudged him to get his attention. "You don't know who I'm supposed to be, do you? Tell him, Nicky."

It tickled me that she recognized my superior deductive skills, so I used them. Deductive skills? Of course. Aunt Zali said she was prepared. Prepared for what? The last time we were at Inglenook, a man had died. Murdered in his guest room.

The aged relative had been convinced it was a game. A murder game. She was prepared to win a murder game. Since I hadn't seen her in the Ballroom tonight, I assumed the idea for her costume had come to her after she heard about the murder.

"Miss Marple."

"Spot on! I knew you'd figure it out. We think alike."

Edward disguised his laughter as a coughing fit.

Zali caught sight of Detective Sykes and exclaimed with joy. "I remember you! You're Detective Jonah Sykes."

"Yes, ma'am. It's a pleasure to see you again."

She peered at Timms and Michaelson. "You're familiar, too. You were judges last time. Have you brought Detective Sykes in case you have to break a tie? You'll need an impartial judge."

Sykes kept his surprise from showing. When he caught my eye, I made a slight motion to let him know I'd fill him in later.

Edward put an arm around Zali's shoulders and kissed her on the cheek. "It's nice to see you again, Miss Zali."

"It's Aunt Zali to you and Nicky. You're practically family. Or just Zali if you'd rather."

I strolled over to Sykes and stuffed my hands in my pants pockets. "Where do you rate? She introduced herself to me seven times before it took."

"Isn't it obvious? She seems, um, simple. I'm probably the only black person she knows."

I nodded. "Could be." I studied Zali chatting animatedly with Edward. "But I think there's more to Zali than meets the eye. Like the iceberg that took down the Titanic."

"Miss Inglenook," Timms began cautiously. "We're having a private consultation about—about the rules."

She grinned at him. "Oh, goody, because my question is about the rules. Are we allowed to choose two murderers?" She rested her index finger on her chin. "Or maybe I mean two victims."

Sykes gave a start, while Timms offered a condescending smile. "You'll have to narrow it down to one each."

Her shoulders lifted as a warm-up to a tremendous sigh. "I thought so."

Turning her attention to Edward, she asked if the clues would be in plain sight again. Not, say, hidden in any of the guest rooms. He assured her everyone had public access to all the clues, and she left, disappointed.

"Thanks for humoring her," Robert said.

Sykes came out of his trance. "She really thinks it's a game?"

Patting his shoulder, I said, "You better watch it, or she'll ask you for hints."

Since Robert was available, Timms leaned on the counter and asked some additional questions.

"What were you doing before Nicholas Harlow came into your office?"

"I was balancing the books."

"Was anyone else around? Anyone who might have been headed toward the library?"

"Sure. People pass by all the time. I mean, there's nothing unusual about that. Nothing to notice." He pointed in the direction of the library. "The washrooms are that way."

"What about your sister? Did you see her?"

"When I first went into the office, my sister was in the hallway with Joshua Breen."

"Where did she go?"

"They both moved down the hallway in the direction of the bar." Which was also the direction of the library.

Timms jabbed a finger at my brother as he crossed the lobby. "I want you to show me exactly where you left the sword." As the detective grasped the doorknob to the Ballroom, he nodded at Sykes. "Last chance to back out."

The San Diego detective assured him he had no intention of bailing.

When the five of us came through the doors—Timms, Sykes, Michaelson, Edward, and me—the teenagers, Brandon and Makayla, were finishing a duet of *You Don't Bring Me Flowers* to the accompaniment of the band.

The girl had a clear voice with a huge range, and she

tossed in a lot of trills as is popular these days. Brandon's steady tenor kept up with her. They finished to a round of applause.

One guest spotted us, then another, until the remaining fifty or so people grew quiet. A tall black youth who wasn't old enough yet to fill out his uniform reported to Timms. He gave Sykes a cursory glance.

"Keller and I made it through most of the guests, sir." He motioned to a stocky blond man in uniform taking Snow White's statement.

"Quick work, Davis."

Grateful for the compliment, the young officer continued. "We took names and addresses and then compared them to a list of invited guests we got from Ms. St. Armand before we let anybody go. The ones that weren't staying here and had to drive home have already left, sir. At least, most of them." The words spilled out. He spoke fast and nervous, and I wondered if this was his first murder case.

Timms grinned at Sykes. "Looks like our night might not be as long as we thought, Detective."

As soon as Davis heard Sykes addressed as *Detective*, his eyes glazed over, and he stared at the man as if he were a superhero in his spare time. The young officer should have seen Sykes in the Dalmatian costume.

"What are the rest of the guests still doing here?" Timms said.

Davis tore his gaze away from his hero. "They didn't want to leave, and you didn't say to order them to their rooms. I will if you like, sir."

"Listen up!"

Timms shouted, which wasn't necessary since they were already staring in our direction.

Sykes leaned in. "The charity depends on donors like these. Please be careful how you word your request."

It didn't appear as if Timms heard him, but he changed his tone. "We are sorry your evening had to be interrupted, and we're grateful for your help. You are all free to go back to your rooms."

Apparently, the donors interpreted *free to* as they were free to stay put. Someone, uncertain if Timms' speech demanded a response, clapped a few times, but the rest returned to their conversations.

The wait staff, who had paused in their rounds, moved through the crowd again with their smiles stretched extra wide with pity for the guests and a smidgen of superiority reflected in their eyes.

Latoya St. Armand crossed the room with Shauna Sykes. When the latter saw her husband had changed out of his costume, her expression adjusted itself to somewhere between irritation and resignation.

"Gentlemen," Latoya said. "I hope you come bearing good news."

Timms shook his head. "I'm afraid the night's just getting started for us. Is there somewhere we can talk?"

She looked over her shoulder. "I don't want to leave my guests or the children."

"Use my table," Edward offered. "Let us get a few more chairs. Nicholas?"

As we headed across the room to the cluster of tables against the wall, I said, "Why are we being so accommodating? We meaning you."

"I'm merely being polite."

"Does this have anything to do with you providing the murder weapon?"

"It wouldn't hurt to hear what line the detectives take."

"As long as it doesn't lead to Claudia?"

"Why would you say that?"

"Because it's obvious she has something to hide. Why else would you try so hard to see her before Timms?"

Resting his hands on the back of a chair, he lifted his chin, dripping rectitude from his pores. "I merely wanted to break the news to her in a gentler fashion than I suspect Timms will employ."

I lifted two chairs. "Right."

We carried them back, and my shoulders relaxed now that we were on the same page. Sticking close to see if it would require any maneuvering to keep Edward in the clear. I had the additional concern about Claudia on my mind, but my brother didn't need to know that.

While the detectives and ladies got seated, Edward swept the remaining books out of their way and told me to pack them up. Except as soon as I loaded one into the cardboard box, Edward took it out, allegedly to check for damage inflicted by the guests. He was futzing around with things that didn't need to be futzed to give us an excuse to stick around.

Timms, never one to waste time with niceties, gave Latoya St. Armand a nod. "How long have you known Benedict Hamilton?"

"Oh, dear. Is that who died? The officers didn't give us any details."

"Right. Benedict Hamilton is dead. Murdered."

She gasped. "Are you sure?"

Before Timms could put it bluntly, Sykes stepped in. "There's no doubt, Latoya. Someone killed him."

After taking it in, she nodded and answered Timms' question. "He first donated about a year ago. It was a large donation, large enough that I wrote him a personal thank you. About a week later, he showed up at my office. He wanted to be on the board." She smiled. "There are many who think of being a board member of a charity as a way to plump up their resumes. It gives them prestige."

"You were wary?"

"It's not often that someone volunteers for the position. Aside from the monthly meetings and financial oversight, they help me brainstorm on fundraising ideas, hold their own fundraisers, try to find new donors, and help wherever needed. I put it to my other board members. We took a vote, and he was in. I think some members thought another person would help lighten their own duties."

"And did he do a good job?"

She nodded, but she took her time about it. "I believe he saw the potential of our mission." She took a deep breath and folded her hands on the table. "Why don't I skip to the part where I tell you I didn't like him."

"Latoya," Sykes said in warning. Timms turned his head.

"Maybe this interview is too personal for you."

A waitress interrupted, offering a tray of snacks. I took a few for me and Edward. He glared at me.

"What? I'm hungry."

I noticed he ate the miniature skewered meatball I offered.

As soon as the employee left, Latoya picked up her thought.

"Jonah, the truth never hurt anyone. Benedict Hamilton was an annoying man. Persistent. He had to be to get where he was, I suppose, but that didn't make him good company. I should take that back. It's not that I didn't like him, I just wouldn't invite him to a purely social event. Like I said. He was annoying."

Timms grunted. "Ambitious?"

"Tea for Teens doesn't need ambition. It needs love. It needs understanding. It needs to remain personal. That's how we help people. It's about more than filling in government forms and paying staff."

"Do you get paid?"

"I'm the executive director."

Shauna rested her hand on Latoya's arm. "This woman worked for free for many years. The amount she's paid is not excessive for the work she does, and she'd do it for free if she had to."

"Are you on the board?"

"In name only." Shauna sighed. "Latoya gives me more credit than I'm due." She waved off her friend's protests. "I live in San Diego, and I don't have the time to make a real difference. Not like Latoya."

Timms pulled out the soft soap. "I appreciate what you do, both of you, and the other volunteers and board members. It's a good thing to help kids get on the straight path before they veer off too far."

Latoya bowed her head to accept his compliment.

"I was there when Benedict Hamilton called a meeting for tomorrow morning. Was that unusual?"

"It wasn't usual, thank goodness."

"Do you know what the topic was?"

Her gaze faltered, but then she looked Timms in the eyes. "He didn't share that with me."

"Did you have any guesses?"

"I didn't make it to where I am today with guesses, Detective."

"What if I told you he planned to replace you as executive director?"

She sat back and smiled with her head cocked to the side. Then she let loose a throaty laugh. Hearing it, I couldn't hold back my grin.

"That would surprise me. A lot. I don't think Benedict had any desire to take on the responsibility."

Timms waited for more.

"Detective Timms, have you ever sat outside on a beautiful evening, but there's this fly that keeps landing on your hand? You brush it away, and it lands on your arm. That goes on for a while, and it gets annoying, but you're enjoying your evening, so you don't get up. You don't leave. You just acknowledge this pesky little insect is going to keep annoying you and it's not worth getting upset over.

"Yeah. And?"

"Benedict Hamilton was my pesky little fly. He would go away for a while, but he always came back, and he always would. I decided not to get upset over him, because the evening is beautiful."

"That didn't answer the question."

"Fair enough. Did I know what Benedict had planned for tomorrow morning? No. He was always surprising me."

"But he *might* have been voting you out of your position."

"Excuse me, ma'am."

Edward elbowed my ribs while I waited for her to acknowledge me.

"Is your charity a membership corporation with you as the sole member?"

She stared, and I got the feeling she didn't like me right then.

"No. It's not. Yes, that makes me vulnerable, but I only bring people I trust onto the board ."

"You brought Hamilton on," Timms said, "and it doesn't sound like he was trustworthy."

"I'm allowed one rotten apple." She smiled. "I'm not a stupid woman. I know what you're getting at. I think you're wrong about Benedict, but even if he were to try a stunt like that, I know my board members. He never would have succeeded."

Her glance took Edward and me in. "You heard what he

said. That he had the votes. That's the third time he's told me that in as many months. He had the votes to change the charity's name to The Young People's Tea Association. He had the votes to switch from the accountant who has handled our account since it began to a friend of his. He had the votes to change the location of our monthly meetings and to make them bi-weekly. Most people don't like conflict. When they were face to face, some members would agree with him just to make him go away. Then they would tell me what he was up to. When we'd meet and it was apparent things weren't going his way, he would find something else that he wanted to address so he'd have a win. So, you see, I wasn't worried."

"Miss St. Armand?" Makayla stood next to Latoya St. Armand's chair. "How much longer before we can go?"

Latoya scooted around and took the teen's hand. "Oh, sweetheart. You've had a long day." She checked her watch. "Just a few minutes more, okay?"

The girl nodded and left.

"Those children have been here since early this morning, lending a hand. I would like to take them to their rooms."

Timms looked thoughtful. "Except they're not children, are they? What if Brandon found out Benedict Hamilton was threatening you and took matters into his own hands?"

Her flaring nostrils were the only sign that the executive director had heard him. Otherwise, she sat so still she might have been a statue.

He didn't wait for an answer. "One last question. Did you leave this room at all tonight?"

"No."

"Thank you, Ms. St. Armand."

The men stood as she left, taking her friend with her.

"I don't know if you've noticed," I said, "but the door to the lobby isn't the only way out of here. Was Ms. St. Armand with someone the entire night? Did she ever wander out onto the patio?"

It was interesting to note that Sykes' growl had a different timbre than my brother's. A richness in tones bordering on a pleasant noise, if that noise hadn't meant he wanted to kill me.

"I didn't think Ms. St. Armand could kill anyone, but after the look she gave you..."

Timms scoffed. "Everyone has something they'd defend to the death. It gives her a motive, but the wrong one unless Hamilton threatened the teens, but I doubt he even noticed they existed."

He strolled up to Edward. "And this is where you left the sword?"

My brother tapped a spot near the wall. "Right here."

The bartender scrambled to take care of his customers. The only way he'd catch sight of the end of the table, even out of the corner of his eye, would be if he made at least a ninety-degree turn to the left, which didn't make him much use as a witness in my book.

"Michaelson, tell Williams to meet us in the unused office we used last time. My feet are killing me, and I don't feel like traipsing back to the Gold Room."

The back office. Ah, memories.

CHAPTER 14

Before heading to the spare office, Timms led the contingent to the swinging doors behind the photography backdrop. Before Edward and I could follow, a small crowd surrounded us. Some I recognized from dinner; some were fans of Aunt Civility who had spent time at the book table tonight.

Rico hung out on the periphery, interested but not willing to join the fun. Josh stood farther back, alone. Female Dracula and Scrub Girl were sticking close to their mates, but I couldn't hear any fear in Female Dracula's voice when she asked, "What's going on? Someone's dead? Who?"

The crowd expressed their interest with murmurs and nods. They seemed to expect Edward to tell them, so he did.

"A man has died. The circumstances are, um, unusual, and so the police must question everyone. It's just routine. Nothing to worry about."

"But *who* died?"

I turned my back on the gathering. "Let Timms tell them. In fact, we should get moving before he says something we'll regret not hearing."

But Edward, always honest, felt compelled to answer. "A man named Benedict Hamilton died."

Most reacted with sighs of relief. It wasn't someone dear to them. Rico, however, showed signs of one affected by, if not grief, shock. An unfocused stare. Lips pressed tight.

Jennifer stood by his side, her arms folded over her chest and chin held high as if waiting for us to name the killer so she could wipe the floor with him.

Someone called out. "Are you going to figure it out like last time?"

I'd hoped Edward's fans had forgotten about that. I also hoped that didn't mean we'd find two more bodies.

My brother raised his voice. "We will help the police in any way we can, just as you all should."

"What's the first question *you* would ask?" That came from Fur Coat Lady, who had ditched the animal skin for scrubs that hung off her skinny frame.

I stepped in front of Edward.

"He wouldn't ask *any* because he's not involved. Just like you people, we're here by an unlucky coincidence."

When Edward answered her question, I don't think he meant it for public consumption, but his murmur could carry across a basketball court. "I'd want to know how the killer got in and out of the library without being seen."

The Hispanic fairy godmother wiggled her long, sparkly nails at him. "Do you think we're in danger?"

"No, no. I'm sure you're all perfectly fine."

Holding up his hands to quell the additional shouted questions, my brother edged his way over to the swinging doors behind the English garden backdrop with me close on his heels.

As we went through, some man called out, his voice raised. "Not involved, huh? Liar. Then why are you following the police?"

The door closed on his last words. Timms and the other detectives were still in what I called the serving kitchen. It shone with aluminum counters, sinks, and trays.

The staff stood along the edges of the room, some leaning against the counter, most with their arms folded in defiance, murder being one more headache they didn't need. They still had to clean up, and if I understood the rules of serving party food, they couldn't expect any tips from this crowd.

Timms finished his speech, stressing their responsibility to let him know if they thought of anything else. They gathered their trays and headed back out to the Ballroom, careful not to run into the backdrop as they passed through the swinging doors.

There room had two additional doors. One exited into the lobby, but the door opposite the Ballroom led into the kitchen proper. Here was the original room that came with the building, where Mrs. Beckwith did the real cooking.

She was a fixture at Inglenook, having been a family employee for decades. When Claudia and Robert launched their business, she came out of retirement.

It was like stepping back to a time when a full staff scurried around to serve The Family. I could almost smell the roast turkey and trimmings for Thanksgiving dinner.

A large stove, modernized about thirty years ago, stood before a brick wall that served as the backsplash. Cast-iron pots and pans, arranged by size, hung from hooks over galvanized steel countertops. The lingering odor of roasted meat took a backseat to the sweet treats baking in the oven.

We found the cook seated at a large rectangle pine table blowing on a cup of tea. At the sight of us, her face creased with lines and wrinkles as her lips puckered into a scowl.

Mrs. Beckwith didn't like me. At least, she thought I was a pain in the side because every time she'd spoken to me it had been in relation to a dead body.

"I know you've got to do your duty, but mind you touch nothing." She sent her glare to me. "You, especially. Last time you were in here, a body fell out of the dumbwaiter."

Sykes shot a startled glance at the small door in the wall and frowned at me.

Timms, having met her before, wasn't intimidated. He pulled out a chair and sat. "Here we go again."

"Nasty things like murder only happen when these two are around." She jerked her head in our direction, but her expression softened on Edward. "Well, I suppose it would have happened anyway, especially to *that man*."

"Why do you say that? Did you know Benedict Hamilton?"

She picked up her teacup with her hand around the bowl, as if planning to throw it at someone. "He's the one who came in here and insulted me. Asked me where I received my training."

She tapped hard on the table with her index finger, reminding us how strong her hands were from years of kneading dough and wielding cast-iron pans. "My mother taught me everything I know, and anything she didn't teach me isn't worth knowing. That's what I told him. Smarmy little so-and-so."

"Have you been out of this room tonight?"

She sniffed. "I had to oversee the staff tonight. When there's a big event, we bring in extras from an agency, and they're not always worth their pay."

"Did you meet them all?"

"Not formally." She tapped the table. "I was *not* pleased with their level of service. First time I looked out some saucy young woman was eating a strawberry off a tray. There were dirty dishes left on the counter a few steps short of the sink. Lazy. Some gal even sassed me. And I had to shoo off one young man who was hitting on Miranda."

Edward frowned. "Miranda Evans? I thought Robert said she was a maid."

"She is. She only works weekends as she's in high school, so when there's a chance to pick up some extra money, she volunteers. A hard worker. And one of those temps was flirting with her." She huffed. "Her mother only lets her work here because she knows I keep an eye on her."

Her look invited us to share her disappointment.

"Did you notice anyone pass through the kitchen tonight who didn't belong?" Edward gestured toward the serving kitchen for the detectives' benefit. "I don't know if you noticed, but there is another door that lets out into the hallway."

Timms nodded. "Good point. Did you?"

"Not as far as I saw, but the staff have to go that way to reach the washrooms. Since I spent most of the night slaving away in here, you should ask the servers and temps."

"I will, but most of them are kids. I thought you'd notice more."

After that compliment, she gave it some additional thought but still couldn't come up with anyone out of place.

A timer went off. Using the table for leverage, she pushed herself to standing, grabbed a potholder, and pulled a pan of cookies from the oven. Sugar and cinnamon wafted through the room, and my stomach growled.

She sent me a look that said you couldn't expect more from a man and, using a large, flat spatula, moved a couple of cookies to a napkin.

After the warm explosion of butter and spices tickled my taste buds, I might have groaned. Noticing the envious glances of my comrades, she served them samples, too.

Timms didn't get any further by re-interviewing the kitchen staff as they returned with empty trays, though it's hard to be intimidated by a cop munching a Snickerdoodle in between questions.

Bottom line? They'd all been too busy working to notice each other, and only a few of the temporary staff had worked together before. All of them were certain they would have noticed anyone in costume hanging around.

CHAPTER 15

The hallway behind the front desk led past Robert Inglenook's office and ended in the back office. I use the term *office* loosely.

The Inglenooks used the twelve-by-twelve room for storage. Boxes in various sizes, both empty and full. Unused chairs and furniture. An old typewriter.

They had cleaned it up some since the last time I was in here, but it still smelled musty, like mildewed cushions and moldy cardboard. Fortunately, the office desk and a couple of chairs were still there.

Since Edward and I hadn't been told to shove off, I moved a second chair behind the desk for Sykes, retrieved another one for Edward, and took up a position leaning against the wall next to Michaelson.

"You know your wife's friend better than we do. Was she lying about the meeting Hamilton called?"

When Timms posed the question to Sykes, that worthy detective took time to consider his answer. "I'd like to think not."

Timms grunted. "Who have we got next, Michaelson?"

The sergeant glanced at his notebook.

"Davis is rounding up regular guests, meaning the ones who didn't come to the event but might have seen something in the lobby or halls tonight."

I raised my hand. "What about the woman Benedict Hamilton was with? She seemed to be his date. Both of you must have seen her. You might jar something out of her if you talk to her now."

Timms glared at me. "Are you running things? What's your obsession with this woman?"

To diffuse the situation, Sykes agreed that starting with the guests was a good plan.

The first person Davis ushered in looked as if the officer had pulled her from her bed. Mussy hair. Wrinkled clothes. I thought she should have either begged off or taken the time to comb her hair and pick out fresh clothes.

"I saw a few people dressed in costume walking through the halls. It's undignified for people over twenty."

When he asked her to describe them, she could only name the costumes. They could have been anyone.

The next two guests saw the same thing. One man had come down to the Welcome Room to get a cookie and some tea before settling down to read a delightful book. I'd seen him playing sticky fingers with the cookies.

"Who else was in the Welcome Room?"

"I didn't pay attention. The people watching television were already there when I walked in."

Another man caused some confusion because he hadn't seen Zorro enter a room but exit. A few more questions clarified the room he'd come out of had been the bar, not the library, and he thought the guy had gone directly to the gent's room.

When the last guest came in, he brought a new angle. "I heard a woman cry out like she was in trouble. Or maybe in pain. When I looked, I saw the pretty redhead who works behind the desk." He wiped a hand over his mouth. "A good-looker." He spread his grin around the room. "Don't suppose she'd fraternize with the guests, but a guy can dream."

Taking a casual step forward, I rested my hands on Edward's shoulders to keep him in place. I could feel his muscles tensing through his shirt.

"Where exactly was she?" Timms asked.

"The next room down from the Welcome Room. She was past the doorway."

The library.

"Was she alone?"

"Yeah. She looked like she might be sick. You know, leaning on the wall and taking big gasps of air. Probably had too much to drink. She looks like a quiet one, but those are the ones you have to watch out for." He wiggled his eyebrows up and down. "I thought she might be a party girl the first time I saw her, if you know what I mean."

Edward's muscles tensed again, so I leaned my weight on him.

The guy jerked a thumb my way. "Then this guy sneaks up on her and scares her enough that she went running."

The urge to pop him one passed quickly, and I focused on keeping my features neutral.

Edward craned his neck to frown at me.

"Oh he did, did he?" Timms said.

The guest grinned. "You should have been more subtle. The ladies like that. You might have had her eating out of your hand like *that.*" He snapped his fingers.

I wasn't sure how I was going to keep my brother from committing a second murder. I was working out the details when Claudia walked in followed by Officer Williams.

She had changed into a simple blue dress and her thick auburn hair hung loose. Her skin was so pale that if I had any worries about Inglenook being haunted, I would have run from the room.

Edward easily brushed me off and hopped to his feet, which showed the difficulties I would have had restraining him.

"Claudia."

At the sound of his voice, she jerked to a stop but avoided looking our way. Then she approached the table with her gaze directed at Timms. I don't think she even noticed Sykes, who she'd met in Citrus Grove.

"You wanted to see me."

After eying Claudia with a knowing glance, our witness vacated his chair. "Can I go back to sleep now?"

"Thank you," Timms said. "You were very helpful."

Claudia replaced him in the chair.

"You made things tough for Officer Williams."

"You're suggesting it was intentional," Edward put a throaty growl behind his words.

"Eddie, I left my glasses in the Gold Room. Can you get them?"

Timms didn't wear glasses. At least I'd never seen them on his face.

Now that he had Claudia in his sights, my brother balked at leaving her. "I'd prefer to stay here."

"And I'd prefer it if you'd get my glasses."

"Why don't you send Officer Williams?"

She stepped forward. "Sir?"

"Because I'd like *you* to get them for me, Eddie. Now."

Claudia spared a quick glance for him, followed by one for me, and then she turned away as if I were Medusa and she might lock eyes with one of my serpent heads and turn to stone.

I lowered my voice. "You're going to get us both thrown out."

Understanding the benefit of having at least one witness at the interview, Edward agreed and left.

Timms looked Claudia over. "You're a hard woman to track down. You've heard about what happened?"

"I did."

"Who told you?"

"I-I just heard. People were talking."

"When?"

"Just now. When I came with Officer Williams."

"You seem to be taking it calmly."

Her lips trembled when she smiled. "This is a horrible thing that's happened. I can't imagine anything worse. I could cry if it would make you feel better."

The last guest said he had seen Claudia and I together in the hallway, but, unlike me, he hadn't seen her exit the library. At least he hadn't mentioned it. Was that why she couldn't look me in the eye? Did she have something to hide?

Between her exit from and my entrance into the library, there hadn't been time for a third party to rush in and kill the developer. It seemed likely she had met with him and done something unladylike.

There was another possibility that made me uneasy. What if she was protecting someone else who had been in the room? Joshua Breen? Edward?

My brother turned up right after I found the body. If he thought his girlfriend needed protecting, he would voluntarily sacrifice everything to defend her.

The detective tapped his fingers on the table. "Where have you been? Other than in your room."

"That's it. Just in my apartment. As you can see, I changed out of my costume."

"Why?"

"Because I've had a headache all day. I had to be there at

the start of the ball to make sure everything went smoothly. After that, I left."

"How long have you known Benedict Hamilton?"

She wrinkled her brow. "I don't *know* him. I've met him." When Timms continued to stare, two red patches appeared on her cheeks. "Mr. Hamilton thought he could give me some advice on Inglenook. It wasn't advice I asked for, but I couldn't very well insult a guest with his influence. So, I listened."

She'd decided to lie. Good for her.

"What kind of advice?"

She motioned toward the stacked boxes and furniture cast-offs. "This was wasted space. Mr. Hamilton was big on the value of square footage. Changes to the lobby that he thought would attract a more exclusive clientele. Changes I'm not interested in making."

"And that's all he wanted?"

"Yes."

It both pleased and worried me that Claudia lied so easily. And so well.

"In his time here, did Mr. Hamilton have any arguments? Did he seem worried about anything?"

"I don't keep close tabs on my guests. Nothing that I witnessed."

"Did Edward Harlow have anything against Benedict Hamilton?"

I looked up, uncertain where Timms was going with this.

"Edward? Why are you asking me about Edward?"

"Because Hamilton was killed with Edward Harlow's sword."

For the second time tonight, a woman fainted. I caught her before she slumped out of the chair and lifted her easily. I glanced around, looking for somewhere to put her down, and I'd just decided the desk would have to do when she came to.

Her eyes fluttered open. "Nicholas?" Then they opened wide as if remembering, and she wiggled and kicked her legs to get down. I set her on her feet and stepped back.

After pulling her dress straight, she reached for the back of the chair to steady herself. "I'm fine. Thank you."

I shook my head. She didn't sound like she meant it, and her breathing had picked up, almost to a pant.

Sykes gestured to the chair. "Why don't you sit down before we continue."

"I'd rather stand, if you don't mind." She gripped the back of the chair with both hands. I stuck close in case her knees buckled.

"Suit yourself," Timms said, and then he fired his shot. "What was going on between Edward Harlow and Benedict Hamilton?"

"Nothing. Edward is the guest of honor. Mr. Hamilton is one of the board members."

"Did they ever meet before tonight?"

"I doubt it."

It's better to stick close to the truth before skirting it, so I stuck in my oar. "We saw him in the Ballroom earlier today, when we were talking to Ms. St. Armand."

"Talking about what?"

Technically, I didn't talk much. Hamilton was the one who insulted Edward, which I was not about to admit. "Not much. He interrupted us and said he needed to speak with Ms. St. Armand. Privately."

"About what?"

"Board business. Apparently, that information is restricted."

"How did Ms. St. Armand feel about it?"

I laughed. "If you expect me to tell you how any woman feels about anything, you've got me pegged as a magician."

"What did you think of Hamilton, Nicky?"

"He was rude and obnoxious. What's not to like?"

After giving me a dirty look, a look that told me he thought I was kidding, Timms went back to Claudia.

"Several people have mentioned that you seemed distressed earlier tonight. You were outside the library door. Why?"

She finally glanced my way, and I scratched my ear to hide the slight shake I gave my head. She seemed to understand. If I hadn't known her better, I would have believed that, when she tilted back her head, she was trying to recall.

"Oh. I remember. I was heading back to my room to get an aspirin when I had an especially painful migraine. It caught me by surprise. That must be what they were describing."

"Did you see Nicky in the hallway?"

She looked down and bit her lip, stalling. Just then, Williams knocked on the door and waltzed in with Cinderella. Even under the mask, her eyes looked tired, as if the night had turned out just as she'd expected. Rotten.

"I found another guest."

Timms straightened up so fast his chair jumped back, and Michaelson, leaning against the wall next to me, sprang to attention. I studied the woman with more interest.

She sent a friendly smile around the room, as if to acknowledge it wasn't our fault that her night had turned out so rotten. Then she nodded once at Timms.

"Hello, Fergus."

CHAPTER 16

"She's your wife?"

They sent Myra Timms out of the room with a request from Sykes to make herself available. As soon as the door closed, Sykes posed the question.

Timms nodded. "Yeah. Want to make something of it?"

"Sounds a little personal to me."

Michaelson stepped forward. "Sir, I believe you have a conflict of interest and should step down."

Timms twisted his neck to look over his shoulder. "You think that, do you?"

Sykes seconded the motion. "Your sergeant is right."

"Who asked you?" Timms snapped.

Sykes didn't take it personally. He just watched and waited.

Timms drummed his fingers on the table. "You said they were short-handed at the station?"

"Yes, sir," Michaelson said, wary.

The detective's jaw clenched like he was trying not to scream. "Call them and explain the situation. Now."

When Michaelson left the room, I clarified a point. I hesitated because it's not fair to kick a guy when he's down. "Does this make you a suspect?"

By the way Sykes didn't react, he had considered that possibility.

"Last time we visited this murder-friendly resort, you two had split. Have you seen her since then?"

I was trying to help, since if he had no relationship with her, it wouldn't matter if she danced the night away with Zorro. I wondered if Timms would admire my brilliance or take off my skin, but a sudden image of Edward trying to head off Claudia followed by her lying her fanny off about her relationship with Hamilton distracted me.

The two of them knew something I didn't, and until they filled me in… Excusing myself, I jogged after Myra Timms and caught up to her on the stairs.

"Mrs. Timms. We haven't met. My name is Nicholas Harlow."

She beamed at me. "You must be Edward Harlow's brother."

"Yes, ma'am. I am. I have an unusual favor to ask of you."

"Oh, my. Sounds interesting." She giggled, and I wished I could see her face under her wraparound mask. The walnut-brown eyes that met my gaze reflected intelligence and humor. "Ask away."

I was taking a chance, one that might backfire in a big way, so I had to be careful with my approach.

Myra Timms had come to a weekend event with a man, not her husband, yet I couldn't assume her loyalty wasn't with Timms. She could run to him with my suggestion to score points. *In trouble* wouldn't cover my position then.

"I make this request under the assumption you didn't kill Benedict Hamilton yourself."

She drew up her round shoulders. "Certainly not."

"Good. There are some, er, circumstances that have come

up. I'm afraid the police may misinterpret the actions of two knuckleheads of my acquaintance. I need time to sort out what's going on, and I wondered if you could refrain from declaring your innocence right away. Nothing definite. Just be vague in your interviews with the police."

I clarified. "I need a distraction."

At first, I thought I'd misjudged her, but suddenly she grinned. "You mean make myself a suspect by not clarifying certain things right away? Let Fergus sweat a little? Sounds exciting."

I could have hugged her, but I didn't. Instead, I returned to the back office, my walk more confident now that I'd taken steps. Just as I entered the room, Michaelson announced the results of his phone call.

"I have orders to relieve you of this case."

Timms nodded at the expected verdict. "Do they want me to leave the premises? Do I have to lock myself in my room?"

Michaelson locked gazes with his superior. "The phone cut out. If there were any instructions, I didn't hear them."

The former detective in charge motioned to his chair and took a position against the wall next to me. The sergeant remained standing, and he studied the floor. "Thing is, sir, I think I better follow the book on this one. Any variations might put you in a worse spot. At least until we clear Mrs. Timms of any suspicion."

Timms sputtered. "Suspicion?"

Michaelson gestured to Sykes. "How well do you know Latoya St. Armand?"

The San Diego detective considered the question for a full minute before he answered. "I don't, really. She's my wife's high school friend. In the eight years we've been married, I've seen Latoya St. Armand four times, including tonight."

Michaelson nodded. "That sounds alright."

Timms walked out without another word. Since I was a variation, I followed. Sykes stayed to give the sergeant moral support and the benefit of his experience on Michaelson's first case. And, I assume, because he wanted to be on the inside track as long as his wife's friend was a suspect.

"Hey Timms," I said when I caught up to him, but he was mad and kept walking. That didn't bother me. My strides were longer than his, so I had no trouble keeping up.

My brother, returning from his errand, met us by the elevator. "Your glasses, the ones I've never seen you wear, weren't there."

The detective glared at Edward as if it were my brother's fault Timms even had a wife. "What about it, Eddie? You were wearing the same outfit that Hamilton died in. Does someone want you dead? Did you tick off some woman by telling her not to wear white before Labor Day?"

He wished, since if Edward were the intended target, he'd be back on the case.

"Before Memorial Day and after Labor Day. Not that I know of."

The detective turned on me. "And you. Why didn't you mention you'd seen Claudia Inglenook in the hallway?"

Edward leveled his gaze at me. "Yes, Nicholas. Why didn't you mention that when I asked you?"

"I must have forgotten."

"You forget nothing," Timms growled, but his thoughts had already moved on. He glanced around the lobby and, finding it empty, put his hands on his hips and glared at my brother. "Another thing. I didn't want to mention it in front of this Sykes guy, but he's going to find out eventually. What's the deal with this duel?"

"Duel?"

"It's all over the Ballroom. Edward Harlow challenged

this guy to a duel. From the description, they were talking about Hamilton."

Edward spread his hands. "There's nothing to it. Benedict Hamilton made a joke, and I said something about duels being interesting."

"Then he winds up dead with your sword in his back. I gotta tell you, it doesn't look good, Eddie."

"Duels use guns," I said to be helpful.

"I'm not saying you had an actual duel, but there were unfriendly feelings between the two of you. He leaves the room. You leave the room. Suddenly, he's dead with your sword in his back."

"Other people left the Ballroom," I said. "And some weren't in it to begin with."

My brother straightened to his full six-foot-two, shoulders back, and chin lifted. "I give you my word I wasn't wearing my weapon when I left the Ballroom."

"So you say."

I made a rude noise. "Hamilton was a jerk. I doubt anyone had friendly feelings for him except three people."

Interesting that Timms didn't ask me to name them. He eyed my brother for a full minute and then let out a sigh, brushing his hands through what little hair he had. "I must be losing my mind. The idea of you killing someone is nuts."

"I'm glad to hear it," Edward said.

"I'm just worked up." Timms shook out his shoulders. "It's embarrassing. Thrown off the case by my subordinate."

I explained the appearance of Myra Timms to Edward.

"It sounds as if Sergeant Michaelson is concerned about protecting you from any improprieties."

"Improprieties my eye. And now that Sykes guy is working on my case. What if he knows his friend is lying and he's covering for her?"

"Detective Sykes is on vacation. He will be an impartial

observer who might help the sergeant since this is his first case without the benefit of your expertise."

Timms glared at me. "Does your brother always say black when you say white?"

"Every time."

"Well, I'm not going to stand around and do nothing while my wife is a potential suspect. Hell. I'm a potential suspect."

I patted his shoulder. "Don't feel bad. So is Claudia."

My brother thumped me between the shoulder blades and sent me stumbling forward. I straightened up. "And so am I, Latoya St. Armand, Edward, and the entire board of Tea for Teens if you go by people who didn't like the guy."

Timms seemed to feel better now that he had company on the suspect list. He laughed. I took advantage of the momentary camaraderie. "You just happened to win tickets to the same event your wife was attending with her new boyfriend?"

The detective swelled up, and I thought he might explode, but then he released the air in a huff and deflated.

"Yeah. Pathetic, isn't it? I heard she was coming and wrangled the tickets out of the real winner. Cost me a hundred bucks. Myra's come back to me and left me three times since I last saw you guys. This last time was twelve days ago. I thought if she saw me having a good time, she might reconsider her opinion that I'm a workaholic who doesn't think about anything but criminals."

"I know the Harlequin outfit won my heart."

Then I took advantage of his vulnerable spot, which might make me a bad person.

"You know, Timms, just because we're out of the official investigation doesn't mean you have to sit on your laurels. Maybe the three of us could work the case on our own. It would please your wife to know her husband risked everything to clear her name. Women like that."

I knew darn well he planned to investigate on his own. He was probably worried we would drag him down, so I gave him extra incentive. "And if you don't solve the murder, you can blame it on us. What do you say?"

My brother took a sudden step forward. Claudia Inglenook stopped walking, glanced at him, and then gave me a look that said she'd love to stop and chat if only I didn't make her sick to her stomach.

Just then, Joshua Breen exited the corridor that led to the back office. If Michaelson had interviewed him, he'd made it quick. He headed our way, spotted Claudia, and changed direction.

It was too much for Edward. He strode over and I followed. When we got there, we interrupted Josh's condolence speech.

"Claudia. May I speak with you?" Edward made his request polite.

"I'm very tired."

"Why don't we give them some privacy," I suggested, and Josh moved to join me.

"No." Claudia blinked a few times, holding back tears. "I need to take an aspirin and lie down."

Edward took her hand. "I want to assure you I will do everything in my power to find out what happened tonight. You don't need to worry."

She pulled her hand away and rubbed her forehead. Maybe she really did have a headache. "Let the police handle it. I mean it, Edward. This is one case you should leave alone."

"At least let me see you to your room."

"No, thank you."

He frowned. "I see. Will you at least allow Mr. Breen to

accompany you? I don't think you should be alone right now."

She agreed to that, and Josh said he'd make sure she was alright.

"I need to get out of this costume." My brother turned and headed for the stairs. "I feel like a fool."

Timms looked after him. "Looks like it's just you and me, Nicky."

Still shaken by almost finding Edward dead, I preferred to keep him in sight, at least for tonight. "Why don't we meet you later? I'll find you."

He rubbed his chin. "I would like to talk to Myra."

Since his wife was in the wing opposite ours, we parted at the top of the stairs. I wasn't looking forward to the conversation I had planned, and my brother wouldn't like it either.

CHAPTER 17

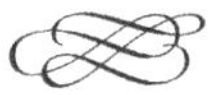

Since I hadn't put on a costume, I didn't need to change. I gave it ten minutes before knocking on the communicating door between our rooms.

While I waited, I put order to my thoughts. Claudia coming out of the library when Hamilton was dead on the floor looked bad. For now, that was my secret.

Edward's sword in Hamilton's back looked even worse, but there was an explanation that, while not great, should satisfy the detectives.

Claudia's lies about her relationship with Hamilton didn't bode well. What if she kept her mouth shut because she'd done it? And if *she* hadn't, there were only two people she would cover for, three if I counted her brother, Robert.

As far as candidates for killer, I could dismiss my brother. I thought Robert unlikely, but would the police agree with me? Neither Timms nor Sykes were fools.

When Edward answered my knock, I let myself in. My brother finished knotting a dark gray tie with a pattern of lighter circles that went with his sea moss green shirt and matching V-neck sweater. He'd switched out the black costume slacks for a pair of black slacks that looked identical but weren't as flimsy as the former.

"Why aren't you in your pajamas? Don't you plan on sleeping?"

"Not tonight."

Which meant I wouldn't get any sleep either. At least I could get my concerns off my chest. I'd already prepared my approach, but Edward didn't give me a chance.

"I want to know everything I missed."

"Are you ready for this? You want to grab something from the mini-bar first? Because there are angles you haven't considered."

His tone got sharp. "Stop stalling, Nicholas. I need to know everything about what happened between you and Claudia in the hallway."

"Which hallway and which time?"

He growled at me, so I told him about Claudia storming out of the meeting with Hamilton, gave him a description of how she acted when I met her in the hallway before finding the body, and I filled him in on the bits he missed after Timms sent him away. As I let the story unravel, his expression grew grimmer with each detail.

"When she came to and saw you were holding her, she seemed…startled?"

"She kicked and wriggled like a cat. The only reason my voice isn't an octave higher is I set her down right away. More interesting is her meeting with Hamilton."

He didn't agree. "Before you saw her in the hallway, before you found Hamilton's body, you were in the Welcome Room next door?"

"I took a quick peek inside, just long enough to take a head count. Then I slipped in a puddle—of what, I haven't decided—as I was coming out the door. It's possible I startled her."

My brother thought about it for a minute and sighed. "We need to speak with Claudia."

"She refused to let you escort her back to her room. What makes you think she'll answer the door?"

"Because I suspect I know what's bothering her."

"What about what's bothering me? I have some concerns, Edward, and I think we should discuss them."

He walked out the door, leaving me to follow.

I trotted to catch up with him so I could keep my voice low. "Seriously, Edward. Seeing Claudia is not going to help. It might even hurt. If the police think there's a chance you're involved in this mess, even on the periphery, they'll have their eyes on you. You're not good at hiding your emotions. They'll pick up on your, um, concern for a certain person and wonder *why* you're so concerned. They may even draw certain conclusions. Like I have."

It made sense to me, but he refused to say anything more as we trotted down the stairs, walked through the lobby past the amenities and a block of guest rooms. We finally reached the door to the private apartment of Robert and Claudia Inglenook. And Zali.

Edward knocked. "Claudia?"

I leaned my back against the wall because I thought it would be a long wait before she answered, if at all.

He knocked again, and this time he added some dialog. "Claudia, we need to discuss why you think Nicholas killed Benedict Hamilton."

While I gaped at him, the lock turned, the door opened, and Claudia Inglenook, the rims of her eyes red, peered out.

Two emotions fought to take over—incredulity and anger. When she glanced at me, her eyes widened, and for a minute, I thought she might slam the door.

"What for?" I demanded.

"Be quiet, Nicholas. May we come in?"

She hesitated, but then she held open the door and stepped back, and we entered her lair.

A short hallway opened into a spacious living room shared by the siblings. Thick, champagne-colored carpet led to glass shelves that held a collection of ballerinas in various poses.

As I passed the bookcase, I picked up one of the many trinkets, this one a calico cat.

"Does Robert live here?"

I heard a laugh. In front of a gas fireplace burning low sat a large sectional couch. I noted the couch was white, just like ours at home, except ours didn't come with a life-sized Joshua Breen. He had his arms stretched over the back cushion, and he looked over his shoulder as we came in.

Claudia gestured for us to sit, but I remained standing, my hands on my hips.

"Why in the name of all that's holy—"

"I said be quiet." Edward sat down and patted the couch next to him in the manner of one coaxing a shy squirrel to step forward and take the nut.

She suddenly cried out and threw herself on him. "Oh, Edward!"

He wrapped his arms around her and rubbed her back while she sobbed on his sea moss green sweater. When her crying subsided enough to allow her to speak, she kept her face buried in his sweater, so I had to strain to hear.

"I've been so worried." She still couldn't look at me.

"Tell me what happened."

She removed herself from his chest and sat upright, twisting her fingers together as she spoke. "I left the Ballroom with Josh. We—we talked, and then he suggested we take a walk to—to continue talking. I went to fetch my coat from my apartment."

"A walk outside? It's too cold."

Josh rubbed the knuckles of his right hand. "That's what I told her.

"How long did it take you to get your cape?"

"Five minutes. Maybe ten. Probably not that long. I was searching for something that would go with my costume."

I snorted. "I assume that's before you got a headache."

She glared at me, but Edward focused on the photographer.

"Did you come with her?"

"I stayed in the hallway part of the time and then I wandered into the bar." He gave us a sheepish smile. "The bartender had a radio tuned in to the Northwestern game. I've got fifty dollars on them to win the tournament."

My hands dropped off my hips. There were more important things than being angry about a murder accusation. "Who's ahead?"

"Could we stay on topic please?" Edward squeezed Claudia's shoulders. "You were saying?"

"Just as I stepped out of my door, I saw who I thought was Josh walking into the library. I turned to lock the door, realized I didn't have my key, and by the time I got it and followed, I found Benedict Hamilton lying on the floor, dead."

"So, you admit you were in the library?" I nodded my head as if I'd just proved something. What, I don't know.

She gave me her snippy tone. "Of course. How else would I have seen him?"

"You poor kid," Josh murmured. "You must have seen me walk into the bar and thought it was the library. Did you think the body was me?"

Her smile trembled. "Only for a moment, but then it was obvious."

Without looking, she reached out her hand for Edward's knowing he would take it, which he did. "I had to get out of there. I thought I might be ill. Then I heard something, turned around, and saw Nicholas. He was *right there,* and I thought—"

"You thought I'd killed a man. Nice."

"You'd just been arguing, and you obviously didn't like him." She made a noise of frustration. "You're a hothead sometimes. I thought maybe things had gotten out of hand, and in my hurry to get out of the library, I missed seeing you."

I shook my head. "That won't do. I would have had to bring Edward's sword with me intending to use it. You think I'm capable of cold-blooded murder."

"When you put it like that, it seems silly."

"Silly?"

"Nicholas, you may be able to look at a dead body without flinching, but Claudia isn't used to that sort of thing and she's upset."

The look Josh sent me said he was reevaluating me. I firmed my jaw as if I ogled corpses for a living.

Edward kissed her forehead. "My poor sweet." She gazed up at him, her eyes shining.

Now it was my turn to feel ill.

Claudia straightened her shoulders. "I'm sorry, Nicholas. If I had been thinking straight, I never would have thought for a moment that you could...you know."

"Don't sweat it."

Since I didn't like Claudia on principle, I didn't see the harm in ignoring the specifics. I'd remind Edward of this moment the next time I approached him for a raise.

The sound of a key in the lock made us all turn our heads

toward the hallway. Robert walked in and stopped when he saw us staring. "The police have contacted Benedict Hamilton's attorney. He promised to be here by tomorrow afternoon, latest."

"I thought his attorney was dead."

He responded to me with a laugh. "Moldy or not, he's coming. They got the name from Frederico Agosti."

"What else did the private secretary have to say?"

"Nothing that I could hear. They got him on the phone in his room. Right now, they're going through Benedict's suite." He shook his head. "They really shouldn't have these conversations on speakerphone. Innocent people can overhear them."

Josh cleared his throat. "There's something I need to tell you two." The two were Edward and me. "I've been looking for the right moment, but there doesn't seem to be one."

He stood. "When they were questioning me, they asked if either of you had a problem with Benedict Hamilton. I told the cops not as far as I knew, but then they said they had a witness who told them you guys had argued. I had to explain about how he'd been rude to you and your brother. I told them you were more restrained than I would have been if he'd talked to me that way. They moved on to the next topic, but I thought I should give you a heads up."

Just as Edward thanked him, Zali joined us. She came out of a short hallway that I assumed led to the bedrooms and greeted us with a pleased grin.

Claudia guided her to an armchair, and once the elder had settled her rump on the cushion, she posed a question.

"Eddie, about the rules..."

"Rules?" Josh raised his brows, and Claudia shook her head gently.

My brother hesitated. "I will be happy to answer if I can."

"Can the murderer and the victim be the same person?"

That made us all pause.

"There are certain logistical problems."

"Yeah. I thought so, too. What's the prize this time? Or is it a secret like last time?"

"I don't honestly know."

She accepted his answer and asked her niece for a hot cocoa. "And don't forget the whipped cream." She rolled her eyes. "She always forgets the whipped cream."

CHAPTER 18

About a half hour later, Edward and I took our leave. Josh had already left to transfer his photos to his computer. By the time he went, the knuckles on his right hand were red and swollen.

"What happened to you?" He looked puzzled, so I pointed at his hand. "You've been trying to rub the skin off all night."

His expression cleared. "Arthritis. Hazard of the job. I can't wear gloves when I'm shooting, even when it's freezing. Sometimes it takes hours of waiting to get the perfect shot."

"Ah. The hazards of the Himalayan goat. That's a tahr to you laymen."

He thought that was funny and chuckled his way out the door.

Robert and I might have slipped away next to give the couple some privacy, but Zali had fallen asleep in her chair. As it was, Claudia settled into deep thought punctuated by impatient sighs, so she wouldn't have been much fun for Edward anyway.

Even so, he seemed pretty chipper. With his determined step and slight swagger, he was back to the old Edward.

"That's one problem solved."

"You say that as if you were cleaning up after me. I didn't do anything except keep my mouth shut about seeing your girlfriend walk away from the murder scene."

"You should have told me."

"Nuts."

"I assume the weekend schedule will go on as planned. Unlike last time"

"If Latoya St. Armand is available. It's obvious she lied about not knowing what was on the agenda for the morning meeting."

"You're making an assumption."

"I wonder if Shauna Sykes knows her friend well enough to be certain she's not a murderer. How well can you say you know someone?"

"That's not a question I'm prepared to ask a stranger."

"Of course not. I'll ask."

"You will not."

"Okay. Do you think the cops forced Joshua Breen to tell them about our little argument with Hamilton, or do you think he volunteered it as a distraction?"

"I don't suppose it matters."

"It might. Timms knew about the duel, but now Michaelson and Sykes might look into it."

"I'm inclined to think it was a mistake. After all, Joshua told us what happened."

"Maybe he wanted to get in there first. And did you notice the way he was rubbing his knuckles? Didn't that forensics guy say someone had punched Hamilton before he died?"

Edward grunted.

"And another thing. I know he's a cop, but Timms seems to like his wife. Enough so that he dressed like a clown and paid good money for the privilege of watching her dance with another guy. Maybe the steam built and he had to find a release. You'll notice how he kept steering me away whenever I mentioned Cinderella. He didn't want his fellow cops to know about her. Maybe he doled out a serving of his own justice to Hamilton."

"By killing him?"

"Why not? And then there's you."

"You're not serious."

"Serious about you killing someone? No. Serious about you being a suspect? Let me tell you how serious I am."

But before I could do so, Joshua Breen, sitting in one of the lobby chairs, stood up and approached us. When we met him halfway, he only had eyes for Edward.

"I'd like to speak with you."

"Something else you need to confess?" I asked.

He sent me an apologetic glance. "Privately."

Taking the hint, I climbed the stairs. Edward said the thing he'd most like to know was how the killer got in and out of the library without being seen.

Out was easy enough. All he or she had to do was walk out the French doors to the walkway and run for it. But if the killer was one of the guests, how did they get back in?

Alfred said no one had entered the front doors other than me. If they went around to the courtyard, which was the only other option, we'd never prove it.

When I reached the landing, Timms hailed me from the wing opposite ours.

"I can't believe my luck, finding you alone. I assumed the two of you were joined at the hip. Follow me."

"Is Michaelson letting you be his errand boy?"

"One of these days, Nicky…"

"I know. *To the moon, Alice.*"

"Sykes had to step away, and he wants another person present."

"A witness? Are you planning to torture me?"

"I wish."

I'd never been in this wing. At first glance, it was identical to ours, with a maid's nook the first room down the hallway, only this room was on the right side, closest to the lobby.

The statues housed in small nooks along the wall were different from ours, and I expanded my knowledge of bad art as I followed the detective into Benedict Hamilton's room.

Inside, fat, forest-green leaves infested the wallpaper, with the curtains, coverlets, and pillowcases in a lighter shade.

"The Jungle Room?"

Timms grunted. "Ivy."

"That's some aggressive ivy."

The police had done a neat job with their search. Hamilton's clothes were folded on one bed. On the other, paperwork and personal items were set out in a pattern, probably those of no importance versus things worth going through.

I shivered, but not because I was looking at the remnants of man's life. To save a few dimes, the Inglenooks had turned off the suite's heat.

Cigar smoke permeated the air. A discarded stub surrounded by thick chunks of ash rested on a plate from the breakfast buffet. I moved to take it outside to the balcony, but Michaelson called out, "Over here."

The sergeant sat on a green love seat the color of broccoli gone to seed. On the coffee table, Hamilton's brown briefcase lay open. The sergeant flipped through the contents of a thick manila folder. Pulling the top sheet out, he handed it to me. "Please tell me what you think."

It took a minute to recognize Inglenook Resort. In the schematics, several walls had been moved to make room for a game room boasting a pool table and a bar, a children's entertainment room with bumper pool and ping-pong, a cigar lounge, and a spa.

The Ballroom had been cut in half with a sliding screen to allow for multiple events. The library and the Welcome Room had disappeared as had the Inglenook's private apartment, which was now an executive suite.

I handed it back. "It's a tarted-up Inglenook."

"That's what we thought." He tapped the page. "Yet Miss Inglenook states Benedict Hamilton only suggested some improvements to her. This is a lot of work for someone who hasn't had a serious conversation about buying the property."

"Says who? Maybe Hamilton got a CAD program for Christmas and liked playing with it. Maybe he always worked out the possibilities before he approached a property's owner. Even if I'm wrong, so what? I once had a guy try to sell me a stolen Rolex. I didn't have to buy it. Maybe he asked her and she said no. Maybe she's keeping the conversation quiet because she doesn't want a rumor started."

The sergeant didn't like that I disagreed with him, and I braced myself for a dismissal, but Frederico Agosti provided a distraction when he burst through the door.

Michaelson stood. "I asked you to remain in your room until we got to you."

The private secretary gestured at me and Timms.

"I saw them come in here, and I couldn't wait." He brushed his fingers through his thick, dark hair. "Benedict is really dead. I can't believe it." He sat on the couch with his head in his hands and the sergeant joined him. "What a mess." He looked up at me. "What are you doing here?"

"Nicky and his brother are helping out on the investigation." Timms smirked. "They're our unofficial advisers."

"That's right. Someone mentioned it in the Ballroom. Is that proper?"

"Sure. We often get help from the public, and these two

are more helpful than most. Now, why don't you forget about him and answer the sergeant's questions. Then you can be a helpful member of the public, too."

Rico suddenly noticed the open file on the coffee table and snatched it up. "That's confidential information."

Michaelson held out his hand. "There is no such thing in a murder investigation."

"His business has nothing to do with the murder."

"Oh. It doesn't?" Timms took a seat next to him. "Then why don't you tell us what it has to do with?"

Rico held up a hand. "I don't know. Maybe it had to do with his love life. I know he was meeting someone here. Maybe he rejected her, and she killed him."

Timms' face got red. "Watch your mouth."

"I think you better let us decide what's important, sir," Michaelson said to stop the coming tirade.

The private secretary had a private debate with himself and finally relinquished the file with a nod. "You're right. You need to find out who did this." He let out a long breath of air.

"I don't know what I'm supposed to do." He looked at us with a wry smile. "My contract didn't cover what steps to take on the death of your employer. It's just…overwhelming. Anyway, I need to talk to you about—"

Michaelson held out the schematics. "Do you know what this is?"

Rico barely glanced at it. "Golden Fields Lodge."

I gaped.

"I'm not crazy about the name either. You can't tell right now, but wheat fields surround this place. It's beautiful in the summer. And I know it doesn't look like a lodge, but Ben liked the masculine sound of it. He thought he could attract family men to bring the whole brood. A spa for the wife, a games room for the kids, and a cigar lounge for the men."

"I know a woman who smokes thin cigars," I said.

"Doesn't sound feminine, but with the way she does it, it works."

Rico assumed an officious tone that would go far in intimidating minions. "The cigar lounge was to attract men, not repel women."

"Had Mr. Hamilton discussed these plans with Mr. and Miss Inglenook?"

"Why? Does it matter? There are more important things I—"

Timms growled on his sergeant's behalf. "He wouldn't ask the question for fun."

"I can't say if he talked to Mr. Inglenook, but he has had several discussions with Claudia Inglenook. One this afternoon, in fact. But it was only a matter of time. Once Benedict set his sights on something, he usually got it."

Michaelson and Timms glared at me. I spread my arms.

Since they hadn't specifically asked if I'd ever seen Claudia and Hamilton together, I hadn't had to describe the scene when Claudia huffed out of the Gold Room. I wanted to keep it that way.

"What? Am I in charge of her schedule?"

"How serious was he?" Michaelson asked.

"Benedict liked to toss ideas around. I was his sounding board. He'd get hot on something, but after a week of thinking about it, he'd go cold on the idea and it was like it never happened. I never took notes because it would have been a waste of my time. With Inglenook? I took notes."

"I'd like to see those notes," Timms said, and then he gave Michaelson a guilty glance and waved his hand. "Or you would."

The typically stoic sergeant had a gleam in his eye as he enjoyed his boss's discomfort.

"I'll put them together for you." Rico froze, and his eyes

opened wide. "Oh. You mean that Claudia Inglenook might have resented Benedict's tactics and killed him?"

"Tell us about Mr. Hamilton's tactics. We heard from Jennifer Proctor that you did research for him."

He rubbed a hand over his mouth. "Yes. I did. Inglenook is in a bad way financially. I can see how he might have backed her into a corner, and she might have resented it."

Both detectives looked my way.

I shrugged. "Or, she might not have."

"Did your brother know about this?" Michaelson asked, tapping the folder.

My jaw stiffened up, and I had to pry the words out. "I can't say."

"Can't or won't?" Timms demanded.

"Can't."

The detective lost the frown and looked sorry for me. "Oh. It's like that."

Michaelson tactfully moved on. "Do you know what your boss planned to say at the board meeting tomorrow morning?"

Rico sent a guilty glance my way. "He wanted to bump out Ms. St. Armand and replace her as executive director. He thought she managed the charity like a small family business and it needed a, um, less emotional person at the helm."

"And did Ms. St. Armand know this?"

"I assume that's what he wanted to talk to her about in the Ballroom. Earlier, when they were setting up."

"Mr. Agosti, do you know of anyone else who has a grudge against your boss? A serious grudge. Someone who might have been here for the ball? Or did you recognize one of the other guests, maybe in the hallway or at dinner? Someone your boss might have had dealings with?"

"I don't want it to sound like I'm accusing anyone of

murder, but his former attorney is here. Melvin Gardner. I saw him tonight."

"Here?" Timms demanded. "At the ball?"

"He wasn't in costume."

"Did they have an appointment to meet? Was his being here arranged?"

"If he did, it's not on my schedule. But you can forget Melvin. He's a lawyer. He'd sue Ben if he got angry, not kill him."

"Who else is there?"

The private secretary leaned back and rubbed his eyes.

"If you want anyone who had reason to resent Ben, he negotiated with everyone from real estate agents to contractors. He went for the best deal he could get, which means the other party might have felt they'd lost out on something. And when it came to buying properties, he had an instinct for people's weaknesses."

"Weaknesses?"

"There were owners who swore they'd never sell. The land had been in their family for generations. He had a knack for finding the one thing that would make them change their minds. But that's how this business works. That's how the world works. There are winners and losers in every interaction. I worked for a winner."

"You should put that on a t-shirt."

I shouldn't have said anything because they asked me to leave.

Back in the Blue-Bell Room, I paced until I heard Edward unlock his door. Without knocking, I entered his room.

"We need to talk. Now."

CHAPTER 19

In the seconds it took Edward to close the door and stroll over to me, I adjusted my approach. Frontal attacks never worked on my brother. He was bigger, smarter, and knew me too well. So, I came at the problem sideways.

"What did Joshua Breen want?"

"Nothing much," he muttered, pulling the balcony door open a crack. A great-horned owl hooted, and the fine mist of rain hissed on the balcony.

Since I didn't care what Joshua Breen wanted, I dropped it. Instead, I tried to get him on my side.

"Can you believe Claudia thought I would kill someone?"

"She explained her reasons."

Edward slipped off his sweater and folded it on the bed. A department store employee couldn't have done a neater job.

"So, with reasons, you think anybody is capable of murder?"

My brother hesitated. "Possibly."

"Even me?"

"Of course not. But Claudia doesn't know you as well as I do."

"Come to that, she doesn't know *you* as well as I do. She knows the Aunt Civility Edward. I admit you've been doing it so long it has become a part of you, but only a part. How about the guy underneath? The one who yells."

"I don't yell," he murmured.

"The one who used to scatter chip crumbs on his sweatshirt while he yelled at the television. Sorry. I brought up yelling twice. How about the one who wanted to be a sports reporter and enjoyed hanging out with the guys at the bar?"

He blinked. It looked like a flinch, but I decided it was only the lighting. "I was much younger."

"So you were. Unfortunately, you're still as naïve."

He glanced at me, wary, as he unbuttoned his shirt. "Naïve?"

As much as he needed to hear about Claudia's deceit, I didn't enjoy breaking his shiny bubble. I wandered to his writing desk and picked up the manila envelope, but my brother lunged across the seven feet between us and snatched it from me.

"You had something you wanted to tell me before Joshua Breen interrupted us." He returned the envelope to the drawer and locked it.

"Sure. There are lots of things I want to tell you. For instance, Frederico Agosti thinks Latoya St. Armand knew Hamilton planned to replace her if he could get the votes."

"When did you speak with him?"

"I just came from Benedict Hamilton's room. Timms and Michaelson are there, too. The private secretary also said that Melvin Gardner, the attorney Hamilton fired, was in the ballroom tonight."

He shrugged off his shirt. "Was he an invited guest?"

"I just know it surprised Agosti to see him here. Though

he made it clear he didn't want to accuse the guy of anything."

"That's prudent."

"He was more forthcoming about Claudia Inglenook and her dealings with his boss."

He turned back from hanging up his shirt. "What do you mean, *dealings*? Did he use that word?"

"Dealings. Meetings. Getting together to do business. Same difference. Remember how I said you were a naïve infant?"

"You didn't use those exact words."

"Well, I do now. For instance, if there were something questionable about Claudia, say, if she lied about Benedict Hamilton threatening her, you'd ignore it until it hit you upside the head."

"Are you accusing Claudia of something? Spit it out."

"I'm only looking out for you."

"I appreciate that, Nicholas, but your worry is misplaced. I know what I'm doing." He sighed. "And right now, I'm going to bed. We have a long day tomorrow."

I crossed my arms. "It's worse than you think. Agosti told the cops Claudia met with Hamilton *several* times. They've even got schematics of what the new Golden Fields Lodge would look like."

"Golden Fields Lodge?" He chuckled. "That was presumptuous of him. Claudia would never sell Inglenook."

"Exactly what I thought, but their conversations have gone further than a few decorating tips. She lied to the police about her talks with him—one of which I overheard part of —and right about now, she's looking like a wonderful choice for a suspect."

"I admit it was foolish for her to lie—"

"You missed another point."

I was about to get into the reasons I'd asked Myra Timms

to distract the police for a while. After taking a deep breath, I let it out.

"Jennifer Proctor described what she saw in the lobby when she looked out. She saw the Halls and the Jenkins. She saw me. She thought she saw Benedict Hamilton go into the library, which means she did more than just lean her head out the door since you can't see the library from the Ballroom door. Even though she had a good view of the hallway, she *didn't* see Claudia Inglenook. Where was she, Edward?"

"Retrieving her cape."

"For ten minutes? Where was it? In storage? Now, before I say it—"

"Don't say it."

"I'm going to say it because you need to start thinking like the cops. What if Claudia was in the library waiting for Hamilton? Red seems to have anger issues when she's crossed. Weren't you listening to her sorority sisters?"

He took a step toward me. "I told you not to say it."

I held my ground. "Okay. If you don't like that scenario, how about this one? What if the person Jennifer Proctor saw walk into the library *wasn't* Hamilton? Maybe Hamilton was already in the library."

"Then who was it?"

"Claudia *says* she saw Josh walk into the library—"

He became still. "Joshua said he went into the bar."

"Come on, Edward. The bar is two doors down. So, maybe she *did* see him, but he'd left by the time she found the body. Meaning he's the one who supplied the corpse."

The gleam in his eye said he liked the idea of Joshua Breen as a killer, but he shook it off. "We should assume Joshua is speaking the truth until there are facts that dispute his statement."

I growled. "Why are you cutting him slack? It seems

obvious something funny is going on, and I prefer the cops focus on him. Not you."

"Me?"

I hesitated. "What Claudia actually saw was someone in a Zorro costume. It could have been *you* Claudia saw going into the library. You were wearing a Zorro costume." When he goggled at me, I hurried to add, "Not that I think so, but Timms has considered the possibility. He asked Claudia several questions about your relationship with Hamilton."

"And she said we didn't have one."

"And they would believe anything she said, especially after the way you kept trying to see her before she talked to the police. Maybe to warn her? To coach her?"

"I would never—"

"For Pete's sake, Edward. Timms even asked you about the duel. Now that they know she lied about her talks with Hamilton, you can see how the police might think you went in there to settle things for your girlfriend. Maybe you didn't tell her what you planned. When she saw what happened, she got upset, which would be natural. Then she sees me and decides it's better to believe I would do such a thing than you."

"Do you believe that nonsense?"

"I'm showing you what Michaelson might think if he gets around to it because if I've come up with it, so will he. Timms already has. So would you if you had your head on straight."

"There are things you don't know—"

"Yeah. Trigonometry."

"Things you don't understand."

"Anti-American politicians and pro-Communist anybody." I took a deep breath and sighed. "So, fill me in."

He shook his head slowly. "Trust me on this."

"I trust you with the big things like my life, Edward, but

it's the little things, like the fallout of this murder, that's got me worried. And your unwillingness to talk to me isn't giving me confidence."

As usual, I was the first one to look away. "If you think about it, the same question I asked about Shauna Sykes and Latoya St. Armand applies to you. How well do you know Claudia Inglenook? Joshua Breen knows her better. You've only known her just over a year."

"What are you getting at?"

"You met last year and rushed into a relationship. Most of that time has been spent on the telephone. Did you notice how people aren't really themselves on the phone? Not like they are in person."

"That may be true, but I still don't see your point."

Neither did I. I seemed to have veered off the tracks. "Maybe you should slow things down and get to know her better. There are more important things than friendly feelings, Edward. Like making a living so you don't have to spend dates on a park bench sharing an apple. I've never known you to miss a book deadline."

He yanked his burgundy silk pajamas out of the drawer. "It's not an ideal situation, but I'll rectify it when I get back home."

"But will you? Not if Claudia Inglenook keeps butting in. She's driving you mad, Edward. The phone calls, the fights, the makeup phone calls. They're all keeping you away from your work."

I crossed my arms. "You'll notice they don't keep her away from *her* work. When your career tanks, she'll still have Inglenook. You may not care, but what about me? I like my job, most days, and I like having a paycheck so I can buy things, like food. You go down, you're dragging me along."

He stared at me for a long minute. "If you didn't have

your job with me, you'd still land on your feet. You're like a cat that way."

I dropped my arms to my sides and gaped. "So, I'm expendable. Are you firing me?"

Edward got agitated and paced the floor. "I don't know how this conversation started, but it's done."

"No, it's not."

"And none of this matters because I'll figure out who did this deed before it becomes an issue." Off my glare, he held up a hand. "*We'll* figure it out."

"Fine. Let's figure it out, starting with the obvious."

But if I thought we were going to have a serious discussion, Edward nixed the idea by pushing me out of his room and locking the connecting door.

I didn't like the way things were headed, but other than walking away, the only choice I had was to follow my brother's lead. I just hoped his feelings weren't clouding his judgment because I refused to let Edward take a fall for the she-devil.

After pulling my pajamas out of the armoire, I looked at my watch. It was a quarter to eleven. I tossed my PJs on my bed and grabbed my key. If Edward refused to look out for himself, I'd have to do it for him.

CHAPTER 20

Robert ordered our second round of drinks before I put the question to him. It takes time to work up to telling a man his sister is a liar and possible murderer.

When I found him, he was closing the front desk. After setting the night ring and putting out a sign that gave guests a number to call in emergencies, which was his cell phone, we took two stools at the end of the bar. The advantage of drinking with an Inglenook was my drinks were free.

We spent the first round unloading our shared experiences with the lovebirds. Robert confessed he often volunteered to work the front desk alone because it gave him some peace from hearing both praise and complaints about Edward.

I liked Robert, and it was a shame we couldn't sit at the bar and enjoy our drinks like normal people. Instead, Claudia and Edward's issues bled into the conversation.

"Did you imagine when they got together that they'd still be an item one year later?"

I had to admit that I did. "Edward doesn't play free and fancy with his emotions."

Robert grunted. "Neither does Claudia."

"Do you think they'll ever marry?"

After emptying his drink, Robert wondered if that might solve our problems. "Of course, they'd have to live here."

Once I finished choking, I asked why.

His eyebrows went up. "Because she works here. Edward can write anywhere, but Claudia can't wait on guests or manage the staff from San Diego. And I can't do it alone."

"You could train Zali."

A grin played at the corners of his mouth. "Funny you say that. She's been asking us to put her to work. We've found some odd jobs for her to handle, but she either forgot about them or tangled them up. But it makes her happy, though her dream is to work the front desk and interact with the guests."

"Ye gads."

Raising his hand to signal for two more drinks, he nodded. "I know."

Raucous laughter came from a booth to our right as the guy on the end fell off his seat. The bartender paused mid-pour to evaluate the situation. One of the friends who faced the bar caught the look and motioned his friends to calm down.

When the last of my first whiskey trickled down my throat, I chased it with some salty peanuts. And that's when I asked the question.

"Did you know Benedict Hamilton was talking to Claudia about buying Inglenook?"

"Know? I sicked her on him. She's much better at dealing with pains-in-the-neck than I am."

My heart rate picked up, a stress reaction. "Were you actually going to sell this place?"

He waited until the bartender set down our fresh drinks and walked away before answering. "Not a chance."

I sighed with relief.

"At least, that's what I would have said a few months ago. Now, with the expenses out of control and people canceling because of the flu outbreak, it's something I at least want to research. Just in case."

"Did Timms ask you about this?"

"No."

For the second time, I sighed with relief prematurely.

"Michaelson did."

"And what did you tell him?"

"Exactly what I told you. Why?"

My molars ground together, so I forced my jaw to loosen up. "Your sister and my brother are a pair of fools. I assume Claudia told Edward. He decided not to tell me. While he's been making a spectacle of himself trying to get his story straight with Claudia before the police get to her, she's been lying her fanny off and telling Timms, Michaelson, and Sykes that the only thing Benedict Hamilton offered her was advice."

He rested his forehead on the bar. "Good grief."

"As long as we're admitting to lies, I neglected to tell the cops I saw Claudia exiting her interview with Hamilton. Her last words were, 'Over my dead body. Or yours.' It didn't seem like something they needed to know."

"Thanks for that. I wonder what got her so angry?"

"If I ask, she'll take pleasure in telling me to mind my own business."

"True. So, I'll ask."

We talked about this and that until Robert stood, stretched, and said he was beat. "If she's up, I'll ask her and let you know."

Even though my drinks cost nothing, I left a tip. About to leave, raised voices caught my attention.

In the second booth from the front sat Jennifer Proctor and Rico Agosti. She had her shoulders hunched up, ready to launch herself over the table and strangle him.

"And there's no reason BanHam, Incorporated can't continue in Ben's memory. No reason at all. Between the two of us, we could make it work."

He shook his head. "Why can't you understand? I don't have Ben's skills at negotiation."

"You could learn. Or *I* could learn."

He gave her a sad smile. "Look. I know you cared about Ben and the company, but he had a special genius that made him recognize a property's potential value. It was instinct. It's not something a person can learn."

Since they weren't keeping the conversation hush-hush, I joined them. "My instincts aren't great either, so I sympathize."

Rico looked up with interest. "How's the investigation going?"

I shrugged. "I assume it's going. I haven't been invited to the party."

He leaned back and smirked. "They've been letting you sit in on interviews. What are you? Private detectives on the side?"

"You heard what Timms said. We're the public."

"He also said you were more helpful than most."

"We seem to have developed a knack for solving crimes," I admitted, and then I gave in to an urge to brag. "Edward's the brains. I'm the peon who feeds the brain by handing it information I've gathered. It's not as prestigious, but I prefer to get the exercise. And Edward would never strain himself to do any real investigating. It's undignified."

The personal assistant rose from her seat. "Then you know who killed Ben?"

"It's early days. Isn't that what they say? But we'll figure it out. Give us a minute."

Rico scooted out of the bench and Jennifer told him to wait. "There's nothing more to say." To me, he said, "Good luck. I hope you catch the ba—"

"Lady present."

He glanced at Jennifer as if he'd never considered her in that role. "We both hope you catch whoever killed Ben." As he walked away, she looked after him with a firm chin and narrowed eyes, as if his leaving had decided nothing.

"Do you still have a job?" I asked politely.

"I'm working on it." Then she jerked her head up to look up at me, her eyes bright with passion. "It could work. I know it could. If we could get investors interested, and I don't see why we couldn't, Rico and I could keep Ben's company going. It would be a way to honor his memory."

My brows went up. "Look at it from Rico's point of view. Committing to running a multimillion-dollar company is an excessive way to pay tribute to a boss. Maybe your associate has his own dreams."

Her hands clenched into fists. "Nothing could be more important than BenHam, Incorporated. It's a sure thing, whereas any ideas Rico might have are just that. Vague ideas. He can't throw over a certainty without a good reason. He just can't. Too many people depend on Benham." She flushed. "I mean employees and—and clients."

"Have you spoken with the attorney? Who are the board members?"

"Ben was the sole shareholder, and he served as secretary, treasurer, and president. Whoever he left the company to will have to see the sense of what I'm proposing."

"Good luck with that." I moved on because something she

said was niggling at my brain, and I wasn't liking it. When I returned to my room, I liked Robert's phone call even less.

"She's not talking."

"Not even to her own brother? Skip that. My brother isn't talking to me either."

He apologized for his lack of success and I told him not to give it another thought. "Whatever she's hiding will come out. We'll probably laugh about our concern."

When I hung up, I wasn't laughing.

CHAPTER 21

At six o'clock the next morning, I awoke to pounding. About to tear into whoever had ruined the best dream I'd had in months, I swung open the door, surprised to see Timms.

"I got news. Get dressed and meet me in the Atrium. And bring your brother."

I knocked on the connecting door knowing that Edward would already be up and performing his morning ritual.

"Just a minute! Ninety-eight. Ninety-nine. One hundred."

When he opened the door, his breathing had almost returned to normal. That's what happens when you do sit-ups, jumping jacks, and push-ups, a hundred each, before breakfast. I'd have to try it sometime.

"Timms wants us downstairs, pronto. He has news."

He gave me a brief nod and bounded off to the shower. It took me five minutes under the spray before I had the desire to bound, and even then, I controlled it.

We exited our rooms at the same time, and when I saw him, I made a noise of disgust.

"I'm changing."

We'd both put on chocolate brown worsted wool suites with butter-colored shirts. Only our ties differed. Mine was burgundy, and Edward's had a two-tone diamond pattern in ocean-blue and chestnut. And he had a butter-toned kerchief in his breast pocket.

About to head off, Edward noticed an envelope on the ground. Stooping to pick it up, he flipped it over and saw his name handwritten across the front. When he read the contents, he frowned.

I gave him a polite smile. "Something I can file for you?"

He tucked it into his inside jacket pocket and strode to the landing. "We don't have time to change. And we look nothing alike. I have flap pockets and yours are jetted."

As we passed through the lobby, we walked side-by-side, which made us look like a Doublemint gum commercial, except for Edward's beard. The other option was to let him lead, but then I'd look like my brother's shadow, which would be worse.

Timms had already filled his plate and taken a table at the back of the Atrium, a room with so many potted plants that I expected to spot Joshua Breen hunting some rare jungle animal with his lens. Sunlight winked through the foliage against the window, promising a respite from the rain.

A few early birds had already grabbed seats at the cast iron cafe-style tables, including a family of four with two children under ten. What kind of parents dragged the kiddies out of bed to meet the dawn? The smaller child, about four, whined over a pancake soggy with syrup. Mom leaned in and asked, "Don't you want to see Grandma?"

That explained it. Grandmas are notoriously early risers.

Since Edward went directly to the buffet, I followed and took a few pieces of bacon, potatoes, and a side of eggs. Then I waited with a plain bagel behind a woman using the toaster. When she turned around, I recognized Shauna Sykes.

"You're up early."

She glared and then decided I wasn't the enemy. "Good morning."

"Taking breakfast up to the hubby?"

The glare came back.

"Jonah didn't get in until late. This was *supposed* to be a vacation. A vacation my husband desperately needs."

"I'm sorry to hear that, ma'am. A cop's life sounds tough. On both of you."

She wasn't interested in sympathy, and she straightened her shoulders and excused herself. While I waited for my bagel to heat up, I decided if Sykes hadn't got in until late, either he'd been working all night and finally given up, or they'd solved the case.

When I got to the table, Timms looked from Edward to me and smirked. "As I live and breathe, it's the Bobbsey Twins."

"What's the idea of dragging me out of bed?" I demanded as I sat down. "Don't you sleep?"

Timms smirked. "Joshua Breen has a possible motive."

Edward's brows went up as my jaw dropped.

"Things are finally moving." I bit off a piece of salty bacon. "Tell all."

The detective needed a hobby. From the way he took his time spreading cream cheese on his bagel, making us wait with a gleeful grin on his face, he obviously hadn't had this much fun in ages. He finally set down the knife.

"When Michaelson interviewed Breen, he was soft on him. Didn't want to upset the famous man. He *did* ask if he'd ever met Benedict Hamilton before, and Breen gave him an unequivocal *no.* Now, my Sergeant is no slouch, and he didn't like that no, so he did some research."

Edward stopped him before Timms got to the good part. "How did you find this out?"

"Sykes told me. He's a good guy."

"He has a vested interest in redirecting your attention. From what I understand, his wife's good friend is a suspect."

"Whatever his reason, it worked for me."

He took a bite of his bagel and chewed. We had to wait until he got it down before he continued. I almost choked him to help it along.

"Since Michaelson was trained by the best, he had the wherewithal to ask Rico Agosti to search his boss's records for anything to do with Joshua Breen." Timms pointed his bagel at me. "I've always thought Breen was a little too good to be true. Handsome. Athletic. Charming. Top of his career."

Except for the career part, he'd just described Edward. And me if you exclude the career again.

Timms held up a finger. "We've already got the means. Your sword, Eddie. Was Joshua Breen around your table at all last night?"

"Several times, but I would have noticed if he had grabbed my sword from its scabbard."

"You'd think so, wouldn't you? But I've found people can be sneaky about things if they want."

I snapped my fingers. "The photos. He took pictures of the guests last night with his cell phone without anyone noticing. I think it's called being subtle, but I like sneaky."

Edward shifted his chair to face me. "There's a big difference between wielding a cell phone and a five-foot-long sword."

I disagreed. "It's relative. That magician made the Empire State building disappear. Or maybe it was the Statue of Liberty. It was something big. My point is, once you know how, size doesn't matter."

Timms showed he appreciated my support with a smile and a nod. "Also, he exited the washroom around the time you found Hamilton. That puts him in the vicinity when

Hamilton was killed. That's opportunity. All we need is motive."

He dropped his hand onto the table. "Anyway, thank you for the cloud. Rico was able to access the office records. Lo and behold, there's this contract over two decades old between the famous photographer and Hamilton. It was a grant. I went over it twice. I'm no lawyer, but I saw nothing that could make a man kill except the repayment clause. It used words like 'the method of our choosing.' My point is, Joshua Breen lied, and where there's a lie, there might be a motive."

He sat back and waited for our applause.

"Twenty years is a long time," Edward said. "If it were a grant, the money may have come from Mr. Hamilton's company. Joshua Breen might never have heard Benedict Hamilton's name."

I frowned. "I thought you didn't have to pay back a grant?"

The detective looked from one brother to the other. "You two are a downer, you know that?"

"I'm not saying you don't have something, and congratulations for being a clever cuss. I'm saying I don't get it." That mollified him, so I continued. "Not to get you riled, but doesn't Joshua Breen have an alibi?"

"He says he was in the bar listening to the basketball game with about twenty other men, many of them in costume. Four of them in Zorro costumes. The bartender can't swear he was there, and those who say they *think* they saw him can't be sure of the times. Another thing. The witness who saw him step into the hallway had to think long and hard before he decided Breen was exiting the bar. Too long and hard for my taste."

"It sounds perfect. And it lets Claudia out of it. Stop glaring, Edward. Robert told the cops all about how he sicked his sister on Hamilton."

Timms laughed. "Sicked. That's the word he used." He had pity on my brother. "I know all about the Inglenook woman's conversations with Hamilton. She doesn't sound like someone he could easily back into a corner, and that's the only motive I can think of for her."

Edward's shoulders relaxed, but he wasn't satisfied. If Claudia was cleared of suspicion, then, by gum, her childhood friend should be too. Anything to make the wench happy. "What did Joshua Breen say about the grant?"

"We haven't asked him yet. Michaelson has a lot on his plate, trying to work alone. I don't want to pressure him."

"I have to tell you, Edward, it makes sense. He has means, motive and opportunity."

"We don't know about his motive yet."

I slapped my hand on the table. "What is it with you and Joshua Breen? You keep defending him. You should be happy Timms here has a suspect. One you don't know personally."

Timms made a noise. "Oh. That's another thing. You know that manila folder I showed you?"

I jerked my head toward my brother. "I told him."

The detective made a noise of disgust. "I should've guessed. Well, it's missing."

"Missing as in mislaid?" Edward asked.

"Missing as it was in the spare office last night. When Michaelson got there this morning, it wasn't. The Inglenooks swear no one went back there last night to their knowledge, but it's not as if they're watching the front desk all night. Of course, I can't imagine anyone would want it other than the Inglenook pair, since it's about Inglenook Resort."

"How can you be sure that's all the folder contained," Edward argued. "Did you examine the contents before it went missing?"

"Michaelson had it, but it was definitely all about them."

"That's bad." When Edward glared at me, I shrugged. "It is."

It's possible my next comment came from a desire to prove my brother wrong about Joshua Breen. "Ask the famous photographer what happened to his knuckles. He said he has arthritis, and maybe he does, but I thought you'd want to ask."

"His knuckles, huh? Thanks. I will."

Timms finished his breakfast and pushed away his plate. I poked Edward's bacon with my fork and asked if he was going to finish it. I needed to cover the taste of bland scrambled eggs. He let me have it, and then his gaze went to the detective.

"I hate to pry, but may I ask how your wife met Benedict Hamilton?"

Timms drummed his fingers on the table, the only sign that the question bothered him. "It's not a secret. She started helping with Tea for Teens. Myra has always been good at jumping in when anyone needs volunteers. She did such a good job they made her a board member. Anyway, she met him there."

Suddenly, his fist came down on the table. "I don't get it. I was a good husband. I took care of her. Myra was always independent. I didn't want to smother her with my opinions, so I always let her decide things. Where she wanted to go for dinner. What movie to watch. I thought she *liked* having a say. You can't tell me Benedict Hamilton gave her the same consideration."

"Sometimes women don't want to paddle the canoe alone," I said. "Maybe you should try putting an oar in the water. But don't listen to me. I'm not married." I glanced at Edward. "We've dodged that bullet."

Edward stood. "Why don't we speak with your wife now?"

Timms looked up. "What? All three of us?"

"Did you sit in on her interview with Sergeant Michaelson?"

The detective growled. "He wouldn't let me, but he's confirmed she's a person of interest. She refused to give him straight answers to simple questions. My wife. A person of interest!"

Hurrah for Myra. I had to fight back a grin.

Edward persisted. "Don't you want to hear what she had to say?"

"I already asked her. She doesn't want to talk about it."

"She may be more forthcoming if we're there because it won't be personal. If you think she'll be awake. It's only going on seven-thirty."

The detective leaned his head back and studied Edward. "What do you want to ask her?"

"Nothing tasteless."

Timms shook his head. "I don't like the idea. It might embarrass her."

"Do you think I would embarrass a woman intentionally?"

I think Timms was happy for the opportunity because he scooted back his chair, stood, straightened his jacket, and led the way.

Dragging my feet, I wondered where I could escape to if Myra Timms emptied the bag for her husband.

CHAPTER 22

It surprised me that Timms' wife wasn't ugly without the mask. Not that I expected her to have fangs, or a hairlip, or a drooling problem, but studies show that like attracts like. Since the detective was average in looks—skirting perilously close to below average—I figured his partner would likewise scrape the bottom of the curve. I admit I might have taken off points for the ginger ring of hair on his head. I'm not a fan of tonsures.

I'd call her cute, in a matronly way. Without the Cinderella mask and costume, she had a straight nose, good skin, a friendly smile, and humor in her brown eyes.

Mrs. Timms had already dressed in navy-blue polyester pants and a blue-and-white patterned sweater. She'd done her makeup and hair, too.

She was on the plump edge of curvy, and I liked her voice. It had a gurgle to it, as if a gentle nudge would start her giggling. Then she set spotted Timms and some of the humor left her.

The room's theme, Tender Tulips, suited her. Splashes of

pinks and yellows on white wallpaper gave Claudia the basis for the color palette.

The bedspreads were a pale, creamy yellow, while the powder pink curtains matched the cushion on the single chair in front of a small, round, white table featuring a vase of the dreaded gardenias. I could smell them the minute I walked into the room.

The balcony door stood open, and the whir of a lawn mower drifted in the window.

When she invited us in, she motioned toward the beds and said, "You'll have to fight for the chair."

This must have been an economy room because there wasn't a love seat or couch available for guests.

Edward insisted she take the chair. He and I remained standing, but Timms plopped down on the end of one bed, which didn't make my brother cringe. After all, they were a married couple.

She picked up her coffee cup from the television stand and paused. "Would anyone like coffee or something to eat? I could order."

"You don't need to entertain them," Timms said.

She shook her head at him and, once seated, opened her eyes wide. "I'm surprised I warrant all this attention. First, your sergeant and that good-looking detective from San Diego, and now you three. Are you here officially?"

"Yes and no," Timms said, though the answer should have been an emphatic no. "These two helped me out last winter. You remember the case?"

She nodded. "I do. I remember being jealous. We'd been talking about going to the opening of Inglenook. You said you couldn't take time off from work."

She placed her index finger on her chin. "I think that was the last straw, the one that made me leave you the first time. Then, I heard you had taken a case here. So, I was jealous."

"Three people died," Timms said in his defense.

"True, but I didn't know them. I think I still would have had a good time."

Timms, unaware that I had already met his wife, introduced us as Edward and Nicholas Harlow. His wife did fine, greeting me with a handshake and beaming at Edward.

"I'm so happy to meet you. Fergus and I used to read your aunt's column all the time. Then we'd try to guess the responses and see how close we could get." She smiled fondly at Timms. "We did alright. Ninety percent of the time we agreed with her. I still do. Read the column, I mean. People are funny."

"They certainly are," Edward agreed. "I regret that we're meeting under awkward circumstances. In fact, we intend to make it more awkward by asking you a few questions, if you wouldn't mind."

Timms stood, tugged on his lapels, and made an announcement. "These gentlemen are not official, so you don't have to answer their questions."

"Oh, Fergus." She dismissed him with a wave. "Ask away." She wriggled in her chair to get more comfortable and winked at me.

That antagonized Timms, and he cut off Edward's question. "Just so we know where we all stand, do you remember seeing this man," he pointed at Edward, "leave the Ballroom?"

"Of course. I was looking in that direction because Ben had just left."

"You mean he followed Benedict Hamilton out?"

She considered the question. "No. I wouldn't say that. Of course, I can't be sure, but it didn't seem like it. Miss Inglenook and Joshua Breen—you know, Fergus, the famous photographer? They left around the same time, too."

"They did, did they?"

"But I don't think they were following Ben, either."

The second mention of Hamilton's name was too much. Timms shouted the next question. "Was Mr. Harlow wearing his sword at the time?"

"How could I tell you that? He was Zorro, and Zorro wears a cape." She smiled at Edward. "And you made a particularly good Zorro. Very handsome."

That left the detective speechless, so Edward smoothly stepped in.

"Do you mind telling us about Benedict Hamilton?"

"Not at all, though I don't know how much I can tell you. We were on the Tea for Teens board together along with eight other people. Anytime you get a board together, everyone is fighting to talk, or posturing, so you don't get a feel for them the way you would if you had coffee together."

"True. Er, did you and Mr. Hamilton have coffee together?"

She gave him an impish smile. "Are you asking me if we were dating? This *is* awkward, with my husband sitting on the bed in my hotel room. Maybe you better leave, Fergus."

His jaw dropped. "But Myra. I'm protecting your interests."

"I don't need protection from these nice, young men."

When all three of us stared at him, he got up with as much dignity as he could muster and left the room.

"That's better." She glanced at me. "I assume it's safe to talk in front of your brother."

"What's that?" Edward glared at me.

"Oh. Maybe not." She covered her mouth with her fingers.

"He's okay, but don't go into details."

She nodded, satisfied. "No. We weren't dating, but Fergus doesn't need to know that. In fact, I haven't told David yet. I mean Sergeant Michaelson. I thought you wouldn't want me to." She smiled at me, and a rumble started in the back of Edward's throat.

"But I'll tell you because somebody needs to know the truth to solve the murder. You can let the others know when you're ready."

She avoided eye contact as she told us the next part.

"Benedict asked if I was coming to the masked ball. I rarely come to the social events because it's not much fun alone, and I can never get Fergus to take the time off. Even if he's off, he says he's tired, but you don't care about that. Anyway, I thought, why not? And then because we *were* each alone, we danced together a lot."

She gave my brother another impish smile. "You'll notice we have separate rooms."

"I wasn't suggesting—"

She interrupted him with a cascade of giggles. "I'm teasing you. Fergus needs to learn a lesson. He takes me for granted. Never instigates anything. I'm always the one who says, 'Would you like to go to a movie, dear?' or 'Would you like a hamburger for dinner?' It wears a woman out. It's tiresome making all the decisions, and sometimes, it makes me feel he doesn't care. And I know he cares. Of course, he does, or he wouldn't come home every night. He's actually an exceptional husband."

Her contradictions—that he took her for granted but was a good husband—endeared her to me. And now that we weren't stepping into a love triangle, Edward relaxed.

"Did you notice anything odd about Mr. Hamilton this weekend?"

"He was his usual, energetic self. I had a good time dancing, but I'm paying for it. My feet hurt."

"Were you aware he planned to force a vote to remove Ms. St. Armand as director and take over the charity himself?"

She put her hand on her cheek. "Was he really?"

"Does that surprise you?"

"He didn't seem to be a managing sort of man. More of an instigator. He had an incredible amount of energy. Non-stop. But I would have called him an idea man. Doesn't a charity director have to do the hard work?"

Recalling what Latoya St. Armand had said, I nodded. "Maybe he didn't realize."

"Oh, well. He probably expected to delegate everything Latoya does now. He would have had a surprise coming."

"Had he mentioned the possibility of taking over before?"

She made a zipping motion across her lips. "The information discussed in the meetings is top secret." Grinning, she added, "Though most of it is pretty boring. I would think they could shout it from the rooftops and the only response they'd get is who cares? So, I'll tell you. No. Not specifically, but he was always going on about how we should fix this or change that. Now that I've thought about it, your suggestion doesn't surprise me."

"And I'm sure they have asked you where you were at eight-thirty?"

She approved of the question. "David asked me that first thing. Or maybe it was the second question. He'll make an excellent detective. I didn't leave the ballroom all night. Ben and I were sitting out a dance—I told you my feet hurt. Not that I needed him to help me sit, but he doesn't have a lot of friends, so he stuck around, which was inconvenient. I was hoping Fergus would ask me to dance. I would have, even though my feet hurt."

I smothered a laugh, and she grinned.

"Of course, I recognized him, the silly goose. But I don't suppose you want to hear about that, either. Ben and I had been sitting for about five minutes when he looked at his watch and excused himself. It wasn't long after you challenged him to a duel."

Edward made strangling noises, so I took over. "Did he say where he was going?"

"Not exactly. He said something about unfinished business, but he looked pleased. Maybe I should say victorious, because that implies a little snottiness, and Ben could be snotty."

"How well do you know his assistants? Frederico and Jennifer?"

Here came a cascade of giggles. "Don't let Rico hear you call him an assistant. That young man is in love with himself." She added under her breath, "And poor Jennifer was in love with Ben."

That explained a lot.

Edward took over. "After Mr. Hamilton left the room, did you notice where your husband was?"

Myra Timms narrowed her eyes. "The sergeant asked me the same thing. I wouldn't like to repeat what I told him."

She let that thought linger so we'd get the point.

"That said, I knew exactly where my husband was all night. He didn't leave the room until Latoya said there had been an accident and would we please remain in the Ballroom." Her features softened. "I remember thinking it's too bad he never gets to stand around with the rest of us and make guesses about what's happened. Guessing can be exciting. The reality isn't."

So, Mrs. Timms was up for some light fun at her husband's expense, but she knew where her loyalties belonged. I wondered if she'd change her mind about helping us now that Edward had shown how it might affect her husband.

She looked out the window at the expanse of muddy lawn

leading to some outbuildings. "I know you're going to repeat what I said to Fergus eventually, but make him work for it, okay?" Her smile had sadness around the edges. "This is the first time in a long time I've had something he wanted."

Edward didn't skip a beat. "Madam, I thank you for your time and your honesty. I hope we meet again under better circumstances."

She sat forward and reached out to him. "You're not leaving, are you? I mean the resort. I'm looking forward to your talk this afternoon."

My brother gave a small bow. "And I look forward to seeing you there."

I said, "Me, too," as I followed him out the door, almost tripping over Timms in the hallway.

"What were you laughing at?" he demanded.

"How do we handle this, Edward? We should keep the lady's confidences, right?"

"You'll keep my foot up your bum if you don't start talking."

I shook my head slowly. "For shame. A police officer threatening a citizen."

"That's enough, Nicholas. Detective Timms, your wife is a perceptive woman."

"If you mean I never got away with anything, you're right. Not that I tried."

"It surprised her to hear Benedict Hamilton was interested in being in charge of the charity, but when she thought it over, she decided it would have been just like him."

The detective/husband's face turned red. "She knew him that well, huh?"

Edward sighed. "May I make a suggestion?"

"You will anyway, so let's hear it."

"Stop worrying about a dead man and start thinking about your wife."

It was a great exit line, and so Edward left. Naturally, I followed.

CHAPTER 23

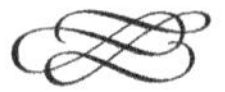

We didn't make it far before Frederico Agosti approached us and asked if we could speak in private.

Timms, who had caught up to us, glanced down the hallway to where Michaelson was hard at work in Benedict Hamilton's suite. I could hear the commotion in his skull as his conscience struggled.

Since Rico had seen Timms together with his sergeant last night, he wasn't aware Timms was off the case.

My conscience was on vacation until this murder wrapped up, so I invited them to my room. Timms and Rico took the blueberry couch, Edward pulled up a chair, and I sat on the edge of the closest bed.

"There's something you need to know," Rico began. "I tried telling you yesterday, but you guys kept cutting me off."

"If you had something to tell us, you could have."

"I tried several times. And then I thought maybe I should think it over again before telling you."

"You mean get your story straight."

Rico shook his head. "Oh, no. My story hasn't changed.

It's the repercussions I was thinking about. You see..." He cleared his throat. "My last name is Agosti because that's the name of the guy who adopted me. He was doing my stepmother a favor, but he never liked me. My dad was dead by then, and to a twelve-year-old, things like names don't matter. To my new father, it did. He even had my name changed from Frederick to Frederico." He smiled. "Everyone called me Freddy before then."

"This is interesting, but what's it got to do with our murder?"

The private secretary swallowed hard before continuing. "Have you ever seen that movie where the parents get divorced and they split up the kids? That's what happened to me. My dad kept me, and my mom took my older brother. My real dad's name was Blazer. His ex-wife remarried, and she became Mrs. Hamilton."

"You mean..." Timms frowned. "What do you mean?"

"Ben and I are brothers."

"How long ago was this?"

"When they divorced, I was five and Ben was twelve."

"Did Ben, er, Mr. Hamilton know?"

When Rico nodded, he didn't smile, so I imagined it wasn't a joyous family reunion. "After high school, I knocked around at different jobs. Mostly with automobiles. Garages, repair shops. I kept track of my mom because..." He shrugged. "She was my mom."

"So how did you wind up working for your brother?"

"I heard Ben was doing well, and by then, I was sick of having grease under my fingernails. I looked him up. We met. He was looking for a private secretary. I think it amused him to have me working for him, but I didn't mind the job at all. I kind of enjoyed it."

"He didn't introduce you as a relation," Edward said.

Rico darted a glance his way. "No. I was his dirty little

secret. He said it was because he didn't want to be accused of nepotism, but I think he kept it quiet because competitors were always looking for a way to get at him. Anyone who dug into my background...well, I got into some trouble as a teenager. Petty theft with my friends. We stole a car and went joyriding. That kind of thing. If anyone found out about me, it would tarnish his reputation. I can understand that."

"You can?" I asked, surprised.

"Not all of us are as lucky as you."

"I am?"

Edward reached over and jabbed me in the ribs, and that made Rico smile.

"I envy you for your relationship with your brother. How you guys joke and get along. I didn't have that with Ben."

"We've been looking for you, Mr. Agosti, though we thought you were a half-brother." Timms stood. "Michaelson needs to know."

Rico looked up. "Will this have to become public information? I mean, it's embarrassing. Besides, I guess I owe it to Ben to keep it quiet."

"We'll see."

The two left and Edward stood and stretched. "I hope you realize how lucky you are, having me as your brother."

"I break into song just thinking about it." I scratched my chin. "This wouldn't be the first fratricide. If you started treating me like that, I could see killing you."

"Hilarious. Now tell me what's going on between you and Mrs. Timms."

I knew he wouldn't let that go. "Don't know what you're talking about. I introduced myself to her before, that's all."

"Her answers seemed to suggest the two of you share a secret."

I met his gaze. "What kind of secret would I keep from

my brother?" I expected a guilty expression. Maybe a confession. Instead, he turned it around on me.

"You mean like not telling me you'd seen Claudia in the library?"

"Coming out of the library. It's a fine point, but an important one."

"Don't start that again."

"Fine. Who else should we concentrate on? We seem to have a surfeit of suspects. Claudia, for reasons we won't go into. The same for you and me. Joshua Breen, if Timms can find a solid motive. Latoya St. Armand trying to stay in charge of her charity. Timms, jealous of his wife. Timms' wife, jealous of Jennifer. Jennifer jealous of Myra Timms. Rico, just because it's convenient."

"There wasn't anything between Mrs. Timms and Benedict Hamilton."

"Since when do you believe anything a suspect says?"

"You can remove Timms and his wife from our list. If she had her eyes on him all night, you can be certain he was watching her. Ridiculous."

"What do you think about the attorney, Gardner, showing up for the ball? If he wanted to argue Hamilton out of firing him, he could have found a better time to do it."

"You think so? Benedict Hamilton would have found it more difficult to ignore Gardner at a public event, especially one where he wanted to make a good impression on the other board members so they would vote his way."

"But did the lawyer know about that?"

"I would think so. Taking control of a charity from the woman who founded it would need adroit handling, or at least legal advice."

"Unless the current executive director of that charity decided to keep him from doing any handling."

"There is that. Timms said many people saw Latoya St.

Armand throughout the evening, but they are vague on times, which is natural. Most people don't look at their watches at a party. If only we could find someone who was bored, or didn't want to be there."

"But *Hamilton* checked his watch and said he had a meeting. What if it was with Gardner? He said he had unfinished business."

Edward sat on the edge of one bed. "That could be it. Definitely."

"Or the unfinished business could be board business with Latoya St. Armand. Or with Claudia about the sale of Inglenook."

I expected a roar, but he didn't even squeak. He clasped his hands. "He had a point."

"Who?"

"Mr. Agosti."

"Rico? What point was that?"

"It must be difficult to work for your brother."

"Are you about to make it easier?"

"I just mean you had plans of your own."

"We saw how they turned out."

Edward surprised me with some sympathy, which is not his strong suit. "It must be difficult to follow someone else's direction after owning your own business."

"Are you dragging my face through that again?"

"No, no. But you were your own man. Not at the beck and call of another. Free to do as you wished."

"And what I did was get into a partnership with a crook who stole all our assets. What's your point, Edward?"

"Don't you want another chance? Your idea was sound. Maybe it could still work."

"Thanks, but no thanks. First, I'd need capital—"

"I could back you."

I gaped.

"Within reasonable limits, of course."

In my surprise, all I could say was, "I'll think about it."

He nodded as if that settled it. "You realize that just because Frederico Agosti came and told us about his relationship with Hamilton, he still could have killed him."

"And his motive?"

"Just what you'd think. Benedict Hamilton was a wealthy man."

"Fair enough. But do you think the private developer would leave his worldly possessions to a brother he hadn't seen in years?"

"He might have."

I shook my head. "They've only known each other for two years. Wouldn't it be suspicious if the two met up, Hamilton changed his will, and then suddenly he's dead? Rico strikes me as smarter than that."

"He seems intelligent. Or at least clever."

When someone knocked on my door a few minutes later, it was Timms, and he wanted Edward. He made it clear it would be a private conversation, so I left.

CHAPTER 24

With Timms and Edward having a private chat, I had to find other ways to occupy my time.

As I trotted down the stairs, Officer Davis escorted a man through the front doors of Inglenook. It was the bald guy who had shown an interest in Benedict Hamilton Friday night. He followed Davis around the corner leading to the back office.

He hadn't been the only person not in costume last night, but the way he'd been studying Hamilton made the odds good that his name was Melvin Gardner, attorney-at-law. Since I didn't have an excuse to follow them in, I stopped just outside the back office door.

Michaelson and Sykes sat in evenly spaced chairs behind the desk. I assumed that meant the San Diego detective was now on equal footing with the sergeant. The opportunity to crash the party presented itself when Michaelson said, "So, you're Melvin Gardner."

The man took a seat in the chair facing the desk and crossed his legs. "I am. I understand from Officer Davis here that you were looking for me. May I ask why?"

Davis, standing by his side, kept his expression stoic and professional.

"Where did you find him?" Sykes asked.

"At home, sir!"

I smothered a laugh over Davis's enthusiastic response.

Gardner looked up at the young officer, more annoyed than concerned. "Do I need a guard?"

Sykes, the hero, intervened before Michaelson could banish Davis from his first interrogation. "Could you take notes, Officer Davis?"

Davis snapped a salute. "Yes, sir!"

Gardner caught sight of me over his shoulder. "And who is this?"

I strolled to the chair and looked down at him for ten seconds. Behind his black-rimmed glasses, the attorney had no eyeballs. It might have been the light reflecting off his thick lenses, but I'd swear I couldn't see any irises. Because it was creeping me out, I averted my gaze to Sykes and Michaelson.

"That's him," I said, as if they had called me in to identify him. "That's the guy I saw watching Benedict Hamilton on the night of the ball."

"Watching him?" Gardner sputtered. "I was waiting for a chance to talk to him."

"What was so important it couldn't wait until Monday morning?" Michaelson asked.

I eased back to lean against the wall, hoping they wouldn't notice me.

"It was a private matter."

"You mean it had nothing to do with Mr. Hamilton firing you two weeks ago?"

Gardner jerked his index finger at the sergeant. "If you repeat that in front of witnesses, I'll sue." When he shot me a glance, I shrugged.

"I don't count."

Michaelson opened his mouth, but Sykes, the more experienced police officer, didn't want to lose the momentum by dealing with my intrusion. "Why did Mr. Hamilton fire you? It's not attorney-client privilege because he's no longer your client and he's no longer alive."

Gardner leaned forward. "Ben's dead? When?"

"Last night during the ball. You were there. When was the last time you talked to him?"

For a moment, Gardner looked nonplussed, but then his inner shark came through.

"I refuse to answer any more questions."

Michaelson nodded. "That will look good for you. Local attorney needs an attorney regarding the death of his former client. Kind of a warning to your current clients."

I was impressed. This was the first I'd seen of the sergeant's sarcastic side.

"Are you threatening me?"

"No. But don't you think it would be easier—and less public—to answer our questions? You haven't even asked us how he died." The sergeant sounded offended.

Gardner took a handkerchief out of his pocket and wiped his brow. "Does it matter? I figured someone would get him eventually if he kept pushing people."

He took the time to fold his hankie before returning it to his pocket. "That's what our argument was about. Ben thought I was getting soft. I thought he should exercise some common sense. He wanted to know how far he could go, legally, in paying someone—I don't know who—to get financial information about a privately owned company. The stuff that's not available to the public." Gardner threw up his hands. "You can't go threatening people, even if it's not an outright threat, without somebody snapping. Looks like I was right."

If he mentioned the duel, I'd scream.

"Who was he threatening?" Sykes held up his hand to stay the response. Even he had his limits on sharing information, and he asked me to leave.

No one wanted to play with me, so I stopped by the Ballroom to see if Latoya St. Armand needed help for the upcoming talk on teas. She seemed covered.

The Inglenook staff had moved a few eight-foot-long tables to the front of the room and covered them with white tablecloths. A brunette woman pulled boxes of tea and teapots and other props from a cardboard box and was arranging them.

At the side of the room, employees disassembled the photographer's backdrop. The chocolate fountain was long gone along with the table it sat on, and our book table had gone back to the crypt.

Mrs. Hall, dressed in a sweat suit covered with sparkles, greeted me as I entered. "Are you here to help? That's kind."

"I had some down time and wanted to be useful."

The board member looked toward the front of the room at the executive director. "We all need to rally around Latoya. We can't allow this unfortunate event to put a damper on this weekend. It's too important."

"Trouble? Excuse me for being so blunt, but is the charity in trouble?"

She paused, perhaps realizing she'd said too much. "Not in trouble, exactly, but it takes money to offer the program for free, and Latoya insists the schools and juvenile halls that use our program not pay for our services. Not that most of them could afford to pay. It would be a shame if we had to cut back."

She had been watching Latoya interact with the teens, but now she turned to me and made a harrumph noise. "Ben thought he could do a better job. Wanted to turn the board of directors into a boardroom and run Tea for Teens like a business. No one would ever put in the time or the love Latoya does."

I nodded knowingly, as if she hadn't just confirmed something for me. "The meeting he called. Took some nerve to bring it up during the ball."

Her eyes snapped open. "I know. I was so embarrassed for Latoya. Ben, too, because he made a fool out of himself." She gazed fondly at the executive director, who was surrounded by Makayla, Brandon, and Claudia Inglenook.

I grunted. "Well, it won't happen again."

"No, it won't. And I'm glad. Does that make me a bad person?"

"I'm sure no one could call you that. I better see if they need any help."

When I arrived, I realized the red hair belonged to Jennifer Proctor. It seemed she had taken on the position of Latoya St. Armand's personal assistant. She ordered the Inglenook staff and volunteers around like a drill sergeant, and I almost reconsidered my offer, but I had an objective.

"I'm at your service," I said to Latoya.

"Thank you for the offer, but you're too late. Ms. Proctor has been a godsend."

Jennifer blushed, which brought out some freckles. It made her look less like Claudia. "Keeping busy keeps my mind off things. As long as you're here, you could help me arrange some chairs at the front of the room."

I agreed, and we moved to pull them from around the dinner tables and into rows in front of the display tables.

"Here we are again, moving chairs."

She loosened up enough to give me a smirk. "But no tables."

Putting two sets of chairs back-to-back, I hauled the four of them to the center of the room. While I moved, Edward's words niggled at the back of my brain. Setting up the Gold Room. Making reservations. Typing letters. Moving chairs. All menial tasks.

In working for Edward, had I settled? It hadn't felt that way before, but maybe I'd gotten too lazy to give it a thought. Maybe he was right. I should get back out there and make it —or fail—under my own name.

"Not there. There." Jennifer pointed to a spot about fifteen inches to my left, and I complied.

"Are you hoping to get a job with Tea for Teens?" I meant it as a joke, but she didn't laugh.

"Until I know for sure what's happening with Ben's will, I'm keeping busy. Rico got hold of the new attorney. He's coming to talk to the police, and they asked Rico to be there, too. I don't understand why they won't let me come. Don't I have a right to know what's happening?"

It wasn't my place to share Rico's messy family history. "Sure."

As we worked, I asked her what kind of boss Hamilton had been.

She paused with her hands on the top rail. "He was everything I hope to be someday. Strong. Focused. Powerful."

"Huh. What about kind? Generous? Flexible? Those are important, too."

"I suppose so." She said it like she was trying not to hurt my feelings, which I guess made her kind. "I'll be honest. I wanted Rico's job. Not that I'm trained for it yet, but I figured he'd leave someday, and I'd be ready. But now..." She shrugged.

"We don't have any other employees, so I'm in charge of myself. Edward expects the world from me. How about Benedict?"

A grin broke through. "I don't think I disappointed him.

I'm a fast learner, and believe it or not, Rico is a wonderful teacher."

"You'll find something. You seem to have a good skill set. For instance, you're observant."

"I had to be in my job."

"Did Benedict seem worried about anything this weekend?"

When she scrunched up her face, it made her look like a moppet. "I would have noticed."

"How about nervous? Did he seem nervous around anyone present?"

That made her laugh. "You couldn't intimidate Ben if you tried."

I set down another pair of chairs. "Why did you think the person entering the library wasn't your boss?"

She waited until she had moved her own chair in place before answering. "I was wrong."

"You didn't seem so sure when you were being interviewed by the cops."

"Give me a break. I was stressed out."

"Does stress affect your eyeballs?"

"I made a mistake. I thought—he had removed his hat, so I didn't think it was him. I expected to see his Zorro hat, and when I didn't... Let's just say I'm sure now."

"We can say it, but I don't think it's true. If it was Ben, why didn't you follow him into the library?"

She opened and closed her mouth, searching for a suitable response, and then decided she didn't need to answer me.

I let the next few minutes pass in silence. Her frown and the furrow between her eyebrows meant she was using her brain. I gave her a few uninterrupted moments and then said, "Penny for your thoughts."

Picking up another chair, she walked away. "I keep

thinking if only I'd followed him, Ben wouldn't have been alone. Then maybe the killer wouldn't have hurt him, and he'd still be alive."

"Or you'd be dead, too."

She paled. I reached out to steady her, but she waved her hand. "I'm alright. It hadn't occurred to me."

"Well, don't let it keep you up at night."

This time, she looked directly at me. "I won't. No one will ever take *me* by surprise. Not now."

Fifteen minutes before the presentation, there were only a few chairs left. I decided I'd done enough manual labor.

In the lobby, I spotted Brandon at the bottom of the stairs, looking as awkward as any teenager trying to fit into an adult world.

To prepare for the first event, he'd changed out of his yellow Tea for Teens t-shirt into a mauve suit with a matching shirt and a patterned tie. He didn't see me coming because he was fiddling with the tie. I sympathized.

"Here. Let me give you a hand."

He angled his torso away from me. "I can get it."

I tapped his shoulder. "I'm still tying Edward's ties for him. Let me take a shot."

First, I undid the knot he'd worked up. Then I held up the two ends and told him to listen up. "This is the tree. This is the rabbit. The rabbit goes around the trunk twice. He's running from a fox, but that's kind of violent, so we'll just say he had an impulse. Then he hides under a bush."

I twisted one end behind the other. "And then he jumps in his hole." Finished, I slipped the knot up, jerked it straight, and stepped back. "There."

He pulled his head back and looked down. "A rabbit, huh?"

"You could make it a squirrel, but I think their holes are in trees. It wouldn't work."

"Thanks." He strolled to the Ballroom doors, straightened his shoulders, and went inside.

Ah, youth. Pretty soon he'd figure out that he was an attractive young man and he'd start leaving the tie a mess so young women, instead of middle-aged men, could straighten it for him. Then again, women were unpredictable. He might be better off learning to tie it himself.

CHAPTER 25

It didn't surprise me to find the library empty. The cops had finished with it and left the lights off and the curtains drawn shut, which left the room in shadow. The darkness suited me fine, especially as I didn't want anyone to join me.

My feet didn't want to cooperate after the first few steps inside the scene of the murder, but I told them the body had been gone over twelve hours and there wasn't any such thing as ghosts. Still, I changed direction, moving right to the recessed bookshelves by the fireplace. I flicked on the torchiere lamp next to the armchair and perused the selections.

Leather spines with gold foil lettering boasted the classics. Austen. Tolstoy. Dickens. Bronte. Dostoevsky was in the original Russian, and Alexandre Dumas, who I always thought was Alexander, had a few of his works represented in French. Amazing what a classical education will do for you. They were in pristine condition, but I knew they were old by the smell of old paper. Coffee, chocolate, and hints of smoke.

The bookshelf to my left held what Edward would think of as light reading. *Howard's End. Rebecca. The Age of Innocence. Moby Dick.* I pulled down a copy of Mary Shelley's *Frankenstein.*

The spine cracked when I opened it, confirming it was there for show, not enjoyment. As I flipped through the stiff pages, some of them sticking together, I decided I'd have to read the original sometime and see if it lived up to the movie. For now, I put it back.

After flicking the light off, I wandered the room, deep in thought. This murder had some strange elements. Edward and Claudia's motives had legs, enough so that I, who knew them well, could imagine them killing Hamilton. Also, aside from my natural animosity toward Claudia, I liked most of the suspects.

Latoya St. Armand and her throaty laugh. Jennifer was just a goof. Even Myra Timms, should she be lying about her relationship with Hamilton, would get my sympathy vote. For a quarter, I would pack our luggage and leave without caring if Timms caught the killer.

Even as I thought it, I crossed off the possibility of letting the murderer of Benedict Hamilton run free. Killers, if they get away with it, tend not to shy away from killing again.

Also, those who were suspects now would never escape the stigma. *They never arrested Latoya, but who's to say she didn't do it?* And people who said murder suspects were innocent until proved guilty had never been subjected to curious stares and whispering. Finally, Edward would never put up with the scales of justice hanging out of balance.

Well, my brother should be happy. When next I saw Edward, I'd have some good news. Gardner suggested there were hordes of people who would cheer if Benedict Hamilton died. Maybe he included himself in that group.

The danger of Hamilton taking over Latoya St. Armand's

favorite charity and her desire to stop that from happening increased as the Tea for Teens funds decreased.

And Jennifer Proctor had a secret. Had she seen Hamilton's killer? If so, why not say something? It probably wasn't anything that dramatic, but she might have a clue that would help tag the murderer. I'd let Edward sort it out.

A sofa table with a fancy lamp rested against the back of a burgundy couch. Skirting around the end of the table, I dropped down and closed my eyes. The stiff brocade fabric and ultra-firm cushions didn't invite company to linger, but I'd come here to think, not take a nap, so that was okay.

Ever since I'd talked with Jennifer last night in the bar, I'd been pushing aside an uncomfortable thought, one that tied in with Edward's response to Wannabe Lifeguard. He'd talked about a responsibility to people who depended on you, and Jennifer had talked about putting aside dreams and sticking to the sure thing because people were counting on you, which sounded like the same thing.

I rubbed the back of my neck. This weekend, I'd noticed something new. Or not new, but new to me.

I'd never noticed how condescending some of Aunt Civility's fans were, addressing my brother as if he were merely the errand boy. I didn't mind being treated like a secretary, probably because I was one. Edward should have been the star of the show, but he'd never be able to shine as long as fans saw him as an elderly lady's lackey.

Was that how Edward saw Aunt Civility? As a certainty he couldn't let go of to pursue his dreams? Edward didn't harbor any dreams that I knew of, but would I know?

My brother and I had grown apart after he left for college, which was only natural. By the time I joined him, he had a set of rowdy friends. Some of them were Journalism majors itching to expose the world's secrets or find work at ritzy magazines. Edward had seen his degree as a means to find a home in a press box at sporting events.

When I followed him three years later, the people I hung out with were more casual acquaintances than friends. Fellow Business majors who were earnest about making their first million before they were thirty.

The only place Edward and I bonded had been on the football field. There, we were the Harlow brothers, and we had each others backs, as one group of sore losers from a visiting team learned to their detriment.

And then he'd graduated. Except for holidays and the occasional weekend, we saw little of each other. We didn't share the details of our lives except on a surface level. And then I'd gone into business with Derick Kaye.

My brother had warned me to stay away from the guy. Said he was trouble. I'd told him he was jealous, since I was sure our new business would be a success. And then Edward was proved right when Derick absconded with our funds.

It was at that low point my brother offered me a job. He was in a bind, as his secretary had just left him without notice, so I'd thought we were helping each other out. It wasn't as if I'd begged for the job. Edward had talked me into it.

I'd never seen myself as a responsibility before, except when I was a kid. As a grown man, I didn't want anyone to think I relied on them. In fact, I thought Edward relied on me, since I was on call twenty-four hours a day, seven days a week.

The job I performed ran well over the description, enough that government agencies would be on my side if I ever complained. But I didn't, not seriously, because I liked my job.

It was a blow to find out Edward thought of me as a hanger-on. Did he make up stuff for me to do to keep me busy? My embarrassment would have sent me out the window if this wasn't the first floor.

Should I quit? Would that open the way for Edward to make his move? Freed of any brotherly guilt, he could afford to live off his savings until he got on his feet doing…what?

I nixed that idea. My brother was a grown man. If he wanted me to quit, he could tell me. Or had he? Was that why he suggested going into business for myself? To get rid of me? Usually, he came right out with his intentions, but he'd been secretive lately.

It irked me I'd lied to the police about seeing Claudia in the hallway, and all the while, Claudia and Edward had been lying to me.

Of course Edward knew about Hamilton's interest in Inglenook. As often as the couple spoke on the phone, it must have come up. Yet he hadn't seen fit to share that information with me. Why?

Did he think I'd blab? Had the harpy convinced him I wasn't trustworthy? It would serve her right if she got nailed for murder. What kept me from going to the police and telling them about the conversation I'd witnessed was the certainty that Edward would never forgive me. I wish he'd fallen for someone I could like.

Opening my eyes, I ran my hand over my jaw and realized I hadn't shaved this morning. The Harlow men got their five o'clock shadows by noon. If I didn't watch it, I'd have a full beard, and then Edward and I *would* look like twins.

Light from the hallway illuminated a path to the thick curtains in front of the French doors. I crossed the room to pull them open and look outside. Whoever killed Hamilton had gone out this way. They must have. Reaching for the door handle, I heard a rustle behind me.

I caught motion in my peripheral vision and jerked back, but not fast enough.

Something heavy slammed down on the side of my head and sent me reeling into the sofa table. Instinctively, I made a swipe for the lamp but missed, and we both crashed to the floor at the same time. As I was lying there, I heard the French doors open and felt a blast of cold air.

After the stars stopped blinking in my vision, I made it to my hands and knees. Once there, I stayed where I was and waited for the room to stop spinning.

"What the devil are you looking at down there, and in the dark?"

Sykes' voice answered my brother. "I think he's injured."

The San Diego detective and Edward each grabbed an arm and hauled me to my feet. I winced when someone flipped on the lights. Timms walked to the open doors, leaning out for a look. He closed them and came back, frowning.

"What happened to you?"

Embarrassed, I shook off my two supporters. "I'm fine, I'm fine."

Then the room swayed, and I went with it, so they led me to one of the armchairs by the fireplace. Sykes said he'd be right back, and Edward leaned over me.

"Look at me."

"I'm fine. Just got the wind knocked out of me."

"I said look at me."

Carefully, I lifted my head, and since my brother kept splitting into three of him, I focused on the center one.

"I'm fine."

He snorted, wandered to the sofa table, and bent over to pick up the pieces of the broken lamp.

When Sykes returned, he brought his wife with him. I knew that because I heard them talking when they entered the room. With my head in my hands, I focused on the floor and willed myself to not be sick.

"Shauna is an ICU nurse."

I couldn't have looked that bad because Sykes' voice reflected pride, not concern.

She cocked her head. "You fell." She said it like a nurse who has heard many excuses from patients and wasn't in the mood to play games.

"Not until after someone hit me."

"Show me where."

I pointed out the spot, and she went to work.

"With this?" Timms held up one of those tubes filled with sand that people used to keep out drafts. "I bet it could pack a wallop." He struck the palm of his hand with it to demonstrate. "Too bad we can't get fingerprints." He tossed it on the sofa table.

While Shauna Sykes looked into my eyes and felt my head, Michaelson walked in.

"What happened?"

Still fighting the urge to be sick, I held up a hand so he would give me a minute. Edward, ever impatient, answered for me.

"The lights were off when Detective Sykes, Detective Timms, and I entered the room. I assume they were off when Nicholas walked in. Well, Nicholas? Were they?"

"Yeah." I took a deep breath and exhaled. "I saw it coming and tried to get out of the way. Obviously, I didn't."

"What were you doing at the time?" Timms asked.

"I pulled back the curtains over the door to look outside. That's all."

The sergeant got out his notebook. "I don't suppose you got a look at the person."

"Not a chance. They came from behind."

"Why were you here?"

"I thought I'd be alone."

"If you hadn't moved, the blow could have landed right

here." Shauna touched the base of my skull. "If that had happened, a coroner might be here instead of me. I suppose it's useless to ask you to go to the hospital for an ex-ray."

"No, thank you, ma'am. I've been hit harder playing football."

"Wearing protective gear." She put her hands on her hips. "I could have my husband wrap you up and haul you to our rental car."

Sykes roared with laughter, tickled by his significant other's suggestion.

"If I may say so, ma'am, that's not playing fair."

She shook her head as if sorry for me. "Too bad, so sad."

"Will you all stop fussing over him?" Edward snapped, which showed me he was worried. "The man can't breathe."

When Sykes took a step toward me, I was on my feet, though not steady yet.

His wife smiled sweetly. "Does that mean you're going voluntarily?"

"Under protest, but on my own feet."

The attack had an upside. It meant Edward and I were on the right track. Now if only I could figure out which track had provoked the killer.

CHAPTER 26

We missed the tea demonstration. It took twenty minutes to get to the small local hospital, and on the drive there I got a view of the scenery. Flat. Flat and more flat. The abundant grass, a deep green from the rains, was pretty to look at, but then you got used to it and started wishing for a hill. Maybe a cow.

The hospital waiting room wasn't much larger than a veterinarian's office. Soft yellow walls, speckled tile floor, and about a dozen chairs lining the room. While Edward paced, Shauna and Jonah Sykes sat in a corner, whispering. She sent over an occasional glance to check on me. By the third one, I made a face.

A middle-aged mother plunked down, exhausted, in the plastic chair one down from me and rocked a crying baby that smelled like poop. Between the noise, the odor, and my pounding skull, well, I'd had better trips to the ER. To make myself feel better, I imagined some creative acts I would perform on the SOB who attacked me.

For the fourth time, Edward approached the middle-aged Hispanic woman behind the counter and asked how long the doctor would be. She gave him the same sympathetic smile she had the last three times he'd asked, but the wattage had decreased, showing her impatience.

"A doctor will be with you as soon as possible."

As soon as possible turned out to be another twenty-five minutes, and it was another hour before they kicked me out with instructions to keep my head away from hard objects.

"I told you not to fuss." In his relief, Edward beamed. "Nicholas has a head of rock."

"You heard the doctor concur with my wife that the blow, placed a bit lower, could have killed your brother."

"Bah. Why dwell on what didn't happen?" Edward said, though he put a lid on further comments.

On the drive back, I skipped the scenery and closed my eyes. When Sykes pulled up to the front of Inglenook in his rental car, he let Edward and me out. His wife went with him to park the car.

For once, the door was open before I reached for it. Alfred stood on the threshold, gaping. As I walked through the door, he took a step back.

"Did you think we'd skipped out on our bill?"

He moved his mouth like a fish, and I had to nudge him out of the way.

There was an unusual number of guests milling about the lobby and murmuring in funereal tones. Many of them held tea cozies or boxes of tea. Prizes and purchases from the tea demonstration.

A small man in a light gray three-piece suit spotted us first. It took a minute to recognize Mr. Periwinkle from Classical Reads, Edward's publisher.

"You're not dead!"

That brought the chatter to a halt.

The publisher scurried up to us and repeated:

"You're not dead."

Since he was staring at Edward, my brother answered him.

"Why would you think so?"

Michaelson and Timms joined us. By that time, Sykes and his wife walked in.

"Someone started a rumor that you'd been seriously injured, and they didn't expect you to make it." Timms swept his glance over me. "How are ya doing, Nicky? You look alright to me."

The ICU nurse took offense at this sunny prognosis. "The doctor agreed with me. He *could* have been killed."

"But he wasn't," my brother said through gritted teeth.

"I still say he should take it easy."

Periwinkle motioned toward Shauna Sykes. "Are you a nurse? Oh, my. How sexist. You may be a doctor."

Shauna took pity on him and smirked. "I'm an ICU nurse, which is in a class all its own."

"I ask because you may wish to check on Ms. St. Armand. She heard the news, and she doesn't seem well. She retired to her room."

He didn't have to say it twice. Sykes' wife skipped the elevator and headed up the stairs to her friend.

Periwinkle squinted his eyes at me, trying to place me. He must have remembered the hanger-on who accompanied Edward to his meetings. "Does that mean you were the intended victim Mr., um…"

"Nicholas Harlow. Edward's brother."

"Of course. How forgetful of me."

"Intended or not, I'm the one that got hit, but as you can see, I'm fine." I gave Edward's brown suit a pointed look. "*Were* you the intended victim? If so, they must not have noticed the pockets."

Bystanders surrounded us, congratulating Edward for surviving what sounded like an assault by armed ninjas.

A shapely woman with gray in her blond hair held out a paper and pen. "Can I have your autograph?"

Some guy called out. "Can't keep Aunt Civility's nephew down. Maybe she'll show up next and dole out some justice. Don't mess with family."

Between the laughter and cheering and butt-kissing, my brother gave up trying to explain what really happened, though he got through to one woman.

"*You* were the one who was attacked?" She eyed me with disbelief. When I agreed, she trotted off to tell her friends. "Nothing to fuss about. Mr. Harlow's fine. It was some other guy."

"Who?" her friends asked, agog.

"I don't know." She made a half-hearted gesture my way. "Him."

Several people wanted to know if the police had captured the culprit. When Michaelson responded in the negative, a man in a sweater and chinos appointed himself spokesman.

"Do you need police protection, Mr. Harlow?"

Edward declined and shot me a guilty glance. "I don't believe I was the intended victim."

As the crowd disbursed, Robert hailed us from behind the front desk. Edward made our excuses to the publisher.

"I tried to explain to people that I'd seen you walking out of here, but once a rumor like that gets started… I have some more bad news."

"How much worse could it get?" I demanded.

"Mr. Periwinkle will be joining us for a few days, and we're out of rooms. I need you both to share the Blue-Bell Room."

Edward didn't argue. He didn't even growl. So, when Robert thanked us for understanding, he put his heart into it.

"You'd better go see Claudia first. She hasn't been around

since the rumor started, so I don't know if she's heard. But if she has..."

Since the cops were still trying to trace the source and were interested to hear what she had to say, we traveled as a group to the Inglenook's private apartment. Edward moved to knock, but I held up a hand.

"If she's heard, and she's in shock, seeing you, not to mention your posse, might make it worse. Step aside and I'll let her know."

Keeping my knock gentle, we waited until the door cracked open. I grinned at the eyes looking up at me.

"Good afternoon, Aunt Zali."

"Claudia's not at home."

"Where is she?"

"She's here, of course, but that's what they used to say when the lady of the house didn't want visitors. *Tell them I'm not at home.*"

"Tell her it's me and that she's going to want to talk to me."

Claudia must have heard my voice, because she pulled the door open and rested a hand on Zali's shoulder. She looked worse than I felt with her red-rimmed eyes and lips pale from shock.

"You heard about what happened, but I'm the one that—"

That's all I got out before she threw herself into my arms, sobbing.

"It's true! If not, Edward would be here!"

Obviously, I'd misjudged the approach we should take.

"I couldn't get any information. Is he—is he—"

I gave her a gentle shake. "Who told you Edward was dead?"

"Does it matter?" she wailed.

"Yes. Because they lied."

She pulled in her breath so fast she choked. And then she

dropped. I caught her before she hit the floor, and when I noticed how soft and warm she was, I immediately handed her off to my brother, covering a shudder of distaste as I did so.

"That went well," he sneered as he carried her into the apartment. Zali called after him.

"I'm glad you're not the body, Eddie. It wouldn't have been fun playing the game without you. But why is there more than one body? Does that mean there's more than one killer?"

Looking from Sykes to Michaelson to Timms, I asked if they wanted to give the couple some privacy.

"We need to know who started that rumor," Michaelson insisted. "It might be the same person who attacked you."

They wouldn't have had privacy anyway because Joshua Breen had taken up residence on the couch. He stood as Edward placed Claudia down and removed her shoes. A flash of annoyance crossed his features before they smoothed out into concern for Claudia.

Edward rested his rump on the edge of the cushion and tapped her hand.

"I think you should throw a bucket of cold water on her," Zali said. "It works in the movies."

Josh stood over the back of the couch. "Claudie," he said, gently. "Claudie, wake up."

Her eyelashes fluttered.

"Come on, Claudie."

Slowly, she lifted her lids. "Joshua?" Then her eyes opened wide. "Edward?"

She popped up to sitting and threw her arms around my brother's neck. "I thought you were dead."

He patted her back, but he didn't squeeze her tight like I would have expected. He seemed embarrassed to do so in front of the company.

"It was only a rumor."

"What a horrible thing to do." She shuddered.

I made a fist. "Not as horrible as what I'm going to do to the guy that clobbered me."

"Calm down, Mr. Harlow. Revenge isn't your best course." Michaelson leaned back his head. "Do I need to lock you in a room?"

"Eddie, why do you think the rumor was about you and not Nicky?" Timms asked. "He's the one that got hit."

"It may have been mistaken identity, as Nicholas suggested." Edward avoided looking at me. "Most likely the person used my name for a bigger effect. I'm fairly well known," he added modestly. He glanced up at the other celebrity in the room. "I'm happy Mr. Breen was here to comfort you during your distress, Claudia."

She pulled back. "Are you serious?"

"Of course." He set her aside, stood, and nodded at Josh. "I'm glad you're here." He glanced at the detectives. "There is something we need to clear up. Claudia, could you excuse us for a moment?"

"Really? In my own home?"

"You're right. That was insensitive. Gentlemen, if we could step outside."

Josh caught something in his expression and moved, but Claudia grabbed his wrist. "Don't leave on my account. I'd like to know what's going on as much as any of you."

Edward ground his teeth. "I'm trying to spare your friend embarrassment."

"Oh." Josh gently extracted himself from Claudia's grip. "I appreciate that, Edward."

"Not at all."

The cops started to move, and Claudia got to her feet. "Fine. I'm going with you. There is nothing you could say that would make me think less of Josh, so just say it."

Timms caught Edward's eye.

"Don't look to him for permission," she snapped. "I'm standing right here, and I give you permission."

Michaelson sighed. "Okay. If you could all take a seat."

The cops and I remained standing, but Claudia sat on the couch bookended by Edward and Josh.

"Mr. Breen, you once signed a contract for a grant from Benedict Hamilton."

The photographer clasped his hands. I noted the swollen knuckles on his right hand. "From his company, BenHam, Incorporated. But it was Ben who talked to me about it. I was a junior in college and had an opportunity to join an expedition to Mexico. I'd never been out of Illinois, and it sounded exciting. They wanted me to photograph an excavation of a Mayan trade route. I was over the moon, but I didn't have the money to join them. Then I met Ben at a dinner for college donors and a few select students. I told him about my dilemma, and he offered me a grant. I couldn't believe my luck. I signed on the dotted line, joined the excavation, and my photographs were so well received that I never looked back."

"Then you lied about not knowing him?"

"Obviously."

Before Michaelson could continue, Claudia grabbed Edward's hand. "And you didn't want me to find out and think badly of Josh. Thank you."

"Well, it didn't seem fair."

Frowning, she said, "Fair. That's an odd word to use."

It *was* an odd word to use, and I could tell by my brother's expression he wished he hadn't used it.

"It wouldn't be fair to you, that this revelation should taint your impression of your friend."

After rolling that idea around, she let go of his hand. "No.

That makes little sense. Why should you care what impression Josh makes on me?"

We were on perilous ground. Edward knew it. Josh knew it. Even I knew it, and I had no idea what they were talking about. I stepped forward. "Come on, Edward. We need to go over your notes."

He nodded, grateful, but she held onto his arm. Then she pulled out her secret weapon. She looked him directly in the eye.

"Tell me what you meant."

I'll give him credit for resisting it as best he could for ten seconds, but then he folded.

"Mr. Breen made his intentions known to me, and I thought—"

She turned to Josh. "Your intentions."

Helpless, he shrugged. "I want to win your heart, Claudie. I thought it fair to let Edward know."

Timms winced, Michaelson chased away any expression, and Sykes stared in wonder.

Her gaze was back on Edward. "Josh told you he wanted to win me over, and you agreed to let him?"

"It's not a question of let—"

"You agreed I was some—some prize? Winner takes all?"

Every woman expects the man who wins her heart to think of her as the Grand Prize, so that was bunkum.

"Thank you for your time." Michaelson headed for the front door. Timms and Sykes, as married men curious to see what annihilation by a female looked like from the outside, stayed where they were.

"And was I going to get any say in the matter?"

"Well, of course. It would be your decision."

"Oh, how freeing. I get to decide." She tapped her chin. "I've decided. Neither of you."

Josh protested. "Claudie, it wasn't like that."

"Both of you, get out."

"If that is your wish." Edward led us out of the apartment. As soon as we made it out the door, Timms snickered.

"You boob. Don't you know the first rule of survival in a relationship is never spill everything?"

Sykes shook his head. "Shauna will not believe this."

"Yeah." Timms snorted. "That's a good idea. Tell her all about it, and then she can corner you and ask if *you* have anything you'd like to share. Take it from someone who's been married thirty years. Keep your trap shut."

The San Diego detective deferred to his counterpart with a nod.

"I'm afraid I bungled that," Edward told his rival. "I apologize."

Josh, a little miffed, accepted the apology.

"He can't help it," I said. "Telling the truth. It's hard to bear sometimes."

"I suspected as much."

When Edward stopped walking, the rest of us waited for him. "There's something I've been meaning to show you."

He reached into his inside pocket and pulled out the envelope he'd found outside his door. "Of course, I thought it was nonsense when I read it." He avoided looking at me as he handed it to Michaelson.

The sergeant took it and pulled out a sheet of paper. "Stay out of this or you will lose everyone you love."

"Gee, Eddie," Timms said. "That sounds serious."

"I thought it was someone blowing hot air."

"From what Detective Sykes says, your brother almost got killed." Michaelson waved the note. "If he'd known about this threat, he might have been more alert."

Exactly what I was thinking.

"And you don't know who might threaten you?

"No."

The cops exchanged glances. "It," Michaelson said. "Stay out of it. That must mean the murder."

"I assume so."

My jaw clenched, but I kept my mouth shut.

"Nicholas, let's go. We need to move my things to the Blue-Bell Room."

He made a stop by the front desk and had a quick word with Robert. The two of them leaned their heads together, and when they finished, Robert picked up the phone.

As we climbed the stairs, I realized the police had never gotten around to asking Claudia who had told her about the rumor.

CHAPTER 27

Since Edward left the key to his room with Robert, we entered Darling Daisy through my room via the connecting door. Edward marched to the closet, grabbed a handful of suits, lifted them to get the hangers over the bar, and then yanked them out in a bundle.

"It would have been nice to have had a warning." I kept my tone polite. "Like the warning in the note you carried around all morning. I was there when you found it. That might have been a good time to share."

He carried the bundle through to the Blue-Bell Room and dumped it on the bed as I watched from the doorway. I suspected his mood had nothing to do with the attack on me and everything to do with how he botched things with Claudia.

"That's nice. You're too big to sulk, and you've got no one to blame but yourself." I moved to the desk to pack up his stuff, but he cut in front of me and barked out orders to get the rest of his clothing.

First, I snatched the roses from the vase and shoved them in the wastebasket. Petty, but it made me feel better.

"Is that the latest thing to bug you? That you had competition for Claudia's affections?"

Yanking the computer cord from the wall, he made a scoffing noise.

"What competition? To compete, you need to be on equal footing."

I didn't think he was giving Josh enough credit, but I preferred feisty Edward to depressed Edward.

"Then why did you agree to it?"

"Because Claudia deserves the best."

Pausing with a handful of socks, I wrinkled my brow. "You mean you wanted to prove to Claudia she had the best by showing her what else was out there?"

I carried my haul into the Blue-Bell Room just as Edward locked the drawer of my writing desk and pocketed the key.

"I admire your confidence. Josh is, by female standards, a hunk. He's successful, famous, and a nice guy. Personally, I would have chosen someone with crossed eyes, or at least bad breath."

I set his socks in a drawer. "Speaking of people with strange eyes, I met Benedict Hamilton's old lawyer. The one he fired."

Silence.

"Did you hear me?"

"Indeed."

"Yeah. He sounded surprised to find out Ben was dead. Apparently, he's the one lawyer with a conscience. He warned Hamilton off doing unethical things like digging up financial information he didn't have a legal right to on companies he wanted to conquer."

"Indeed."

"Yeah. Indeed. You're taking this in, right?"

Edward roused himself enough to ask, "Did he say who?"

"I got kicked out before he gave a name, but I can guess.

Also, I had an interesting conversation with Jennifer Proctor. She's now certain that the man entering the library was Ben, but she got confused because he took off his Zorro hat. When I asked her why she didn't follow him if she was so sure, she didn't have an answer. Also, she's brave. She says no killer could scare her. Not now."

"Not now?" He narrowed his eyes. "What exactly did she say?"

"She said she regretted not following him because maybe he'd still be alive. I pointed out that maybe she'd be dead, too. When she got pale, I told her not to worry about it. And she said she wouldn't. *No one will ever take me by surprise. Not now.* So, if you're thinking about sneaking up on her, don't. She may be armed."

"It sounds as if Jennifer Proctor is playing a dangerous game." He tossed down the undershirt he'd been folding. "You finish up here."

"If you're going to talk to her again, I want to be there."

"I'm meeting Mr. Periwinkle in the bar."

"Now? We haven't even discussed the murder. Well, I have, but I don't know what *you're* thinking, other than you don't think Claudia did it and you're afraid to consider Josh as a suspect because it might appear you're jealous of your rival."

"It's certainly awkward," he agreed. "Why don't you think about it while I'm gone, and we'll talk later."

As he strolled out the door, I glanced at the heap of clothing and thought it would serve him right if I left it there to wrinkle.

It took some finagling, but I got Edwards' suits into the armoire with mine. Then I moved all my foldables and delicates to one drawer to make room for his stuff.

After hauling in his luggage and checking under the beds, I took one last tour of the room to make sure I didn't miss anything, including the bathroom. I even opened the shower curtain to make sure he hadn't left behind his favorite shampoo. Then, after locking the connecting door to keep nosy publishers out of our room, I called the front desk and said room service could have at it.

About to leave, I realized I had an opportunity. I'm not as thick-headed as Edward pretends to believe. I'd made a connection between his fluctuating moods, odd behavior at home, and a certain package he'd received this week. It might hold answers, and I knew right where to look.

As we were leaving the house in San Diego, the mailman made his delivery, which included a large manila envelope. Before I could take it, Edward snatched the mail away. He wasn't fast enough.

I'd seen the word *Press* in the return address. Since we went directly to the car, and I hadn't seen him open anything on the plane, I figured the grand reveal had waited until after we'd arrived at Inglenook. That envelope contained a certain letter he'd refused to hand over to me. He should know it's not advisable to make me curious.

He'd locked the desk drawer, which was naive. A few minutes with a paper clip and I had it open. After taking out the envelope and studying the return address, which was Field Press, I hesitated.

I had an uneasy feeling that to look inside would expose Edward's guts. No man should have his guts exposed, even if he isn't aware it's happening.

Since I had to know what was bugging him, and I wasn't a mind reader, I told my inner voice to shut up and pulled out the contents. On top was a letter addressed to my brother.

Dear Mr. Harlow,

While we appreciate your interest in Field Press, we believe our readers would not appreciate a book written by a man whose specialty is etiquette. This is not a criticism of your current profession. We admire anyone with expertise, whether in our field of sports or in the rules of a civil society. Incidentally, our readers don't hold those rules in high esteem. Also, our readers are fanatical in their devotion to sports, especially baseball, and might find the opinions of an amateur insulting. (Unless shared among friends at the local bar.) That and your lack of writing credentials make it impossible for us to offer you terms. Thank you for thinking of Field Press, and we hope you continue to be a fan of our publications.

An acquisitions editor signed it, or the guy's secretary. The handwriting looked a little feminine to me.

I chuckled. When it came to sports, my brother was anything but an amateur. One reason he got the job writing the Aunt Civility books was his uncanny ability to memorize facts. I've mentioned the catalog of statistics he holds in his skull. I'd put Edward up against any sports editor in a trivia contest.

I set the letter aside and held up the manuscript. *Monday Never Ends.* Okay. He might need help with the title. I flipped through the first few pages and settled back in the chair to enjoy a few more.

Edward had written an homage to his favorite Cubs player, Rick Monday. Being Edward, he dedicated a chapter to stats including Monday's personal record-breaking year in nineteen seventy-six where the player hit career highs in home runs, RBIs, total bases, slugging percentage, and OPS, which naturally made him the team's MVP. But it was more than a report on the man's career.

My brother had captured the mood of a country giddy with optimism and pride over the bicentennial. Red, white, and blue fire hydrants. The American Freedom Train. Operation Sail. Johnny Cash as Grand Marshal of the U.S. Bicentennial Parade. I would have liked to have seen that.

Using everybody's favorite medium, he reflected a time when we didn't talk things to death but did them.

Representing diversity on television with *Chico and the Man* and *Sanford and Son.* A time when humor helped expose the prejudices of Archie Bunker in *All in the Family* and the chauvinism of Mel in *Alice*. Humor that addressed the frailties of the human condition while acknowledging that people were complex, but not monsters.

Sexuality on the rise as seen in Cher's costumes on *Sonny and Cher* and the risqué—at the time—*Three's Company.* Good versus evil, with good always winning, in *Columbo, Quincy,* and the always watchable *Charlie's Angels.*

He reminded us how we loved our heroes, from the fictitious *Rocky* to the very live Nadia Comaneci and her perfect score on the uneven bars in the Olympics. Without intending to, I started humming *Nadia's Theme.*

Edward had cut through the rubble of a current, ill-mannered society and let through the light of human potential that still existed, if we'd only stop yelling and look.

The manuscript ended with Monday's rescue of the American flag from a fool who wanted to burn it on the field of Dodger Stadium. I was stirred by Monday's quote about not allowing its destruction because he'd seen the broken bodies of too many veterans who had defended it. I might have had a tear in my eye.

When I finished, I felt proud to be an American, and proud of Edward. Sitting there, I enjoyed the afterglow of Edward's story. If it sounds like I'm making a raunchy reference, then you don't understand a man's relationship with sports.

So, this was Edward's dream. I could see myself as secretary to a famous author. One who was famous for his own authoring. One who didn't have to hide his talent.

Once I shoved aside any guilt I felt over reading his manuscript uninvited, I had a problem. I couldn't bring Edward's dream up in conversation, so we couldn't discuss a way to make it happen, and I was determined to make it happen for him.

I looked at my watch. It was twenty-five after two. Edward would notice my absence. Jumping to my feet, I scrambled to put everything in order and popped it back into the drawer.

The ignoramuses at Field Press had the nerve to return the manuscript just because my brother had to make a living. I was sure they hadn't even looked at it. It out-shone anything I had read in a long time, and as far as I could see, my brother had only one stumbling block. Aunt Civility.

CHAPTER 28

Once downstairs, I acted on an idea. It was an impulse. Otherwise, I would have worn a coat.

Stepping outside, the biting wind cut short any benefits of the increase in temperature brought on by the shining sun. Hugging my suit jacket shut, I turned right and walked along the cement walkway around the side of the building that housed the amenities. Maybe the killer had re-entered the building from the outside through one of the other rooms.

The recent drizzle left a fine mist of wet on the cement. The air smelled clean, and the birds were out in full force. The rat-a-tat chirp of a cardinal reminded me of the laser gun sound effects from a movie. *Star Wars*, I think. Then I looked up at the nearest balcony ledge and saw it was a mockingbird. I should have remembered that nothing was ever as it seemed at Inglenook Resort.

The first set of French doors I came to belonged to the bar, but it was useless to try to open them as a booth ran along the door, blocking access. I kept going past the windows, noting that Periwinkle had kept his appointment with my brother.

When I got to the doors outside the Welcome Room, a quick pull on the handle confirmed the door was locked. The old guy in the Cubs cap looked over and made a move to get up, so I shook my head and moved on.

Timms must have locked up after we'd left the library for the hospital. Whoever hit me had used these doors as an exit. I wondered how easy it would be to unlock them earlier in the evening and creep in from the outside. Simple, so long as none of the staff checked the locks. And why would they?

The Atrium doors were unlocked, but there were so many heavy potted plants blocking the way, if the killer entered through this room, we'd be looking for someone with a broken leg and scratches on his face from the branches. They probably left the Atrium doors open during the day so the gardener could access all the plants with a hose.

Turning right at the end of the building past the Inglenook apartments, I came to the patio outside the Ballroom. The cleaning crew had pushed the lamps into an inside corner and removed the tables.

Someone had abandoned the job of taking away the chairs and had left them in a few stacks. With luck, I found the doors leading into the dining room open and stepped inside.

Silverware clinked as servers reset the tables for dinner. They didn't acknowledge me as I moved back into the lobby.

I walked into the bar, ordered a scotch, and headed for the corner booth occupied by my brother and Mr. Periwinkle, intending to crash their party. In the first booth I passed, Rico and Melvin Gardner had their heads together, and when the private secretary spotted me, he got up and blocked my progress.

"Could I speak to you for a minute?"

He gestured for me to join them, and I slid in next to the attorney.

"Are we swapping secrets?"

He laughed. "You're a smart-aleck. I can put up with that."

"Are we going to be here long enough for either of us to put up with something?"

"I have a proposition."

"I'm not that kind of guy."

Gardner chuckled, which made me suspicious because it sounded forced. Rico only pressed his lips together in irritation, so I held up a hand. "Okay. I'm done. What did you need?"

After studying his drink, Rico took a sip. "I've been talking to Gardner here. Melvin Gardner."

The man held out his hand, and we shook. "We haven't met formally. I'm Ben's former attorney."

Up close, the lawyer's eyes didn't look any better. Colorless. Lifeless, like a dead man's eyes. I realized I was staring and looked away.

"The thing is, I don't think Ben should have fired him."

The lawyer snorted. "He certainly shouldn't have."

The bartender set down my drink, and when Rico offered to pay for it, I declined and handled the bill myself.

"See," Rico continued after I'd tasted my scotch, "Melvin and Ben had known each other forever. Melvin's a good guy. We were talking..." He sat up. "I forgot. You haven't heard. I met with Ben's attorney, the current one, for the will reading. The cops were there, too. I wish they hadn't been, especially when he said Ben left everything to me."

I whistled. "I guess he liked you better than you thought."

Gardner cleared his throat. "The will doesn't specifically name you, Rico. Your brother never updated the will he made with me fifteen years ago." He leaned his head back and squinted his eyes, recalling. "It instructed his assets be liquidated and divided among his surviving relatives."

"Which leaves me."

An awkward silence hung over the table. Rico cracked open a peanut from a bowl on the table and popped it in his mouth.

"Did you know about the will?"

Rico's eyes widened. "Not a chance. I thought he might leave me something, but I didn't think about it. He wasn't an old man, and as long as I've been with him, he's never even had a cold."

Running my finger over the rim of my glass, I said, "Before this conversation goes any further, I have to ask. Did you kill him?"

Gardner exploded. "That's totally uncalled for! It's slanderous! If you—"

Rico stopped the flow by holding up his hand. "It's a fair question. And the answer is no."

"Well, that's good news then. Congratulations."

The two men raised their glasses, but I didn't join in.

"Like I was saying, I talked to Gardner. I might be able to keep everything as is. The business, I mean. I know all about what Ben did, but I know little about running a business. And that's where you come in."

He took another swallow. "Even though I haven't had much time to think about it, I have done some research online. You have a business degree. You even went out on your own. I could use someone like you."

"You want to hire me?"

"I want you to partner up with me."

The attorney put in his two cents. "The details will have to be worked out, such as responsibilities and the ownership percentage."

Rico was handing me a chance to go out on my own. An

opportunity that would cost Edward nothing. To be my own boss. Well, at least a partner in an established business that, should Rico have the right stuff, would pay off nicely.

"I hope you'll give it serious consideration."

I scooted sideways to get them both in view, since I assumed Rico shared his finding with the attorney. "If you did your research, then you know my partner stole our assets. I don't appear to be a competent judge of character."

The new heir leaned forward. "I also know you went after him. I need someone who doesn't let people walk over him. Besides. I have enough suspicion for both of us."

"And what does Jennifer think about bringing me on? Shouldn't she be here?"

Gardner dipped his head and smirked. "Miss Proctor is a fine young woman, but I don't think her input is necessary."

Rico slumped back in his seat. "Jen is…I don't want to get her hopes up in case it doesn't work out. She cared for Ben, and she cares for BenHam, Incorporated. She'll be an asset."

Gardner nodded at Rico's fine tribute and then spoiled it by opening his mouth. "That said, she is an employee of the company, not an owner. I think it would be more appropriate to tell her about it after we settle everything."

"What happened to Ben's gift of intuition? Something you don't have. Isn't that what you told Jennifer?"

"I'm willing to give it a shot if you are." Rico raised his glass. This time, I drank with him.

As soon as politely possible, I moved to the corner booth. Mr. Periwinkle wasn't in sight. I slid in, checking the motion halfway in because of the expression on Edward's face. I'd seen homeless people in the emergency room waiting area with more optimism sketched on their features.

"How'd it go?"

He finished something in a tumbler that I assumed was alcoholic.

"As expected."

"Were you negotiating your contract early?"

"You could say that."

"Because you're pretty valuable to Classical Reads. Their best-selling author."

"That's what Mr. Periwinkle said."

Edward pronounced it as a death sentence. He set his glass down so hard the ice clinked.

"Will you stop? Even I can see whatever is wrong has to do with your writing. Spit it out. How bad could it be?"

And this is where I thought he'd tell me about *Monday Never Ends* and we'd get to work on making it happen. I was wrong.

His gray eyes studied me. "I was trying to get out of my contract, Nicholas. Or work out a compromise. But it isn't possible at this time." Then he waited for my response.

Suddenly, it all made sense. Locking his office while he worked on his book in secret. Chasing down the mailman and racing me to the phone, hoping for a reply from publishers. Then the kick in the teeth from Field Press to follow the one from his girlfriend. All of it pointed to an unstable, unpredictable Edward.

Something told me not to bring up his unpublished manuscript, possibly a preservation instinct dating back to when walking out the front door could get you eaten. I nodded my head slowly, absorbing the news. "Okay. Have you checked every angle?"

He rubbed his thumb over his forehead. "I thought I had." Then he realized who he was talking to. "Is that all you've got to say? If I give up writing Aunt Civility, *if* that happens, you lose your paycheck. Or you'd at least take a pay cut while I, er, worked on my career. Doesn't that worry you?"

Ah. Nicholas the dependent. The responsibility. Maybe not for long.

"I hate to break it to you, Edward, but you're a grown man, and we're not married. Though siblings getting married may be next."

I made a brushing motion. "If that's what's holding you back, forget it. You've got to do what makes you happy. Don't worry about what anyone else thinks. That's the job of teenage girls. And teenage boys. They worry about other people's impressions, too, especially those of teenage girls. And grown women. They tell you they don't care about any man's opinion, but then they get mad if he has one. I can't speak for gay men since I've never been one, but I'm inclined to think their reactions are split. Maybe—"

"Are you finished?"

It wasn't really a question, so I skipped my answer. "Anyway, you shouldn't worry about what I or Claudia or anyone else thinks."

"Claudia doesn't enter the picture."

"So, it's like that. You're sure your banishment isn't temporary?"

His jaw muscle twitched. "Not so far as I'm concerned. She doesn't have time to wait around for me to reestablish myself. Not if she wants, er, a family."

I shuddered at the thought of little Claudia's running around. Then my eyes narrowed. "That's why you've been pushing her on Josh. No wonder she's mad at you."

"You're really okay with this?"

I shrugged. "I assume you won't kick me out until I find a place to live. Maybe I could move back in with Mom and house sit while she travels with her friends."

That made us both chuckle. Not because our mother traveled a lot, though she did, but because one of the happiest days of her life was when her nest got emptied. She likes her privacy.

And then reality hit me.

On the outside, my demeanor remained calm. Inside, where my fears, insecurities, and anxieties met for drinks, it felt like the floor had dropped out of the room.

Was I seriously considering a partnership with Rico? Would Edward's decision force me to make that choice? My brother might be obnoxious sometimes, but he gave me a *familiar* pain in the side. I knew what to expect from him and what he expected from me.

I knew Rico like I knew how to speak Russian. Not at all. What if I said yes and the partnership blew up in three months? Where would I be then? My worries must have made it to my expression.

"You don't need to rush. It wouldn't happen until my contract comes up. Three more books, including the one that's overdue. The publicity afterward, maybe six months. You would still work for me in the interim, I assume."

If I hadn't been distracted, I would have thought before the words came out. "Good gravy, Edward. You're talking three years from now. Your book—"

Nuts.

"You were saying?"

I squirmed on the bench. "The thing is, Edward, I read your manuscript."

"You what?" His voice had that deadly calm that makes the hairs on my arm stand up. "You had no right."

"Really, Edward. A locked drawer in a hotel room is not a good hiding place."

He slammed his fist on the table and my drink spilled. I scrambled to get out of the way, but by the time I stood, I had a wet spot on my left pant leg.

My brother took his time standing and loomed over me. "You had no right."

"It's good. Really good. As good as anything I've ever read. The guys at Field Press were fools to turn you down."

My compliment seemed to make him angrier. I could tell by the way he spoke through gritted teeth.

"Did it not occur to you I might have a plan? That I'm not looking for pity?"

"Honestly, I'm not sure how it works. You were already writing the Aunt Civility books when I started working for you. As for me handing out pity, give me a break." I held my arms out to my sides. "If it will make you feel better, hit me."

His fists clenched. "No. Because if I let loose right now, I'm not sure what would happen."

Since I wasn't suicidal, I left.

CHAPTER 29

My progress upstairs was impeded by my curiosity, which was aroused when I glanced into the corridor past the front office and saw Robert Inglenook lurking. I say he was lurking because he had taken a position outside the closed back office door and was leaning against the wall in an attitude of listening. And taking a detour gave me an excuse not to run into Edward before he calmed down.

Moving silently, I crept up beside him. "Boo."

He jumped.

"Who's in the hot seat now?"

He put a finger to his lips, and unable to resist the invitation, I joined him by taking my position against the opposite wall. He glanced at the damp on my pant leg and raised his eyebrows. I shrugged in response.

"You can't prove anything."

The voice belonged to Joshua Breen.

"It's quite a coincidence, though. You with the swollen knuckles, and my corpse with a bruise on his face."

Pursing my lips, I nodded. Nice to know Timms listened when I spoke.

Michaelson led the interrogation. I wished it had been Timms, as his voice carries. I leaned in and considered cracking the door open but decided against it.

"I told you. I caught my hand in the door. End of story."

I shook my head at Robert. Arthritis my Aunt Fanny.

"Okay. Let's move on."

Papers rustled.

"Where did you receive your degree in photography?"

Mumbling.

"You didn't? That clearly violates the terms of your grant, which meant Benedict Hamilton could collect from you in the manner of his choosing. That's what it says here."

It sounded like he flicked a finger at a piece of paper.

"How did he plan to collect?"

After a moment of silence, Josh answered. *"I offered to pay him back with interest."*

"And he accepted your offer?"

Another pause. *"No."*

"What did he want instead?"

"You'll find out anyway, probably from Rico. Benedict wanted an associate producer's credit on the television show I've been offered, and points. They weren't interested. I tried to explain their position to him, but he wouldn't listen to reason. He was so smug and self-satisfied. Nothing I said mattered. I got mad, and I punched him. I'm ashamed I lost control and wish I hadn't done it, but that's all I did. I walked out and left him there, alive."

"The problem is, sir, we don't have anyone who can verify that Benedict Hamilton was alive after you left him."

"Which means you don't have a witness who can tell you he was dead when I left him."

Touché.

A chair creaked, as if someone had stood, so Robert and I tiptoed down the hall and into his office.

"Interesting."

Robert immediately turned his sympathy toward his friend. "Poor Josh."

"Do you think he would have lost the TV show?"

Robert gave a half-shrug. "I mean, a show is nice, but it's not as if Josh needs it. He's got plenty of work. I've got to tell you. The more I hear about Benedict Hamilton, the less sorry I am that he's gone."

Narrowing one eye because everyone knows that helps you think, I reconsidered Robert as a suspect. Maybe Hamilton had pressured Claudia past the point of endurance. He stood to lose just as much as his sister if Hamilton won that battle, as Hamilton was wont to do.

He noticed my scrutiny. "What?"

"I'm just wondering where *you* were when Hamilton was killed. You know, your sister would never tell on you. She'd be much happier to see me go down for murder."

Always a nice guy, Robert didn't get angry. "That's probably true, though if they arrested you, I like to think she'd step in."

"I notice you didn't answer my question."

"I was where I always am from six in the morning until ten at night, unless I'm off fixing something, or attending to a problem in a guest room, or, if I'm lucky, grabbing a meal. Give me a break. No one leaves me alone long enough to commit murder."

"That's probably true, but I've got my eye on you."

He grinned back at me.

Heavy footsteps sounded in the corridor. As Josh passed by, I called out. "How's your arthritis?"

Adjusting his course, he entered the office.

"You heard all that, did you?" He dropped into a chair. "Embarrassing."

"More than embarrassing if it means he likes you for murder."

Josh waved his hand. "Not a chance. He just wanted to razz me for lying about it. My career took off after that dig, and there didn't seem to be a point to getting my degree. Not at the time."

"Always read the small print. That's what my granny used to say."

The photographer rubbed his hands over his face and then through his hair, which was loose today and made him look like a cover model for a romance novel. "I meant it. That I wished I hadn't hit him. It brought me down to his level."

"Speaking of levels, did you knock him to the ground?"

"Nah. I didn't hit him that hard."

"Were you going to lose the program if he didn't back off?"

"Maybe." He made a face. "Probably. The channel doesn't clear much after paying everyone. I told them to wave my fee. It was a charity project. Something to help people who can't afford classes to learn how to take great photos with a camera. Believe it or not, some people still prefer cameras."

He looked up. "I think that made it more insulting. I was doing it for free, but he wanted to squeeze them. If anyone wanted to kill him, it would have been the producers of the show. If the project didn't move forward, I would have been disappointed, but not devastated."

I glanced at my watch. "Speaking of devastated, Edward will be if I don't get back to him to regroup before the show."

"If you don't mind, I'm going to pass on it."

"No problem. See you around."

In hindsight, it was lucky Josh didn't come to the lecture.

There might have been bloodshed on top of everything else that happened.

After nodding to Josh and Robert, I headed back upstairs, wondering if I still had a job. While Edward had indirectly threatened to kill me, had he also fired me? I hoped not. Now that I was free to take Rico up on his offer, the job didn't appeal to me.

As I unlocked the door, all my anxieties from the weekend crowded in on me, fighting for the spotlight.

Edward's recent behavior.

Finding Hamilton in the library and thinking it was Edward.

Working to cover for Claudia Inglenook and then finding out she thought I'd killed a man.

Edward's book.

His disappointment with Aunt Civility.

My own uncertain job prospects.

And then I opened the door.

CHAPTER 30

The first thing that met my eye as I walked into the Blue-Bell Room was my bedspread. Not the spread itself, but the dozen tiny liquor bottles scattered over it. Empty liquor bottles.

I sucked in a breath through my teeth, which is a manly version of a gasp. Edward can hold his liquor when he's in practice, but he rarely took a drink these days outside of wine with dinner. Not to mention the effects of mixing liquors.

I checked the bathroom, but he wasn't there.

A strong smell wafted to me from our balcony.

"Who gave you that?" I demanded. My brother leaned against the railing in black slacks and a white shirt open at the collar, smoking a cigarette.

He tapped the ashes off the tip. "Mrs. Timms."

By the time I got to him, he had finished. He flicked the butt over the railing. When he gave me a withering look and stepped back inside, stumbling over the doorjamb, my jaw dropped.

He'd shaved off his trademark trim goatee. It had been

twelve years since I'd seen his face. Latoya St. Armand had been spot on. It was almost like looking into a mirror.

"Let me finish dressing and we can go."

He wasn't slurring, but his voice was thick. After I closed the door, I stepped close and smelled his breath. Smoke and whiskey. "You're not going anywhere. I'll make your excuses to Ms. St. Armand."

He shook his head hard enough that it sent him off balance and he had to reach out for the television and steady himself. "No."

"Then I'll give your talk. I know it as well as you do. I have notes."

He swayed a little. "Not going to happen, little brother."

Edward lumbered to the armoire, pulled open the door, and yanked a tie from the hanger. When he put it on, he had trouble with the knot. It came out lopsided. I automatically straightened it. As I did so, I remembered I didn't want him ready for his talk, pulled apart the knot, and jerked the tie off him.

"I'm fine. You worry too much."

That made me mad. "I don't give a rat's butt if you think you're fine. You're not showing up in front of a room full of fans in your condition. You'll embarrass yourself."

He stood tall and puffed out his chest, mocking me. "How can I do that? I'm the great Aunt Civility. There's nothing I can do that would make Classical Reads look on me as anything but their brilliant cash cow." He leaned forward. "Can I tell you a secret?"

"Sure."

"I *hate* Aunt Civility. She's cutting off my air supply." He grabbed my lapels. "I'm choking. Literally choking." His hands tightened on the fabric and he shook me. "I'd like to wring her scrawny, wrinkled, sanctimonious neck."

I grabbed his hands and wrenched them off me. "Well, if

you don't care about your reputation, think about me and Claudia. I still need a paycheck if you haven't fired me, and Claudia owns this place. Your embarrassment would be her embarrassment."

"I'm sure she'll get over it."

When the world seemed cruel, Edward retreated to his dark place where apathy and lethargy were best friends. One of the hardest duties I had was to steer him away from that place as soon as I saw the signs.

This wasn't his dark place. I didn't know what this was. I admit it scared me because I'd never witnessed him give up control before, so I wasn't sure how to handle it.

"Nicholas!" He frowned. "Why do I call you Nicholas? Too uptight. Nick it is!" He rummaged through the fridge, pulled out a whiskey, and cracked it open. "To Nick."

When I grabbed the bottle by the neck, we struggled before I got it away, and it spilled on his shirt. That gave me an idea.

"Edward, you're a mess. You can't greet your public with a stain on your shirt. Put on a fresh one." I reached into the closet and pulled out the closest one.

He looked at me, uncertain, but he unbuttoned his stained shirt like a good boy. When he started to button the fresh one, I shook my head.

"You're crooked. Go look in the bathroom mirror."

Once he was inside, I bumped the door closed. Then I slipped his key off the television stand, exited the room, and locked the door from the outside.

This had once been a home, and since the Inglenooks hadn't updated the locks, he couldn't get out. I had a flash of him jumping from the balcony to escape, but I couldn't worry about everything.

"It's for your own good, big brother," I muttered as I headed for the stairs.

CHAPTER 31

I ran into Claudia in the hallway leading to the Gold Room. As soon as she saw me, she rushed over.

"Where's Edward? He's not here."

"There's been a change," I said as I entered the packed room.

After making eye contact with Latoya St. Armand, I steered Claudia back by the conference table to where a middle-age man had claimed one of the office chairs. I kicked the wheels.

"There's a lady present."

He glanced up resentfully. "I got here first."

"You can either offer her your chair or I'll offer it for you."

He decided against a scene and I rolled it over to Claudia so she could sit down.

Latoya made her way back to me. In as few words as possible, I explained the situation. We moved to the front of the room, and she held up her hands for quiet.

Everyone stared, curious. All those eyes fastened on me. Waiting to hear my every word. Rabid fans of Aunt Civility waiting to catch my mistakes. I ran a finger around the inside of my collar, pulling it loose.

"Mr. Edward Harlow is indisposed, but we're lucky enough to have his secretary and brother, Mr. Nicholas Harlow, to take his place."

Ignoring the protests, I pulled out the copy of Edward's notes I'd previously placed on the podium shelf and flipped through the pages. Only three. Three scanty pages. Leaning over, I felt around the shelf to see if I'd missed any. It seemed like more when Edward practiced his talk.

At a quick glance, no fewer than four women were glaring at me. Vultures waiting for me to die onstage so they could pick apart my corpse. My pulse pounded in my ears.

I'd never put the same feeling into it as my brother would. Nothing that would satisfy them. It would be like reading a book report. A bead of sweat trickled down my temple.

I had to raise my voice to be heard since, in my preoccupation with Edward, I had forgotten to set up the portable microphone.

"I could give you the planned talk, but I wouldn't do it as well as my brother. Instead, why don't you ask any questions you might have? I'll answer as best I can."

The man I'd separated from his chair shouted a question. "Why do women get the chairs if they're late? How is that fair?"

"Good manners aren't about being fair." I decided to let him save face and make him the hero. "Or maybe they are. You gave up your seat to the lady because you're a gentleman and respect her as a woman." When people applauded, he had no choice but to acknowledge them with a smile.

"Then there's the practical side. We men like to see women in heels, or at least I do, and since they're wearing them for us, it's not fair to make them suffer through standing in them." That got me more applause from the women. "You look healthy, but if you're sickly, you can always take it back. That would be fair."

He blushed a little but moved to rest his rump on the conference table. Unfortunately, his question got us off the subject of masked balls, so I couldn't refer to the notes.

However, as we moved along, I discovered my excellent memory wasn't limited to things that interested me. I had my brother's books and his lectures stored up and I pulled them out without difficulty, but that didn't mean I enjoyed it. At one point, I sniffed a few times, disconcerted, and realized the offensive odor was my own sweat.

Most of the questions were complaints offered by women. The last one came from a female in her early forties.

"I can't remember the last time a man opened the car door for me. Why not? Is it out of fashion? I mean, it's nice to be treated as if I were special and not one of his buddies riding shotgun."

The guy next to her objected. "Women complain all the time they're not treated as equals. I wouldn't open the door for my buddy. Why should I open it for you?"

I held up my hand. "When you're using your manners, you're rising above expectations. The arguments for and against don't matter. You do it because you're a man and you want to let her know she's a woman. That doesn't mean she's incapable of opening the door herself. If she wants to argue about it, find a girlfriend who isn't so petty."

"She's not petty. She's smart."

When I heard Edward's voice, I sent a startled glance toward the door and saw him leaning against the frame. "It's all phony-baloney. It doesn't make a damn bit of difference."

He looked around at the faces of his captivated audience through bleary eyes. They didn't recognize him at first without the beard. When they put it together, the muttering started.

His gaze landed on Claudia. He gave her a sardonic smile, and she looked away. That seemed to egg him on.

"I mean, seriously. What difference will it make in your life if you walk through the door and let the woman behind you make her own grab for it? Even if she's ticked, you'll never see her again. Big deal."

His voice was still thick, and I could swear he was imitating the way I talk. I grimaced and swore because I hadn't checked the mini fridge for additional booze.

I pulled air into my lungs. If Edward's reputation tumbled off a cliff and shattered into a million irretrievable pieces on the rocks below, it wouldn't be because I hadn't grabbed a branch to try to keep us from going over the edge. I held out a hand and introduced him.

"Edward Harlow, ladies and gentlemen. He's arguing for the opposition so you can see how their talking points don't stand up. For instance, what if the door is heavy? Or she's pregnant, or not feeling well? Instead of feeling cared for, she'll just be another nameless number walking alone through life. Every encounter we have with people should leave them feeling a little better."

One woman nodded her agreement, but when Edward made a rude noise, her expression said she'd just failed a test.

"Better than what?" my brother demanded. "If she's pregnant, she'll still be pregnant after she walks through the door."

Sober Edward wouldn't have spoken the word pregnant in mixed company. Not even hypothetically.

"And if she's feeling blue, maybe opening her own door will give her the knowledge that she can get through life with no one's help. Because we are all alone. Fussy bits of etiquette will not alter the fact that we're by ourselves in our misery for the rest of our days."

A woman gasped. "What would Aunt Civility say if she heard you?"

He straightened up and glared at the people in the room. "For the love of Mike, woman, I *am* Aunt Civility! Stick that in your pipe and smoke it."

The room went still. I forgot to breathe.

A woman cried out. "No Aunt Civility? It's like she's dead and you killed her. You monster!"

No one could talk to Edward like that except me. A surge of anger warmed my chest.

"Get your priorities straight, lady," I snapped. "Nothing has changed except you learned something new." I gave them all a dose of my glare. "I don't get you, anyway. None of you. You come to this fundraiser to give money to a charity that actually helps people, but you have to have a party before you'll do it."

I flung my arm out toward Latoya St. Armand. "And while some kids this lady helps are trying to figure out where their next meal is coming from, you obsess over a bunch of little things that don't make a bit of difference to anyone's life."

"Which salutation should you use? Isn't it keeping in contact with your loved ones that counts? I don't think they'd throw out your letter just because you said Miss instead of Ms. and vice versa. Which fork is the right one for your salad? Don't make me laugh. Would you sit there and stare at your lettuce all night if yours was missing? And if someone ate their dessert with a soup spoon, would you faint?"

My voice trailed off because of the way Edward was staring at Claudia. He must have been lurking in the hallway during my encounter with Chair Guy because his next move was to grab the back of her seat and dump her on the floor.

Then he picked it up in one hand and held it out to the original occupant. "Here. This belongs to you."

The guy must have seen something dangerous in Edward's expression because he declined and stepped away. When they saw Claudia's tears, the holdouts who thought this might be part of the act changed their minds and decided they'd prefer to get the hell out of there.

Now I know what an uproar sounds like. Some remained in their seats, some stood and waived fists in the air, but they were all yelling by the time I made my way around the departing audience and helped Edward's ex to her feet. Something flickered in his eyes when I did so, but it went out so fast I might have imagined it.

She was in a kind of shock, where she couldn't speak and didn't want to look at him. I couldn't deal with two nutcases at once, so I handed her off to Latoya St. Armand, who had followed me back. But by then, Edward had left.

"Would you like to explain what just happened?" Latoya St. Armand struggled to keep her tone reasonable.

"I really would," I said with feeling, "but I can't right now."

People were pulling at my jacket and yelling in my face, and it took a few minutes to shake loose. When I caught up to Edward, he was getting ready to crash. He had a hand on the stair railing and had paused to let the room stop spinning.

I steered him to the elevator and, after shooing off three guests who must have missed the episode in the Gold Room because they weren't disgusted by him, I propped him against the wall with my shoulder and prayed that his knees wouldn't buckle before we got back to the room. I was so mad, I couldn't speak.

They didn't. His legs, that is. Outside my door, I pulled my key out of my pocket and saw it wasn't necessary. Splinters of wood surrounded where the lock should have been, the lock now on the hallway floor.

"So that's how you got out."

He leaned against the wall. "That wasn't nice to lock me in. I told you I was going."

"That you did."

Once we were inside, I let loose. "If you wanted to tell everyone you were Aunt Civility, couldn't you have chosen a better way? Like in the question and answer session?" Then I noticed the bathroom door hung from the top hinge. "Nice. Very nice. You are aware the bathroom door locks from the inside, right?"

"When I heard you lock the door, I got angry. And slightly confused."

Someone knocked.

"The Inglenooks are probably going to toss us out of here. I hope you're happy."

The door threatened to fall off the hinges when I yanked it open, ready to chase away any critics. Instead, I stared into the face of Sergeant Michaelson.

"Come with me, please. Just you."

CHAPTER 32

"I need to stay here." I jerked my head toward Edward, lumbering his way to the back bed. "I have a patient."

"I heard. But I'd still like you to come with me. If you would."

At his continued insistence, I finally agreed. Edward stretched out on the bed and closed his eyes, so I figured he'd stay put, but I told him not to move, anyway. Once in the hallway, I took a deep breath and asked the sergeant, "What's up?"

"I have a request."

Request didn't sound as intimidating as order. Or demand. "Okay."

"I'm about to interview Claudia Inglenook, and I would prefer it if she had someone with her. She doesn't want your brother or Joshua Breen, and she's declined an attorney."

"Why me?" I tried not to whine like a little girl. "What about Robert? She *is* his sister."

"He's dealing with an emergency furnace issue in the cellar, and this can't wait."

On our walk down the stairs, I asked him for the status of the investigation. "Are you closing in on anyone?"

But the sergeant wasn't a gossip.

"Does Gardner have an alibi? Did anyone see what time he left the Ballroom?"

"We're checking everyone's alibi."

"Even mine?"

He didn't answer.

"Stop being so chatty. You're hurting my ears."

Down in the lobby, sunlight flooded through the transom window above the entrance, making a path to the corridor next to the front desk. He led me to the back office and closed the door behind me.

Claudia sat in the same chair as last time with her arms folded across her chest. She barely glanced my way. I noticed the rims of her eyes were red, but I wrote that off as being left over from Edward's stunt with the chair.

Michaelson went behind the desk and sat down. He held up a manila folder.

"You found it. If that's the missing folder."

He gave me a glare. I zipped it.

"Miss Inglenook, do you recognize this folder?"

"It's a regular manila folder, just like the ones we use in our filing system."

He ran a finger over the label. "Except this one says Inglenook. It's the file that went missing from this office last night."

"And it's no longer missing."

"That's correct. Do you know where we found it?"

She pushed her hair back over her ear. "I couldn't guess."

"I think you could because we found it in your bedroom."

While I absorbed this news, she went on the attack. "You had no right to go through my things!"

Her yell reminded me I was here on her behalf. "Did you have a search warrant?"

The stoic sergeant had a handsome smile. "I didn't need one. I merely told your Aunt Zali what I was looking for and asked her to keep her eyes open and let me know if she found it."

Claudia shifted in her chair. "That was low."

"I don't agree, but we'll skip that." He pulled out a slip of paper and held it up. "Is this what you wanted to keep from us? We'd already seen it, and we could get another copy."

He looked up and caught me chewing on my bottom lip. I didn't want to know what that piece of paper said, especially after Michaelson's smile. Doing without another piece of bad news might even make me happy. To me, that piece of paper dangling from his fingers looked like a weapon.

"Miss Inglenook took out a secured loan on Inglenook."

A-a-nd the hammer descended.

"It's temporary. Only to help us through this slump." She seemed more interested in keeping up Inglenook's image than saving her skin.

"She went through a private lender," Michaelson explained, "which, on paper, I can see why she did. However, Benedict Hamilton set up the company to make hard money loans for quick purchases of properties he wanted to buy, giving him an up on the competition. He wouldn't have to wait for a bank's approval process. Did he approach you personally and offer you the loan?"

Claudia refused to answer, so he turned the letter around and scanned it.

"It must have been a shock when he called in the loan so he could get his hands on Inglenook."

She pressed her lips together and tears streamed down her face, but she didn't whimper. At the sight of a woman crying, even Claudia Inglenook, my muscles tensed and I clenched my jaw, but without knowing how much Edward knew and if a bigger story lurked behind the accusation, I held back, uncertain what to say.

"Miss Inglenook," the sergeant said, his voice kindly, "you have to see this gives you a motive for murdering Hamilton."

That decided it. I stepped in front of her. "So far I've counted five people with motives outside of Claudia, including your boss."

He gave me a sharp glare.

"So, she didn't like the guy. Neither did Latoya St. Armand, and she stood to lose control of her charity, not to mention worrying about what would happen to the kids if Hamilton took the program overseas and abandoned her charges in the States. Rico Agosti might have known darned well Benedict Hamilton was leaving him everything, and Claudia's loss of a white elephant can't compare as a motive to the receipt of millions and a business guaranteed to bring in more. Joshua Breen stood to lose his television program, and he admits to hitting Hamilton."

Claudia gasped. "He what?"

"Let's not forget your brother," Michaelson countered, "who might have known about the loan and decided to help his girlfriend."

Claudia interrupted. "I'm not his girlfriend."

He closed the folder. "Miss Inglenook, the only way I can find the person who did this is to collect information. If you didn't do it, you have nothing to fear. Now, will you answer my questions?"

"Edward can find you a lawyer," I said. "If he can still afford it."

"I don't need any help from your brother, thank you. And I don't need an attorney. I've done nothing wrong." She narrowed her eyes. "Am I under arrest?"

He hesitated. "No. But please don't leave Inglenook until

further notice." He glanced my way. "That includes you and your brother, too."

Exiting the corridor into the lobby, I had a dilemma. Usually, the person I unloaded on was my brother. That was out. I stood in the lobby, ignoring passing guests, while I tried to order my thoughts.

Claudia had a good reason to stop Hamilton. What if there had been no one else in the hallway? What if she just said she'd seen Josh knowing that he'd gone into the bar and had an alibi? I rubbed the back of my neck and tried to decide my next move.

Someone tapped my shoulder. Still skittish after the attack in the library, I tensed and spun. Sykes took a step back, and I forced my shoulders to relax.

"I'd like to speak with you, if you have a moment."

He motioned me inside the bar. We ordered, and by the time we got our beers, a trio of ladies left a booth and we snagged it. Once seated, Sykes looked me in the eye.

"Your brother is Aunt Civility."

After unclamping my jaw muscles, I answered, but I kept it vague. "That's what he said."

"But you couldn't tell me that during a murder investigation. You referred me to the publisher."

"And you solved the case without an answer to that question."

"You worked hard to keep his identity a secret. Your brother must have had a good reason for exposing himself."

"Call it an impulse."

He shook his head. "I don't believe you or your brother do anything unintentionally. So, what's the story?"

"It would be long and boring."

"I've got plenty of time. Shauna is with Latoya."

"I can't tell the story because it's not mine to tell. But you can tell *me* something. What do you think of Melvin Gardner? And while we're at it, Rico Agosti. Would you trust either of them? I have a reason for asking that has nothing to do with murder."

He shook his head. "I couldn't reveal that kind of information."

"Why not?" I demanded. "You're not officially on the case."

"It would be a betrayal of Sergeant Michaelson's confidence."

I pulled back my head and made a face. "Did you promise? Pinky swear? Become blood brothers? Then what's the problem? He probably expects the information to get out."

He gave me the kind of glare Edward gives me when he wants to show he's irritated, but not that irritated. "Personally, I don't like Mr. Gardner."

"I was hoping for something more factual."

The detective kept his topaz eyes fixed on me. "Are you going to tell me why your brother made a fool of himself in front of seventy people, including his boss?" He held up a hand. "I know what you said, but there's more to it."

Since Sykes hadn't given me anything new, I figured his contribution didn't entitle him to my information. And besides, I was mad. So, I said Edward had his reasons and left it there.

He studied his drink. "I've taken classes you know."

"Huh?"

Sykes nodded. "And training, continuing education, not to mention over twenty years of experience."

"Congratulations."

"Your brother *isn't* trained and could easily get in over his head. That could be dangerous since this person has already killed once. And then there's the note. I assume you're a loved one. You were lucky you weren't killed in the attack on you. You heard what my wife said. A little lower and to the right and we'd be having your funeral."

"You mean you'd come?"

"Only to make certain you were really dead." He sighed. "I'm serious. And what if the attack had been meant for your brother? The two of you are dressed alike."

Inside, his speech worried me. On the outside, I told him Edward could take care of himself. "And he has Robert looking after Claudia."

"Just tell your brother to watch his back."

If he intended to bring up an image of Edward with a sword buried between his shoulder blades, he succeeded. So, I changed the subject.

"How is Ms. St. Armand holding up?"

"Fine."

"I mean, are the police, the other police, hassling her? It seemed pretty clear to me she knew what Hamilton was up to."

If Sykes planned to make me pay for that remark, a female voice interrupted him.

"I knew."

Sykes twisted his head to look at the newcomers. Latoya St. Armand took the spot next to me once I scooted over to make room, and Shauna sat next to her husband. He didn't make as much room as I did, but I think it was deliberate.

"Benedict wanted my charity bad. He liked percentages, and we have a wonderful success rate. But that's all he saw. Numbers and a chance to increase those numbers."

"But is that a bad thing?" I asked. "As long as there were people on the ground like you to give your customers the personal touch, did it matter how the money man saw them?"

She was an honest woman. "I suppose it didn't. I hadn't really thought about it that way." She looked at her friend. "Is my ego getting in the way of doing what's best for those kids?"

Now, it might have been pure emotion, but right then I pegged Latoya St. Armand as an innocent party. No one who could ask that question would have the arrogance it took to snuff out a life. Then again, I'd been wrong before and it almost cost me my life.

When Shauna Sykes finished assuring her friend that she was being silly, Sykes delivered a few stern words.

"You should have told the police."

"Says the policeman," she retorted. "And then they would have trussed me up and carted me off for murder."

He almost smiled. "No, but now that they know you were aware but didn't say so from the beginning, they might question you again."

"Is this conversation unofficial?" I asked Sykes.

"I'll keep it off the record unless one of you admits to murdering the man."

"Then we can be frank. As far as we know, the suspects are Ms. St. Armand, Claudia, Edward and/or Josh sticking up for Claudia, me sticking up for my brother, Josh trying to save his television show, Myra Timms overcome with passion, Rico wanting to take over the business, or the attorney seeking revenge for having been fired. Or his executive assistant, assuming she thought Hamilton and Myra Timms were an item. We can rule out you, Ms. St. Armand, along with Claudia, Edward and me."

"Why you two and Miss Inglenook?" Sykes asked.

"Okay. You can have Claudia, but my brother and I didn't kill anyone. Timms and his wife had each other under surveillance all night, so we can rule them out as well. That leaves Josh, Rico, Gardner, and Jennifer."

Sykes held up a hand. "Back up. Jennifer Proctor has a crush on her boss?"

Shauna Sykes pursed her lips. "Definitely. Of course, that's just a woman's opinion."

Whenever ladies say that, it's meant as a passive aggressive statement.

Sykes grinned. "You mean she was making googly-eyes at him?"

His wife dipped her head. "Have you ever seen anyone do that for real? No. She glared at Mrs. Timms while she danced with Mr. Hamilton, and she was very attentive to him."

I'd seen the same thing. Glad to know I had female corroboration.

"She was his personal assistant. She was paid to be attentive to him."

Shauna rolled her eyes. "Not that attentive."

I sipped my beer. "Do we gang up on her and demand she reveal her true feelings for her boss?"

"That would never work." Both women said this with the conviction of people who have their own approach in mind.

"What would you suggest?"

Shauna Sykes drew her fingertip down her husband's arm. "The woman's approach. Some girl chat."

He covered her hand. "No. She might be a killer."

Latoya St. Armand smiled. "That's why we'll approach her together."

Sykes had the look of a man experienced at losing battles. He sighed. "Be careful. Both of you."

The women slid out, and we both stood. When they left, I said, "I better check in with my brother."

Before I passed the front desk, I took a right and headed into Robert's office. I could see Claudia through the window helping a guest at the front desk. For once, I was happy to see her. I asked Robert how she was holding up.

"If I'd known what kind of roller-coaster ride she'd have, I never would have given your brother permission to court her."

He referred to Edward's old-fashioned move to clear the ground with Claudia's sole male relative before dating her. Claudia's response had lacked feminine feelings, and their relationship had almost ended before it started.

"It's not us. It's this place. Inglenook Resort is bad luck."

"Who do I give my solution to? You know. For the murder."

I looked down to find Zali at my elbow. I wasn't up to humoring her.

"Robert's a neutral party."

Proudly, she handed him a sealed envelope. "It was tricky, but I think I'm right." She sighed. "No one ever talks about the prize. Not that it's not fun to do the puzzle, but it would be nice to know what I was working for."

Robert winked at me over her head. "Winner gets free room and board at Inglenook for a month."

She frowned. "I already have that." Then she grinned up at Robert. "Maybe I could pay you for my room and board now, so winning would be worth something to me." She scrounged through her Miss Marple bag, pulled out a crumpled bill, and handed it to Robert.

"Thank you, ma'am." He bowed. As soon as she left the room, he slid open a desk drawer full of similar bills and tossed it inside, along with the envelope.

"Every once in a while, Zali contributes to her upkeep even though we tell her it's unnecessary. One of these days I'm going to open a savings account for her. I'm waiting until I reach a hundred dollars."

"For a hundred dollars, I'd leave Edward here and let him stew."

Robert laughed. "He's certainly off his stride this trip." He raised his head so he could look down his nose at me. "I'll have to withhold my permission for them to date until he gets another job."

"I'm working on that. But first, I need to knock some sense into him."

He stopped laughing when he saw I was serious. "You break it, you pay for it."

CHAPTER 33

As I left, I considered what to say to Edward. How much to tell him. Heading for the stairs, my steps became more determined, but when I got to our door, I paused.

Alfred, the doorman, was putting the final touches on a new strike plate. He'd already installed a new doorknob and deadbolt after replacing the broken frame with scrap wood.

"It's not pretty, but it will hold. The bathroom door is a loss. I put up a piece of plywood as a temporary fix, but you won't get much privacy."

"I'm impressed." And I was. So much so that I tipped him a twenty. He handed me two keys and hauled his tools away.

I closed the door and tested the lock a few times. Edward was still stretched out on his bed. He snored softly, the sleep of the innocent, in the shadows of the clouding sky. I strode to the side of the bed and tapped his face, not lightly.

He swiped at me, but I moved out of reach. "Get up."

"Leave me alone."

"I said get up, you damn fool."

He stared at the ceiling for a minute. When he suddenly

swung his feet off the bed and stood so he could intimidate me with his glare, he did it in one smooth move. He wasn't as bad off as I'd thought, which was a relief.

"Your pity party is officially over. I need you sober. How close are you?"

I leaned in and looked into his eyes. They held my gaze for ten seconds before blinking. His breath smelled like he'd been chewing on dirty socks, and a haze of alcohol surrounded him.

"Close enough. There's a lot going on right now, some of it your fault, and it's too much for me to handle by myself."

"Surprise."

When I slapped him hard, he was so shocked he dropped to sitting. I jabbed my finger in his face.

"Yeah. I need help, and I'm not too proud to say it. Unlike you, you fathead."

I swiped my hand over my mouth because a rant wouldn't help. I held up a finger.

"Latoya St. Armand and your fans did nothing to deserve the blow you gave them, so you're going to have to figure out a way to make it up to them."

"What happened to not worrying about what other people think?"

"That's not the same as kicking them in the teeth and expecting them to like it."

"None of those people will think twice about me after tomorrow."

He started to recline again, but I grabbed a fistful of shirt, pulled him to sitting, and put my face close to his, speaking through clenched teeth.

"Listen up, brother. I've had enough of your moping. You didn't like your job? Then you should have handled it like a man. Hired a lawyer. Not made an ass of yourself in front of people who depend on you."

"Like you?" he growled.

I let go and straightened my jacket.

"I can take care of myself. In fact, I've been talking to Rico Agosti about partnering up with him on Ben's business."

His eyes widened. "You're not serious."

"I said we're talking about it."

"You want to go into business with a murder suspect. Nicholas, Nicholas, Nicholas."

Nothing ticked me off more than when Edward repeated my name with a heavy dose of condescension, but I held in my feelings.

"Forget about me. What about Tea for Teens? They're in financial trouble. I wonder how many donors will reconsider giving this weekend after your performance."

"Where did you hear that?"

"Mrs. Hall. A board member."

"I'm sorry about that," he mumbled, "but the damage is done."

"It sure is. You've also put Periwinkle and Classical Reads in a pickle after they took you on with no experience. Some gratitude. And Ms. St. Armand knew the subject of the meeting Hamilton called, so that puts pressure on her from the police. She doesn't need to deal with your mess, too."

"If Michaelson suspects her, he's a fool."

"Why would he need to focus on the charity director when Claudia Inglenook makes such a good target? And she refused my advice about getting a lawyer, so she's defenseless."

"Why would she need a lawyer?"

"You tell me."

My glare remained steady until he looked away.

"If she wanted to talk to Benedict Hamilton about what price Inglenook would fetch, that's her business. She shouldn't have lied about it, but it's not a motive for murder."

"No. But Hamilton being the owner of a recent loan and calling in that loan to force her to sell is a motive. A person with her back against the wall is apt to lash out."

His head jerked up. "What are you saying?"

"I thought it was clear. Hamilton owned the loan. He called it in. She doesn't have the money to pay him back. Inglenook was the collateral. Bye-bye Inglenook. And Michaelson likes that motive."

He scrambled to his feet so fast I stepped back.

"Is she under arrest?"

"Not yet. But if you continue to sit on your fanny and moan about how cruel the world is, she will be. And she's not eager for your help. Not after you humiliated her in front of a crowd."

Without another word, he headed straight to the bathroom and turned on the sink's cold-water tap. I thought, *this is more like it.* I knew the routine from our college days when the football coach would call a surprise practice after team members had spent the night drinking.

"I'll order coffee and juice."

His head wouldn't fit under the tap, so he turned on the shower and hung his head and shoulders under the spray.

After arguing with the woman on the other end of the line about the convenient self-serve coffee and juice in the Atrium, which meant I should stop bothering her and fend for myself, I convinced her to send up a carafe of each.

Edward strolled out of the bathroom toweling his hair, then tossed the towel to me and quick-changed out of his damp shirt and into a cable-knit sweater in blues and browns. Then he did some jumping jacks to get his blood pumping until room service showed up. He sat on the edge of the bed and gulped down the entire pitcher of juice before talking.

"Give me the details and leave nothing out."

I repeated the scene in the office between Claudia and Michaelson verbatim.

"Why was she alone? Why wasn't Joshua with her?"

"Will you stop with Joshua Breen? He's got his own problems. He followed Hamilton into the library and decked him because Hamilton was about to ruin his television deal, but he says he left him alive. Also, he's not her boyfriend, you are. At least you were before you demonstrated your ability to lift a chair with one hand." I shook my head. "You've got a lot of making up to do."

He stared at me, then let out a sigh and cradled his head in his hands. "Nicholas, I've been a fool."

About to say something crude, I changed it to, "No kidding."

"I don't know what happened to me. It's as if an alter-ego from the dark side took me over."

"I think it was just ego, Edward."

"This desire to secret away certain facts from the police like some black-hearted criminal shying away from the light..."

"Maybe black-hearted criminal is too strong," I muttered, but my brother's romantic imagination had broken free, and he was enjoying himself.

"I was aware of what Claudia was up to with Benedict Hamilton. I felt, and obviously she felt the same, that their dealings would not get a fair appraisal from the police. Then Hamilton reaches from the grave with a compromising financial deal and drags poor Claudia to her doom."

"Michaelson hasn't doomed her yet. He's just suspicious."

He nodded his head with vigor. "And well he should be. I'm so ashamed. And then there's the way I treated you. My own brother. Instead of sharing my hopes with you and allowing you to take part in my tension and fears—"

"Sharing is overrated. I've got enough of my own tension and fears."

"My behavior has been abominable. Will you ever trust me again? Will Claudia?"

"It's called a mid-life crisis. I'm afraid you were being predictable. And nobody cares. Just get over it."

I heard a man's voice cry out. We exchanged glances.

"I thought I heard—"

This time the cry came with pounding fists. I strode over to the connecting door, unlocked it, and as soon as I turned the handle, Mr. Periwinkle tumbled into the room.

"She—She—" He looked from Edward to me. I pushed him aside and entered the Darling Daisy room. Nothing seemed out of place until I got to the bathroom.

Her body slumped over the edge of the tub, with her auburn hair touching the floor.

Edward followed me in and let out a strangled cry. "Claudia!"

I shoved him back, and as I knelt in front of her, my brother expressed his frustration by punching a hole in the wall. "Why did I wait to give Timms that note?"

"Edward."

"And where the hell is Robert? I'll kill him."

"Edward."

He ran his hands over his face. "He said he'd look after her."

"Calm down. It's not Claudia." I looked up. "It's Jennifer Proctor.

I held back her hair. Edward stepped closer and gazed at her face. Around her neck, tied so tightly that I couldn't get a finger behind it, Edward's red Zorro sash looked like a bloody gash.

"Should we call Michaelson, Timms, or Sykes?"

My brother narrowed his eyes and growled.

CHAPTER 34

All three detectives came, though there was a delay. Edward insisted I call Robert first and make sure Claudia was okay, since he didn't think she'd take his call.

The scene of crime people bustled around Darling Daisy, something I could see through the open connecting door.

Since Edward had emptied our mini bar, he had to call down for a drink. When a waiter came up with a tall glass of scotch, he handed it off to Periwinkle. The publisher accepted, grateful.

I had a vague thought about where the man would spend the night, but then my attention turned to the detectives as they returned to our room.

Sykes shook his head at us. "You boys must wear trouble magnets."

Michaelson took the desk chair before Edward could claim it. Mr. Periwinkle, after a large dose of the scotch, took off his shoes and jacket and made use of my bed, though he stayed awake and stared at the ceiling while he answered questions.

The sergeant was not intimidated by my brother, and he immediately took off the kid gloves. "Tell me why you couldn't have killed Ms. Proctor before you went to the Gold Room? You were drunk. Maybe you didn't intend to. Maybe you grabbed her a little too rough. I notice your hair is wet."

I raised my hand. "Let me answer. Because Edward left his room key with Robert. Because I checked Darling Daisy to make sure nothing had been left behind, including bodies. I specifically opened the shower curtain to make sure my brother hadn't left his shampoo. Seventeen dollars a bottle. Then I locked the connecting door and told Robert he could send up housekeeping."

"Do you still have your key?"

I patted my pockets and produced the key. "You're right. I could have helped my brother dispose of the body, but you still have the problem of the maid. I assume she would have noticed a body in the bathtub, and going by the time that's passed since we emptied the room, I assume Periwinkle moved in as soon as she finished. And for the record, Miss Proctor and the bathtub were dry when we discovered the body."

"You noticed that did you?"

Crossing my arms over my chest, I said, "Yeah. I'm observant that way."

The sergeant transferred his gaze to my brother. "How did the killer get hold of your sash?"

We knew it was Edward's sash because we checked the box the costumes came in, and it was missing.

Edward grunted. "If someone could get into that room with a body, I'm sure they could have taken my sash."

Michaelson grunted back. "Different rooms."

"So? What's one more break-in?"

"But then they would have known the Darling Daisy room wasn't yours, so it wasn't a frame up job."

"Not necessarily," I said. "As Edward's secretary, I handle things for my brother. Why not his costume?" I struggled to remain polite. "I'm sure you remember the last time you were at Inglenook. The maids all have master keys, and the Inglenooks have grandmaster keys."

"Interesting you remember that."

"Interesting how? Are you complimenting my memory? Or do you think the first thing I did after checking us in and setting up the Gold Room and typing responses to fan letters was to ask about the key situation? And how did I go about it? Excuse me, ma'am. Could you tell me how many doors your key opens? And where exactly do you keep those keys?" I waved a hand at him. "You're reaching."

Turning my back on the sergeant, I walked over to Timms. My nose took in a new scent. The detective had on cologne. I made a note to razz him after the interrogation if we were still on friendly terms.

Squeaky wheels announced the arrival of the Gargoyle and her cart. She didn't look like someone who'd been shocked by a corpse as she glared through the open door. "They said you wanted to see me. What do you want?"

The sergeant left the room to speak to her, pointing at Edward's door. She shook her gray curls. Then he asked another question, and she patted herself, reached for a spot on her cart, and frowned. She lifted towels and sifted through cleaning supplies.

Officer Davis moved in to help her. After shaking the bag of garbage that hung from the handle on her cart, he got excited and dumped the tissues, candy wrappers, newspapers, and discarded cups, and bottles onto the floor. Victorious, he held up a set of keys.

While the sergeant talked to her and she gesticulated some, Davis cleaned up the mess and asked permission to wash his hands in our bathroom sink.

Timms gave him the go-ahead, and I preceded the officer into the room and pulled down a fresh hand towel from the rack above the toilet. Deep blue to match the room's theme.

I returned to the main room just as Michaelson came back from his talk with the maid.

"Her keys weren't where she usually put them down on her cart, but they were there."

"Someone could have borrowed them after she cleaned the room and before Periwinkle moved in," I noted.

"I suppose it's possible. But how would someone drag a body through the hallways with no one noticing?" He eyed Edward. "You wouldn't have to drag anybody. You could have carried her."

"I'd like a clearer image of that, please." I swept my arm toward Edward. "Would he have carried her kicking and screaming into the room? Or is she supposed to have been dead already? *What's that you've got in your arms, Mr. Harlow? Oh, nothing. Just a piece of luggage I forgot to unpack.* Give me a break."

"Your brother could have arranged a meeting with her."

Nodding, I said, "You've got something there. He's had no contact with her, but she willingly meets him alone in a room when she knows there's a killer on the loose. After she told me she had her guard up."

Timms finally spoke. "When did she say that?"

"I was helping her set up for the tea demonstration. She said no one would get the jump on her now, meaning now that her boss had been killed, I assume."

Sykes spoke up. "If that's so, Jennifer Proctor trusted the person she planned to meet. Who did she trust? Rico?"

"They didn't strike me as being chums," I said. "She wanted his job. Honestly, she didn't seem like a woman who trusted anyone but herself and her dead boss. Another thing. Why would Rico do it? If he killed Hamilton for money and wanted to off anyone who threatened his inheritance, he wouldn't have bothered with Jennifer. She didn't own stock."

An idea occurred to me. "Jennifer cared about Ben. She would have wanted to see his killer punished. Maybe the killer, knowing this, told the personal assistant he or she suspected there was a clue in the Darling Daisy room. No. That wouldn't work. We're back to someone she would trust, which is no one."

Timms scratched his chin. "Why that room?"

Sykes directed a question to my brother. "How many people know you moved in with Nicholas?"

Michaelson started. "You mean someone *was* trying to frame Edward Harlow?"

I like that idea. "Possibly. Or scare him. Remember the note? Aunt Civility will lose everything she cares about. Jennifer Proctor resembles Claudia a great deal. Maybe the killer mistook her for Miss Inglenook."

Michaelson wasn't ready to buy it. "I've heard you and Miss Inglenook are having difficulties."

Edward lowered his head like a bull ready to charge. "Don't even go there."

I lined up next to my brother. "Edward would do anything to protect Claudia Inglenook. He's chivalrous that way."

"He dumped her on the floor in front of a roomful of people."

Timms covered a snort of laughter.

"That was him being dramatic. And he had impaired judgment. He was drunk."

Michaelson jumped on the last bit and brought the conversation back to Jennifer's death being an accident caused by Edward's lack of control.

"Will you get off that kick? Jennifer's death? Not an accident. Not caused by Edward."

I couldn't read Michaelson's expression as he held my gaze, but the sergeant finally transferred his attention to the publisher. "Why are you here, Mr. Periwinkle?"

Periwinkle lifted his head off my pillow. "I came because I heard about the murder." He gave a delicate cough. "The first murder. And then I arrived and heard that Edward Harlow was dead."

Edward snorted with disgust. "This is a farce. Nicholas. Make a note."

I pulled out my pocket-sized notebook and readied my pen.

"Mark the date. In fact, mark the entire weekend. We have had the privilege of encountering the most inept, bumbling murderer in history. He passed me a message threatening my loved ones. You might qualify for that role, Nicholas, as I am fond of you, but since the rumor that swept through the lobby, a rumor we assume the killer started, hinted that it was I who had been mortally injured, it appears he missed his mark. Then, after finding me alive and well, he takes steps to further warn me off by killing Claudia and leaving her in what he thinks is my bathroom. Only it was no longer my room, and the person killed wasn't Claudia. It was Jennifer Proctor."

He snorted, this time like a bull. "Are we certain Benedict Hamilton was the intended victim? Maybe the killer meant to take out Joshua Breen, who was also in a Zorro costume."

I closed my notebook without writing anything down.

"So, maybe Jennifer was the intended victim all along?" Michaelson asked, trying to keep the conversation straight. "Why her?"

"I might have an answer." The sergeant frowned at me. "Nothing definitive. It's just, when she first said she saw someone entering the library Friday night, she said she didn't think it was Ben. When I spoke with her this morning, she was absolutely, positively certain it was Ben."

"So? She thought it over."

"And went from *I didn't follow the man I'm in love with because I was certain it wasn't him* to *I'm certain it was him.* You'll note in the second case she still didn't follow him into the library."

"You think she gave it serious thought and figured out who the killer was?" Timms snapped his fingers at Michaelson. "Who else was in a Zorro costume?"

The sergeant grimaced. "There were a lot. Offhand, Edward Harlow and Joshua Breen. Some of the board members. I'll have to check."

"Wait a minute." Everyone turned my way. "There were other people around. People who weren't important. Why couldn't it have been one of them?"

Timms shot down my suggestion. "She said none of them were with Benedict Hamilton."

Michaelson closed his notebook and included Periwinkle when he said, "You're free to move about. But I need to ask you to remain at Inglenook until further notice. All of you."

The list of permanent Inglenook guests was growing by the minute. Maybe Robert was the killer, and his motive was to increase business.

As the detectives left, Claudia Inglenook pushed past them and entered the room.

After giving her a curious look, Sykes closed the door to give us some privacy. I wished he'd left it open. It would have given me somewhere to run.

"It's true." Her glance strayed to the connecting door through which she could see the cops at work. "Jennifer Proctor is dead."

Edward, relieved to see her alive and kicking, stared at her as if she were a holy apparition, so I answered. "Yes."

"That's two people dead this weekend. In my resort. The head of the charity I invited for the weekend is a suspect. I'm a suspect..."

Putting the back of her hand against her forehead, a giggle escaped, first quietly, and then louder, with tears streaming down her face. She stepped forward, and clutching my lapels, leaned her forehead against my chest.

I held up my hands around shoulder height while she cried. To be fair, I was the closest to her.

I looked to Edward for a hint. She wasn't my girlfriend. Hugging her was out. So was slapping her to bring her back from the edge of hysteria. But she wasn't his girlfriend either.

"For the love of Julius Caesar, Edward, do something."

"Why are you walking about unescorted?" he demanded, and then he reconsidered his approach.

Just as my brother was about to make a move toward his lady love, Periwinkle got up and asked her if she'd like a hug. She fell against his shoulder, which came up to her chin, but she made do with it while he patted her back. When she got hold of her emotions, she stepped away.

"There, there. Do you feel better?"

"I do." She brushed his shoulder. "I'm so sorry. There's lipstick on your suit."

His lips curved in a shy smile. "That will be one for the books."

Under the tailored suit and fussy manner, Periwinkle had a sense of humor.

"I don't know what came over me. These last few days have been...difficult."

"That's an understatement," I muttered.

"It's just—" Claudia began, "I just wanted to see if it was true."

Now she was the one waiting for Edward to do or say

something, but he didn't. With one last glance at my brother, she left. I let loose.

"We need to stop this guy. Jennifer Proctor was a pain, but she didn't deserve to die, especially not like that. Some crumb decided she was a threat and had to go. He's the one that's going to go."

"A woman could have done it using the sash."

"I'm open to equal opportunity punishment."

Periwinkle started muttering. "Oh, dear. Oh, dear." He looked up at us and seemed to decide. But first, he put on his shoes and jacket to make it an official statement.

"This is so awkward, but considering what's happened here," he cleared his throat, "the murder and most especially the unexpected revelation about Aunt Civility, I feel Classical Reads is no longer in a position, that is, I feel we can no longer continue with the Aunt Civility books. I'm terribly sorry, Mr. Harlow."

He really seemed sorry. He blinked a few times, possibly holding back tears for the loss of their bestselling series.

"I understand." Edward patted the man's shoulder to show there weren't any hard feelings.

Mr. Periwinkle adjusted his glasses. "This is very unfortunate, and to add to my discomfiture, I'm uncertain where I shall spend the night. Certainly not in there." He peered into Darling Daisy and shuddered.

Edward raised his eyebrows at me, and I sighed.

"It would be my pleasure to let you use my bed tonight." Then I picked up the phone and dialed the front desk. "Have you got a spare cot for the Blue-Bell Room?"

CHAPTER 35

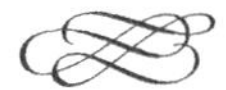

Though I offered to eat in the room with Edward to spare him embarrassment, my brother said that would be the coward's way out.

Three men getting ready for dinner in one small room was too much to handle, so I did a quick clean-up and waited in the hallway while Edward used the shower to wash away the smell of booze and cigarettes and Periwinkle made last-minute adjustments, like getting rid of the lipstick smear on his suit.

When they came out, Mr. Periwinkle's suit pants were a little wrinkled, but we hadn't figured out how to get at his clothes since Michaelson locked the connecting door and took my key.

Since the publisher had severed relations with Edward, my brother wouldn't have to make a good impression. So, I didn't mind discussing the murder in front of him.

"What I was saying before we were interrupted by yells and dead bodies..."

Periwinkle's cheek twitched. "I apologize for that."

"We still need to address those issues."

Edward zeroed in on the one most important to him. “Michaelson didn’t mention suspecting Claudia.”

“He wouldn’t, but it’s the simplest explanation. Claudia has a grand master key and could get into the room easy. She would know you had moved in with me.”

“And her purpose?”

That stumped me. “Maybe the anonymous note you got wasn’t from the killer, but she wanted the police to think it was. So, she killed Jennifer Proctor to keep that illusion going.”

“And the attack on you?”

“For Claudia, that would be a bonus.”

Edward nodded. “Pretty good reasoning.”

Periwinkle stopped walking. “Are you talking about that nice young woman who visited your room? You think she’s a murderess?”

Edward barked out a laugh. “Of course not.”

I explained. “We’re trying to think like the police so we can head them off.”

My brother led the way onto the landing. “How was the loan worded?”

Since Edward knew my ability to memorize came in second only to his, he expected me to rattle off the entire document.

“I didn’t get that close, but Michaelson said Hamilton called in the loan, so there must have been a clause allowing him to do so.”

“Who says he called in the loan?”

When I halted to consider, my foot dangled over the second step. “Good point. Was he just guessing? If so, Claudia didn’t deny it.”

“From your description of the conversation, she, er, didn’t sound as if she were thinking logically.”

“She wasn’t thinking at all. Just reacting. You should have

seen her face when I said Josh had punched Hamilton. Complete surprise."

Periwinkle squeaked. "Someone's been punched?"

"If Latoya St. Armand, or Joshua Breen, or Rico Agosti, or Myra Timms, or Timms himself killed Jennifer, they must have had a reason."

Periwinkle grabbed Edward's arm. "You're accusing a police officer of killing someone?"

I spared a glance for the publisher. He looked like he needed to sit down, but I kept moving. "Jennifer wasn't stupid. If she suspected any of them, she never would have agreed to meet them except in a crowded room."

"It's him!"

Standing in front of us, blocking our way into the Ballroom, a small group of elderly women surrounded us like aged hyenas coming in for the kill.

"You should be ashamed of yourself." A hunched gnome jabbed Edward's ankle with her cane.

"It's a crime, that's what it is," another said. "We should get refunds on all our books. They were all lies."

My brother had never met with anything less than adulation from Aunt Civility's fans. His brow wrinkled and a forlorn expression crept into his eyes. "The information in your books was accurate."

"But it didn't come from *her*." A woman with horned-rimmed glasses jerked her head with each word for emphasis. She reminded me of the Lollipop Guild from *The Wizard of Oz*.

Latoya St. Armand broke through and took Edward by the hand. She smiled and nodded at the ladies, who receded like vampires exposed to sunlight.

As she led us into the Ballroom, I wondered how she had anticipated our need for her, and then I saw the expressions worn by the other diners.

The nice ones looked away as we passed. Others glared. Muttered comments about Edward's nerve in showing his face reached my ears and, I'm sure, his. Periwinkle clung to my jacket and followed close behind. I think he expected another riot.

Once safely at the VIP table, I noticed we were down a few members. Jennifer and her boss weren't using their seats. The other board members at Edward's table and the Jarvises from my table had gone home. Periwinkle, me, and the Halls took the empty chairs, and Josh joined us a few minutes later. Rico and his attorney chose to dine at another table.

I wound up sitting between Periwinkle and Josh. No one commented on the missing personal assistant, so I assumed Michaelson had kept Jennifer's death quiet. But then Josh asked where she was.

"She said she had a headache when I saw her earlier." No one questioned why Jennifer Proctor would have shared this information with me.

Shauna Sykes leaned toward my brother. "How are you doing?" It took a woman to offer sympathy to a man who had made a drunken fool of himself.

"I'm well, thank you." He tried to ignore the elephant in the room, but it reeked of martyrdom, so he sighed. "These things have a way of sorting themselves out."

Sykes bit the olive from his martini and pointed the toothpick at Edward. "I was of a mind to offer you a police escort into the room."

Mrs. Hall dabbed her lips with her napkin and looked at me. "I was shocked by what you said today, Mr. Harlow."

Periwinkle stifled a sob.

She dropped her napkin on the table. "But I'm glad somebody had the nerve to say it."

Edward frowned at me. He might not remember how I came to his defense by insulting his fans.

She smiled and nodded at the other guests. "It takes the pressure off. All those expectations about which spoon to use and when to wear a hat and when not to. And my word, if I never have to handwrite another letter again in my life, well, I just might break into song."

My brother's frown turned into a glare.

Her husband rubbed her back. "Does that mean I don't have to open your car door for you?"

"Don't you want to?"

With his hand over his heart, he said, "It's my honor."

She blew him a kiss.

"It's the little details that drive me crazy. Don't you find that's so?"

Since she addressed her question to the publisher, he had an obligation to respond. I could sense the struggle taking place. To keep it polite, he should agree with the nice lady. To defend his bestselling series meant arguing. Which would he choose?

"I'm afraid those details as you call them have become second nature to me, so it's difficult for me to be objective."

That satisfied the lady, since that meant the poor schlep couldn't help himself. It also gave me an opening to launch an idea I'd been tinkering with ever since Edward botched his career.

"It's interesting you say that." I shifted my chair to see her better. "Because Edward and I have been talking about a new direction for his books."

My brother coughed water out his nose and quickly covered his leaky faucet with his napkin.

"What's this?" Periwinkle said, using his outside voice.

I grinned at him. "Sure. Let's face it. Most of the etiquette books out there focus on men and women, mostly women, who have a certain position in society. That doesn't mean your average Jane and Joe aren't interested in manners, but when are they ever going to attend an afternoon tea or a costume ball?"

Shauna slipped her hubby a smile. "Keep going."

"We'd also love to hear what the ladies think, not just tell them what to do."

"Here, here!" Mrs. Hall clapped.

"Do they love the customs, or is it a pain in the side adhering to them? How much pressure does it put on them? Do they even care? For instance, it doesn't take much more than basic manners for ladies not to wear white to a wedding, but what if it's the second marriage? Or third? Or what about hats?"

Shauna Sykes narrowed her eyes. "Don't mess with my hats."

The detective chuckled. "My wife's collection is taking over our closet. I'll have to move all my suits to the kid's room."

She smacked his arm and turned her head away from him, and he put an arm around her shoulder and pulled her close.

"Come on, baby. You know I love your hats. Especially that one with the—is it chicken feathers?"

Her jaw dropped. "I'll have you know they're pheasant feathers."

He nuzzled her neck. "Poor pheasant."

"They're fake. Except for the one I inherited from Aunt Sophie."

"The one that smells funny?"

Periwinkle had been absorbing the idea behind the new book, and as the implications hit him, he sputtered. "You mean you want to change the rules?"

I turned my hand palm up. "Why not? If you remember the topic of Edward's talk, it was on what the etiquette *used to be* for social dances. That means it changed. Take Ms. St.

Armand. If she was at a dance and had an attraction to a particular person, why should she be limited to four dances with him for the night?"

Edward's lecture notes were seared into my brain. Now that I didn't have the pressure of performing, I pulled them up easily. "Why should she have to dance with someone with two left feet who smells funny just because his name is on her card?"

"Ooh." Latoya grinned. "I like it."

"And what about a bunch of guys at the corner bar? If a woman walks in, should they grunt at her like they would any other man? Or should they all stand? For the ones that have been there all day, that could be dangerous. Is there something in between that would acknowledge her status as a woman but not put anyone in danger?"

Josh laughed and shook his head.

"Another thing. Now that more women enjoy watching sports, or are more open about it, what are the rules for events? Or how do you pull off a neighborhood potluck? Or what if your niece, the one who couldn't hit a note if her life depended on it, offers to sing for your anniversary party?"

"You mean everyday situations." Mrs. Hall thought about it. She grinned. "Yes. Yes, I think that would work."

Her husband cleared his throat. "I have to say, it bothers me when I want to relax at the pool hall and a woman wants a game. Do I let her break because she's a woman? And do I always have to rack up the balls because I'm the man?" He rubbed his belly. "Leaning over the table can be a pain in the patootie."

I wouldn't have pegged him as a pool player, but why not?

Sykes rolled his eyes. "How will I keep track of the new rules?"

I leaned forward. "That's the genius of it. We'd keep track

for you. We could take polls after the books are released and post the results on the website."

Edward, dazed by my suggestions, roused himself. "Online?"

You'd think my brother chiseled his books on stone tablets.

"We haven't worked out the details yet, but it's in the works. We're still tossing around ideas."

The publisher adjusted his glasses. "I don't know if that would fit in with our image."

I patted his arm. "That's alright. There are other publishers itching to put the book out."

Everyone seemed to agree it was a bright future for the former Aunt Civility. Mrs. Hall offered a toast. "Or isn't that appropriate? You know. With Ben's death."

Latoya set down her drink. "It's difficult to keep priorities straight. A board member has died, yet all I'm thinking about is the demonstration tomorrow."

She sent a guilty glance around the table. "The teens were looking forward to showing off. Makayla loves the dress I got her to wear for the demonstration, and though Brandon would never admit it, I can tell he thinks he looks pretty smart in his new suit."

"And that's when you planned to give your pitch." Mrs. Hall smiled at the rest of us. "After people see how the charity works, they are at their most generous."

"I suppose I'll have to do it." When Latoya St. Armand sighed, the sadness in it didn't fit her upbeat personality. I hoped she didn't need to sigh like that often. She shook off the glums and grinned. "It will be just like the old days when I wore *all* the hats."

I raised my hand. "Excuse me, ma'am, but aren't the stars of the show Makayla and Brandon?"

She nodded. "You're right, but I don't think they would

enjoy being in the lead. That's a lot of pressure to put on them."

"I don't see why Edward couldn't guide them from the background and be there for questions that come up."

Edward hadn't heard a word for the last two minutes. He had his gaze fixed on our waitress as she delivered the salads. She noticed him watching and smiled. When he didn't smile back, she looked away and picked up her pace.

"Edward?"

I had to say it twice before he acknowledged me. He blinked a few times, clearing a thought away. I caught the glint in his eye. He was onto something, but after replaying the table chatter in my head, I couldn't figure out what.

When he agreed to handle the demonstration however Latoya St. Armand wished, she sighed again, this time with relief. "I think it will work. We'll keep everything as planned. And, I'm sorry to say, some donors may return to get a look at you once the news gets out."

"Where are Makayla and Brandon, anyway?" Shauna asked.

"The teens prefer to eat pizza with Ms. Zali in her apartment." She grinned. "She has a television set. They enjoy her company, but they are getting a little confused by her questions about some competition." She tilted her head toward Edward and waited for an explanation.

"I'm afraid Zali believes Benedict Hamilton's death was make-believe. A murder game."

"I wish it were," Shauna muttered.

Her husband grinned down at her. "She asked me," he gestured to Edward and me, "I should say us, if the victim and the murderer could be the same person. That would be a unique crime."

"She did." Edward stroked his chin. "She also asked if there could be two murderers, which is interesting."

Latoya laughed. "Isn't one enough?"

As several of us left the table after dinner, Edward pulled Joshua Breen aside.

"I heard about what happened in the library."

Josh sighed. "I'm never going to live it down."

"Was Benedict Hamilton wearing his hat when you found him?"

The photographer grinned. "I knocked it off him when I punched him."

"And you were wearing your hat?"

"I was."

"Thank you."

Josh stared after us.

As we passed a table at the back of the room where Rico Agosti sat with Melvin Gardner, Edward stopped and greeted them.

"I understand you've made an offer to my brother."

The lawyer spoke up. "It's not an offer yet. There are negotiations and details to settle. My client was testing the waters."

"You look out for your client," Edward said with approval.

"I like to think so."

Then my brother looked squarely at the Italian American heir. "Just as I look out for my brother's interests."

Rico's expression didn't quite make it into a smile. "That's what brothers are supposed to do."

As Edward led the way out, I thanked him for his concern. "I feel just like a five-year-old held tight to his mother's bosom. Safe. Protected. I wonder if they'll address all future correspondence care of you, so you can read it to me and make sure I understand the big words."

Instead of heading to the bar or back to our room, Edward strolled down the hallway to the area just before

Claudia's apartment where the back stairs came out. He turned with his hands on his hips and studied the view.

"Do me a favor, Nicholas. Walk into the library."

I did as instructed, waited in that room for a few minutes, and when Edward didn't join me, walked back out. He wasn't in the hallway, but I found him in the Welcome Room. A few guests were grabbing cookies and tea, and the television set blasted a nature special.

The program was a documentary on birds of prey. The only two takers were my brother and an octogenarian man in a Cubs baseball cap who was telling his life story several decibels louder than necessary, unless he wanted the bartender in the next room to hear.

"We used to collect the bodies of hawks after the farmers killed them. We stuffed them and sold them to museums."

Edward nodded. "Interesting. Did you kill any of the hawks yourself?"

"Kill 'em?" The old man wrinkled his puss, disappointed in Edward. "Nah. Who would want to kill a beautiful bird like that?"

"Farmers."

The aged one's head jerked toward my brother. He pointed at him and grinned. "That's right! You're quite a card."

Stationed behind the man, I caught a whiff of something unpleasant and hoped Claudia had a strong cleaning solution that wouldn't damage fabric. Then I stepped around the sofa and Edward looked up.

"I could use a sweet. Why don't we have my brother get us something from the treat table? Mrs. Beckwith counts baking as one of her many gifts."

The old man twinkled at Edward. "Why not? You only live once, right?"

Edward, the man who rarely eats sweets, agreed. "That's what I say."

I handed out two cookies apiece and joined them on the couch.

The program only lasted another half hour. By then, our companion snored softly with a sprinkling of crumbs in his lap and drool on his chin.

After we crept to the doorway, leaving the television on, I asked if we should notify someone he was here.

"They know Henry. The staff look after him."

I followed Edward back down to the private apartments. "Do you think she'll talk to you? She's pretty mad."

He knocked. In less than a minute, Aunt Zali answered the door. My brother beamed down at her.

"You're just who I wanted to see."

CHAPTER 36

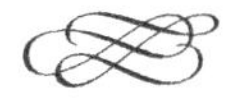

Zali, happy to escape her guardian, slipped outside and stood at attention.

"What do you need, Eddie?"

"Could you show me where you were when you saw both, er, victims, or killers, enter the library?"

She pursed her lips and clasped her hands behind her back. "That's my edge over the competition."

"But we're judges, Aunt Zali, not participants. And both of us would give you our word of honor not to reveal your secret."

When she slid me a glance, I tried to look trustworthy, but I think what decided her was my brother's use of *Aunt.* That made him family, and you must trust family.

Taking five steps to her left, she plopped down on the third step from the bottom of the staircase. "Right here." She ran her hand over the wall. "As you can see, I have cover." She leaned forward. "And it's easy to peek when I want to."

"And you saw two people walk into the library? What did they look like?"

"Both of them had capes, hats, and silly little swords on their belts."

"They were both dressed as Zorro?"

She gave us a raspberry. "Tried to be, but they couldn't very well be Zorro without the mustache, could they? Or at least a beard like—hey! You shaved it off. I like you better with it on. More dashing."

"Er, thank you. Was there anyone else? This is important."

"Only a member of the serving staff, but they're supposed to go around to the different rooms and pick up any plates or trash people leave around. People are pigs."

"Was it a man or a woman?"

"A guy."

"How long was he in there? This is important, Aunt Zali, because it will help narrow down the time the killer had to make his move."

Her face scrunched up. "I had moved on by then and couldn't see the library anymore. Let me show you."

She trotted up the stairs at a speed that made me aware of how fast she could strike if I got on her nasty side. Edward bounded up the stairs close on her heels, and I followed at a reluctant distance. It seemed like a waste of energy since half the time Zali resided in La-La Land.

At the top, which was the back end of our hallway, she looked up at us. "You can't tell Claudia. I mean, ever. You'd ruin the only fun I have."

We both swore, but we had to cross our hearts to satisfy her. To my surprise, she led us straight to the maid's nook. The Gargoyle had locked up, but Zali jiggled the handle and did something with her hip against the door and it popped open.

Inside, she shoved the cart aside and went to the towel rack against the wall. By towel rack, I mean a large, metal chef's rack with dividers to separate the stacks of towels by color. That way, if someone called from the Red Rose Room, the maid could access the deep red towels, the blue ones for the Blue-Bell Room, and so on without having to dig them out.

I wrinkled my nose at the smell of bleach, and then I forgot all about the sting when Zali pulled out the tangerine towels from the middle of the rack and set them aside. Gesturing with a sweep of her hand, she stepped back.

"Oh, my word," Edward whispered as he bent down and leaned in. "It's a peephole."

"Let me see." He stepped aside, and I squinted through a hole about the size of a walnut. Pressing my face close and angling my head, I could see Claudia behind the counter with a male customer who was checking out or checking in. He had on a jacket, and his luggage rested by his feet.

Their conversation carried in slightly muffled tones, though I distinctly heard the words *enjoy your stay.* Or maybe it was *enjoyed your stay.*

"There's one in the maid's room in the other hallway, too. Grandad was a peeper. Liked to keep an eye on visitors coming in so he'd know if he should make himself scarce. And he was always watching the staff, especially the pretty ones. There are holes all over this place."

After I put the room back in order and Zali had relocked the door with a reversal of her earlier performance, Edward thanked her for her excellent memory and willingness to help.

"I need to think," she told us, "so I'll leave you now."

She never explained what she needed to think about, which was one of her appealing traits. As for us, we stopped by the Blue-Bell Room to have a think ourselves. Periwinkle wasn't around, so I reclaimed my bed, kicking off my shoes and stretching my legs out while I leaned against the wall.

Edward settled in the chair by the writing desk and leaned one arm on it while tapping his knee with the other.

"Does this change anything?"

"It clarifies," he murmured.

"What exactly? We already knew two Zorros walked into the room."

"Two Zorros and a waiter."

"Zali's right. People are slobs. There are always empty cups and plates on the snack table in the Welcome Room. So, why were you staring down the waitress at dinner?"

"What? Oh. There was something familiar about her."

I sat up. "You mean the murder was a two-person job? She's related to the killer and helped him out?"

After that, he fell into deep thought and stopped answering me. Silence and inactivity aren't my friends, so I got playful.

"Some weekend, huh? Colonel Mustard in the Library with a knife. Say, did you know Clue is called Cluedo in the UK? Miss Scarlet makes the first move in the game. Miss Scarlet is obviously Claudia. Or Claudie. Your preference. Although if Claudia murdered anyone, it would be me."

Edward made a noise, surprised. "Claudia cares about you. Like a brother, of course."

"Yeah, right."

"She submitted to police harassment rather than tell them she thought you killed Hamilton."

After thinking it over, I had to agree. "By gum, you're right. Still, I'm the brother she begged her parents to return to the stork. Okay, what about Joshua Breen? He's Mr. Green because it makes me sick how wonderful he is. Also, it rhymes."

Edward snorted a laugh, and I grinned. Feigning deep thought, I rubbed my chin. "Maybe he was cleaning up in the bathroom because he got blood on him from stabbing Hamilton in the back. After he punched him, of course."

"He would have been standing behind his victim. I don't think blood would have spurted anyway because the sword never left Hamilton's back. And you said there wasn't anyone else in the washroom except Mr. Hall?"

I snapped my fingers. "That's an idea. Mrs. Hall wasn't pleased with Hamilton's treatment of Latoya St. Armand. Maybe he was trying to keep his wife happy."

"Unlikely."

"Who is Mrs. White and who is Mrs. Peacock? We've got Latoya St. Armand and Myra Timms. Peacock sounds silly, and Ms. St. Armand is anything but silly, so she's Mrs. White."

"Mrs. Peacock is a dignified, elegant woman, and Mrs. White is the housekeeper."

"Okay. Switch them. Maybe Latoya St. Armand killed him. She knew what the meeting was about, and maybe she stopped Hamilton from taking a vote."

"And Mrs. Timms?"

"Deeply in love with Hamilton." It wasn't a bad idea when you put the two murders together. "And then she killed the competition, Jennifer Proctor."

He didn't answer.

"Or do you still think the second death had something to do with the anonymous note you got? And why send the note? We're not cops. I admit we've had some success helping the police, but the verdict rests with a jury, not us."

My brother had drifted back into silence, so I continued. "Colonel Mustard is a suspect, so he can't be Benedict Hamilton, but he could be Frederico Agosti. Mr. Boddy was always the corpse."

Even while thinking deep thoughts, Edward couldn't resist showing off. "In the UK, Doctor Black is the body."

"I like the sound of Mr. Boddy better. Who did I miss?"

"Professor Plum."

"That's Detective Timms. Speaking of Timms, that would be ingenious. Kill your wife's boyfriend and then take over the case. I wonder who he picked as the fall guy? But I suppose we should give him the benefit of the doubt. Gardner can be Professor Plum. His motive is easy, and I didn't have an eye on him the entire night. He could have arranged a meeting, slipped into the library, killed Hamilton, and then exited through the library doors. I should have checked his shoes for salt stains. That's if they salted the walkways."

I hesitated before touching on the hot topic. "Sorry about your career and, you know, reading your book. And slapping you."

"I'm sure you were just talking to hear yourself, but the guests at the table seemed interested in your book idea. Or should I say ideas? It wasn't clear if there was one theme." He got up and walked over. "I apologize if I was hard on you about reading my book." He cocked his head. "You really liked it?"

"Not liked. Loved it. And I'll cross my heart if you want me to. Seriously. Don't give up on it."

"I don't intend to."

"Not that it's the most important question of the day, but now that you're unemployed, can you still afford to pay me?"

"We'll see."

He looked at me for a long moment and then suddenly pulled me to my feet and gave me a tight hug. Wary, I tensed up, waiting for the knuckle rub that usually followed Edward's hugs, but he released me and clapped my shoulder.

Embarrassed, I shrugged and shivered, like I was passing off a batch of cooties. "What was that for?"

"I should do it more often. Mother would approve."

"Mother thinks hugs are sentimental slop."

"True."

"So, have you got any ideas about our unhappy situation?"

"I do." He went to the mini-bar and opened the door, and I only relaxed when he grabbed a bottle of water.

"You know, we could always leave it to the cops."

"And remain prisoners here?" He twisted off the cap and took a long drink.

"The drop from the window doesn't seem that bad. One of us would survive, though we'd leave an imprint on the muddy flower beds."

He choked on his drink.

"Is it tap water? That wouldn't be ethical to refill the bottles from the sink, but the Inglenooks are saving pennies. I find my own standards drop along with my ability to pay for things."

I turned to find him staring at the rug. There wasn't anything there, so I nudged him.

"If you're wondering if they've skimped on cleaning the rooms, I heard a vacuum going this morning."

"Actually, I was thinking about water." He made a noise of frustration. "My mind has been elsewhere this weekend. I should have seen it before."

"You mean you know?"

"Not with certainty."

"Who?"

"I said, not with certainty."

"Okay. It would be a coup if you solved the murder before the police. Aunt Civility needs the goodwill. What will it take to be certain?"

"We need to see Joshua Breen."

CHAPTER 37

I wondered who had snagged the Red Rose suite. My last memory of this room was waking up in the dark to find Amanda Mayfield standing over me with a walking cane. That was right before Edward intervened and dragged me to the adjoining Darling Daisy room. Being democratic, she took a shot at him.

In daylight, the dark rose wallpaper looked kind of classy. The vase of roses on the coffee table went with the theme, but I still felt Claudia had deliberately dissed me with the geraniums.

Joshua Breen repeated Edward's request. "You need to look through my photos. Can I ask what you're looking for?"

"I want to confirm something. I'll know it when I see it."

The photographer set up his laptop on the coffee table in front of the couch—a sprinkling of baby roses on a cream background—and my brother and I sat on either side of him. When he opened the camera roll on his screen, we all leaned forward. Josh used his fingers to enlarge the photos.

"I'm interested in the pictures after Benedict Hamilton's announcement." Edward reached out to swipe the screen, but

Josh didn't like anyone touching his toys and nudged his hand aside.

Naturally, there were photos of couples dancing. Hamilton swung Mrs. Timms around while she looked over his shoulder at the grumpy Harlequin seated against the wall. Jonah and Shauna Sykes slow danced, with her laughing as she tugged on one of his dog ears.

Latoya St. Armand, as proud as any mother, beamed at Brandon as he led her in a dance, while Makayla covered her mouth in a fit of giggles from the sidelines.

I made him pause on the picture of Edward and Claudia. He'd done something with the exposure that made them look as if they had stepped back in time.

The next picture had Jennifer seated in the back of the room after she'd asked Hamilton to dance. Josh had chosen black-and-white. While her lips pressed together in a pout, and her arms crossed defensively across her chest, the closeup captured the wistful expression in her eyes. It was painful.

"Probably not a candidate for the Tea for Teens Newsletter."

We moved forward a bit to filler stuff. The trumpet player's cheeks puffed up as he blew a solo. A woman laughing as her chocolate dipped strawberry dribbled on her chin. The Halls seated in front of the backdrop pretending to drink tea while Rico, dressed as Dracula, looked on in the company of Tinker Bell, alias Jennifer. Josh had made it look as if her wings sparkled.

I spotted Dracula Woman and Scrub Girl with their husbands. In another shot of an unknown couple dancing, I leaned forward to squint and confirmed the man in the background was Melvin Gardner.

Then Josh got a picture of Edward at the book table. My brother sat alone, hands folded on the table and staring at a copy of his book with an expression of morbid distaste.

"When did you take that?" I asked.

"While you were dancing with Claudie."

"Can I get a copy? For old time's sake?"

Edward growled.

Josh moved through the rest of the photos and sat back. "That's it. Do you want to see them again?"

"No." Edward sighed. "Thank you."

"It looked to me like everyone was accounted for. No one slipping out to commit murder." I nudged aside my disappointment. "The pictures look great."

As the photographer closed his laptop, he said, "I'm sorry it didn't help."

Edward's brows went up. "I didn't say that." He jerked his chin at me. "Let's go. We need to talk to Detective Timms. Or Michaelson. Or Sykes."

Overcome with curiosity, Josh jumped up from the couch and followed us.

We found everybody gathered in the ballroom, at least the people that mattered.

Employees cleaned up the remains of dinner and listened unobtrusively to the argument taking place at the front of the room, featuring Claudia and Robert versus the detective trio.

Their audience included the Halls, Latoya St. Armand, Shauna Sykes, Rico Agosti, his lawyer sidekick, and other guests attracted by the noise. Mrs. Beckwith peered out of the kitchen, scowling, and Mr. Periwinkle, his eyes open wide as if gazing into the apocalypse of manners, was trying to negotiate a truce.

As soon as Edward spotted his lady love, he increased his pace. I had to put out some effort to keep up with him.

"I do *not* have to let you search our apartments or the

office." She planted her fists on her hips and jutted out her chin.

"Ma'am," Michaelson explained, "we'll have our warrant by Monday morning. You're just dragging it out. Why not get it over with?"

"You got something you don't want us to find?" Timms said.

"Stop harassing my woman!"

Everybody stared at Edward's bold choice of words, though I noticed surprised pleasure in the eyes of the females, as if they'd found a beloved object they'd lost and never hoped to find.

"Excuse me?" Claudia demanded.

My brother matched her pose with his fists on his hips. "Enough of this nonsense. Are you or aren't you my woman? And aren't I your man?"

I took a deep breath and held on for the expected cyclone. It didn't come, not exactly. But as expected, no woman answers a yes or no question without qualifications.

"That depends. Are you going to include me in your life? Or will you push me aside whenever things become difficult?" She sneered. "Or try to pawn me off."

Shauna Sykes pursed her lips and nodded, so I assumed Sykes had caved and told her about Edward's gaff.

Claudia let out a frustrated huff. "You never told me you were so unhappy with your job."

"You were unhappy?" Periwinkle wrinkled his brow.

Claudia pointed an accusing finger at the famous photographer. "And you keep steering me toward Joshua, as if I didn't know he existed before you pointed it out. I've known him for twenty years. If I were interested, don't you think I would have acted on it before now?"

"I'm right here," Josh said, but we ignored him.

Edward pressed his lips together and tried to hold on to his dignity. Then he growled. "You're right."

The ladies let out a collective sigh as they captured the win in the battle of the sexes.

My brother shocked everyone, including Claudia, when he pulled her forward and planted a kiss on her that would have made Rhett Butler blush. She responded with enthusiasm and would have kept on responding if Mr. Periwinkle hadn't coughed.

They broke apart, both breathing hard. Unseemly. Mrs. Hall and Mrs. Timms giggled. Shauna Sykes had a smile on her face as she leaned into her husband.

"If you ever do anything like that to me in public, I will have your hide."

"Yes, ma'am."

"Okay. Everybody's friends again." Timms waved his hands around. "But we still need to search the Inglenook apartments."

"No, you don't."

Michaelson looked at my brother. "We don't?"

"Details. We can discuss them later." Edward raised his voice to booming. "Right now, I need to make up for my behavior." He turned to Latoya St. Armand. "I owe you an apology. I've messed up your fundraiser, and I want to make it up to you."

She folded her arms. "I'm listening."

"Let's make tomorrow's tea with the teens a spectacular event. I thought we could have it in here, with the service at the front of the room. Phone the donors on your list and tell them the disgraced Edward Harlow will be here." He showed all his teeth when he smiled.

"Are you sure?" Latoya St. Armand glanced at him sideways. Suddenly, she grinned. "What am I saying? Of course I'll call them."

Mrs. Hall offered to help.

Edward then faced Claudia's discard. "If he would agree, we could have the world-famous Joshua Breen take photographs of the event."

If Claudia's choice had devastated the photographer, he rose above it. "Sure. I'll do that."

My brother snapped his fingers as if a brilliant idea had just occurred to him. "And we could have servers. A man and a woman." He glanced around, his gaze resting on Mr. Periwinkle, then me. "Why not Mrs. Timms and Mr. Agosti? If they wouldn't mind."

They both responded positively, though Timms looked like he might fight it.

Rico brushed his fingers through his thick hair. "I'm happy to help, but I don't know the first thing about waiting tables."

Mrs. Timms placed her fingers on her chin. "It can't be much different from waiting on Fergus at dinner, but I assume you'll show us anything special we'll need to do."

Edward gave her a slight bow. "I will. We can practice with the teens tomorrow morning."

"That's very generous of you," Latoya St. Armand said. "I'll have to ask Brandon and Makayla if they mind the new arrangements."

"I'll go with you."

Edward wasn't about to remove his arm from around Claudia's shoulders, so she went too, willingly it seemed.

Robert strolled over. "Here we go again."

"It was a public declaration with witnesses. We can drag it out whenever they get snippy."

Perhaps in deference to my head, which had already suffered a blow, Timms punched me in the stomach. I doubled over with an *oof,* and Robert's arm helped steady me.

"Fergus!" Mrs. Timms rushed over.

The detective jabbed his finger in my face. "You told my wife to make herself a suspect."

"Leave him alone, Fergus. He was worried about his friends." Mrs. Timms twitched her shoulders. "I enjoyed myself immensely."

He gaped. "You enjoyed being a suspect?"

"I enjoyed your interest in me."

The detective turned red, a combination of anger and embarrassment. His glare softened. "Well, don't do it again."

I coughed. "Got it."

Out of the corner of my eye, I caught Sykes' satisfied smirk, and I detected a hint of envy.

Mr. Periwinkle and I went through the motions of getting ready for bed. Of course, with him being the guest in our guest room, I let him have the bathroom first.

By the time I finished my turn, the publisher's light snores filled the room and Edward had returned.

Since my cot stood in front of the armoire, I'd set out his pajamas on his bed, but he stripped down, folded his clothes over the chair, and slid between the sheets in his underthings. The new, bold Edward.

"You've got a plan for tomorrow?" I slid under the covers to the protesting creaks of the cot.

"The teens are ready, and Mr. Agosti and Mrs. Timms will meet me tomorrow morning."

I plumped up my pillow. "I repeat. You've got a plan for tomorrow? And I'm not talking about the tea."

He glanced at Periwinkle. "I'll fill you in tomorrow morning."

"Did you find what you were looking for in the pictures? Because I didn't notice anyone carrying a sword."

"Use your head, Nicholas."

"Do I need to know anything special?"

He turned onto his side and smirked at me. "You already know everything you need to know. Goodnight."

I'm not sure how he expected me to get to sleep after that teaser, but I managed.

CHAPTER 38

If I thought the attack on me yesterday would move Edward to let me sleep in…I didn't expect it because I know my brother. So, it shocked me when I woke at nine a.m. to the smell of coffee as he walked in the door, fully dressed.

Edward wore his nicest suit, a black double-breasted to which he'd added a white shirt and black tie. He'd even put a rose in his top pocket along with his white handkerchief.

He was planning to wow the audience. He'd even skipped shaving and had a good start on a full beard.

I sat up in my cot and rubbed the side of my head, then decided not to because it hurt. "What day is it?"

He handed me a blueberry muffin and Styrofoam cup of coffee with cream. "Sunday."

Periwinkle, mouth open in sleep, drooled on what should have been my pillow, so Edward left the second muffin and coffee on the nightstand next to the bed.

I almost spilled on my pajamas in my scramble to get to my feet. "The demonstration."

"It's all set up. Take your time getting ready. I'll meet you in the lobby in ten minutes."

"But you were going to tell me your plan," I called out, but he had already closed the door behind him.

One day walking around looking like his twin was more than enough, so I pulled down a single-breasted fawn tic suit with a light blue shirt and dark brown tie and changed in the bathroom. I had a head start on a beard, just like my brother, but I didn't stop to shave.

They say that tragedy attracts human beings, and from the head count in the Ballroom, they had a point. I'm sure we broke fire codes that day. People crowded around the entrance as we pushed our way inside. All heads turned to look as the disgraced Aunt Civility walked to the front of the room.

My stomach flip-flopped. What if my brother made a fool of himself? Again. Once more, he'd left me unprepared for what might come. I didn't like it.

The fathead should have told me his plan. A plan that seemed to include giving Claudia Inglenook my usual spot—the chair at the end of the front row.

The doors to the courtyard stood open, letting in fresh air and a slight chill. I backed up and took a position against the wall near Melvin Gardner, keeping my eyes open and my guard up.

On the other side of the demonstration's setup, Brandon and Makayla stood with their heads together in serious conversation.

I'd already seen Brandon's suit, but Makayla was debuting her new dress. Shiny lavender hugged her budding curves without being vulgar. I thought Latoya St. Armand might have had some say in the length, which ended just below the knees. Her dainty white gloves matched the lace trim on a large-brimmed hat in a darker shade of purple. With the sprigs of tiny white and yellow flowers tucked into the band, it looked perfect for an Easter parade.

When Latoya St. Armand introduced Edward simply as Edward Harlow, without any reference to Aunt Civility, both teens stood at attention and waited to step into the spotlight. They seemed tense. Maybe they had stage fright. I sympathized.

Once he got the okay, my brother stepped in front of a round table dressed up with a lacy white tablecloth and scanned the crowd. A lot of unfriendly faces stared back along with curiosity seekers and the type of people who slowed down at accidents. He raised his hands, and they held their breath, waiting for the first words from the nefarious nephew of the non-existent author.

"This morning, Mr. Brandon and Miss Makayla from Tea for Teens will honor us by demonstrating a proper tea." He stepped aside. "As you can see, the table has been set for *afternoon* tea. High tea is *not* the same thing, and we won't discuss it today." He grimaced and muttered under his breath. "Or ever, if I have any say."

He then went over each item on the table, naming it and explaining its function, and by the time he explained that the handle of the tea cup should point right in the three o'clock position, the faces of audience members reflected disappointed. They probably hoped for a tearful confession. Maybe an apology.

He gestured for the teens to come forward. When the nervous couple joined my brother, the guests forgot their morbid preoccupation with Edward and let out a collective sigh, admiring Makayla and Brandon with some clapping and murmurs of *adorable, darling, how pretty,* and *such a handsome young man.*

Brandon pulled out Makayla's chair for her, and once he had taken his place across the table, my brother again held out a hand.

"Today, we have two volunteers to serve so you can see how the steps are affected should you take your tea in a tearoom."

Myra Timms and Frederico Agosti, dressed in black and white server's uniforms, stepped forward. The white vest seemed a little tight across Mrs. Timms' endowments, but with his dark hair and slim build, Rico looked handsome. Myra carried the teapot in two hands, and Rico held a tiered serving tray displaying an assortment of scones, finger sandwiches, and dainty pastries.

"You'll note that just because there are servers, it doesn't mean they will fill your teacup for you. One of our teens will *play mother*, which means that person will take charge of pouring out the tea."

In this case, Brandon did the honors. Makayla bowed her head and thanked him. When Brandon offered sugar and cream, she allowed him to drop in one sugar cube using tiny tongs and refused the cream.

"Sugar cubes are better," my brother explained, "because they make less mess than loose grains. As for making their selection from the serving tray, it would be polite if the young man allowed the young lady to choose first."

When the swinging door to the kitchen opened a crack, my muscles tensed until I recognized Mrs. Beckwith peeking through the gap. A few faces joined her there. Even the Inglenook employees wanted to check out the subject of the rumors.

Makayla pressed her lips together to hold in a grin, chose the tastiest looking pastry—a fairy cake with yellow frosting—and then surprised the audience when she handed her plate to Brandon. They both grinned as people applauded her gracious move.

The hand-off didn't go as planned. The young lady

fumbled the plate, sending it crashing to the floor. She put her hand over her mouth and cried out.

"I'll get it for you, miss," Rico said, playing up his part. He gathered the pieces, executed a grand bow to the embarrassed young lady and carried the debris toward the kitchen.

Since the swinging doors were no longer hidden behind the photographer's backdrop, no one had to crane their neck to see what happened next.

The door swung open, and Miranda Evans, the young maid/waitress, stepped out. Rico checked his steps. With all eyes on her, the teen grabbed her moment of fame. She placed one hand over her heart and pointed. "That's him!"

Rico dropped the dish and sprinted toward the exit to the lobby, and after the quick second it took for me to react, I headed him off. He altered his course and made for the open courtyard doors.

Edward had anticipated his move and came around from behind. He was waiting by the time Rico hit the cement.

Without slowing down, the private secretary rammed my brother around the middle and hooked his legs in a tackle, but Edward quickly rolled to his feet.

Several women screamed, and Claudia yelled, "Get him, Edward!"

I pushed through the guests blocking the doorway in time to see Rico bounce a chair off my brother's shoulder as Edward side-stepped a blow aimed for his noggin.

When the BenHam heir rushed forward again with the chair held high, I came at him from the side and yanked the weapon from his grasp.

I didn't intend to get involved. Edward could handle himself, and two-on-one isn't a fair fight. Neither is using anything but fists.

As I turned to toss the chair out of reach, Rico sucker punched me and sent me sprawling. I dropped the chair and folded an arm to absorb the brunt of my fall as I landed sideways on the cement.

That made Edward angry. "You'll pay for that."

While the cops encircled the patio, Rico feigned an escape to the right, then to the left, but with Edward's experience on the football field, the moves were child's play.

Lunging forward, he grabbed Rico by the collar, lifted him in the air, and slammed him to the ground. Then he pinned him there with his knee on the heir's diaphragm.

Foolishly, Rico kept swinging, so Edward pulled his opponent's left arm across his own knee and pressed down on Rico's shoulder, effectively blocking any further punches the private secretary might want to deliver.

When Davis approached with handcuffs, Edward released his hold, sprang to his feet, and moved aside. Breathing heavily as he walked over, he held out his hand and pulled me to my feet. "I need to increase my exercise routine. I'm out of shape. Are you alright?"

"Never better. How's the shoulder?"

Edward rolled it a few times. "Right as rain."

"What does that even mean?"

"I do not know."

Timms, back in charge now that his wife was out of the picture, pushed forward. He caught himself in time and stepped aside to let his sergeant do the honors. Michaelson delivered his line in a loud voice tinged with pride.

"Frederico Agosti, I'm arresting you for the murders of Benedict Hamilton and Jennifer Proctor."

As Davis handcuffed the accused's hands behind his back, Rico searched the crowd until his gaze landed on Melvin Gardner. "My attorney will do all my talking."

Gardner shook his head and took a step back.

Rico dragged Davis with him when he rounded on my

brother. "Why didn't you leave it alone? It wasn't your business."

Edward arched one brow. "And allow you to get away with murder?"

"You have everything. A career. Money. Recognition. A woman who cares about you. A brother who's proud of you."

"There are times," I began.

"Shut up!" Spittle flew as Rico screamed. "You have a great relationship with your brother. Ben treated me like dirt. Like I was nothing." He bared his teeth at Edward. "I want those things. I deserve them."

Edward nodded slowly as an idea came to him. "And that's why you threatened to take them away from me."

As my brother considered the killer's argument, I could see him moving toward pity, but then he shook it off. "And you killed for them. You took the life of a young woman who'd done nothing to you. Your brother may not have been an agreeable person, but he worked for everything he had. It wasn't yours to take."

"He was lucky, that's all. So are you."

Rico meant it as a sneer, but Edward grinned. "Yes. I am."

The crowd parted as my brother strolled back to the front of the room, dusting off his jacket, as if nothing out of the ordinary had happened. He swept a hand toward the teens.

"Many thanks to my accomplices, Brandon and Makayla."

As they accepted applause from the crowd, Makayla curtsied, and Brandon bowed.

"You did so well," Mrs. Timms said. "I was nervous. Were you?"

Brandon just smiled, but his counterpart shook her head.

"I'm going to be an actress," Makayla stated. "But only in community theater because I'll be nursing full time."

I cocked my head. "Seriously? Then I have someone you ought to meet."

As the guests crowded in, there seemed to be one theme.

"Did you see the way Aunt Civility's nephew rescued his brother?"

"And so easily."

Though I didn't like the idea of helplessly waiting for Edward to save me from Rico, if it made him a hero in his fans' eyes, so be it.

"I thought I was a goner." I rubbed the back of my head. "Good thing Edward was nearby."

"You were so brave," Fur Coat said, stroking her fingers down Edward's arm.

Thin Lips harrumphed. "Your aunt would be proud of you."

I gaped. "His aunt?"

She turned to me, her lips still not moving when she talked. "Naturally. You didn't expect us to fall for that old rouse. By pretending to be drunk and announcing to the world he was Aunt Civility, your brother put the killer off his guard."

"He did?"

"So clever," Pug Nose murmured, eying my brother as if sizing him up for a cabana boy outfit.

The Gnome nudged Edward's ankle with her cane. "I hope I wasn't rough on you last night, but I wanted to play along, and I thought it should be realistic." She lied without blushing.

"You were wonderful," my brother said. "A brilliant actress." She tilted her head and allowed him to kiss her cheek. Then she blushed.

Mrs. Timms had a gleam in her eye as she gurgled a laugh. "It certainly was clever. With Mr. Harlow *appearing* to be out of the picture, Mr. Agosti put down his guard. Everyone knows how the Harlow boys helped with the last murder, so they made it look like they had other things on their mind. A wonderful idea." She gurgled again and winked at me.

Everyone agreed except Sykes. "How did you figure it out?" He directed the question to Edward the hero. "There were many people with motives, including you."

Fur Coat lady shrieked. "Aunt Civility's nephew would *never* kill anyone." Her posse agreed.

Edward gazed down at her fondly. "Thank you for your faith in me." He took us all in with a glance, and some people moved forward, drawn to one last lecture by Aunt Civility's official representative.

"'There were many suspects, including myself." He gestured toward the head of Tea for Teens. "Ms. Latoya St. Armand for one."

Murmurs and gasps followed this, though Latoya smirked at him like he was a naughty boy.

"Hamilton's desire to take over the charity and move it from the helpful organization it is today to something more corporate and less helpful became an obsession. He used the charity's precarious financial position to apply pressure, which makes him a cad of the first order."

He acknowledged the crowd, who numbered more than the night of the masked ball.

"If you wish to keep this dedicated woman from the clutches of unscrupulous investors, I suggest you make a healthy donation today."

Purses unzipped as he continued.

"I didn't believe murder would be in her nature. A nurturing, caring nature, which made it unlikely anything could move her to kill a person. Also, I couldn't believe she could escape the public eye long enough to commit the deed, so I dismissed that idea."

"I'm glad to hear that," Sykes said.

"The police also suspected Claudia Inglenook, another

victim of Hamilton's bullying. Of course, I never considered that possibility."

She gazed up at him with a soppy expression.

"Then we had the world-famous photographer, Joshua Breen. Hamilton took actions that threatened Mr. Breen's proposed television series. He was seen coming out of the, er, men's facilities near to the crime scene. Mr. Breen admitted to punching the unscrupulous Benedict Hamilton during a confrontation."

A few ladies sighed, and Josh straightened his shoulders and lifted his chin.

"That act alone made it clear he hadn't murdered the man."

"Why?" Mr. Hall frowned. "He was obviously angry. Why stop at punching him?"

Edward, delighted that someone had asked, clasped his hands behind his back.

"If Mr. Breen had carried the weapon into the room, which he would have had to do, would he have then set the sword down so he could hit his victim first? And if he had hit Hamilton, I couldn't see that man then turning his back on Mr. Breen. Benedict Hamilton was, er, stabbed in the back."

Josh rubbed his knuckles. "You make me glad I hit him."

"And," Edward added, unable to hold back the truth, "for reasons I won't go into, I was watching him all evening."

Claudia moved closer and wrapped her arm around my brother's middle. He responded by pulling her close.

"That left my brother—"

I gaped. "Hey!"

"Who I know as well as myself to be incapable of a deliberate, planned murder."

"Thanks for that."

"And—"

Timms grabbed his wife's hand. "Don't even think about it."

Edward passed over Myra Timms. "It left other miscellaneous motives for other miscellaneous people. There was also Frederico Agosti, who inherited Mr. Hamilton's fortune. A particularly good motive. His recently fired attorney was here the night of the murder. Could he have been seeking revenge? Finally, Jennifer Proctor, his personal assistant, was in love with the man, but a mistaken case of jealousy could have pushed her to kill. If I can't have him, no one can. As you know, Miss Proctor was murdered, and that left two viable suspects."

"*I* didn't know about the second murder," Fur Coat said, and several others agreed.

"Sadly, she was. My brother told me Miss Proctor insisted that the person she saw entering the library that night was Benedict Hamilton. That made me think about how she at first *didn't* think it was him. He was in a Zorro costume, so she must have seen someone else in the same costume, someone who didn't move like her boss. That was Joshua Breen. But then she said something silly. She stated she didn't recognize her boss at first because he had removed his hat."

"That's why you asked about the hats," Josh said. "I wondered."

"I think it was a slip. She had seen someone else she *didn't* tell us about. Someone without a hat."

"So, she lied." Michaelson looked at his boss. "Right? She saw Dracula walk into the room. That's the costume Frederico Agosti wore to the ball."

Edward shook his head. "No. She saw someone walk in who wasn't in costume."

Gardner had been quiet, but he squawked when Michaelson took hold of his elbow. "They were in it together? The lawyer here was the only one not in costume."

"Not exactly. Jennifer said there were other 'unimportant people' around. Who does that make you think of?"

"I'm not interested in taking a quiz," Timms said. "Just spit it out."

My brother frowned at the detective's unwillingness to take part. I, however, saw where he was headed.

"No one ever notices the staff."

His grin was as good as a gold star. "Exactly. Aunt Zali confirmed she had seen *three* people enter the room. Two Zorros and a member of the wait staff. The first person was Benedict Hamilton, eager to make a meeting that would settle unfinished business. The second Zorro was Joshua Breen, who, as we now know, punched Hamilton and then left. The third person was a member of the serving staff, which was natural. One of their duties is to walk the rooms and pick up discarded plates and foodstuff. As my brother put it, people are slobs."

That comment earned me several nasty glares. One woman held my gaze longer than the rest, which made me think she was a guilty party. I shook a finger in her direction, and she jerked her head back and looked away, which confirmed my suspicion.

"It wasn't until dinner last night that I noticed the details of the uniforms worn by the servers. It reminded me of something. Dracula. Frederico Agosti wore a Dracula costume. Once he removed the cape, his remaining costume resembled the wait staff uniforms."

Michaelson narrowed his eyes. "Remind me why Jennifer Proctor kept that a secret. Didn't she want to see her boss's murderer punished? After all, you said she loved him."

"I believe she didn't realize the importance of what she'd seen at first. Her mind was preoccupied with continuing

BenHam, Incorporated in Hamilton's honor. At first, she tried to talk Rico into finding shareholders to invest, but he declined to take part in her scheme. Only later did she realize the identity of the waiter. Once it came out that Rico was Hamilton's brother and would inherit, she knew she could hold her knowledge over his head to accomplish her tribute."

Timms squeezed his wife's hand. "She underestimated him, poor idiot."

My brother grimaced. "How simple to remove his cape, leave it in one of the potted plants by the photography backdrop, and go through the kitchen to the library, especially with the backdrop covering the kitchen doors and hiding his movements."

"Why didn't anyone see him come out of the library?" Sykes asked. "Wasn't he taking a chance?"

"Because he didn't return to the kitchen that way. Nicholas slipped in a puddle of water outside the Welcome Room. People have been tracking in rain and mud all weekend, but the Welcome Room is far enough from the lobby that there shouldn't have been a puddle."

"Henry." I shouted the name.

"That gentleman, almost a permanent fixture in the Welcome Room, confirmed a waiter came in from outdoors, collected plates, and returned to the kitchen. Two mistakes that could have cost Rico worked in his favor. He didn't follow protocol and take the dirty dishes to the sink, but that merely confirmed Mrs. Beckwith's opinion that the temporary staff were poorly trained. Then he ran into Miranda Evans. He used his charm to get around her, which made Mrs. Beckwith, and perhaps Miranda herself, believe he was a temp flirting with her young charge. Both actions strengthened the impression that he was simply a waiter hired for the evening."

Edward's expression took on the self-righteousness of a

born avenger. "And when Jennifer Proctor threatened his safety, he killed her. The man is a maniac, and I'm pleased our excellent police have taken him in hand and a jury of his peers will dole out justice."

My stomach growled. People got chatty, and since I hadn't eaten breakfast, I left Edward to his fans and headed to the Atrium for the Sunday buffet.

CHAPTER 39

With everyone fawning over Edward in the Ballroom, the Atrium had several tables available and no line in front of the buffet. Any time I relax after a period of stress, my appetite increases, and the savory smells egged me on. No pun intended.

Sykes and his wife had taken a table with the Timms. So, after I loaded up on French toast, bacon, potatoes, ham, and a glass of orange juice, I sat down at the table next to theirs and leaned in.

"So, what do you think of Inglenook?"

"It could be charming...for a vacation," Shauna said with a bushel of sarcasm.

Myra giggled. "I like it. I like Claudia and Robert. I didn't meet Zali, but I hear she's a hoot. We'll be back, won't we, Fergus?"

He gazed at her with complete satisfaction and patted her shoulder. "Anything you say, dear."

She kept the smile, but then her features readjusted themselves into resignation. Her expression said they were back to the status quo with her making all the decisions.

Our chairs were close enough I was able to kick his ankle, frown, and nudge my head in his wife's direction. He cleared his throat. "Myra, I think we should come back for a relaxing weekend. I have vacation time coming. I say the first week in June looks good. What do you think?"

His wife's eyes shone with pleasure. "Why, Fergus! That would be wonderful. I'd like that. Thank you for asking."

Sykes scooped up the last of his omelet. "I think we'll come back, too. Maybe." He looked my way. "When you're not here."

Timms threw back his head and laughed. "Nicky can be a pain in the, um, butt. That's for darn sure."

I still had packing to do, so I made good time on breakfast. Periwinkle was at the buffet when I left, and I spotted Edward heading down the hallway toward Claudia's apartment, so when I got back to our room, I had space to move my elbows.

The publisher had already taken his luggage down and left it with the front desk. Once I folded my blankets and the cot and pushed them against the communicating door, I got everything packed except our toothbrushes, searched the room to make sure I hadn't missed a stray sock, and left the luggage by the door. I checked the shower twice.

In the lobby, the guests were leaving *en masse*, which is typical of any hotel I've stayed in. Both Robert and Claudia scurried to process the check outs. When I saw they had help, I grinned.

Zali stood behind the front desk, her short, squat frame stuffed into a black-and-white food server's uniform under a burgundy jacket about two sizes too large. Wandering over, I rested an arm on the counter. "I'd like to make a complaint."

"Sorry, Nicky. They don't let me handle those yet. People can be touchy when you tell them they're wrong."

"What's your department?"

"I'm kind of a concierge. I tell people where to go. Let them know if there's a good restaurant in town." She lowered her voice and leaned forward, which put her chin on the counter. "I lie. Tell them there have been rumors about health department visits, and wouldn't they rather try our dining room? And I'm not lying, it's just I'm the one who started the rumors."

"You're good for business."

She beamed.

"Pretend I'm new here. Tell me about the amenities."

"Well, if you're feeling homesick, or you're a teenager dragged here by your parents, you can go to the Welcome Room because it has everything you have in your own living room. Cookies. A couch in front of a big screen television. No game system yet, but you can lose your vision playing those things too much. That's what I tell them."

She narrowed one eye, taking my measure.

"You look like a guy who might want a drink."

She had a point. Since I'd skipped shaving this morning and had more than a five o'clock shadow, I probably looked like a well-dressed bum.

"Our bar has stools, but if you don't want to be seen by your wife or your girlfriend, there are booths you can hide in."

"Sounds perfect. What time do they start serving?"

She craned her neck to look at the clock on the wall.

"Fifteen minutes ago."

I rapped on the counter. "I'll check it out."

"Don't forget to tip."

I took a step but did a U-turn. "Detective Sykes."

"Detective *Jonah* Sykes."

"You remembered him from Citrus Grove."

"I sure did."

"He made quite an impression on you."

"He did."

"Why? What's so special about him?"

"That's easy. He always talks to me like I have a brain. Not like the other detective. That guy sometimes uses the same voice the nurses at the home did. Fake nice. I don't mind *real* nice, but fake nice makes me mad."

Like I told Sykes. An iceberg with hidden depth.

Periwinkle hovered next to me, waiting to speak, but Edward walked up just then, and the publisher transferred his attention to the more important of us.

"Mr. Harlow, I spoke out of turn yesterday. I hope you'll reconsider remaining with Classical Reads."

I tapped his shoulder. "You fired him."

"Well, yes, but I did so without all the facts. It doesn't seem there's been any harm done to Aunt Civility's image. Also, I've been thinking about your book proposal, and though you haven't made a formal submission—"

"My brother has other projects. He might not have time to do the Aunt Civility books, the new series, and his own projects."

Edward interrupted. "There will be time enough for, er, my project. I'm not giving up on it."

"A personal project?" Periwinkle tapped his chin. "What is it? Does it fit into our catalog?"

"Not your field. Athletics."

The publisher wouldn't let go. "Athletes with good manners? There are some wonderful examples, though most are from the past. These days you would have to write about poor examples of good behavior."

"It's an idea," Edward said, though his tone said it wasn't a *good* idea.

"No." I shook my head. "You've got a gem, Edward. Don't settle."

"We could discuss any side projects you wish to do—"

"All negotiations have to go through my *private secretary*." And then my brother winked at me.

"Who's that?" the publisher called out as Edward headed for the stairs. He looked up at me, doubtful. "Is he referring to you?"

Periwinkle accompanied me out of the lobby, eager to start negotiations, but I held up my hands. "Why don't I call you after things have settled down? I'm sure there will be some changes, and I need to deal with those first." Starting with if my new title came with a raise.

After making me promise not to forget about the long and fruitful relationship Edward had with Classical Reads, he agreed.

Robert had his hands full at the front desk, so I stepped into the bar and ordered a scotch on the rocks. Then I decided that, with a knock on the head this weekend, I should stick to something lighter and ordered a ginger ale. The bartender looked at me funny but made the switch.

"Take a look at these."

Joshua Breen held his cell phone in front of me and flipped through his latest album. There were several shots of Brandon and Makayla in their finery followed by a series of Rico making a break for it, but most of them were of Edward's fight on the patio with the killer.

"What do you think? Black and white for some drama?"

I grinned. "Could you let me have copies?"

He played with his phone. "Done."

"Actually, I have a favor to ask."

We discussed it for a few minutes before Josh laughed and agreed to my plan. I sipped my ginger ale and made a face. What a weekend. At least I still had a job. This trip could have turned out worse. I rubbed my head. Much worse.

When Robert finally joined me, I risked a small glass of scotch, one finger full.

"All's well that ends well," I said.

"For the moment."

"Sorry about the crazy weekend. Are we banned?"

"Are you kidding? We are booked solid through the summer."

"I'm glad to hear it. I have to admit I was afraid you'd sell this place and move in with us."

"Give me some credit. Although, you might have to prepare yourself for close contact if Edward and Claudia get serious. By the way, your brother booked the two of you in for another few days."

I lifted my glass. "Let's toast to future bickering and the following estrangement."

"Oh! I almost forgot." He patted his jacket and pulled out an envelope. "Do you want to do the honors?"

He handed it to me.

Handwritten across the front, it read *Zali Inglenook: Private and Confidential.*

"Is this—"

"Her answers. Hurry up and check them before she starts asking me about the prize."

She'd sealed the thing as if it contained the secret to eternal life. Leaning over the bar, I grabbed the cocktail stirrer and used it to slit open the flap. She wrote her answer on a single page. I read it through twice and then threw back my head and laughed.

> *Dear judges, I have decided that the second Zorro was a decoy, and the murderer is the waiter who entered the room. He probably sneaked outside through the library doors, and since Alfred's sharper than he looks, I bet he came back in through one of the other rooms. The Atrium's a pain. I've tried it. The bar won't do because it's blocked. I think he came back in through the Welcome Room. It'd be easy. No one pays attention to the waiters.*

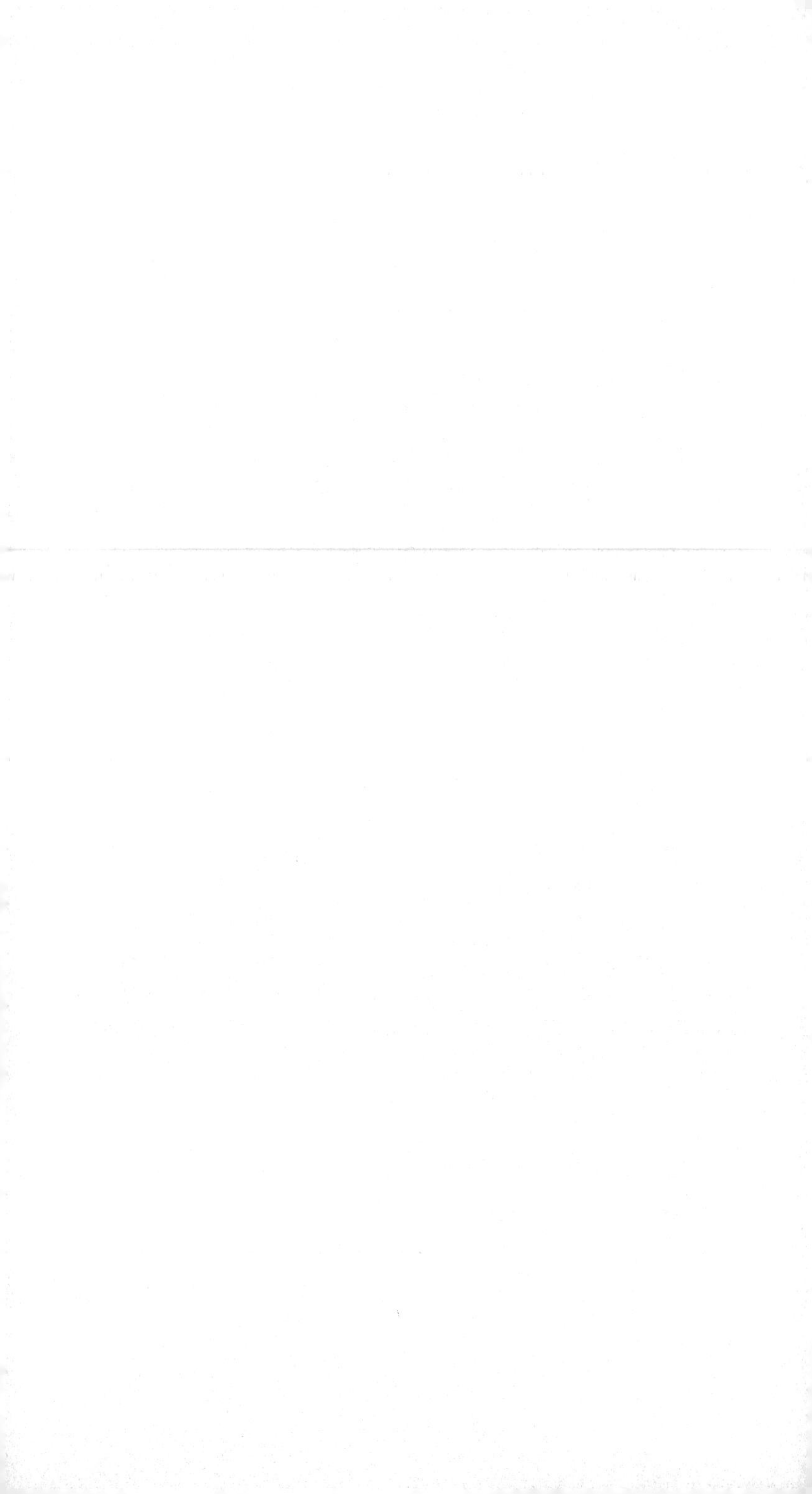

THANK YOU FOR READING DEADLY DECORUM

If you enjoyed this book, please consider leaving a review. Reviews help readers discover new books, and the author, who socializes mostly with dogs, appreciates the human feedback.

Thank you!

Jacqueline

KEEP READING

The End. Or is it? *Unsportsmanlike Conduct* will be available in 2023. Check in at jacquelinevick.com or sign up for my newsletter to get the latest news.

AND DON'T FORGET to download your free story!

THE CASE OF THE COOKED GOOSE

A Harlow Brothers mystery prequel

When Nicholas Harlow accompanies his brother, Edward, to a conference at the Deer Stalker Hotel, he discovers his childhood idol, Sammy Spade, starring in the hotel's production of *Jekyl and Hyde.* During the evening performance, Sammy keels over onstage, poisoned. Unfortunately, Nicholas was the last one to see him alive, and the detective in charge is ready for an arrest.

To Get the Free Story for My VIP Readers, the Mystery Buffs, go to www.jacquelinevick.com/subscribhb

Read on for a preview of the next Harlow Brothers mystery, *Unsportsmanlike Conduct.*

A PREVIEW OF UNSPORTSMANLIKE CONDUCT

CHAPTER ONE

"I don't get it."

Detective Jonah Sykes of the San Diego Sheriff's Department was seated on the white leather couch in the living room of the house I live in and my brother owns on Sunburst Lane in San Diego County. He gestured at my brother with his blueberry muffin. "You broke your hand at a cricket match, but you weren't playing." He took a healthy bite of his breakfast-on-the-fly and waited for a reply.

"It's not broken," Edward snapped. He adjusted his rump in his favorite chair, one of two matching recliners on either side of the fireplace. "I injured it while saving Nicholas's life."

Sykes stopped chewing and frowned at me. "Why?"

"Many thanks," I said.

"I mean why did you need saving? Were *you* playing?"

As the only one standing, I had a good view of them both: Sykes with his trim goatee and short tight curls packaged together with the body of a former college linebacker, and my brother with his trim goatee and dark hair that tended to curl packaged together with the body of a former college linebacker. They could have been twins except Edward's eyes were gray and Sykes' were topaz. And Sykes was black.

"I was trying to stop a woman from getting killed. Or maimed. The ball was headed for Myra's face. Or maybe Bob's."

"You mean Myra Finkelstein and Bob Wallers?" Sykes dusted the crumbs off his fingers and flipped open his notebook, ready to get to work. "They were both at the party last night."

Sykes' visit wasn't a social call. He'd been up all night, working on a murder. The detective had bags under his eyes, and he frowned not from irritation at me but because he was too tired to hold up his lips. He rang our doorbell at six a.m., which was early for a Sunday morning, especially as we just left him at three o'clock this same morning. Five hours after I'd found the body.

Yesterday's cricket match between two software giants—Dark Angel Studios and Executive Suites Business Solutions—was supposed to initiate a weekend of festivities. My discovery of a dead man in the home of Gerald and Gloria Hamilton had brought celebrations to an abrupt halt.

Sykes reached for another muffin; banana nut this time. Since he'd been working all night, I didn't begrudge him a large share of the baked goods left for us by our housekeeper and cook, Mrs. Abernathy, while she visited with her daughter.

I went to the kitchen to refill the tray. By the time I returned, Edward had launched into a lecture on cricket.

"Don't try to understand it," I said, setting the tray in front of Sykes and refilling his coffee. Edward held out his plate, but I turned my back on him. "It makes no sense. You know how you when you watch a baseball game you always know where to find the shortstop and center fielder? These players meander."

Sykes expression cleared. "It's like baseball?"

I shook my head sadly. "You know what they call the batter? A batsman. The catcher's even worse. Wicketkeeper."

"What exactly is a wicket?"

I waived a hand. "There are bails and stumps, and they build the wicket out of them. Like Legos. And there are two of them. The wickets, I mean. You don't want to know."

"Is one a backup?"

Edward, in the middle of adding an apple tart to his plate, cleared his throat. "No. The purpose—"

I interrupted. "Get this. There are two batsmen out there on either side of this strip of dirt they call the pitch. They take turns. Sometimes they run. Sometimes they don't. Nobody steals home plate. What I say is, if the batsman's not excited about hitting the ball, why should I care?" I sat on the opposite end of the couch from Sykes. "Here's a tip. If anyone tells you the game is only two innings, don't get excited. Everybody gets a turn at bat. Everybody. Though at least when they're out, they're out for the rest of the game."

Sykes gave in and took the apple cranberry scone he'd

been eyeballing. "I still don't get it. Why were you there? What does cricket have to do with Aunt Civility?"

My brother ghost writes the Aunt Civility etiquette series. He makes public appearances as the author's nephew, since the nonexistent old lady who allegedly pens the books is agoraphobic. What can I say? It's the publisher's call and makes the fans happy.

I'm his secretary, errand boy, and lackey. I glared at him, as our being there had been a subject of much discussion.

"Absolutely nothing. Edward's hand wouldn't be broken—"

"It's not broken."

"My brother wouldn't have injured his hand if he'd been at the annual florticulture show giving his talk on the Victorian Language of Flowers, which is where we were supposed to be yesterday afternoon."

Sykes eyebrows went up. "You blew off your Aunt Civility fans?"

Edward growled. "I wanted to go to one event where women weren't screeching in my ear."

I made a face. "I've never noticed any screeching."

"Where no one smells."

That made me laugh. "Smells? Who smells?"

"I hate gardenias. It's like they all get their scents from the same perfumer." He raised a finger and nodded as if he'd just thought of a zinger. "And where grandmothers aren't trying to unload their homely granddaughters on me."

Sykes and I stared at Edward. My brother was never intentionally mean.

"That happened once," I said. "Last year. And when Miss Tremont found out what Granny Tremont had done, she was horrified. She had no interest in you. She had a fiancé."

"So, these players are on the field," Sykes said, changing the subject. "How did you manage to get hurt?"

That was a story in itself, and I told it.

At the start of the second inning, when the Dark Angels were up to bat, the bowler had made the kind of flailing run which I'd come to accept as normal for cricket. He delivered the ball to Gerald Hamilton. The head of Dark Angel Studios was early on the swing, and when the bat connected, the ball caught the tip and soared toward the stands, directly at the man and woman seated two benches up from us.

"Heads up," I called out, my feet already moving. There wasn't time to get in a position to catch the ball, so I launched myself in front of the couple, angling my body to face the incoming projectile. I thought a broken rib would be preferable to a broken back.

Edward's left hand shot up, and the thump and mind-numbing pain never came. The woman and man jerked back, the former gasping, though that might have been from my weight pressing on her legs.

"Get off!"

Her shove rolled me onto my knees. While Edward transferred the ball to his right hand, I pulled myself up, jumped to the ground, and stood in front of him.

"Is it broken?"

He gently wiggled his fingers. "I caught the ball in the palm of my hand."

"That's why I asked."

My brother relieved his feeling by throwing the ball back with enough power behind it that the bowler stumbled backwards when he caught it.

Edward made it through another batter before I called the game. For him.

Sykes whistled. "Sounds painful. And the party last night was to celebrate the win of the Dark Angels over the Executive Sweets. Interesting name for a software company."

"Executive Sweets is a play on Executive Suites," I

explained. "They make business software. Dark Angel Studios produces video games. The cricket match was leading up to the launch next weekend of Gerald Hamilton's new release, *Zombie Cricket*."

"So I've heard." Sykes cast his interested gaze on Edward. "And you went to the celebration even though you were, I assume, in a great deal of pain. Why? What's Gerald Hamilton to you?"

"We never met him before last night," I said. "Edward gets lots of invitations as Aunt Civility's representative. I'd declined this particular invite, but Edward, who apparently doesn't trust me to do my job, saw it in my discarded emails and decided to overrule my decision."

Sykes raised his eyebrows again. It's something he did a lot around us.

"Do I need to explain my choices to you?" Edward was talking to me, but Sykes answered.

"Yes. It was an unusual choice for you. I want to know the impetus behind it. Had you met Hamilton before? Or his wife?"

"Why would you say that?" Edward demanded.

At the mention of Gloria Hamilton, I wisely kept my mouth shut. They had a stare-down that lasted a full minute before Edward sighed. "I felt like a change. Something different. A little excitement."

I snorted. "You got that, alright."

Sykes got his notebook ready and looked at me. "You'd better tell me about the party, and don't leave anything out." In the past, I'd given Sykes an example of my excellent recall abilities. It's a family trait, but Edward is smart enough to keep his talent quiet.

Both men were waiting, so I closed my eyes and gave my memory a shake, trying to capture every detail. When I had it, I began.

ACKNOWLEDGMENTS

Thanks to my hubby for his unwavering belief in me.

Kim Taylor Blakemore kept me on track. This book wouldn't be finished without her gentle prodding. Thanks, Kim.

Thanks to those who gave me valuable feedback, including members of the Writers Well, Andrea Voirin and Foster Vick.

Finally, thanks to the Mystery Buffs, a community of readers who love mysteries as much as I do.

Other novels by Jacqueline Vick

Frankie Chandler Pet Psychic Mysteries

Barking Mad at Murder

A Bird's Eye View of Murder

An Almost Purrfect Murder

What the Cluck? It's Murder

A Scaly Tail of Murder

A Scape Goat for Murder

The Harlow Brothers Mysteries

Civility Rules

Bad Behavior

Deadly Decorum

Standalone Novels

Family Matters

The Body Guy

An Unhealthy Attachment

BOOK CLUB QUESTIONS

Deadly Decorum

Nicholas can't stand Claudia, and the feeling is mutual. Should whether they get along or not impact Edward's feelings for her and whether he continues to pursue the relationship?

Edward has a successful career as the author of the Aunt Civility books. Is he a fool to throw that away for a dream that may or may not happen?

Claudia's sorority sisters brought up a surprising college episode involving Claudia. Do you think there is another, darker side to her? Would you like there to be? Does it make her more interesting?

At one point, Nicholas wonders if Edward could ever commit murder. Do you think we all have the potential to kill if the stakes are high enough?

After a few drinks, Edward goes to his presentation and ruins his reputation with an outburst. Was this intentional? Or did he act out of character because of the alcohol?

Edward felt trapped by his contract. Do you think he noticed the way people ignored and disrespected him because he wanted out? Would these slights have bothered him if he had been happy in his job?

Sibling relationships are powerful. No one knows us as well as our siblings. Is it an advantage for Edward to have his brother working for him? Or an obstacle?

In this book, there are two professional detectives working the case, and both have close connections to possible suspects. Do you think having a stake in the solution made Sykes and Timms better investigators?

Edward and Claudia's relationship is long-distance. Do you think a romance can survive when the couple only meets in person every few months?

Nicholas depends on Edward's success. How do you think he would do if Edward stopped writing and he had to make it alone?

ABOUT THE AUTHOR

Jacqueline Vick writes the Frankie Chandler Pet Psychic mystery series about a woman who, after faking her psychic abilities for years, discovers animals *can* communicate with her. Her second series, the Harlow Brothers mysteries, features a former college linebacker turned etiquette author and his secretary brother. Her books are known for satirical humor and engaging characters who are reluctant to accept their greatest (and often embarrassing) gifts. Visit her at www.jacquelinevick.com

Made in United States
Orlando, FL
08 September 2024